Hope you enjoy

Dorothy
Collins

TODAY THE WAITING

DOROTHY COLLINS

Tellwell Talent
www.tellwell.ca

ISBN
978-1-77370-524-8 (Paperback)
978-1-77370-525-5 (eBook)

CHAPTER ONE

*I*nside the homey ranch-style house, the family dinner conversation is at a minimum. The silence was penetrated by the slim boy. "Dad, I hit a home run today. I wish you had been there."

The father looked at him as the front door bell peals loudly. Before his father could speak, ten year old Todd leaped up scraping back his chair, hastening down the hall to the front door. Opening it, he was surprised, vacant space. He stuck his head out looking around but the veranda was empty.

"That's weird, there is nobody out there not even on the street, except for Mr. Maxwell's old Dodge crawling by." Todd slouching into his chair with disgust on his face. Picking up his fork and scooping up a hefty forkful of potatoes, he crammed them into his mouth. Harry looked at him but made no comment.

Again the doorbell rang, Todd around a mouthful of food uttered a cocky. "Dad, it's your turn to go this time." Harry rose from the table with a slight scowl landing on his son. Proceeding down the hall at a quick pace, he twisted the door handle pulling it with a rough jerk. Glancing out, the space outside the door was indeed empty. Harry being a bit perturbed stalked out onto the veranda. Gazing around, his peripheral vision picked up a shadowy figure, then he heard "help us."

Assuming the source of the voice must be some kids playing games, Harry negotiated the stairs quickly. He strode in the direction of the voice. Rounding the side of the house, he spotted a small boy kneeling down beside a little girl causing Harry to hasten his steps.

"Hello, what do we have here?"

Looking up with pleading eyes and speaking with a quiver in his voice, "Hello mister, my sister is sick. Can you help her?"

"Well let's have a look." Kneeling his sturdy frame down beside them, Harry put his hand on the girl's forehead. Her eyes were closed and she was very pale and lying motionless. He brushed her blond curls from her forehead and found it quite hot to the touch. The trail of tears running through the dirt on her face prompted Harry to ask if she had hurt herself. The boy replied. "No, just sick."

"Did she have this sickness for long?"

"Yes for two days now, but today is the worst because now she can't walk any further." His voice held tears in it. "I tried to lift her but I couldn't. We were just going to sit on those chairs. My sister needed to rest." Pointing his finger and nodding toward the backyard. "We are looking for our daddy but we haven't found him yet." The boy stammered sadly.

"Where did your daddy go?"

"He went to work and he never came home," a sob in his voice.

"Let's get your sister inside so I can make her feel better."

Lifting the little girl, Harry navigated the stairs to the veranda, with concerned eyes for the child that lay passively in his arms. A young boy's curiosity had Todd standing at the door shouting questions, "Dad, who are they? Where did they come from?" Moving aside Todd let his father enter.

"I don't know but they need help. Will you get a bowl of cold water and a cloth and bring some soap?" Harry carefully set the girl down on the couch in the living room. Turning to the boy who was following him. "All right son, let's hear your story starting with your names."

"My name is Jason and this is my sister, Bethany. My sister and I were left alone because my sister wasn't nice to Jennifer when she was looking after us. So Jennifer left. Then I was looking after Bethany myself. We got hungry so I made hamburgers, and maybe I didn't cook them right, because she got sick. Today when she was still sick I knew I had to find my daddy."

"Who is Jennifer? Where is your mother?"

"Jennifer is the babysitter and mommy isn't home."

"Didn't Jennifer come back to check on you?"

"No, but Mrs. Clark, who lives across the street came over. But we were quiet and didn't answer the door." Jason responded.

"Why didn't you answer the door?" Accepting the basin of water and the cloth from Todd. Dipping the cloth in the water Harry wrung it out and placed the cloth on Bethany's forehead.

"Because mommy says Mrs. Clark is a busybody and tells everybody our business."

"Where is your mother, Jason?"

"My mother is in the hospital. She is sick too." An anguished Jason responded.

"Do you know where your father works?"

"No, he said it isn't far when he went to work." The tears were trickling down Jason's cheeks. Harry continued bathing the little girl's face, having rinsed the cloth again.

"Who are they?" Todd asked again.

Glancing toward Todd, "I don't know but Jason is telling me his story."

"Do you know where you live, Jason?"

"Yes in a house on Greenley Street"

In a shocked voice Harry exclaimed. "Greenley Street is quite a distance from here. How long have you been walking Jason?"

"All day," Jason replied warily.

"Dad that is impossible for two small kids this size to walk all that distance."

"Well Todd, if you are looking for someone important it might keep you walking longer. Dad's are pretty important right Jason?" Harry's free hand gently squeezed Jason's shoulder encouragingly, although he knew the story didn't quite ring true. He let it go for now.

"Yes, it was a long way." Jason replied woefully having managed to curb his tears. "I am very tired."

Reaching over to apply the cool cloth again Harry observed the slight fluttering of the small eyelids, then the appearance of some pretty blue eyes.

"Hello little darling, back with us are you?"

He kept wiping her face gently with hopes she wouldn't be frightened at seeing a stranger. Jason, who was standing next to Harry, said. "Bethany it is okay, he will make you feel better." He was patting her arm gently. Her eyes filled with tears. Jason soothed, "It's all right Bethany." Now that she was awake Harry proceeded in cleaning her dirty hands, while she let out a quiet sob.

"Dad this story is going to take all night." Todd interrupted anxious for proper answers.

"Todd, be patient Jason just needs our consideration on this?" Jason was still patting his sister's arm soothingly.

"Bethany and I were looking for our daddy because we don't know where the hospital is." His voice cracked noticeably at the mention of the hospital.

"How did you expect to find your daddy, if you don't know where he works?" Inquired an irritated Todd.

"Well daddy used to say it wasn't far when I would ask him. When daddy got in his car, he drove in this direction." Jason said angrily at Todd's remark. Jason just knew he was going in the right direction.

Harry raised Bethany into a sitting position with a pillow behind her. "What is your last name?"

Jason replied quickly. "McKnight I can even spell it. My mommy taught me." "M-C-K-N-I-G-H-T." The spelt word rang clearly.

"Todd, will you get the telephone book and see if you can find their phone number?" With a reproachful voice Todd said. "Dad, no one is home so what's the point."

"Todd, will you just get the telephone book, please? Maybe the father is home from work by now and wondering where they are." Stomping off Todd headed for the kitchen.

"Jason, do you know why your mother is in the hospital? I know you said she was sick but do you know the reason why she is actually in the hospital?"

"No, only that she was having trouble breathing and an ambulance took her away. Jennifer's mother called the ambulance after she came to our house when I told her how sick my mother was."

"Didn't Jennifer's mother come to take care of you when Jennifer left you alone?" Harry found it difficult to understand why these two small children were left by themselves.

"Yes, she came but I saw her coming through the window so we hid from her because Bethany didn't want Jennifer to come back. I guess Jennifer's mother thought someone else was taking care of us, when she couldn't find us. We were hiding under the bed and Mrs. D'Angelo didn't look there."

"You know Jason that wasn't a wise thing to do." Harry said with a quiet reprimand.

"I know. After she went away I was sorry because she never came back." A sob tripping his voice. "We only did it because Bethany didn't want Jennifer to come back anymore. We only wanted our mommy and daddy."

Jason, trying hard not to cry, whispered. "My daddy used to say to me when he was leaving for work 'Son you are the man of the house now so take care of your sister and your mother.' So I was taking care of her." Jason sniffing wiped his eyes with his sleeve.

"You did fine, Jason. I'm sure your dad would have been proud of you."

Looking up Harry watched Todd walk back into the room with the telephone book. "Here it is Dad. There is only one McKnight on Greenley Street. The name in the phone book is Laurie."

"Thank you, Todd. Now you sit with Bethany and watch her while I phone their father." Reaching for the phone in the kitchen Harry dialled the number, after six rings he contemplated hanging up only to hear a gruff voice answer. "Hello"

"Hello is this, the McKnight's residence?"

"Yes who is this?" A male voice inquired.

"My name is Harry Cochrane. I want to speak to Mr. McKnight? Is that you?"

"No, this is the police. Why are you calling?" The police officer adamantly inquired.

"I am trying to locate Mr. McKnight. I have his two children here." Harry said thinking he had better indicate why he was calling.

"So you have them. How did you get them?" The officer asked displaying curiosity in his tone, with a great deal of concern.

"They knocked on my door. They told me their names, and that they were looking for their father. Why are the police answering the phone? Is there a problem? Is their father not there?" Harry enquired.

"This is Officer Johnson. Their mother reported the children missing this morning and there is no Mr. McKnight."

"Really?" Harry was baffled

"I'll explain everything when we get there. What is your address Mr... did you say Cochrane?"

"Yes, Harry Cochrane and I live at 742 Ashley Avenue I'll be waiting here with the children. The little girl has a fever but I don't think it is serious enough to require an ambulance."

The officer said, "We'll be right over." abruptly the phone clicked.

Bewildered Harry went back into the living room. "There is no Mr. McKnight. The police were there and they are now on their way over." Harry said to Todd on entering the room. He immediately turned toward Jason. "Jason, when exactly did your father go to work?"

"He went to work and he never came home a... I don't kn... ow... Mommy said he... he..." Jason was crying in earnest now. Harry went over to put his arm around his shoulders. Jason burrowed into Harry letting the tears flow. Bethany started to cry as well. Todd looking from one to the other wishing that he could help them, knowing how he felt when his mother died. He leaned over patting her hand sympathetically gently whispering. "Don't cry baby, don't cry."

Sitting down with Jason, Harry tightly hugged him against his side. He was gazing down into his face. "Jason, it's all right. You were a very brave boy to look after your sister, that was quite a responsibility your daddy entrusted to you."

Todd was relieved the tears were stopped, except for a little hiccup escaping Bethany's lips and little whimpers now and then. "You are safe with us, little one."

Harry was proud of the way Todd was treating Bethany with gentleness. It suddenly dawned on Harry that since his wife died his son had been deplete of open affection from him. He had centred on coping with Sarah's death. Harry felt his guilt, as he saw how awkward Todd was being with Bethany in his attempt to be consoling.

Bethany sniffing was looking up at him intently.

Looking back at Jason, Harry spoke kindly. "Well Jason, the police will be here soon. Apparently your mother has sent them looking for you both."

Looking scared Jason whispered. "I didn't mean to worry mommy."

"I know but your mom is wondering where you are." Harry said gently.

Noticing the heat radiating from the girl's face, Todd interrupted. "Dad, Bethany's forehead is really hot."

"Maybe we should give her some aspirin and something to drink. Do you think that you could help me, Jason?" Harry asked.

"I think so. We haven't had anything to drink or eat for awhile." Jason said longingly.

CHAPTER TWO

Harry went over to the sofa with Jason trailing behind. Todd was talking gently to the little girl. He was reassuring her that her mommy would be home soon. With bright blue eyes Bethany was staring up at Todd.

"Todd, I'll carry Bethany you go with Jason and put some dinner on a plate for him. Then you heat Jason's and your dinner in the microwave, and pour him some milk too."

Todd strode towards the kitchen with Jason half running behind.

"Come on little darling, I'm going to give you an aspirin along with some juice to make you feel better." Picking Bethany up Harry faintly heard a whisper. "I have to pee."

"Okay, no problem" Harry changed direction and took Bethany towards the bathroom. If Sarah had lived would we have had a sweet little girl like this?

"We will get you fixed up?" Toilet duties taken care of, he looked in the cabinet for some children's aspirin. With the bottle in his hand, he bent to lift Bethany then headed for the kitchen. Harry came to an abrupt stop at the door. Todd was talking to Jason about his own mother going to heaven, and he was assuring him that his father was probably there too. Jason was eating and looking at Todd with amazement.

"Do you mean my father is with your mother?" Jason asked in wonder.

"Well. . . not beside her but somewhere nearby. . . maybe. . . but they are both in heaven." Todd finished quickly. He must have sensed someone listening, because he looked sheepishly towards his father and Bethany. Harry was rather surprised, as Todd had never said anything like this to him.

"Do you want me to zap your dinner in the microwave, Dad?" Todd asked helpfully to cover his embarrassment.

"No Todd. Not right now. The police should be here shortly and Bethany needs some attention first. Don't you, buttercup?" Looking at her sad face Harry continued. "We will get you feeling better real soon."

He reached into the fridge for the orange juice, pouring it into the empty glass on the counter. Grabbing the glass he headed over to the table. Sitting down with Bethany on his lap, he noticed Jason had eaten most of his dinner. The boy had obviously been very hungry from the way he had devoured his meal.

Harry took the bottle of chewable aspirin from his pocket, where he had shoved it while he poured the juice. He squinted at the directions to find the dosage for a child about Bethany's age, then he tipped out one tablet.

"Now chew on this for me then I will give you some juice to wash it down." He put the aspirin on Bethany's tongue watching her nibble a bit then held the glass to her lips for her to drink. She took a couple of little swallows.

"Did it go down?" Harry asked rather concerned. She stuck out her tongue showing it was empty. "That's a good girl. Now drink a bit more juice." After, Bethany cuddled into his chest her thumb went directly into her mouth.

"Jason, I don't think your hamburgers made Bethany sick or she would be throwing up. I think she just has a fever." Jason gave a relieved sigh.

The doorbell rang. "Todd, will you get that it is probably the police?" Jason's slender body sank in the chair a look of dread on his face. "Jason, don't worry they are here to help you. I promise. The police have come at your mother's request to find you." Harry finished reassuringly.

Todd showed the two officers into the kitchen. One officer was very tall and burly while the other was thinner and shorter but also seemed a tall man to Jason as he slumped more into his chair.

"Mr. Cochrane, I see you have made the kids at home. This is Officer O'Donall," indicating the burly cop, "and I am Officer Johnson. I spoke with you on the telephone. We were contacted by Mrs. McKnight. It seems that when Mrs. McKnight called the babysitter to find out how the children were doing, there was no answer. Then she called Mrs. D'Angelo, the mother of the babysitter, only to find out that they were not babysitting these two anymore."

"When we interviewed Jennifer and Mrs. D'Angelo, they said the children had somehow disappeared, so they assumed the mother had made arrangements with family members for their care. Mrs. McKnight was very alarmed to find out that the children were missing. She has been in the hospital with pneumonia, but she is getting better at last and felt well enough to phone, in hopes of speaking to the children. That was when Mrs. McKnight found out there was a problem, when no one answered the phone. You can imagine how upset she was when she heard her children were missing." Officer Johnson said.

"Yes I can imagine." Harry replied quickly.

Bethany had fallen asleep against his chest. Todd was asking Jason if he wanted more wings hoping to distract him. Jason was looking fearfully at the policeman. "Todd just give him some more. I am sure he is still hungry." Looking at the officer, Harry asked. "Do you know when the mother will get out of the hospital?"

"No, I imagine it will be a few days yet before she can leave, the way Mrs. McKnight was talking. Especially since she is deeply distressed about the children, in her weakened condition it might set her back." The officer offered.

Harry looked down at the little girl. "Did you know that the children were looking for their father when they arrived on my doorstep? Bethany was sick and unable to continue."

"Mrs. McKnight said their father was killed in a traffic accident three months ago on his way home from work, so these two children would never have found their father." Officer Johnson replied glancing over at Jason.

Jason was eating absently while scrutinizing the two policemen.

"The problem is that Mrs. McKnight has no relatives nearby, so she was depending on these neighbours to look after them. The babysitter said she only left them for five minutes to go over to her house and when she came back they had disappeared. Mrs. D'Angelo's story was, she didn't go over herself until quite late that night, when Jennifer returned from the mall after suppertime. Jennifer's excuse to her mother was the children had gone missing so she took off."

"Why didn't Mrs. D'Angelo call Mrs. McKnight and ask her if she had made other arrangements?"

"Mrs. D'Angelo said, she attempted to call the mother but was unsuccessful in reaching her. Mrs. McKnight must have been out of her hospital room for some reason or other. Then Mrs. D'Angelo put it out of her mind completely, with the assumption that the mother must have made other arrangements, or why else would the children have suddenly disappeared." Officer Johnson stated. "We have called Mrs. McKnight, to let her know how you immediately took the children in when they arrived on your doorstep but we didn't give her all the details. Now the question is how did the boy get this far especially with his sick sister?"

"His name is Jason and he said they walked but you can question him. Jason did you walk all the way?" Harry asked the boy before the officer could speak in the hopes to reassure him, it was all right to answer.

"Not quite." Jason voice quivered. "We climbed into the back of a Purolator truck. After he had made several stops for deliveries, I was afraid he would discover us. We seemed to be riding for a long time so we got out, after he had made a few more stops. Then we walked and walked. I didn't tell you because my mommy told me not to get into strange trucks or cars." Jason's voice trailed off quietly.

"That explains the mystery of how they got this far. I didn't think they could have walked all this way." Officer O'Donall put in decisively.

Harry replied rapidly. "Officer, I think perhaps they walked further than you are giving them credit for. You would be surprised how resilient children can be when looking for their parents. What are you going to do with the children?" Looking back at Officer Johnson, Harry waited for his answer with interest.

"We will have to take them back to Mrs. D'Angelo."

"You can't be seriously thinking of taking the children back there to them! They sound so irresponsible, especially Jennifer." Harry added in dismay.

"What else can we do, the mother has no one else to look after them. We don't want to get the Children's Aid Society involved for such a short period of time. Mrs. McKnight should be leaving the hospital soon."

"I am off for a few days vacation to help Todd get ready for school. He needs some new clothes and school supplies. So why don't I keep them?"

"That is very nice of you Mr. Cochrane, but their mother doesn't even know you. I can't possibly leave them here." Officer Johnson said authoritatively.

"So, you would rather give them back to Jennifer and her mother, knowing they didn't even bother to pursue looking for the two children after they disappeared?" Harry asked in disbelief.

"Well, we have no choice that is the arrangements Mrs. McKnight made for them."

"What if I call the mother and get her permission to keep them. Will that help?" Harry requested.

Todd piped up. "Yes Dad, we have to keep them. I'll help you with them." Todd said forgetting his earlier resentment of the children in their need. Harry was thankful that Todd was on board. He shifted the sleeping Bethany to his shoulder then stood up. He went to the phone using the number Officer Johnson gave him for the Westside General Hospital.

"Could I speak to Mrs. McKnight please? She is a patient there. I believe her first name is Laurie." Harry waited. "Hello Mrs. McKnight this is Harry Cochrane. You don't know me but I have your two children here." "Yes." "Yes they are okay. Bethany has a bit of a fever otherwise they are both fine." Mrs. McKnight's 'Thank heavens' resounded clearly through the phone.

"I can only assume you really don't want to give Jason and Bethany back into the care of Jennifer and her mother, when they didn't check thoroughly into the children's welfare, when they went missing."

Harry listened as Laurie explained her reasons for having the D'Angelos look after the children, saying she really had no other choice but to return them there.

"Mrs. McKnight, the police are here. They want to take the children directly back to Mrs. D'Angelo's. The children are perfectly happy here and my son Todd intends to help with them. I am going to let you speak to Jason so you can be sure you are doing the right thing." Harry held out the phone for Jason.

"Your mother wants to talk to you."

"Hello Mommy." "Yes, I am okay now. Mr. Cochrane is pretty cool and so is Todd. Bethany has a fever but Mr. Cochrane gave her an aspirin and juice and she fell asleep while he was holding on to her." Jason said.

"But Mommy, Bethany doesn't like Jennifer because she hits her, then Bethany is bad to Jennifer, then she leaves us alone." "I know Mommy but Mr. Cochrane treats us nice and I like Todd too. Todd is bigger than I am." Jason said with admiration in his voice.

"Yes Mommy, I love you too." Jason held the phone out to Harry. "She wants to talk to you."

"Hello Mrs. McKnight, if I get the two police officers to talk to my closest neighbours as to my credibility, will that make you feel better? I also might add my wife and I were at one time in an approved foster-care program." Harry didn't think it was necessary to clarify that they had never actual received a child because of Sarah's unexpected passing.

"Yes, I have the time. I have a few days off to get my son ready for school. I am a widower so I will be taking Todd shopping." "Just a minute." Harry held the phone out towards the officers saying. "She wants to speak to one of you." Harry sat down because Bethany had started to stir with all his movements and he didn't want her to wake up yet.

"Hello Mrs. McKnight this is Officer Johnson." "Yes Mrs. McKnight, it is a well-kept house." "Yes the boy is about four years older than your son." "No I don't know Mr. Cochrane but I could speak to his neighbours like he suggested."

"I think from the relaxed way he is with your children since we

13

arrived, I would say they were in good hands, especially if he and his wife were accepted in the foster-care program. They are pretty carefully screened before approval."

"Yes Mrs. McKnight, we will check in with Mr. Cochrane during the time he has them in his care. Do not worry just you get better. Everything will be taken care of and Mr. Cochrane looks like a genuine caring man by the way your daughter is curled up in his arms sleeping. Just a minute," The officer handed the phone to Jason.

While Jason talked to his mother in the background, the officer turned to Harry. "Well it looks like you have the responsibility for these two for a few days until their mother is released from the hospital. You probably heard that I promised Mrs. McKnight, we would check in on the children, which we will do." Officer Johnson said with a voice that brooked no refusal.

"Not at all, in fact I would expect it. I realize it is unusual to leave two young children with a stranger but I also recognize, under these circumstances the children cannot go back to Jennifer or her mother."

"I agree." Officer O'Donall interjected. "I wouldn't feel right taking them back there either."

"Well, we had better get going. Thank you for taking care of the children, Mr. Cochrane. Don't bother to get up Todd can see us out, won't you son?" Officer Johnson held out his hand and shook Harry's hand. "Good Night."

When Todd came back he went over to Jason and he put up his hand for a high five and Jason put up his hand to receive it with a big grin. He was happy to be with Todd, secretly liking the idea of a temporary big brother.

"Okay you boys finish your dinner and then clear off the table. Then you can watch television for awhile." Harry was glad the two boys were getting along so well and Todd was being agreeable. "Remember Todd, good programs for Jason and not too loud." The boys quickly ate then cleared the table.

Racing for the living room Todd's quick steps were followed by Jason's running pace.

Harry looked down at Bethany who was giving off little sucking sounds every once in awhile, her thumb still held firmly in her mouth.

What had he gotten himself into? What made him offer to take on these two children? Then he knew it was the bravery of these two little tykes walking to find their daddy, that had reached into Harry's heart. If only Sarah was here, sudden sadness choking him.

Easing off the chair he carried Bethany into the guest bedroom, laying her down on the bed after pulling the covers down. He made a cocoon for her of blankets and extra pillows from the closet. Touching the back of his hand to Bethany's forehead, Harry was thankful that her temperature seemed to be lower.

Going to Todd's room, Harry remembered buying two beds in the hopes of Sarah having more children. Recalling with sadness, how much they both had wanted another child. She had died from complications after an appendix operation.

Sarah appeared to be recovering well when suddenly she had developed a fever then a few nights later the alarming call came that Sarah had passed away in her sleep. He had been devastated and he had shut down emotionally. Realizing now his error in ignoring the affection he should have given Todd, which no doubt helped explain his cantankerous attitude at times, Harry felt sure.

CHAPTER THREE

Harry made up the other bed in Todd's room with fresh sheets, as Todd normally just kept it covered with a bedspread to match the one on his bed. The thought struck Harry that this was Todd's room. Perhaps he should be obtaining his permission first; he might resent Jason invading his privacy. Completing the bed, he headed for the living room.

He stood observing the scene before him. Todd was sitting with Jason's head in his lap while he slept soundly. Todd wasn't moving a muscle, so he wouldn't disturb the boy. He must have sensed his father standing there, because he looked up whispering. "He was falling asleep so I pulled him over against my shoulder but he eased down and put his head in my lap and went out like a light. He hasn't moved since." Todd's hand was on the boy in a comforting gesture.

"I came to ask if you would mind that I have made up the other bed in your room for Jason. I could put him in with Bethany in the guest bedroom, if you want." Harry whispered giving Todd a chance to make his own decision.

"No Dad, he'll be fine in my room. I'll listen for him if he wakes in the night, that way you can focus on Bethany more. How is she?" Todd whispered back.

"Thank you Todd. Bethany's sleeping, I think the aspirin did the trick." Harry eased Jason up into his arms and carried him into Todd's room. He undressed him and slid him under the covers without waking him. He stood peering down at Jason in the spare bed.

Harry realized he had always meant to remove that second bed. But when Sarah first passed away the significance of the empty bed was only too clear. However, he just couldn't remove it because somehow it seemed so final, and he couldn't do that to Sarah and their dreams.

Over time, the bed had become useful as a racetrack for Todd's collection of racing cars, which was his main hobby. Todd's collection had grown greatly over the years.

Obviously very tired, Jason was deeply asleep after his traumatic day that ended on a stranger's doorstep. Harry was touched by this little boy who was the stand-in man of the house and protector of his sister. He wondered why these two little tykes had reached into his heart so much, feeling somehow more alive.

Harry went back into the living room feeling that he had to explain himself to Todd. He sat down beside him placing his hand on his arm wanting to make contact. "Todd, I am sorry that I haven't shown you much affection since your mother died, but part of me shut down I think. I just realized that, when I put the two children to bed. I am so sorry."

"That's all right Dad. I knew we were both hurting for Mom so I do understand. Are Bethany and Jason both asleep now?"

"Yes, I hope Bethany will be okay in that big bed by herself. We can only hope that she sleeps through the night. I piled lots of pillows and blankets around her making a cosy nest." Harry reached around Todd with his arm and pulled him into his shoulder. It had been too many years since he had done that. Todd amazed him by resting against him and the two continued watching the TV neither breaking the connection.

The next morning, Harry heard the boys' voices escaping from Todd's room. After checking on Bethany who was still asleep, he followed the voices. The sunlight was filtering in the window, illuminating the racing car collection. Jason was watching and listening intently, as Todd described each car's features. He had many books on race cars and racing, so his knowledge was extensive and interesting. Jason wasn't touching any of the race cars, just looking on with total rapt attention to what was being shown to him.

"Well did you two have a good sleep?" Harry said as he entered the room.

"Hi Dad, I am showing Jason my racing cars. He really likes them." Todd said in response to his father's arrival. Jason was still looking at Todd with hero worship before he eased his eyes towards Harry. He said. "Yes, I slept well. How is Bethany?" Jason's voice held concern.

"Your sister is still sleeping and her fever seems to be gone. She must be really tired after the walk yesterday. Do you two lads want breakfast now?"

"We will be there shortly; Jason wants me to show him a few more of my special racing cars." Jason's eyes fixed back on Todd. The two boys were soon deep in concentration on the colourful racing cars. Harry stood observing them, experiencing gladness that Todd had taken to these two children, who had disrupted their weekend.

Returning to the kitchen, Harry poured the preset coffee and carried it to the table to sit and relax with the paper. A paper that Harry had to regularly search the bushes or lawn for, as the paperboy's throwing arm usually missed the veranda. A normal morning ritual while awaiting Todd to put in an appearance. Perusing the first page of the newspaper, Harry heard a cry from the bedroom. Setting aside the paper, Harry headed down the hall towards the sound at a quick pace hoping to stave off an intense bout of weeping.

Bethany was fully awake and kneeling on the bed. "Hi there, wee darling. Time to get up is it? Well we had better get you washed and dressed before we have breakfast." Harry carried her into the bathroom.

When they arrived in the kitchen it was to see Todd serving cereal to Jason, telling him the benefits of this oat cereal over the sugar ones, that so many kids seem to prefer. 'Too much sugar isn't good for healthy teeth' Todd was saying. The toaster popped up with some brown toast. Todd went to retrieve the popped up bread and brought it to the table. "Do you want me to butter the toast for you, or will you do it yourself Jason?"

Jason looked at Todd fixedly then he made his decision. "I can do it I am a big boy." Todd gave him the plate and a knife and placed the butter dish close at hand.

"Careful, don't put too much butter on your knife. Too much butter isn't good for you either."

Harry stood there listening with a tightness in his chest. He was hearing his son echoing his chants that he gave to him each morning. Obviously Todd had taken-in the message. He noticed a big change in him from the day before, into a responsible boy despite his not having a mother to nurture him. He felt proud he had achieved this unknowingly.

Harry spoke to Bethany. "Apparently these lads are well attended. How about I make you something to eat would you like that? What does Bethany usually have for breakfast, Jason?"

Since Jason had issued his claim on Bethany as her protector, Harry thought he should consult him. "She likes peanut butter on her toast."

Continuing Harry asked, "If I drive you over to your street, will you have any trouble finding your house Jason?"

"No. It is easy to find." Jason answered in a positive voice.

"I think that if you two are staying here we need to search out some more clothes and things from your place."

The trip to Jason's house was uneventful, however as Greenley Street came into view all conversation ceased. Todd with the realization of the distance the kids had traveled, and the children with their memories of their long escapade to find their daddy in their mother's absence.

Jason directed them along to Mrs. D'Angelo's with positive guidance. She answered the door so fast it was as though she had watched them get out of the car. Harry left Bethany in the car with Todd.

"Hello Jason. I see you are okay. Where did you go? Is your sister with you? Your mother phoned here really worried." Her voice wasn't unkind but did hold a note of accusation of bad behaviour on Jason's part.

"My sister and I went looking for my daddy." Jason stated in a sad voice.

Harry placed his hand on Jason's shoulder. "You don't have to explain any further Jason. Mrs. D'Angelo, Mrs. McKnight gave me permission to look after the children. I am here to pick up their clothes and things so please may I have the house key? My name is Harry

Cochrane if you wish to confirm with Mrs. McKnight?"

"No. . . No. . . aah. I'll get the key for you." Her face had a closed expression, as though Harry was being critical of her. She quickly came back with the key, trussing it at him. Without another word to Jason, the door was shut firmly in their faces.

"Come on Jason. We'll go to your house now." Harry steered the boy back to the car without a backward glance, although Harry felt sure Mrs. D'Angelo was peering out from behind the lacy curtains.

Arriving at the house, Harry saw a cute little home with a white picket fence. The flower garden was out in full bloom, but they were vying for space amongst some extra healthy weeds, showing the evidence of their absent owner, who normally gave them attentive care.

The front door held a wreath of various pretty dried flowers in a welcoming colourful invitation. This added touch made the house look cheerful. "Todd, you and Jason open the door and I will bring Bethany."

"Yoo-hoo Jason how are you?" A voice permeated from across the street. "Where have you been?" Jason whipped around in his path to the front door. His face went white.

"It's okay Jason. Is that the lady you told me about?" Jason shook his head yes.

"It's okay Mrs. Clark; the children are staying with friends." Harry immediately turned away before she could call any further inquiries. Jason was now running after Todd who had hopped up on the veranda. Jason wanted to be the one to open the door. They all quickly stepped in. Harry and Todd were casually looking around. It was an attractive place with lots of bright colours evident in the decor against light rose coloured walls. The furniture was old but not threadbare.

Looking in the kitchen, Harry observed two cereal bowls and an empty milk carton. Jason had mentioned the kitchen was relatively clean.

"Let's go see about the clothes for you and Bethany. Jason you lead the way." They all trouped to the bedrooms. The first bedroom was small in size, a little bed with a white and pink coverlet and a ruffled pink skirt all around sat under the window. The small side table held a Bo-peep lamp painted white and pink with blonde curly hair showing under the bonnet. This was so feminine and pretty, Harry easily recognized this had to be Bethany's room.

"I'll pack Bethany's clothes while you two go pack Jason's." Harry had brought paper grocery bags with handles. Grabbing for some bags the boys took off down the hall.

Harry glanced at Bethany. She was peering up at a picture of a woman, he surmised was her mother with Jason and Bethany enclosed in her arms. It looked like the mother was bending to receive them in her embrace, just as the picture was taken with a blissful smile on her face, catching the moment for a lifetime. Tears were trailing down Bethany's cheeks, a soft mewing sound emitting from her mouth.

Harry went over to her and put his hand on her shoulder. "You miss your mommy don't you, pet? Well she is missing you too, I am sure. If she could be here with you she would be. Your mommy loves you very much." Harry's voice was quiet but reassuring.

Down the hall Jason was quickly pulling out drawers while Todd glanced around. There were a variety of airplanes hovering overhead suspended from the ceiling.

"Wow! Jason these planes are really neat. Who gave them to you?" Jason turned and looked up at the soaring planes. "My daddy and I made them. Daddy mostly did the handiwork. I just got to hand him pieces but I did glue some pieces together every now and then." Jason said proudly.

Todd was impressed at the intricate detail on some of the planes. Then he cast his eyes around the room until they came to a large shelf beside the bed. There were ships in full sails and rigging; replicas of Clipper ships from long ago. Todd knew Jason's father must have built these too.

"Dad will have to come and see these, Jason. They are nifty. Your dad was really expert at making them, wasn't he?" The detailing of the sails and the elaborate rigging on each ship was very impressive. Jason was busy packing the bags while Todd was looking around in wonder.

"My dad and I spent most of our weekends building planes or ships when we weren't visiting the park or the zoo. Bethany liked the zoo best. My dad has assembled ships in bottles too, but they are special and mommy keeps them on the shelf in the living room." Jason spoke with such pride about his dad's endeavours.

Harry walked in with Bethany following him like his shadow. It had taken no time at all to pack her things and put them by the front door. "How are you doing in here? Almost packed yet?"

"Dad, look up and around you." Todd said in admiration. "Jason helped his dad create these."

"Jason these are wonderful. You and your father have real talent. It shows in the explicit detail in which they were assembled." Jason was grinning with pride now that Harry too admired them.

"Yes, my dad liked to build things with his hands. He was teaching me how to do them too." There was a catch in his voice as he said this last comment.

"Jason, I think Todd and I could help you, if you have something that you and your dad might have been working on. Why don't you bring it along?" Harry was looking at Todd for support.

"Yeah Jason, bring whatever needs assembling. I would like to help you." Todd reached down for the bag that Jason was filling. "Is there anything more to be put in here? "

"No that should be enough."

Jason went to the closet door and opened it. He looked up longingly. Harry had followed him to the doorway. "Is this box up here holding something you want to bring with you, Jason?" Jason was wagging his head up and down decisively. Harry reached up for the box, which held a half-finished clipper ship. It looked exactly like a replica of the famous Bluenose Schooner Harry had seen in a magazine.

"Todd, you carry this and Jason can carry the bags." When they were ready Harry noticed Bethany was missing, heading for the front door there she was on the floor playing with a Raggedy Ann doll. There was a stuffed dog peeking out of the bag beside her.

"Next stop Westside General Hospital." Harry eased the big car into the roadway. "You mean we can really go see mommy?" Jason said in awe.

"No guarantees but we'll try." Harry said hopefully.

CHAPTER FOUR

When they arrived at the hospital Harry told Todd who was sitting in the front seat, to watch out for Jason and Bethany while he arranged to have their mother appear in the window of her room, so they would be able to see each other.

Harry located the information desk, asking for Laurie McKnight's room. He found out she was in 311.

"Hello Mrs. McKnight. I am Harry Cochrane." He walked over to the bed. Reclining against some pillows in a half sitting position on the raised bed, was a petite blonde lady with a cautious look on her face.

"Mrs. McKnight, I have your children in the car. My son, Todd is with them until I get back. I brought them here because I promised that they could wave to you. If you are able to get out of bed that is, and move to your window. They want to see that you are getting better. They are both missing you greatly."

"Mr. Cochrane, I want to thank you for taking the children into your home. How are they adapting? I have been so worried about them. When they went missing, I didn't know what to think." The worry was still etched on her face. "Especially when Mrs. D'Angelo said they had been alone for three days, but you didn't have them that long did you?"

"No Mrs. McKnight. The children hid under the bed when people came in after the babysitter left them alone. They didn't want Jennifer to come back, as she was mean to Bethany, Jason said. Then they left to go find their father." Harry heard her draw in a hurt breath, knowing what was coming next.

"But their father was killed three months ago."

"I know but children that are as young as Jason and Bethany don't always comprehend death. All they remembered was their daddy went to work and didn't come home. At their age, given the circumstances at the time, they just knew they needed their father, when they didn't know where the hospital was." Harry said compassionately.

She looked so sad, it was disconcerting to him. "I didn't mean to upset you. I just wanted you to understand Jason's reasoning. He was a very brave boy to travel that distance. I live quite far away from your house." Harry ended softly. "How are you doing Mrs. McKnight? The children will want to know?"

"I am getting better at last. I hope the doctor lets me leave early next week if not sooner. I want to be home with my little ones."

"Well you are not to worry about Jason and Bethany. Todd and I are taking good care of them, not that Jason needs much as he is quite the lad. I have to get back now as they are waiting in the car. The nurse will be coming in to help you over to the window, so the children can wave to you. Take care, Mrs. McKnight." Harry moved to the window looking down on a floral garden with a fountain, then glanced back to the bed.

"Please call me Laurie. Thank you again. I appreciate what you are doing for me. You can tell the nurse I am ready for her to help me. Please come again if you have the chance. I need to know how my children are doing."

"You're welcome Laurie and please call me Harry. I will keep you informed about the children." He ducked out of the room and signalled to the nurse that was looking his way. It was the nurse that offered to help Laurie.

"I'll go down and get the children in place." Entering the stairwell, Harry was too impatient to wait for the old elevator. When he approached the car, he could see their eager faces watching him hopefully. He nodded his head yes and grinned, and their faces lit up like hundred-watt bulbs.

Todd was out of the car and held the back door open. Jason leaped out before Harry reached the car. He opened the door and released Bethany, picking her up to speed their passage to the floral garden and their waiting mother.

Todd and Jason were running ahead and Harry was yelling directions. He went as fast as he could without jostling Bethany. He reached the floral garden. Jason was leaping up and down waving and yelling, "Hi Mommy."

Harry was directing Bethany to look up, to wave to her mother. When Bethany spotted her mother, she began to cry, reaching out her arms and struggling, "Mommy! Mommy!" Harry was trying to hug her back into him, as he was afraid of dropping her.

Then he looked up and somehow he knew, even before he saw Laurie's face, that she would be crying too. He felt emotional watching this family reunion. Jason had stopped jumping. His face had lost its excitement staring up at his crying mother. Todd had his arm around him, comforting him. "It's all right Jason. Your mom is just crying because she wants to be with you." Jason swallowed deeply but one small sob still escaped. "I want to be with her too." His voice trailed off but he didn't openly cry.

Harry was feeling wretched that his idea had turned into disaster and made things worse. He had not taken into account that these six and three year old brave tykes, who had crossed a town looking for their daddy; whom they would never have found, would fall apart seeing their mother in tears. So near, but separated from them behind a pane of glass in the towering building.

Seeing their crying mother in the window was hard on Todd too. He thought he was over missing his mother, but his heart now wished that the pretty woman had been reaching out to him too.

• • •

The day of Laurie's leaving the hospital had finally arrived. Harry had been to the hospital to see Laurie a couple of times to report on the children's progress. Today, he had left them home with his next-door neighbour to watch over them. During the trip home Laurie would no doubt be eager to glean information about the children from him.

He would tell her Bethany was now talking freely, and she had become Todd's little shadow. Todd didn't seem to mind being big brother to these two waifs. He was going to miss them, when they went back to their home. The boys had finished the schooner. Jason would be taking the model home with him.

Their next trip to the mall would include Todd picking out a clipper ship to build, Harry surmised.

During his drive to the hospital, he was practicing his speech in preparation for inviting her to stay at his house with Todd and the children while recovering. She would need to get stronger before she should be on her own was his sound reasoning. The fact that hospitals were restricting as to exercise, she would still be in a weaken condition and could do with help for her and the children for awhile.

'Face it Harry' he thought 'you just couldn't bear to lose those two little tykes so soon.'

He approached the room as the candy stripper brought a wheelchair for Laurie's exit from the hospital, being a normal hospital procedure. Her face was animated with warm smiles at his approach. He took pleasure in looking at this beautiful woman with her bright blue eyes and her dazzling smile, radiating her pleasure at being released to be reunited with her children. Her hair was falling in waves around her shoulders in a shiny aura, which framed her pale face. Harry enjoyed the sight, as he had only seen Laurie with her hair tied back at the nape of her neck.

"Are we all set Laurie?" Harry smiled at her. Then the nurses were giving her a send off of wishes for a good future and a little joke of don't bother to hurry back.

Noting the empty car, Laura tried to disguise her disappointment at not being reunited instantly with her children. Harry told her the children were with his neighbour.

He wanted her alone to suggest his plan to detain her from going home, but instead, to convalesce at his place. He was doing some fast-talking overruling her protest. She slowly gave in, being too weak to argue with his sensible point of view.

The children leaped off the veranda before the car eased to the curb. The sprinting bodies were like projectiles in their flight across the lawn. Their feet hardly touched the ground in their haste and their chants of "Mommy! Mommy!" were chorused as they ran.

Laurie had stopped part way up the walkway and waited with wide-open arms to receive her babies. Todd lagged behind watching those open arms ready to engulf them. This was something that Todd truly missed.

Laurie was kissing, hugging and exclaiming how much they had grown, when she glanced up at Todd. She held out her arm and Todd went forward to be drawn into her embrace hugging all three of them. She thanked Todd for looking after her little ones. She kept her arms around all three as she looked up at Harry and thanked him too. He was admiring the picture they made missing the completion of a loving family.

· · ·

The days flew by and Laurie revived under Harry's care. She was making overtures of wanting to go home. He was back to work after extending his time off to be with Laurie and the children for a few days.

The day had dragged significantly for him as he wanted to be home with his newly acquired family. To that warm place that his home had become. It was the end of the day but he had one more meeting with a client. He hadn't given his complete attention to the plans spread out on his drawing board. Tom Baker was discussing some changes for his new company complex, and Harry slowly altered the path of his thoughts to concentrate on Tom's suggestions of modifications.

Tom was adamant that the changes were reasonable and must be made to facilitate the expansion that he was expecting for his company in coming years. Harry finally agreed, but made limitations, so the changes would not alter the concept of the outer design of the building, which was what drew Tom in the first place. The agreement of changes were finalized. The cost rehashed to reflect the difference.

Harry was trying to politely end the lengthy meeting, while regretting his neglect of a client in his need for speediness. They agreed to another meeting when the modifications had been completed.

Arriving home Harry felt disappointment, only to see Laurie sitting in a chair on the veranda surrounded by the standing children, their boxes of clothes and a suitcase piled near the stairs in readiness. Looking like they couldn't wait to leave.

He couldn't help the feeling of hurt, to see that she was so anxious to go home. When he got out of the car and walked towards the house, Bethany and Jason ran to him. Bethany's little arms encircled his leg and Jason's arms were grasping his waist. Harry was overcome by this show of affection that would soon be lost.

He ruffled Jason's hair and bent down to pick up Bethany. She planted a big smacking kiss on his cheek surrounding his neck with her chubby arms. He looked at Todd and Laurie and said 'Hi' adding. "It looks like you are already packed to go home." He paused, and then continued looking into Laurie's eyes as though wanting to find some regret. "Can you give me time to shower and change my clothes?"

He was trying to read Laurie's expression. *Was she glad to be going? Would she and the children miss Todd and him as much as they would miss them? Will they ever be together again like this past week? No it couldn't end this way.*

"Sure take your time." Laurie said with a sweet smile. She knew in her heart that she would really miss them both.

Harry went into the house to shower and change. Laurie certainly seemed very eager to leave. He knew he was being unrealistic. He liked having a family to come home to. He really missed being a family since his Sarah died.

When he came back out his hair was still damp and curling at the ends in an masculine way. He had on a polo top and chinos in blues.

"Well shall we be on our way? Everyone grab something and we will have the car packed in no time. Todd you strap Bethany in her car seat. Jason, you are in the center." The children were laughing and giggling in their excitement of the excursion home. Harry took Laurie's arm and her suitcase. "The door is open on your side Todd. I will put everything into the trunk." The children had piled the boxes on the sidewalk beside the trunk except for the finished schooner, which Jason was carrying in a box, he wanted to hold it on his lap.

Harry entered the car. "Everyone buckled in? Laurie, I thought we would go to Maffeo's for dinner. They make good pasta and their seafood dishes are to die for. Their dessert Tiramisu is out of this world. Would you like that?" Hoping to sell her on the idea. "If not, we can go to a place of your choice?" Harry glanced Laurie's way.

Laurie smiled. "The children love pasta so that would be fine." She was watching him. He was such a nice caring man. How many men would take in two small children that were strangers and look after them? She appreciated that he had taken her into his home for her convalescence too. Not many men would have, and certainly not any that she had occasion to know until now.

Harry noticed Laurie studying him. *Will he be able to keep seeing them? Maybe it would be best if I stay away from her and let her keep her independence. Was that why she was in such a rush to get back to her own home?* Then there was the obvious fact that it was too soon since her husband died, to expect more from her. Besides she probably didn't want to out stay her welcome now that she was stronger.

During dinner Laurie and Harry had been quiet, as though waiting for the other to set out guidelines for their future. The children had kept up a lively dialogue with their incessant talking.

When they finally pulled up in front of their home, Laurie glanced around at the garden. "I have my work cut out for me for the next month. The garden is overgrown with weeds again, since the landscapers were here." Jason piped up at that moment. "We are home Bethany isn't that great?" Bethany yelled "Yes."

After unpacking the car and the groceries, that had been bought on route, they all stood on the veranda looking at each other uncomfortably not knowing how best to end this recently formed connection.

Todd gave Jason a high five and said. "See you around." Then headed back to the car feeling too choked up to delay the goodbyes. Laurie picked up Bethany, relaying her thank you to Harry, expressing her appreciation for his help with the children and her own convalescence.

"Think nothing of it. I guess we should be going so you can settle in. Sounds like the children are happy to be home at last." The warmth in his voice evident. He reached out to give Bethany a kiss on her cheek. He placed a hand on Jason's shoulder and squeezed. "Take care, Jason."

Laurie said lamely. "I guess we should go in and get unpacked. The children will be happy to be back in their own beds again."

"Hopefully I may see you around town sometime soon." Harry said expectantly. Laurie replied a weak yes.

"If you need anything, anything at all; be sure to call me anytime." Harry added as he patted Bethany then headed down the stairs and walked to the car.

Todd and Harry gave them a wave as the car slowly drove off. A silent car ride ensued.

CHAPTER FIVE

Several weeks passed and Harry didn't hear from Laurie and the children nor had he seen them in town. He had gone unnecessarily to different stores nearby Laurie's place hoping that she might be there. He had called a few times but the ringing was never interrupted by a voice.

Once he drove by the house in high hopes, but there was no one about, it had a sad look of abandonment. Why hadn't he been more insistent they keep in touch, when they parted? He at least thought Jason would try to contact Todd. Definitely Todd had tried calling Jason but he was unsuccessful too.

Harry couldn't believe it had ended this way. He was kicking himself inwardly for letting them disappear out of their lives. That short time of family unity had made him yearn for more.

Todd and he had kept up the bonding connection induced by Jason and Bethany's stopover. Often Todd would remark on how quiet the place was without them. Harry would agree with him, not admitting completely how melancholy he was feeling. That would be when he would try to give Laurie another call. Eventually the ever silent telephone had a message that this line was no longer in service.

Todd and he had resumed their lives but neither had completely forgotten those two little ones that had burrowed into their hearts, and for Harry the mother too, in the nine days their lives touched. A little bit of sadness in both of them was evident. During this time Todd's fleet of Clipper ships grew, sometimes even with Harry's assistance.

One day when he came home there was a letter from a lawyer. It was addressed to Harold Benjamin Cochrane. That was his father's name. Harry never wanted to use that name although it was his name too. He always figured that Harold Sr. had died of meanness, but really it was his heart that gave out. Harry never had a close relationship with his brusque father, nor did Harold Sr. bother with his relatives either. Due to his father's terse behaviour no one seemed to visit them and his parents never visited anyone nor did his father deem to discuss them. At least that was his impression of his youth.

When Harry opened the letter, it said that he had inherited a house in Lambton Mills, Ohio. Apparently it had belonged to his Aunt Elsie, his father's sister. He had a dim memory of a pleasant cheerful lady. Harry remembered meeting her a few times at funerals. Aunt Elsie hadn't talked much at his father's funeral. He surmised, she couldn't think of anything nice to say about his cantankerous father or their childhood together. He always wondered what it would have been like to live in a close friendly family. In his youth, Harry had always promised himself that his family would be a loving one, but he felt guilty that he had failed to live up to that after Sarah died until recently.

Harry's mother lived in Joyceville five miles away. Their relationship was more open with each other now that his father was dead. His mother's parents had been to visit them a few times in the early days. They lived in Florida now. His father's behaviour had discouraged the grandparents from coming too often.

The other funeral at which he had seen his Aunt Elsie was at his grandfather's. Harry thought that maybe that was the last time he had seen Aunt Elsie as Harry's grandfather outlived his son.

"Who is that letter from Dad? You are really studying it."

"It seems I have inherited a house. It is located in Lambton Mills, Ohio. It belonged to your Great-Aunt Elsie. I have never been there. How about we travel there on the weekend to check it out? Then we can look the place over thoroughly and decide what to do with it? Are you game?"

"Yes. Hey Dad that might be kind of neat. Does it describe the house? I wonder what it is like. Where is Lambton Mills?"

"Lambton Mills is about forty miles west of Dayton, Ohio."

"Dad that is quite a ways from here isn't it." Todd actually liked to travel in the car. They went to see his grandmother fairly often, although this trip to Ohio sounded so far away to Todd.

"Well we could drive up real early Saturday and if the place merits a stay we will. There must be a hotel or motel close by. We could always sell the house and use the money for a trip some place." Harry added thoughtfully. "I haven't travelled much with my job since your mother died because I wanted to be here for you. When your mother was with us, I used to do a lot of travelling. Your mom never liked that aspect of my job and I regret that now." *Why didn't I refuse some of the out of town jobs? Why didn't I spend more time with Sarah?* Harry was silently kicking himself now.

"We could go to Disney World or someplace like that." Todd suggested.

"That might be a good idea. Your great-grandparents still live in Florida. Maybe we could stop in and visit with them." Harry said thoughtfully. It was something he had told himself he would do someday.

"They must be pretty old."

"Yes I imagine so, but your grandmother says they are still living in their own home."

Harry was trying unsuccessfully to bring a picture of them into his mind. Their visits had been too few and far between.

The weekend trip went speedier than they imagined. Maybe it was the expectation that helped make the miles disappear. When they arrived in Lambton Mills, they easily found the lawyer's office on Main Street. The sign in the window depicted the message. 'In case of emergency call 988 1666.'

"This isn't an emergency but maybe he might not mind if we call under the present circumstances." They stopped at the phone in the restaurant entrance.

A female voice said. "The Hamilton residence."

"Could I speak to Mr. Hamilton please?" Harry asked hopefully.

A gruff voice answered the phone. "Hamilton here. What can I do for you?"

"I am Harry Cochrane. The letter from you mentioned that I had inherited a house belonging to my Aunt Elsie Cullen. Can you direct me there?" Harry fumbled in his pocket for a pen. Thoughtfully he had shoved the pen in his breast pocket before leaving home. "Yes I have a pen."

"It is 795 Hager Street, three blocks off Main St. on Roe Hampton. You can't miss it. It has orange shutters. Why would anyone put orange shutters on a home is beyond me?" The gruff voice muttered then continued. "I have the key in the office. I can meet you there in say. . . fifteen minutes." He must have been studying his watch the way he hesitated.

Mr. Hamilton was the perfect picture of a lawyer. Well dressed in a suit even though it was a Saturday. His hair was neatly groomed with a bald dome. His tie was very conservative and he had a stern look on his face. He didn't even smile when he greeted Harry and Todd. Maybe he wasn't happy to be bothered on his day out of the office. He whipped out a key chain with numerous keys jangling on it.

They followed him in, going directly to a large office holding countless file cabinets and a desk. Under the 'C's he extracted a bulky file folder and returned to the desk, setting it down. The name on top was Elsie Cullen in big letters.

Harry felt guilty that he hadn't even known his Aunt's married name when she was alive until he had received the lawyer's letter. "How did my Aunt Elsie die?"

"She just died of old age quietly in her sleep. She was always on the frail side but wiry in her later years. Elsie lived for her floral garden." Mr. Hamilton remarked. "Here is the key and the deed. I will arrange to have this property re-registered in your name. There were some funds in a savings account but that was left to her companion, Mrs. Davies, who stayed with her during the last five years." Harry thanked the lawyer as he signed some papers.

When he slipped into the car, he said to Todd. "I have the key and a copy of the signed papers for the new deed so I guess we are the proud owners of a house with orange shutters."

"Orange shutters ugh!"

"Well they can always be painted over. Besides we don't intend on keeping the house, do we?"

"But Dad we haven't even seen it yet? Maybe we will want to keep it."

"Lambton Mills is too far away from my office, Todd."

"Maybe we can use it as a weekend retreat or for holidays." Todd said in a helpful way.

"I don't know about that. Let's go take a look." Harry drove down Main Street in the direction that the lawyer had indicated.

Turning onto Hager street, spying the orange shutters Todd exclaimed. "Dad, they aren't so bad."

"No actually I kind of like the colour on this particular house." Harry said craning his neck stopping in front of the home. "You know this isn't bad. It seems to have character. Don't you agree?"

"Character says it all." Todd replied studying the house.

They went up the front steps to the dark brown front door. The grounds were weedy and the grass needed a trim. Nice flowering shrubs were decoratively spaced. When they entered, the house gave off a slight odour of abandonment.

"Leave the door open and we'll open a few windows to air the place out." Peering into the first room, Harry observed a living room. The furniture was French Provincial in shades of beige, pink and greens in a well cared for condition. Tiffany lamps residing on scrolled tables bordering the formal couch with an antique Axminster rug on the floor. Harry's impression was that he had stepped back in time.

He crossed to the window to open it. The view was of some well cared for homes across the street with an affluent look. He was taking it in, as he heard the click of the window locking into place. The windows were more modern, so they must have been replaced fairly recently.

Harry continued looking around noting the ancestral grandfather clock that was due to chime the hour but was silent. It was a magnificent piece with its immobile pendulums in an intricate walnut cabinet, patiently awaiting the key to release it into mobility.

There was a picture of a gentleman sitting at a pedestal desk over the mantel. He looked like he was admiring the artist with a gleeful look in his eyes. Harry wondered if the artist had been his aunt. How little he knew of his Aunt Elsie feeling a little regret.

Just as he went to step through the French doors into the dining room, Todd yelled. "Dad come here, you have to see this?" Harry followed the voice upstairs. Todd was standing in the doorway of a room. Harry joined him stopping in admiration of a amazing bathroom with gold fixtures. An ancient bathtub with clawed feet and a cabinet with the look of the fourteen century, graced the one wall. The sink was like a rose ceramic bowl with gold taps jutting out from the wall. Whoever designed this house had a past era in mind. The towel rack was a podium in gold with handmade lacy edged towels pleasingly draped there. The toilet was vintage style and the huge bowl seemed to be suspended from the wall.

Harry and Todd stood transfixed gazing their fill of an era past. Harry wished he could have visited his Aunt Elsie, now more than ever. He was sure she had quite a tale to divulge. She must have been quite the lady in her day, which her husband must have pandered to, as he looked around.

Todd was running from room to room observing the grandiose decor. He announced. "Four bedrooms with abnormally large beds and small boudoir chairs like you see in olden day movies." He ran back into the master bedroom. "Dad, there is a pond in the backyard with running water spouting from a dragon. I can see fish swimming around amongst the lily pads."

Harry came to pause behind Todd. The garden was an imposing sight with its multitude of floral blooms with flagstone walkways; forming a path and encasing the pond. The furniture was a scrolled white wrought iron table and chairs placed invitingly near the lily pond. There were stone benches tucked in amongst some shrubbery on the pathways.

Harry turned from the window to observe the massive bed with its huge armoire and dresser matching but not dwarfing this huge room. There were two boudoir chairs, which indeed were small in stature. Harry figured the furnishings must have been passed down through generations. He knew it wasn't his family so it must have been Mr. Cullen's. Just maybe, the antique furniture was the directive for the home's design.

Todd had gone downstairs to the kitchen. "Dad, the kitchen at least seems more modern." He broadcasted. Indeed when Harry viewed the kitchen it was to see modern day touches throughout. The sizable windows looked out onto the splendour of the abundant garden. They walked out onto the patio, which held a table, chairs and a drooping umbrella.

Harry's impression was, the house was awaiting its owner who had gone away perhaps on a long trip. His eyes drifted to the pond. Todd was kneeling gazing into the pond, watching the fish weaving in and out under the leafy water plants. "I think there are ten but it is hard to count, because they keep moving in and out, hiding under the water foliage." Todd called out to him.

Harry was glancing back at the house, wondering if selling it would be very difficult with its unusual past era motif, especially the unique bathroom. Was it possible to find someone that would actually appreciate its appeal?

The furnishings would have to be put in storage until Harry located other living relatives of Mr. Cullen's. What had been his name Uncle. . .? He would have to ask his mother if she knew anything of Mr. Cullen's family. Otherwise he would have to sell the furnishings, as these antiques certainly wouldn't look appropriate in their current home. It would be a shame, as there were some wonderful pieces here. Would it be possible the new owners would want them?

Todd watched the expression playing over his father's face as he approached the pond. "Dad, what are you thinking?" "Well Todd I was thinking, could we find a buyer for it and what in the world to do with those furnishings?"

"Could we keep it for awhile? We could come on weekends." Todd said hopefully. "I really like this fish pond. I wish Jason were here to see this?" Todd finished wistfully.

"Me too." With a sigh Harry wished that Laurie and Bethany could be with them too. He still missed them a great deal. *Where had they disappeared to?* "Come on let's find a restaurant for something to eat and discuss the possibilities."

Todd said viewing the Eatery Grill menu. "I would like a hamburger." The waitress looked at Harry who said a hamburger would be fine for him too. During the meal they talked about the house. They puzzled over the possibilities. The agreement they finally struck was putting the house up for sale with the closing date in three months, so they had time to enjoy the place. They could come weekends for their pleasure and do some weeding and such. Their decision made, they headed for the real estate office up the street.

The real estate office was open, a sparking smile from the young lady who enquired if they were looking for a house. When Harry said they wanted to sell one, she directed them to the end office. When they looked inside there was a cheerful face waiting to greet them having been informed by the receptionist. She smiled broadly. "Can I help you?"

"Yes, I am Harry Cochrane and this is my son, Todd. We would like to talk to you about putting a house on the market."

She stood up and held out her hand. "I am Annette Brice. Please take a seat." At the same time, she was waving her hand towards the fabric chairs. They sat down while Annette stationed herself in readiness. "What property are you referring to?"

"795 Hager Street, it belonged to my aunt but she passed away and I have inherited the property. It is not feasible for me to keep it, as we live in Indiana."

"I know that property and I knew your Aunt Elsie, a dear sweet lady. My condolences to you on your Aunt's passing. I hadn't heard." Annette was chiding herself for missing this information as she usually skimmed the obituaries, as they were potential sales but at the same time sad at Elsie Cullen's passing.

"Thank you." Harry acknowledged her condolences. "We were thinking of selling. Have you been inside?" His voice held scepticism.

"Yes, I visited your aunt on occasion for afternoon tea. I seem to recall the unusual bathroom, which is what you are probably thinking about?"

"Yes, unusual is putting it mildly." Harry answered.

"You could of course promote its unique decor but then it would certainly deter some people looking to buy. You could renovate but I feel that if we get the right buyer the bathroom will appeal to them." Her eyes were animated with the opportunity of selling this unique house. "Shall we drive out there now?"

Harry stood up. "Yes, we were just going back there."

"I will meet you there in thirty minutes. I have a few things to attend to first. That will give you time to look around some more before I arrive."

Harry and Todd drove back to the house while discussing their potential weekends there. Annette arrived shortly after.

Walking through the house, she expressed her point of view, from a woman's perspective. She particularly liked the ornate bathroom as a feature in the sale. Harry could see a speculative look on her face at this. *Did she have a client in mind already?*

Annette was saying that the houses in this particular district were selling for a significant amount right now. She believed Harry would be pleased with the proceeds of the eventual sale. They walked back into the large kitchen, and she displayed information from her briefcase on the counter top of recent sales in the district.

After browsing over them, Harry invited Annette to sit down at the table near the window. He noted Todd was laying at the edge of the pond dragging his hand in the water as though hoping the fish would swim near him.

He was receiving vibes of a special affinity with this house, but it just wasn't feasible to keep it. He was thinking over the material Annette had shown him. The amounts were more than he anticipated for a small town like this. She mentioned it was the proximity to Dayton and the easy daily commute.

Harry asked if there was anything that he could do to make it marketable in the meantime. Annette indicated he only needed to spruce up the gardens and the house would sell itself as the market trend was a seller's market. "There aren't many houses for sale in this particular area, being a high demand neighbourhood." Annette started gathering her papers and returning them to her briefcase.

"Mr Cochrane, I will take some measurements and some particulars then I will be going back to the office to make up the listing. I'll be having two open houses. The first open house will be a weekday, and then the next on a weekend. I will let you know when I am able to schedule them. We will start about ten thousand over current market price only because the type of prospective buyer I have in mind, will leap at it even at that price. I assure you I have a good feeling about this house." Annette voice oozed confidence. "How does that sound?"

"That's fine by me. Thank you, Mrs. Brice. Feel free to take all the time you need. My son and I plan to enjoy it for three months. During that time I will pack and remove my aunt's personal belongings." Harry assured her.

Annette held out her hand to shake his hand. "Please call me Annette. Thank you Harry." He stood at the window watching Todd while Annette obtained measurements of the rooms. Todd was playfully trying to attract the fish to his hovering hand. Harry envied Todd his absorption in the fishpond that he had missed in his own childhood, not having visited his Aunt Elsie during her lifetime.

CHAPTER SIX

Harry headed for the back garden to talk to Todd. He looked up as his dad approached him. "Dad the fish were coming to nibble on my fingertips. Not nibbling really just opening and closing their mouths." He added pensively.

"Todd, Mrs. Brice might be having an open house next weekend. She will be advertising it in the paper, which should bring people looking. I'll need to hire someone else to groom the gardens. I thought we could do it ourselves next weekend but the open house takes precedence."

"That's okay Dad there will be other weekends."

"I very much doubt it will sell that fast," glancing back at the house. "The closing date is for three months unless the new owner insists on an earlier closing. I am going to ask Mrs. Brice about a possible landscaper for the grounds, should the opening be next weekend."

Annette was very accommodating, she said she would take care of it for him. Leaving shortly afterwards with a confident air that she would indeed sell this unique house.

Todd spent the rest of their weekend making up imaginary stories, had they come visiting when Aunt Elsie lived here. Harry sure wished now that he had made the effort to come, despite his own father's attitude. He was openly surprised at the great scenarios that Todd was coming up with, facilitated by photos in some albums he had discovered in one of the bedroom closets. Todd believed Aunt Elsie must have loved her garden, as the pictures of the current blooms were similar but somehow different over the years.

The weekend had waned. Todd spent one last time with the fish lazily dragging his fingers invitingly in the pond, while Harry sat close by idly watching. Todd finally looked up. "Dad, do you ever think of Jason, Bethany and Laurie and what it would be like to share this with them?"

"Yes Todd, I do think of them periodically. I too wish Jason and Bethany could share the fish with you. I know Laurie would love the house, some of the things in her home would fit in here nicely." Harry glanced back at the house with a sigh. "Time for us to hit the road Todd."

Harry locked the door and they headed back home to Indiana.

* * *

They were into the second week after listing the house. Annette had called with a couple of offers but advised against considering them as they were too low and she felt they weren't the proper persona for their distinctive house. Annette deemed the house needed to be appreciated for its unique charm.

Harry let her know he and Todd were planning to arrive that weekend. Annette's suggestion was to drop into the office to see her as she sensed she might possibly have a potential customer, as she had been sending notices to several past clients. Harry said he looked forward to seeing her then.

The early morning trip was made more speedily according to Todd this time. Harry had found out a more direct route from Neil in the office. When they arrived the drapes were pushed back so invitingly as though someone in the residence was awaiting their visit. The garden had been manicured to resemble the picture albums.

When they went inside the scent of fresh garden flowers permeated the air. Someone had done the cleaning, and flowers were displayed in many nooks and crannies. Going into the kitchen they found flowers on the table and fresh eggs, bread, juice and milk in the fridge. He was sure after talking to Annette about coming that she had arranged this for them.

He had planned on shopping when he stopped at the real estate office but Todd had wanted to come to the house first. Each picked out their choice of bedroom and stored their suitcases there. Harry would make up the beds with clean linen when they got back from town.

Todd happily darted outside. He counted the fish as though they might not have survived without him. Harry gave him a few minutes then called for him to come. It was time to go to the real estate office.

Annette received them with a big smile. "I have an offer that I believe you will be more than pleased with this time. The closing date is sooner but the price is precisely what we hoped for."

Harry had mixed feelings. This house had become more than a house to Harry and Todd. It had become the past they had never attained and now it was passing out of their lives again. He wanted to say no, not yet, we aren't ready but that was ridiculous instead he said. "That is wonderful." Looking towards Todd for the same affirmation but not getting one. "I think Todd wishes we could keep it."

"Well. . . sort. . . ah. . . I like the fish and the fountain is kind of neat too." Todd muttered forlornly.

"I don't blame you, Todd. Shall we look at the offer?" Annette was pulling out papers from a folder. She wasn't about to lose this sale. "Todd would you like to ask the receptionist for a drink of pop and perhaps some iced tea for your father and I. Is that okay Harry?"

"Yes that is fine." Harry was reading over the papers she had set before him. The large amount would be a nice nest egg for Todd's education, along with the vacation to Disney World they had tentatively planned. The offer of purchase in front of him was signed and all the provisions agreed upon in the agreement.

Harry thanked Annette for her proficient handling of the quick sale and the homey touch of the milk and eggs along with the flowers. Annette said, "Think nothing of it and it was only natural to arrange the cleaning of the house, as I was sure of my potential buyer's interest. In the end the selling feature was, the woman had fallen in love with the distinctive bathroom making her ecstatic. The husband had been taken aback with the bathroom but when he had learned about the normal bathroom off the master bedroom, he withdrew his objections.

The weekend departed. On Sunday, Annette dropped by to relate how pleased the couple was that the sale had gone through to both their satisfactions. She inquired if her client could purchase most of the furnishings. Harry had contacted his mother about Mr. Cullen's relatives but there appeared to be none. So Harry agreed as he had dreaded getting rid of the beautiful furniture. He invited her to stay for lunch. The conversation was about the Lambton Mills area and about Annette's husband who she said golfed and lunched with his cronies every Sunday.

Harry thanked her for all her help and for the fast sale of the house, which Annette waved off like it was all in a day's work. She was the top sales person in real estate in this area, Harry had heard. He and Todd saw her off. Todd yelling "Will we see you next weekend?" Annette stuck her head out the window and yelled back. "Sure sport, I'll drop in to see how the fish are doing while you're gone."

Harry and Todd watched her drive away longing on their faces? It was nice to have a woman around again even if it wasn't the woman they both wished for.

"Dad, Laurie disappeared without calling us, why?" Todd asked as if reading Harry's mind. "I miss Jason and Bethany so much."

Harry sighed. "I don't know why son but I would give anything to have them back into our lives too. When we arrive home, perhaps I'll make some enquiries in their old neighbourhood."

After packing up and securing the house Harry steered the car for home. He was thankful, Annette had promised to keep and eye on it and the fish knowing Todd's concern. Todd had spent several minutes assuring the fish he would be back.

The month vanished and their period in time was coming to a close. Annette and her husband Bill had them over for a BBQ on the last weekend. They invited Harry and Todd to drop in anytime they were in the general area, but Harry knew that Lambton Mills was a closed chapter. The final weekend was over, Radford Falls was home.

. . .

Immersing himself in work, Harry was back to the old grind. Todd's fleet of Clipper ships was growing. Harry inquired into Laurie's whereabouts hoping Mrs. Clark or Mrs. D'Angelo might know. All they could tell him was, they moved down south somewhere shortly after they returned home.

The days seemed endless. Harry had drawn so many architectural plans in recent weeks he was seeing shapes and lines in his sleep. Todd was excelling at school. As time went by their evenings and weekends had evolved into planning the dream holiday to Florida and Disney World.

They were going over Christmas and New Years for two weeks so Todd would miss only two school days. Todd's teacher assured Harry that he could easily make it up on his return, as he was an exceptional student. Mrs. North remarked that Todd seemed to be intent in making the honour roll this year.

The trip was to involve three days in Disney World staying at a hotel on the park grounds. Three days of visiting the grandparents. The expectation of seeing them and their enthusiasm over the potential trip made it all the more exciting. The rest of the time they would be touring Florida with Cape Canaveral a must. Todd, with the help of brochures his father provided, had been instrumental in deciding most of the plans, finishing up in Busch Gardens on the Gulf Coast.

During this time Harry had a few dates with Denise Talbot. But he was looking forward more than ever to the trip. Denise was pressuring him into permanency. He didn't want to hurt her and avoided the situation, because he didn't feel the same about her. Harry believed that Sarah was to be his one and only love. He had shared the best moments of his life with her. Then the niggling thought came except for Laurie. He knew he could have loved her if they had just had the chance.

● ● ●

The plane took off and Todd was watching the ground recede. He had been so excited these last few days that his free time was spent pouring over the brochures.

Harry thoughts wandered, he had put off two dates with Denise and was now hoping she would find someone else while he was gone.

She was a lovely woman with a good sense of humour, very attractive, stylishly dressed with a terrific personality but when it came right down to it Denise just wasn't Laurie. Besides he wanted Jason and Bethany as a packaged deal which of course wasn't about to happen.

Harry let out a sigh. Why had she vanished so abruptly? Maybe if he had visited her instead of waiting for an invitation, things could have been different. He had only wanted to give her more time to recover from her husband's passing.

The stewardess came along with the drinks cart. Todd had an apple juice and Harry had a scotch on the rocks wanting to lift his spirits or dim his thoughts. They arrived at Orlando airport at 9:30 pm. Sailing along the highway with anticipation, next stop Disney World. Todd was reading the map as navigator. The red car was a sporty model, a convertible to enjoy the warm weather.

Arriving at Disney World they were soon shown the way to their room and the much awaited trip had begun. Looking out the vista of windows they could see the glittering lights of Disney World spread out below them. Harry had promised Todd could be first in the lineup at the gates in the morning. Todd was tired but he wasn't ready to give in too easily, the excitement making his stomach quiver.

The three days passing like lightening, as they experienced Epcot Centre three times, one part day at Disney's Hollywood Studios, and the rest and best times at the Magic Kingdom. Todd particularly liked the Pirates Cave, so much that they traversed it quite a few times with Space Mountain a close second.

Christmas day was spent in the Magic Kingdom with the special events for the children that Disney World is noted for. The parade had been most entertaining and the fireworks at night spectacular. One night they went to Epcot centre to take in the special fireworks display there. With the daily passes they could come and go using the rail train, to take breaks at the hotel.

Todd liked to swim in the pools and the other many activities the hotel provided for children, in this playground of sun. Todd wanted to avail himself of the sports car also so they did some sightseeing of Kissimmee and other places nearby. The days of Disney World were over and they were more than ready to leave.

The grandparents were at a place called Winter Haven, which were quaint homes of modest means but an attractive community living area with a large pool gracing the lawn. Their pride was showing, while viewing the active clubhouse, which they daily enjoyed with great participation.

Harry and Todd were welcomed with open arms, but Harry soon realized his grandparents weren't very agile so they took a motel in the area and spent only part of each day with them. Harry was thankful that he had been able to see them once more and introduce Todd to them. Aunt Elsie's passing had made him nostalgic it seemed.

They mostly spent the morning with them. The day they tried going in the afternoon, they would be in the middle of saying something then the grandparents would drop off to sleep for ten or fifteen minutes then wake up and continue talking. Then they'd drop off again sometimes independently or together for a few more zzz's as they called them. His grandfather had some interesting stories to tell and his humour was weaving through them. Todd was patient and very respectful which made Harry so proud.

Todd told them about the fish at Aunt Elsie's house and the names that he had made up for them. He told his great-grandfather about his fleet of clipper ships that he had constructed which set his great-grandfather off on more stories about his sailing experiences. Todd took these in with interest.

Harry was sad when he left his grandparents. He was so glad they had stopped even though they weren't agile enough to actively entertain them. His grandmother was an excellent cook and Harry was thankful for the withdrawal from restaurant food. And their stories and memories would live on in Harry's mind and heart.

The next day they started off for Cape Canaveral. The news had revealed a space shuttle was due to take off that day and Todd wanted to be there to witness the launching in person. To experience history in the making and be able to tell his buddies that he was there at that exact moment.

Breakfast was at a restaurant that Harry thought must be considered a truck stop. The food came on colossal platters and just looking at all that food Harry wondered if they could make any headway.

"I think we will be skipping lunch Todd don't you, after this mega meal?" Todd gave it quite the effort but never did reach the plate hidden under the food.

Back in the car Todd was bouncing around in his excited anticipation of the arrival at the Cape. Passing through the gates, they were told the areas that were off limits for today, because of the space shuttle launch.

The guard directed them to the space museum building. He suggested, "There is an observation deck there for best viewing." Todd wanted to go there immediately so he could acquire a place by the window but Harry said not yet. The guard had told him the shuttle wouldn't be taking off for another three hours, as the checking out of all the systems was important. Then if everything checked out satisfactorily and only then, they would start the countdown. The astronauts would converge into the spaceship in two hours approximately.

They looked around outside first. They could see the spaceship that was readying for takeoff in the distance. There was a spaceship separated in sections on a large platform showing the different stages as they would come apart during the flight. Then they went inside the space museum to view past capsules recovered.

Todd was able to sit in one and view the numerous switches on the instrument panels up close. Harry had the camera ready capturing Todd's excitement in these space odysseys. He had to admit that it was special to witness this historic event. He knew he would be doing a little bragging himself, when he told of their Florida trip in the office.

Eventually, Harry gave in to Todd's impatience to be on the observation deck. The deck was filling up fast. Todd did manage to get right at the window for best visibility but Harry stood back being tall but easily kept an eye on him.

Todd would have a clear view as the astronauts strolled to the spaceship even from this distance. Harry had butterflies in his stomach at the thought, and he was sure the astronauts did too. Todd kept turning around to see his father and Harry would give him the thumbs up sign.

Suddenly Harry's eyes alighted on a woman with two children. It was Laurie. A man was directing the children forward so Jason could see well. Was this man with her? Who was he? Was he a relation or just a friend? The man eased Jason and Bethany into position at the window besides lots of other eager children, with the filling up of the deck. Then Laurie and the man stood back but still within easy reach of the children.

The next time Todd looked back at him, Harry directed Todd's attention to the two children. Todd's eyes enlarged like saucers and he moved quickly to intercept them. Jason and Bethany's squeals of delight could easily be heard. Harry was amazed when Todd hugged them both in his arms close to his body. Laurie was straining looking around for him. Harry was slightly behind a pillar so she couldn't see him well. He wasn't sure he wanted to greet her with this man in tow. His shock at seeing Laurie with a male escort, he knew now it would make it impossible to renew their friendship.

Todd was explaining the sections of the shuttle, as they would be falling apart on transition. Jason was taking in every word staring at Todd with worshipful eyes. Todd had kept his arm around Bethany as if to protect her from the crowd that was pushing forward as the room filled up, and the excitement of the astronauts entering the spaceship.

Harry kept his position near the pillar observing Laurie. She was so pretty today. The tall stocky man beside her accentuated her petite figure. He felt taller although the man and he would be approximately the same height. The difference being Harry was more muscular where this man tended to portly. What an odd way to think, he mused for it was unusual for him to be so critical.

The momentum of the excitement was rising as the countdown was near if all systems were a go. The information from NASA's control room was being piped through the speakers into the room. After greeting Todd, every once in awhile Harry would see Laurie crane her neck in his general direction?

NASA's control voice said all systems 'were a go' and the final countdown started. The expectation in the room was causing the crowd to push forward and Harry was concentrating on what was transpiring outside the window. Laurie was forgotten for the moment although he did cast an eye towards the children now and then.

The crowd was counting with the speakers. The crowd finally intoned in unison "LIFT OFF". Harry was really overwhelmed and he could see the boys bouncing around in their excitement. He thought that if the rest of their trip was a bust seeing that shuttle take off was worth every cent, to be privy to the launching and history in the making.

CHAPTER SEVEN

When the shuttle was too high to see it with the naked eye, Harry started towards Todd because the crowd was making a mass exit. His concern was for Todd but also the little ones. People were converging amassed towards the doors.

Then Harry saw Todd being dragged along with the crowd. He caught up with him as they reached the double doors grabbing his shoulder. Looking up at Harry in relief Todd gave him a big smile.

"Where are Bethany and Jason are they okay?"

"Yes the man with Laurie grabbed up Bethany and dragged Jason by the hand before they were swept away."

The fact that the observation deck must have held a hundred or so people, with one set of double doors propelling them all in one direction, the crush was mammoth. When they were outside, he shifted Todd to the side to look at a display till the crush dissipated. Harry was glancing around but he didn't see Laurie and now he was sorry that he had missed the opportunity to say hi. *Fine Harry, now is a great time to have regrets when you more or less hid yourself behind a pole the whole time.* He chided himself.

The NASA space loudspeaker was still giving off the sounds of voices cheering at the perfect lift off with lots of background jubilant laughter and ovation. History in the making BUT not for Harry, he had missed his chance.

. . .

After leaving the Cape, they had motored to Fort Lauderdale. The hotel they chose for the night resided on a beach where they lazed for the afternoon. Todd wanted the experience of swimming in the Atlantic Ocean. The flags today indicated that it was safe to swim.

When the blue flags flew they were a warning sign of Man-of-War sea urchins were in the area, because they are deadly to some no one was suppose to swim. A lifeguard filled them in with this information that the stinging Man-of-War appearance is like a purplish blue balloon. The lifeguard said they resemble jellyfish in some ways but actually are colonies of a different type, propelled by a balloon like float that acts like a sail. The Man-of-War can inflict painful stings causing reactions of severe pain, nausea, and breathing difficulties. People allergic to bee stings or red ant venom, it can be fatal.

Fortunately there were none in the area today which made life easier for the lifeguards. After hearing the lifeguard's narration, Todd glanced sceptically at the water but he still bravely waded in for a brief swim.

Todd like a typical boy was looking at the jellyfish and other visible sea urchins that were stranded on shore as the tide was going out. Harry told him to be careful not to step on anything. After awhile the sun was so hot, he could feel his body reacting. He suggested a cool drink and a cold shower to end their time on the beach. Todd naturally raced up the beach to the hotel. Harry wasn't about to race anywhere. He followed at a leisurely pace.

They spent the evening motoring around discovering the sights of Fort Lauderdale, and had a late dinner in a restaurant overlooking the ocean. They were getting an early start for Tampa the next morning, so Todd agreed to head back to the hotel for sleep.

The next morning Harry and Todd rose early for their start to the Tampa area, with expectations of Busch Gardens and more adventures. As they were ready to get into the car, Todd waved at a car going by. "Dad did you see? That was Jason and Bethany in that car." Opening the car door automatically, Harry glanced in the direction of the speeding car. "No, I missed it." He had been putting the luggage in the trunk at the time.

Todd expressed his disappointment that they hadn't been able to meet with Laurie and the children in Cape Canaveral.

Apparently, they had been in Fort Lauderdale too, but evidently missed bumping into each other. Harry felt sort of guilty. Maybe if he had made more of an effort at greeting them at the Cape, they could have arranged to be together part of yesterday.

The car ride to Tampa was overshadowed and silent by their missed opportunity with Laurie, Jason and Bethany. When they were going past Disney World, they both glanced towards it. The two in the car didn't have the same feeling of expectation that had been with them leaving Disney World for the Cape. Seeing Laurie, and the kids but not being with them had dampened their enthusiasm.

They soon saw some colourful billboards inviting people to go to Busch Gardens. The sign depicted the place as a theme park with rides, animals and beautiful gardens.

Todd perked up and the feeling of anticipation was coursing through him, when a news bulletin on the radio drew his attention. Two children had been kidnapped that morning from Fort Lauderdale. They gave a description of them. Todd's head quickly whipped towards his father. "Dad that description sounds exactly like Bethany and Jason. They say their mother is frantic. Did it sound like them to you?"

Harry started to really pay attention to the newsman's voice. "The children's names are Bethany and Jason McKnight. Anyone knowing of their whereabouts or if anyone has any information that can be helpful in locating these missing children, contact the Fort Lauderdale police."

Todd interrupted the message. "Dad, I saw them in a car when we left this morning, remember? They were in a blue car, it was not new but it was a really nice car." Todd recalled.

Harry was watching the roadway for the next turnoff. "Yes I recall you mentioning it, but I didn't see enough of the car to know the make, but maybe we should go back anyways." Harry responded. They veered off at the next ramp. The red sports car zoomed up the ramp and stopped at the red light. Harry looked for the indicator back to Fort Lauderdale, which was to the left past the overpass. As they re-entered the highway again, the green signs were giving the mileage to Disney World and Fort Lauderdale along with mileage to Cape Canaveral. Harry's single thought was Laurie needed someone to be with her.

"Dad, why are we going back? They will be long gone by now. Look how far we have come already."

"Laurie will need us and that's where we should be." Harry's heart was pounding and his throat was tightening. How could this have happened? Wasn't that man with her able to protect the children? Harry didn't care if the man was going to be there, he just knew he wanted to be there for Laurie. That was his one and only contemplation now.

The sports car ate up the miles easily with Harry reaching the limit and more but staying within the boundaries of safe driving. He wasn't about to put Todd or his life at risk. Now that he had a purpose to his driving, he was making good time. Todd was squirming with an anxious attitude too. "Why would anyone take Bethany and Jason?"

"I don't know Todd. That is what we are about to find out."

When they turned off at the first exit to Fort Lauderdale, they phoned the number given on the newscast. Todd had memorized it because they had repeated it so often. Harry told the male voice on the phone that he had information regarding the two missing children. He said that he wanted to come to the police station to discuss it. The mannish voice passed him off to someone else.

"Detective Reilly here, who may I ask is calling?" The voice was abrupt and stern. "I am Harry Cochrane. I know the two missing children. My son saw them leaving in a blue car this morning."

"Where are you Mr. Cochrane?" Detective Reilly inquired.

"Back in Fort Lauderdale, we just came off Highway I-95 at the first exit. We would like to come to the station to see you. How will I get there?"

"Well the best way is to stay on I-95 south until exit 29, exit towards downtown which is West Broward. Follow that until you come to the Avenue of the Arts intersection then from there it is approximately six blocks to Andrew Avenue and we are right on the corner. It is a large building easily identifiable by police cars parked around it."

They got back in the car. Harry soon executed the turn towards the downtown from the off-ramp at Exit 29 onto West Broward.

"Watch for a main intersection named Avenue of the Arts, then it is six blocks past that to Andrew Avenue, the police are on the corner." Harry prompted.

Todd saw the sign for the Arts then he counted the streets until he sang out. "There it is Dad, right on the corner with all the police cars surrounding it." Harry pulled into the parking lot behind the building. They threw off their seatbelts in their agitation to get inside. He didn't even bother to lock the car. He quickly made for the back entrance and Todd followed running.

Harry approached the first officer they encountered. "Where will I find Detective Reilly?" The policeman pointed down the hall. "Second door down on the right side."

They went to the door indicated but the office was empty. Harry was deflated. Again he looked around for someone to ask. This time he found a policewoman carrying a pile of files. "Excuse me; do you know where Detective Reilly is?"

"Isn't he in his office, the third door on the right?" She waved her head in the direction they had just come from.

"The office is empty. We have already looked there."

"Then he must be in the main interrogation room, go to the front of the building then to your right and down the corridor to the second room." Harry hurried that way with Todd shadowing him. The door was closed but they could hear voices inside. Harry knocked. The door opened and a husky cop stood filling the doorway. "Can I help you?"

"Yes, I am Harry Cochrane. Detective Reilly is expecting us." The burly cop looked over his shoulder but didn't move away from the doorway. "Hey Mike, someone here to see you, says his name is Harry Cochrane."

The voice from inside said. "Tell him to wait out there I'll be with him in a minute." A female voice said something not loud enough to make out. Then the male voice from within said. "Gus, show Mr. Cochrane in."

The husky cop stood aside and waved them in. Harry entered the room his eyes locating Laurie immediately. She had always looked so petite and delicate to him and today was no exception. Laurie looked shattered. Harry came a few feet inside the door. He opened his arms as if begging her to come to him.

Laurie gave a cry. "Harry. . ." She leaped out of the chair into his arms. He closed them like a trap. He was there for her now, to help shield her from her distress. She was crying against his chest. Harry was running his hands up and down her back soothingly.

"Mr. Cochrane, I am Detective Reilly. Will you both come and have a seat? I see Mrs. McKnight knows you."

"Yes, we knew each other back in Radford Falls, Indiana. We haven't seen each other for over a year." Ignoring the detective's request for a bit longer, Laurie wasn't ready to be released yet.

"Perhaps your son can wait outside while we talk." Reilly said in an acknowledgement of Todd's presence.

"It was actually Todd that saw the children in the car. By the time he called my attention to the car, I just saw the tail end and I never thought to look for the licence."

"Well come over here Todd and give me a description of what you saw." Detective Reilly was holding out a chair beside him. "Don't be nervous, because I want you to relax, so you can clearly give me all the details you can remember." Todd dropped into the seat but his eyes were on Laurie. Harry easily could see that he was concerned for her too.

Laurie was still crying but had eased to a light trickle of tears. She turned her head to give Todd a weak smile. He smiled back relieved that she had finally acknowledged him. "Laurie, we'll help you through this. We will stay here till they find them, won't we Dad?" Todd's glance drifted to his father.

"Yes Laurie, Todd and I will be here for you no matter how long it takes." He was looking down into her tear stained face. There were still big tears pooled in her eyes. She was looking up at him but he must have been a fuzzy blur through her tears. "Thank you Harry." Laurie swung around to Todd. "Thank you Todd." Her voice was getting stronger. She was getting her emotions under control.

Detective Reilly asked Gus to bring some drinks. The room was big but the air was stagnating even though two small windows were open. There was a trace of cigarette smoke in the air, although no one appeared to be smoking. The brown marked table held styrofoam cups with dregs of coffee indicating the room had been used for awhile. Gus swept the cups up and left the room.

Harry hated to break the contact but he guided Laurie back to the seat that she had vacated upon catching sight of them. Her unfastened purse was on the table giving the impression that she had been searching for something inside. Harry dragged a chair over beside her and sat down opposite Todd. He was watching Laurie with caring eyes. Todd knew how much she must be hurting because of how he felt at his loss when his mother died.

"Laurie, I am sorry the children are missing. If I had known I would have had Dad follow them. That man appeared to be together with you yesterday, so I didn't realize." Todd said pleading for her understanding of why they hadn't interfered or at least got the licence.

"I know Todd. Dennis was the man with me yesterday, unfortunately I had no idea he had devious plans for Jason and Bethany. He seemed such a nice man and so helpful. I have been seeing him off and on for four months or so." Her voice caught on this last comment. Laurie felt she had to explain to Todd why she had trusted her children to him.

"Todd" the detective interrupted, "I am Detective Reilly and I want to ask you some questions." Reilly was trying to bring things under his control again. His voice was still brusque but in a relaxed way, unnerving Todd wouldn't help.

"State your full name and age; I will have a recorder on so the tape can be replayed later for details?" Reilly looked first at Harry then Todd for objections. They listened to the detective state his name, date and the place. When he stopped Todd proceeded. "My name is Todd Cochrane and I am eleven years old."

Reilly said, "That is good Todd, just talk in a normal clear voice." A knock came at the door and it opened interrupting proceedings. It was the burly cop with the drinks. He had cups in one hand and a can of pop in the other. He placed them on the table and brought out three more cans of pop from his pockets as though he was doing a magic act. "Thank you Gus. What kind would you like Todd?" Trying to put the boy at ease, while Gus gave the iced tea to Laurie presuming she would prefer that.

Todd indicated the coke, reaching for the can and pulling the tab. Harry reached for a cup for Laurie. The top cup had a lid and felt hot so he assumed it was coffee. He placed it on the table in the general direction of Reilly, then reaching for an empty cup to pour Laurie's iced tea. Laurie took the cup in both hands and Harry noted her hands were shaking. She drank as though her tears had drained her. Reilly waited till everyone was settled then re-engaged the recorder. "Now Todd, tell me in your own words what you saw this morning?"

"My Dad and I had just come out of the hotel to our rental sports car when I saw a car race pass with Bethany and Jason in the back seat. Jason was frantically waving through the back window, but I believed it was because he was excited to see us. Honest, I didn't realize he was signalling their distress because I recognized the man Laurie called Dennis driving." He looked anxiously at Reilly then at Laurie.

"I understand Todd, now what else did you see?" Reilly reassured him.

"The car was blue and larger than most cars like a Buick or Cadillac, an older car not a recent model." Todd added.

Laurie piped up. "That wasn't the car Dennis was originally driving when we came here. Dennis said that he had to borrow this one from a friend because his car wasn't working properly. I didn't think anything of it at the time. I just accepted what Dennis said." Her voice trailed off sadly.

"Now Todd, is there anything else that you remember such as which direction he was headed?"

"They were heading north. There was an animal plastered to the side back window. Garfield with its legs splayed out in fright. You know Dad like the one Ricky has in his back car window."

"Yes Todd, I'm sure Detective Reilly has seen them too. They were very popular last year." Harry replied.

"Did you notice the licence plate?" Reilly requested.

"No, not really, except that it seemed deep blue in colour, deeper blue than the car with white lettering. Not a Florida licence." Todd added.

"That is good Todd, anything else?"

Todd paused, thinking back to the scene of the car zooming by him. "No not that I can remember." Reilly turned to Harry.

"What about you Mr. Cochrane, did you see the car or anything that will help?"

"I had just finished putting the luggage in the trunk and was opening the car door when Todd mentioned they had gone by. At the rate of speed the car was travelling, I didn't see much but I did notice the car had a bumper sticker with a saying on it. But I don't know exactly what it said."

"That's a big help. Is there anything else you can add Mrs. McKnight?"

"The car had grey vinyl seats and the interior was also grey. The outside was a medium blue like Todd said. I didn't pay much attention, except it was a four door, because I was putting Jason and Bethany in the back seat, making sure their seat belts were fastened. Before I could open the passenger door Dennis took off." Laurie drew a breath then continued.

"I thought he was joking at first and would stop and back up or at least let me catch up, because he had a sense of humour like that, so I just stood there. But Dennis kept going and he was really picking up speed, turning at the corner of the second block, on squealing wheels. I was immobilized in shock and horror." The stricken look on her face deepened.

"It took me a couple of minutes to grasp the situation. There was a couple coming out of the parking lot and I waved them down and told them what had happened and they told me to jump in so we could follow them. But when we turned that same corner they were nowhere in sight, we just saw a truck and a taxi. That is when the couple brought me here." Laurie's throat was filling with sobs again and she was swallowing hard to control them. Harry reached out his hand to grasp hers. Laurie held on tight.

"Todd, you said that Jason was waving at you franticly yet their mother said they were buckled in?" Detective Reilly reiterated.

"Well Jason was definitely waving at me from an upright position so he must have released his seatbelt." Todd replied positively.

Harry asked. "Have you put out a description of the car yet?"

"No, we didn't have much to go on until you got here. Mrs. McKnight was too upset up till now." Looking at Gus, Reilly said.

"Dark blue licence is Michigan; find out if there was any stolen cars of that description reported within the last 24 hours. We may get lucky and get a licence number. Make sure the full description is broadcasted immediately. Reilly turned to Laurie. "Can you give me any more information about the man?"

CHAPTER EIGHT

*L*aurie looked uncomfortably at Harry then back to the detective. Reilly asked if she would prefer to have Harry and Todd wait outside before she continued. Needing Harry's grip on her hand for the courage to go on she quickly said, "No, it is okay."

"I met him at a party my friends gave about five months ago. He must have obtained my phone number from my friend Janice who held the party. At first I kept putting him off then Janice and Jack had another party and Dennis was there. Again I put him off. Dennis must have approached Janice about me because she called to arrange a double date with her and Jack. I enjoy being with them so I finally conceded."

"His full name is Dennis Simpson. I thought with Janice and Jack being with us, it would be on more of a friendly basis only. We continued with a few dates after that and he did seem quite a caring man. He kept hinting to be invited to a meal, as he said he was single, so I invited him for dinner. I told him I had two children and he indicated without hesitation that he liked children. But now that I think back he didn't appear to be surprised about the children, as though he already knew. When Dennis came for dinner, Jason and he got along fabulously." Laurie paused and looked at Harry because she felt his hand loosen on hers that he was holding. She could see he was bothered somehow about Dennis.

Reilly prompted her to continue. "We had a few more dates. Dennis never appeared to show any particular interest in the children other than to enquire how they were occasionally."

"Then last Saturday, after he had made several hints about enjoying my cooking, I invited him to a BBQ at my place with the children. He talked to Jason about the space shuttle that was due to go up into space on the following Thursday. Jason was enthralled with excitement, his affinity for flying objects with his model planes that hovered around his room. He would naturally have an interest in the space shuttle launch."

"Dennis asked Jason if he wanted to see the next shuttle take off, as it would be during the Christmas holidays. Jason pleaded with me to go and Dennis indicated quickly that the accommodations would be separate. I wasn't ready for an intimate relationship so I was relieved at his suggestion." Laurie went on rapidly. "He had never pressed me for intimacy of any kind. During our acquaintance, we had the occasional casual kiss." She paused, she didn't dare look at Harry then. She felt strange telling this story in front of Harry and Todd.

Detective Reilly pressed for her to continue. "What happened next?"

"Jason was so excited about seeing the space shuttle take off. It was like a dream come true. I too got caught up in Jason's excitement agreeing to go." She did add timidly. "I wouldn't have accepted other than his promise of separate rooms. We arrived at Fort Lauderdale from South Carolina on Wednesday where Dennis had booked a hotel. We took the kids to the ocean for the rest of the afternoon then we had dinner together parting shortly after, so we could have an early rise in the morning."

"The next day we went to Cape Canaveral for the launching. It was wonderful. Jason was so thrilled and happy. He couldn't stop talking about it, plus he and Bethany were excited about unexpectedly seeing Todd there also." Turning to Harry with a tiny smile Laurie said. "I was hoping that we could get together after the launch, with you and Todd. I mentioned it to Dennis but once the shuttle had taken off he grabbed Bethany and Jason whisking us away, saying we would wait for you outside. There was such a crush from the crowd I naturally went along with him." Then swinging back to Detective Reilly she continued.

"However, once we got clear of the doors he rushed us to the car.

When I explained I wanted to see Harry and Todd, Dennis said we wouldn't be able to find them in the huge crowd. I kept glancing around but never saw you." Laurie looked at Harry beseechingly then turned back to Detective Reilly again.

"We went back to the hotel in Fort Lauderdale. When we arrived there, Dennis said he had to make some phone calls and he left us to go to his room. I was kind of glad, not being use to constant male attention."

"While we were in our room suiting up to go swimming in the hotel pool, Dennis called. He specified that the calls he had made resulted in him having to work on some quotes, which would nullify his meeting us for dinner. Once completed the quotes would have to be faxed to South Carolina, so he would be very busy, and would grab something from room service."

"Again I was kind of relieved, but we did make plans to meet in the morning for breakfast in the hotel restaurant. He said we would be going home from there and I was to bring down the luggage when we came for breakfast. He said he had some important business that needed attending to when he got back to South Carolina, making it necessary to get an early start. We had arranged to come for the space shuttle take off only so I half expected this." Laurie picked up her iced tea taking a few sips. Reilly was patient waiting for her to go on with her story.

"The children and I had dinner after playing in the pool for awhile cooling off rather than swimming. We went to our room after, and played games that we had brought with us. The children were tired and I wanted them in bed early. I never saw nor heard from Dennis anymore that night." Laurie took a small breath then continued.

"The next morning we packed and carried our luggage to the elevator and rode to the lobby. I went to the desk to check out but Dennis apparently already had settled the bill. Then we met him at the entrance to the dining room. We stored the luggage in an alcove nearby. Everything seemed normal or so I thought at the time. After breakfast we picked up our luggage and went out to a car, which was parked in the parking lot. Dennis mumbled something about having car problems, that was the reason for a different car. He put the bags in the trunk, while I settled the children in the back seat. He entered the front seat and started the car."

"When I went to reach for the passenger door that was when he took off like I told you before." Laurie had been holding back her tears during her story. She started to cry in anguish. Harry pulled her against him and tried to calm her. "Harry, why would he take my children?" Laurie said looking into his face between sobs.

Before Harry could reply, Detective Reilly resumed control of the interview. "I don't know the answer to that Mrs. McKnight. Did Dennis appear to be overly interested in the children after getting to Florida?"

"No, only in talking to Jason about his planes and his ships. Bethany was always shy so she never really talked to him much." Laurie straightened up as though Harry had given her the strength she needed. She pulled out some tissues from the box on the table Gus offered to her.

Reilly hid his concern for Laurie's tearful state. Turning to Harry. "Now Mr. Cochrane would you mind explaining to me your relationship to Mrs. McKnight?" Detective Reilly requested, giving Laurie added time to recover.

Harry straightened in his chair preparing for his share of the usual questioning. "I knew Laurie back in Indiana. Her children stayed with Todd and me while their mother was sick in the hospital. When she was well enough to leave the hospital, she came to live with us too, till she recovered fully and was able to be on her own. Not long after that Laurie moved away." Harry figured a brief version of their friendship was best in the hopes of protecting Laurie. He didn't want Reilly to know their true relationship had been so brief. "We haven't seen each other for over a year."

"So you haven't been in contact during that time?"

"No. Laurie moved out of state and I had no idea where she moved to. It wasn't that kind of a relationship. Laurie had only been a widow for three months at the time we were together. We were just friends. The children were closer. It was only natural that she came to stay with the children when she came out of the hospital, as she was still in a weakened condition, and no family close by to help her." Harry was avoiding the true story of the children's appearance on his doorstep and not having met Laurie prior to then. Detective Reilly must have accepted his answers because he turned off the recorder. "Jason is such a resourceful kid I can't see him giving in too readily to the kidnapping." Harry said positively.

"I hope so." Reilly and Gus left the room to converse elsewhere.

Todd eyes were on Laurie. "I'm sorry Laurie about Jason and Bethany, I had no idea they were going unwillingly. But I'm sure the police will find them." She looked at him and gave a half smile. She had wiped her tears and was fiddling with her cup turning it around and around but not drinking. Harry gathered her hand into his, pressing it reassuringly. Laurie asked Harry, "Do you think Dennis will hurt them? They are so powerless against him. He is such a big man."

Entering the room Detective Reilly exclaimed decisively before Harry could reply. "Mrs. McKnight, we have had a report of a blue car stolen matching the description of the car that Todd and you described correctly. So now we have a licence number, unless he ditches the car or plates for others, which unfortunately can happen." Reilly turned to Harry. "You were right about the bumper sticker it says 'Honk if you love Jesus.'"

"Now Mrs. McKnight, can you go over Dennis' description once more? I know you told me before Mr. Cochrane and Todd arrived, but I would like you to repeat the information to see if Harry or Todd can add anything useful." Reilly looked directly at Harry. "You don't mind if I call you Harry?"

"No that's all right." Harry replied. Reilly pressed the record button as Laurie started to speak.

"Dennis is approximately 6 foot 3 inches with huge shoulders and on the heavy side, heavier than Harry. He has blond hair and a narrow moustache, with his blondness it was hardly noticeable. I often wondered why he bothered to grow one. He has brown eyes and is good-looking with nice white teeth."

"His hands were huge too but soft like he never did any manual labour. Dennis never told me what he did professionally. He would just say it was too complex to explain. As I never intended to become serious about him, I never pressed him for a great deal of personal information."

"Does he have any notable marks or scars?"

Laurie thought for a bit then said. "Yes he had a finger that seemed crooked as though broken at one time but not properly set. His left index finger I think. Otherwise no other marks that I am aware of. I have never seen him without being fully clothed. Even when we took the children to the ocean when we arrived here, he stayed fully dressed." Laurie's voice trailed off. "That is all I can think of."

Detective Reilly turned to Harry. "Have you anything that you can add?"

"I wasn't that close to him at any time, so I can't really help."

"Todd how about you, did you notice anything about Dennis that would be of significance?" Detective Reilly prompted.

"When he picked up Bethany and called Jason he talked like he had some kind of accent." Todd was concentrating real hard.

Laurie affirmed. "Yes I forgot, that's true but I never figured out where from nor did he offer the information about his background in our conversations." Laurie added feeling a bit inadequate travelling with Dennis and obviously not knowing him that well.

Reilly's hand stopped the recorder. "Well that is all the questions for now. We will try to work from what you have told me. When the man arrives to do the composite drawing, we will have you back here to work with him."

"I know this is hard on you Mrs. McKnight but the more information we can get distributed to our law enforcement, and the surrounding states, as well as into the public sector the better. The faster we will track this man down."

"What are the chances really?" Harry queried.

"Well I'll have to be honest with you. I don't like the fact that he stole a car for this kidnapping. That makes his intent more serious and if he steals another one to escape detection, then he may get away. So we can only hope that he doesn't ditch that car. The first 24 to 48 hours really are the most crucial. After that. . ." His voice trailed off. Neither Laurie nor Harry wanted to hear the rest.

Reilly went on to say. "If we can catch him while he is still in our state, the chances of the children not being hurt is much better. The longer Dennis is out there undetected the longer he has those kids. As we don't have a conclusive reason for him taking them, we can only hope his intention is not to hurt them." So the news wasn't all gloom, he continued instantly.

"From your earlier description of Jason and Harry's remark, I don't think he will keep quiet, if he gets a chance he will speak out. Now this may work in our favour or against Jason, as Dennis may decide to tie him up and gag him in order to restrict him. At this point, we just don't know. It is a known fact in these cases of child kidnappings, that the possibilities are endless for them to disappear without a trace. I am sorry to have to say that but it is true. All we can do is keep trying to locate them quickly."

"Mrs. McKnight, do you want to wait here till we hear something or do you want to go to a hotel? The hotel across the street on Andrews Avenue is nearby and also reasonable and clean. Then you will be close by if we need you. I don't think there will be a ransom request under the circumstances, your being away from home."

Harry suggested. "Laurie, let's go to the hotel and freshen up. We don't know how long it will take but I think you should be away from here. Todd you go first and we'll be right behind you." Todd got up watching Laurie feeling sad for her then turning and leaving the room. Reilly went after him and was asking him about the shuttle takeoff. Todd answered excitedly but not with the same enthusiasm of yesterday, with the sadness of Jason and Bethany's predicament looming over them.

Harry stood up and pulled Laurie into his arms. "Laurie, you won't speed things up by staying here. Come to the hotel. You will be able to freshen up there, then you will feel a little better." He kissed her forehead then realized what he had done and stepped back.

"Oh Harry, he took my suitcase too. I don't have anything to take with me."

"That's all right, we can go out later to pick up some things for you. You could always wear one of my T-shirts for nightwear." Harry was trying but he wasn't sure he was helping.

"Harry, I don't want to be in a hotel alone, I will go crazy."

"Well we will get one with a connecting door, so we can share during the day and be separate at night. How does that sound?" Harry had placed her purse in her hand and was guiding her to the door. When they reached the front of the building, Detective Reilly was there with Todd and another cop. The two men were talking earnestly and Todd was watching them with interest.

Detective Reilly stopped talking when he saw them. "Mrs. McKnight, we will call you at the hotel as soon as we find out anything." Reilly turned to Todd and winked with a stern look. Todd knew he was cautioning him not to tell Laurie what he had just overheard. Reilly excused himself saying he had calls to make.

They went out into the sunlight and down the precinct's front stairs. Laurie turned her head into Harry's shoulder. The bright sunlight was hurting her tender eyes after crying so much. Harry slipped his sunglasses on that he had clipped to his open-neck shirt upon entering the police station. Laurie stopped to fumble in her purse for her sunglasses. Crossing the street, he noted the hotel was three buildings away.

They managed to obtain adjoining rooms on the third floor overlooking the street. Harry had told the hotel desk clerk they would bring up their luggage later as they had walked a distance from their parked car. A bellhop didn't need to be aware that Laurie didn't have any luggage. Hotels are usually suspect with guests without suitcases. The fewer questions the better Harry thought.

After Todd settled in front of the TV, Harry went in to see Laurie. He wanted to tell her about the information Todd had garnered from the two men but he knew Reilly preferred her not to know at this point.

Todd had told him the police had found a car, answering the description of the stolen car Dennis had been driving, near a hotel on the beach up nearer the Cape. They were now checking that area for the possibility they had stolen another car, so that was why Laurie wasn't to know yet. The police felt sure Dennis had made another switch.

"Laurie did the police ask for a description of Dennis' car?"

"Yes I gave a description to them but what good will that do when Dennis said it had motor problems." She automatically replied. Harry was relieved in case Dennis had switched to his own vehicle somehow. Laurie was sitting stiffly in a chair like a zombie. She hadn't moved while he was in with Todd.

"Perhaps Laurie if you freshen up you will feel better." Harry eased her out of the chair.

She leaned against him but then she straightened looking into his face intently. "Harry, do you think they will find my children?" He looked down at her. "They will try their absolute best. Detective Reilly maintains that the first 24 hours are crucial. He seems confident in what he is doing." Laurie wanted to take Harry's positive tone of voice to heart, and let it bolster her sagging spirits.

Entering the bathroom, she looked at her tearful face in the mirror, making some effort to freshen up, knowing he was waiting.

After Laurie had been lying quietly for a few minutes, Harry hoped she had fallen asleep as he turned to leave. She gave a quiet moan of inner pain.

CHAPTER NINE

Turning back he eased down on the bed, Harry was aware of Laurie's shuttered eyes, but felt she wasn't asleep. Then he thought better of it and stood up, her eyes flew open. "Please don't leave me? I don't want to be alone right now." The tears started seeping out of her eyes, trickling down her cheeks. Harry quickly sat down with his back against the headboard and pulled her into his arms.

Immediately Laurie curved into Harry's body and her head rested on his chest beneath his chin. "Laurie, it is hard but you have to be brave and not cry. It will exhaust you too much. You will need your strength for later. The police will recover the children. I have confidence in the police and you must too." He said comfortingly.

"I am positive Detective Reilly will leave no stone unturned." They stayed unmoving for a long time. Harry worried about the children and their possible fate, and feeling guilty at the same time, as his thoughts at the moment were on Laurie wanting her in his arms like this forever. He finally realized with her lack of movement that she had fallen asleep. He eased her down on the pillow and looked in the closet for a blanket to cover her. Pulling the drapes to steep the room in darkness, Harry stood looking down at Laurie in her vulnerability.

Creeping from the room, he closed the door part way so the TV would not disturb her, but still be part of their closeness. Todd looked up at his father, his concern pictured there. "How is she?"

"Laurie is asleep and I hope she stays that way for awhile. Anything newsworthy on the TV I should be aware of?" Todd knew he meant about Bethany and Jason.

"The TV has periodically shown their pictures and given their descriptions asking for help in locating them with a police number flashing across the screen."

"I think I will call Detective Reilly for an update?" Picking up the phone, Harry requested the front desk to connect him to the police station. "Could I speak to Detective Reilly?" He waited awhile listening to the background noises of a typical day in a police station. "Reilly here."

"This is Harry Cochrane. We are in room 312 & 314 at the Hampton Inn across the street. I thought I would call for an update?"

"Harry, how is Mrs. McKnight holding up?"

"She has fallen asleep in the other room out of exhaustion."

"Good. The news is not great. Dennis ditched the stolen car like we surmised he might. No one in the area could shed a light on seeing anything. We are assuming, he has transferred to his own car as it is absent from where it was reported hidden.

Hopefully that is how it played out, otherwise if Dennis stole another car that could create difficulties. In the meantime, we will keep an eye on any stolen vehicle reports just in case. It is viable with the timing and the distance from here to where he abandoned the stolen car, close to the location of his stashed car, makes us quite certain he has his own car now. Mrs. McKnight told us, he was busy the night before so maybe exchanging the cars was what kept him occupied. Anyway, until we hear differently, it is Dennis' car we are looking for now."

"What about the stolen car was it from that area?"

"No but Dennis could have stepped into either a bus or taxi or hitchhiked to arrive where he eventually stole the vehicle he used in the kidnapping. The other possibility being, there is an accomplice. Where children are concerned there is usually a female involved too."

"Another thing Harry, technically the children are not considered missing for 48 hours, then we have to call in the FBI. Kidnapping is a federal offence. There's a legal reason for the FBI to be involved. But if we can get the right break, we will locate the children, before that step becomes necessary."

"Wouldn't it be better to have all the help you can get?" Harry inquired.

"The FBI are well trained in kidnapping. They have a lot of equipment and resources at their disposal. However, some of them have authority issues and they are inclined to railroad people like us or give attitude such as making Laurie feel incompetent, in her care looking after her children. I want to avoid that if possible if you know what I mean?"

"Yes Laurie feels bad enough already without some overbearing FBI agent labelling her incompetent."

"Mind you I don't say all FBI guys are like that but some are, and I don't think we want to take the chance in the wrong type arriving. However, if it becomes necessary I will make the call to them myself unless they get wind of it first, which might happen with our news bulletins." Reilly paused.

"Harry, I have to go I have another call and they say it is important. I will call as soon as I hear anything. When Mrs. McKnight wakes up come to the station, we would like to arrange for a composite drawing to be made with her help. So call me okay?"

"Yes, I'll do that." Harry put down the receiver with a heavy feeling.

Todd and Harry sat discussing their worry for the kids, not wanting to think the worst, but also wanting to alleviate Laurie's fears. Todd wanted to say something positive but didn't know what to say except. "Dad, you know Jason is really smart. He will figure out a way to attract attention if the possibility is there, if this Dennis guy doesn't restrain him."

"I know Todd. Jason is very smart and given the opportunity he will make use of it. Now I am going out to get some drinks and some food. Laurie should eat before she goes back to the police station, for the composite drawing. Will you listen for the phone and for Laurie too?"

"Yes Dad, I'll take care of her. It would be nice if she could sleep till the news is more hopeful."

Harry whispered back. "Dennis has changed cars, Detective Reilly has confirmed." Todd looked as sad as Harry felt. Neither thought this would end successfully any time soon. Harry pondered. "I wished

I knew what food Laurie liked to eat. She will probably need something really tempting."

"Dad, most women like chicken, according to the cooking shows I see."

"Since when do you ever watch cooking shows?" Harry chuckled.

"Flipping channels Dad, you pick up ideas." Todd grinned.

"Do you have a preference?"

"No, whatever you decide is fine with me but I would like some Gatorade. You know the kind I like."

Harry stood with his hand on the doorknob. "I'll go get the car while I'm out and bring up our luggage." After he had left for awhile, Todd peeked into the other room but Laurie was still covered up and her hand was under the pillow in a deep slumber. Todd turned the TV down so the loud commercials would not disturb her.

Sitting down, he noted the news bulletin flashing on the screen. Bethany and Jason's pictures appeared and descriptions of Dennis and his car, also requesting help in locating them. Todd was glad he had turned the TV down. Laurie didn't need to hear this.

His mind was deep into the movie 'Robocop' when he felt Laurie's presence in the doorway. "Hi, did you have enough sleep?"

"Yes Todd. Where is Harry? I mean your father."

"He should be back soon he went foraging for food and drink. Would you like to come and sit here with me?" He quickly turned off the movie.

"Don't do that Todd. You were watching it." Laurie said quickly as she sat on the bed.

"It's okay I've seen it before so I know what's going to happen." Todd said in an offhand manner. His intent was that Laurie wouldn't see the bulletins.

She asked about his and his father's activities since she had last seen them in Indiana. He was dragging it out in the hopes of keeping her mind occupied till his father arrived. Harry would have been surprised as Todd usually talked in an epigrammatic brief manner.

Jumping up at the light knock, Todd opened the door for his father, before he could use his key. Harry strode in carrying a huge brown bag, sending Laurie a big smile. "Sleep well?"

"Yes, I just woke up really. Todd has been bringing me up to date on your home life." She smiled sweetly at Todd. "He has certainly grown into quite the young man from the way he is talking. Your relationship sounds like one to envy." Laurie voice held sadness. *Where are you Bethany and Jason?*

Harry looked over at Todd proudly. "Yeah, I am lucky. We do seem to click most of the time, when he isn't hanging out with his buddies. Who wants sandwiches? I have ham, chicken and salami along with potato and Greek salad. Drinks are Gatorade and iced tea?" Harry looked in the bag. "I guess that about covers it except for some fruit."

He looked purposely at Laurie expecting her to refuse but she said she could eat a chicken sandwich. There was a table in front of the window with two chairs and Todd dragged over the one he had been sitting on watching TV. Harry waited till Laurie ate some of her sandwich, before telling her about the need to appear at the police station again.

"Have they heard anything? Has anyone reported seeing them?" Laurie set the sandwich down her appetite gone, Harry was thankful he had waited.

"Not yet. Detective Reilly asked me to phone when you were awake, to arrange a time for the composite drawing with the police artist." He picked up the phone, as Laurie nodded. When Detective Reilly came on the line, Harry indicated Laurie was ready to help with the composite drawing. Looking at his watch it was 2:30 in the afternoon, Harry felt the day was never-ending. "Yes three o'clock will suffice to be there."

In the meantime, Harry and Todd brought up the luggage hoping Laurie might eat some more of her sandwich while waiting.

When they arrived at the police station, they were taken to a small room down the right corridor, that contained a computer. A man with glasses greeted them at the door in a jovial manner. "Come in, come in, let's get started." Todd held back. Calvin waved him in. "You too, the more the merrier. I'm Calvin." He looked at Laurie questioningly after they were seated. "Well shall we get started?" He explained how composite drawings were developed. "Ready?"

Laurie started talking self-consciously. "Dennis has a long face with high cheekbones and a broad nose." Calvin was pulling up images as Laurie spoke, changing the drawing on the monitor. "He had a high forehead and a receding hairline." Laurie voice petered out, but her eyes never left the screen. Calvin was constantly changing and fine tuning the image as he requested Laurie for more detail. Dissecting the image the chin first, was it rounder, pointed or clear shaven or shadowed as she answered he would press an icon and the image would change until Laurie approved the chin shape. The lips were next. Where they wide, full or narrow, stern or bow shaped?

As Calvin worked his magic, Laurie began to see the image of Dennis expose itself on the screen, cheeks, eyes, forehead, ears and finally the hair. Todd was helping too. He had a good eye for shapes and features. After three-quarters of an hour the drawing had the defined likeness of Dennis.

Dennis had been adamant that his picture wasn't to be taken, especially at Jason's attempt to catch him on camera, during their trip to the beach. Nor during anytime in their relationship, had he supplied her with one, Laurie recalled. But there he was captured on the screen and soon to be projected into living rooms across the nation. Laurie felt gratified that his picture would be a secret no longer.

After the session was over, they were directed to Detective Reilly's office. Reilly asked Laurie more questions about Dennis and his habits and mannerisms. Was he patient? Did he show any tendency to violence? What type of a driver was he? Did he drive short distances or long before stopping? Did he drink coffee or pop when driving requiring him to stop more often?

Laurie really wasn't much help, because their few dates were such short distances making it hard to tell Dennis' driving habits. The trip down wasn't a good indicator either, because of the time element of the shuttle takeoff. It was a long drive with few stops, just to cover the distance in time for the launch.

Detective Reilly started questioning Laurie about the couple that had originally been involved in introducing them. How well did they know him? Would they know Dennis' address or phone number? Laurie had said that morning she only knew the vague direction of the place where he lived. She really didn't know him that well, to have ever gone to his house. She wasn't much help filling in the information the detective wanted.

Laurie kept looking at Harry uneasily wondering what he was thinking about her travelling with this unfamiliar man. She was wishing a bit that he wasn't present to hear her feeble answers. Harry was thinking, how he had been a stranger too when she came to his house from the hospital, and yet she had been trusting with herself and her children.

Perhaps she had accepted Dennis for the same reason believing, he had been like Harry who had instilled his kindness and caring into the brief time, they had spent together. *Was it his fault she had perhaps trusted Dennis?* Although this morning, she had said she didn't think or care much about Dennis because she hadn't intended forming that kind of a relationship. It was only after he enticed Jason, knowing he would be interested in seeing the shuttle takeoff, that she had considered travelling with him.

Finally Detective Reilly said that was all he needed for now, when Laurie seemed to be getting agitated in giving her answers. Was it the missing children, or Harry's presence, in the questioning of Dennis' relationship to her? Reilly was pretty good at reading people and had noticed Laurie watching Harry's reaction to her responses. Her words had become more guarded and vague.

Reilly had also noted there was chemistry between these two that was much in evidence, although they were not physically touching. But he would catch the odd glance or expression between them. Their relationship would have flourished into permanency if she had stayed in Radford Falls, he felt sure. Reilly excused himself to look for Gus.

Gus was keeping an eye on incoming information regarding sightings. The sightings were being investigated along with searching police files, hoping to find a likeness to the composite drawing of Dennis. Gus indicated nothing much so far of worth. He said it was too bad that this guy had never touched Laurie's purse, then they would have had some fingerprints. When asked, she was sure Dennis had never had occasion to touch her purse.

Reilly and Gus knew they needed a break of some kind because Dennis was putting a lot of miles between Fort Lauderdale and his

potential destination with every passing hour. While they were discussing the latest findings apparently the FBI had arrived, Reilly was
informed by Jake when he popped his head in the door. They exchanged
glances. This wasn't the break they were looking for.

Reilly tried to ease his features of dejection, as he needed to go back
now and face the woman whose children had been missing eight hours
without a viable sighting. Things were not looking good. Dennis could
rightfully be halfway through Georgia by now. Even though they
had not heard from the Georgia State Troopers, who were suppose to
be watching for them, at the border. Unless Dennis was holed up in
Florida somewhere.

The unannounced arrival of the FBI was all he needed. The
unfriendly rivalry between the FBI and local law enforcement was
deep-rooted and a hell of a nuisance too. Reilly knew he would just
have to try to work around it. His intention was to keep control of
this investigation.

Getting ready to go back to his office he said to Gus. "Keep looking
for that break we need. I have hopes the composite drawing of Dennis
will turn something up soon."

Gus replied. "Yes, I will keep trying to find something. If any news
comes in I will let you know immediately. Don't sweat the FBI we'll
keep them out of your hair for a while." Gus gave him a knowing wink.
"Thanks." Reilly walked back to his office.

Todd was saying for Laurie's benefit, that he felt Jason would get
someone's attention to their plight knowing Jason the way he did.
Reilly stood there listening to Todd's hopeful words, which were full
of pride for the missing boy's capabilities. There was a definite familiar
closeness, even though they had been separated for over a year.

Reilly also knew there was more to their story than they were
telling, and it wasn't just his analytic mind. He strode forward. "Well
that appears to be all we need. Feel free to return to your hotel and
I will call as soon as we have anything of importance."

Laurie quickly pleaded. "Isn't there any news yet?"

Reilly hated to tell her but he had to. "No I'm sorry nothing yet.
We have nothing significant but we are checking all leads. Now that
Dennis' picture and description along with his car's description is

being broadcast, we feel sure it is only a matter of time. The fact that we haven't heard from the Georgia State Troopers, we feel they are still in Florida. Someone must have seen them, but has not taken the time to contact us." This last was added to give her some hope.

Reilly's hands were tied if they had managed to get into Georgia, because then it would be out of his jurisdiction. He would have to depend on the Georgia State Troopers and the sheriff's office there as well as the FBI taking over, so he was definitely hoping they were still in Florida.

Laurie was quietly sobbing again not hysterically but calmly like she was partially numb. Harry was trying to ease her out of the chair holding on to her arm gently. "Laurie we'll go back to the hotel. You will be more comfortable there. The composite drawing you helped to construct should be beneficial in spotting Dennis." Harry's voice was comforting.

He wanted to ask why the drawing hadn't been done sooner. But he didn't want to upset Laurie further.

Reilly's expression was such that maybe he was thinking the same thing, or maybe the artist just wasn't available. Maybe Reilly had been worried about Laurie's capabilities of thinking straight under her grief. Harry was willing to let it go unanswered for now but later he would make a point of asking?

Reilly said as an afterthought. "The FBI has just arrived. They are called in on all kidnapping cases. If you go back to the hotel I will deal with them." Harry looked relieved.

"I want you to know, although the FBI will want to take over this case it is still mine, and I intend to find the children for you. Someone has to recognize the car and Dennis soon."

• • •

The trip back to the hotel placed them at the corner where people and cars were busily darting here and there. The unconcerned people with their own agendas were naturally unaware of the tragedy that was driving Harry and Laurie's lives at the moment. The nightclub nearby was expelling laughter and music from the early evening crowd domiciled within. The noisy jubilance and excitement of some teenagers walking by who were happy to be free, to roam the streets of this famous Florida holiday spot.

Harry glanced around wanting to shout, 'there are two kidnapped children out there somewhere, how can you be so happy? We three are distraught knowing the circumstance of their kidnapping. We aren't here for pleasure. We are being forced to stay here. But that is life, only the eminent players are involved, not the world around us.

The light changed stopping the traffic that was clogging the road letting them cross the street, taking their tragedy with them. Although the passing people were unaware of them, Harry felt the anger burning inside. *Where were Bethany and Jason?*

CHAPTER TEN

*T*hey arrived at the hotel, Laurie going directly towards the elevators. Harry had tried to steer them to the restaurant before going upstairs. Laurie refused politely. Reilly's words held no encouragement to this ending anytime soon, so he didn't blame her. The last thing she wanted right now was food when she was so upset.

Harry ordered room service of drinks with the food to follow in one hour. He was hoping the brandy he had ordered for Laurie would help bring her out of her numbed state. She had kept saying in a strangled voice she couldn't eat anything. She was sitting at the table by the window, and Todd was in her room watching TV with a low volume. He knew without asking that Harry wanted him to keep track of news bulletins.

Laurie got up to use the washroom. She put cold water on her face and tidied her hair, to make her feel better. When she re-entered the room there was a brandy sitting on the table waiting for her. "Harry, I don't think I can drink the brandy. I find it too strong."

"Laurie you need to drink some to take away the numbness that is setting in. Please do this for me. Just take tiny sips then it won't hit your stomach so hard. You haven't eaten much today." Harry didn't want a drink either, but he just sipped some in the hopes Laurie would respond.

She picked up her glass and put it to her lips and tipped it. The liquid seemed to be poised on her tongue then he saw her throat move in a small way. The brandy must have caught in her throat, because she gave a little strangled cough. Harry took another drink of his to encourage her to take more. She was staring at him sipping. She looked like a little child that was being forced to take her medicine by a vigilant parent. She took a few more sips, before setting her glass down. Harry relaxed he was satisfied for now.

"Laurie, when the food arrives I want you to eat. I know you don't want any, but you need food to keep up your strength for the children's sake. The brandy may have made you feel a bit tipsy, but the food should alleviate that. The children will need you when they are found. They are going to be found I just know it." Harry said positively.

The phone pealed loudly. Harry jumped up and Laurie leaped startled. "Hello." "Yes." "Great that is positive news, when will you know for sure?" Harry was looking at Laurie hoping she was seeing his excitement. "Thank you, Reilly." "Yes." "I will." Harry hung up just as a knock came to the door. Room service had arrived with the food. The delay was annoying, but Harry directed the waiter inside with the dinner cart and tipped him liberally.

Laurie was surveying Harry wanting to ask, but at the same time afraid despite his look of exhilaration. She picked up the brandy and took a sizeable gulp to give her courage, but put it down quickly as she started to cough. The brandy had a definite bite to it when swallowed too fast.

Harry drew the cart nearer the table and at the same time called to Todd. He had excellent hearing and was already on his way into the room. He must be really hungry, Harry observed at his quick entry. Todd had been marvellous in his behaviour under these adverse conditions, he recognized.

While he dispersed the food crowding the small sized table, he stated. "That was Detective Reilly. He wanted to tell us, they had two calls of sightings and both were in Florida. He felt that was really encouraging news, that Dennis was still in Florida. Reilly seems confident that it won't be long before they were apprehended, with these latest sightings."

Todd chirped in. "Good maybe the next call will be to say they've been found."

"I hope so." Harry replied smiling at Laurie. She didn't say anything she just had an unbelieving look on her face. Knowing that she was not ready to get her hopes up too soon, only to be dashed once again.

Harry, hoping to have Laurie eat something, concentrated on the food, letting what he had conveyed sink in. The dinner looked very appetizing and the aroma permeated the air. Todd dived in eagerly. Harry picked up his utensils and napkin and Laurie automatically did the same.

His was roast beef and mashed potatoes smothered in a rich mushroom gravy. Laurie's was chunks of chicken in a white sauce on a bed of rice with a garden salad. Harry enquired politely. "Would you prefer the roast beef? I just assumed you would prefer the chicken. I like both if you would prefer the beef?" Bending over backwards trying to make the food sound enticing to Laurie, he awaited her reply.

"The chicken is fine." Her voice wasn't too enthusiastic. Todd was eating the traditional jumbo hamburger with gusto. He had eaten the Greek salad for lunch so Harry indulged him for dinner. It was sort of a reward for handling himself so maturely throughout the day. He was really proud of him.

Laurie was eating slowly but eating all the same. Harry realized he was hungry too and the delicious roast beef was quickly consumed. She appeared to be eating with more interest than he expected, perhaps the brandy had helped. They were practically finished when she spoke. "Harry I am not letting this latest news excite me. If I get my hopes up too high and turns out not to be them, I don't think I could handle the disappointment."

"I know Laurie. I understand but I am the opposite. I need to think positive because I want Bethany and Jason returned so much." Harry put out his hand covering Laurie's. She turned her hand over into his and grasped his hand tightly. She was trying to smile. She was feeling better for the brandy and the dinner, but until the news was more positive, she couldn't completely shed the fear of never seeing her children again.

Harry was encouraging her to eat a little more. She picked up her fork but laid it down again. He was pleased she had eaten more than he anticipated. Todd asked to be excused. Harry said. "You can watch

TV until Laurie wants her room again but keep it low." Laurie was best not hearing the news bulletins interrupting programs.

Todd made a beeline for the other room. Harry tidied up and placed the cart out in the carpeted hallway. When he closed the door he asked her if she wanted tea or coffee, not having included any when he ordered dinner except milk for Todd. She expressed her desire for tea. He ordered the tea and coffee from room service and some desserts knowing Todd's sweet tooth. If they looked appetizing enough maybe Laurie would indulge in some too.

Her colouring was a little better after the meal, although her eyes were almost sunken in her face. She looked smaller and more vulnerable than he remembered. Her inner grieving was taking a toll that was diminishing her. Harry's heart was going out to her.

Why didn't Reilly phone? Surely they had followed up on those two leads by now. Surely it wasn't a false hope? Were they really still in Florida? Why wouldn't they have left the state? It would be easier to disappear that way. Harry wasn't about to reveal his thoughts to Laurie. He asked her about her life since Indiana. She was giving answers rather sketchily as though she was accommodating him but had no interest in the topic.

Room service arrived with the tea, coffee and desserts. Harry placed the tea in front Laurie. She picked up the pot aiming the flow into the cup. The desserts he arranged in the middle of the table. There was Key Lime pie, Apple Crumble and a Chocolate Torte on small plates. He placed his coffee in front of his chair and sat down. Laurie was holding her cup with both hands, like she was trying to warm herself. Harry took a drink of coffee. It was black and hot the way he liked it. She was studying him.

What was she thinking? Is she thinking what am I doing in this hotel room with this man who is virtually a stranger? Harry hoped that wasn't her direction of thoughts.

Laurie was in deep contemplation. *This is a very caring man. Would we have been closer if I had stayed in Indiana? Why did I move to South Carolina? This would never have happened if I had stayed there, because then I would never have met Dennis. Oh God!* Her breath caught on a half sob.

The phone interrupted the silence of their thoughts. Harry wanted to rush to it but at the same time he didn't want to in case the sightings had not panned out. But he knew it had to be faced whether it was good news or bad. Laurie had a stricken look on her face. She didn't want to know either if it was bad news.

Harry finally lifted the receiver. "Hello." "Mike Reilly here. The two leads I called you about did not amount to anything, but we did have another call that sounds promising. It is from the Tallahassee area. I delayed calling in hopes of something definite, but then I thought it was unfair to keep you hanging, after my last call."

"Did you prove positively the other leads weren't valid?"

"Yes Harry. But I hate to get your hopes up again only to be dashed but I have a good feeling about this one. The break we have been waiting for. You can handle the information how you think best for Mrs McKnight. The best I can say is, I'll definitely keep in touch."

"Thanks Mike for calling." Harry hung up elated and deflated at the same time. His wish had been for more positive news. Todd had come into the room to hear what Harry had to say. He was standing like a deer poised for danger before flight. Waiting for the impact of Harry's news and so was Laurie.

"I have to tell you the two leads Mike Reilly previously called about didn't pan out." Laurie emitted a whimper of distress. "However, there is also a new lead that they are tracing. Mike is confident this will be the break they need. I wasn't going to tell you," Harry said honestly, "because I don't want to dash your spirits if it doesn't pan out either. Mike said he had a special feeling about this one though. I hope he is right."

Harry and Laurie looked at each other both needing that hope. To ease the moment he offered her a dessert. Her hand came out to take the Key Lime pie but the reflex was automatic rather than desire. Todd took the Chocolate Torte.

"Dad is the latest lead in Florida?"

"Yes Todd, up near Tallahassee which is not far from the Florida border. Detective Reilly is hoping they don't cross into Georgia." He was still watching Laurie, waiting for any type of response. She was nibbling on the pie and drinking tea as though she had not comprehended what he had said.

He sat down and pulled the apple crumble towards him but he did it for something to do rather than want. *Should he force the issue of acknowledgement with Laurie or should he just wait until she was ready?*

Todd went back into the other room with his cake. He knew his dad was waiting for Laurie's reaction so he thought he should make himself scarce, and besides he wanted to be near the TV in case they announced the latest lead was a success.

Harry sat eating his dessert and drinking coffee following Laurie's lead. *Why doesn't she say something? Yell or cry or do something?* He wanted to say. Instead his look was beseeching. She laid down the fork, her Key Lime pie plate was empty except for crumbs. Her eyes on Harry were impassive. She finally spoke inconsolably.

"I tried to take in all you said but when you inferred the leads were false, I sort of lost track of the rest you were saying. My hopes were dashed the way I thought they would be. They will never find them. I can just feel it. It has been hours too long." A lone tear drifted down her left cheek and unthinkingly she stuck out her tongue and caught the tear. That tore at Harry's insides more than if she had cried buckets. Feeling choked he had no reply. They sat looking at each other not moving. He realized he had to say something.

"Laurie it isn't too late. It is less than 24 hours. There is still hope, particularly when Detective Reilly is so hopeful with this latest sighting. He knows about these things. Gus, the other officer says the first 24 hours is crucial even up to 48 hours, as long as they stay in Florida and that is where the latest sighting places them."

"Well I can't bring myself to hope any longer and be deflated again. **I have lost them! The car just drove away with my Bethany and Jason!**" Laurie was yelling at him. Then she clinched her jaw and stopped. Her voice went to a dead monotone. "It is hopeless."

He was not going to let that happen. "Laurie come on we are going out. We are going to get you some clothes and incidentals. The waiting is what is defeating you. There will be a message when we get back, I know it." He was gently pulling her up out of the chair. She had such a surprised look on her face, she didn't even refuse.

Harry shoved her purse into her hands saying, "freshen up," his voice brooking no refusal. "There is still time before the stores close and you need a nightgown. Todd come in here, I want to talk to you?" Harry called. Laurie entered her room; she passed Todd just inside the adjoining door. He gave her a tentative look as he continued on to his father.

"Todd, we are going out to replace some of Laurie's things. You have a choice. You can either come with us or stay here and man the phone, while we are gone. I think you are old enough to be left alone, but promise you won't leave the room?"

"Dad, I want to stay in case Detective Reilly phones with more news. Do you mind?"

"No I said, you had a choice hoping you would want to stay for messages. Thank you. Stay in this room now while we are out. Mike will be calling here." Harry's hand drifted toward the phone.

"Laurie will be okay won't she Dad?"

"Yes Todd, she just needs to occupy her mind for awhile, to alleviate the waiting and she does need to replace her things." Todd settled in the chair in front of the TV. Laurie arrived with makeup on and her hair in a ponytail. Harry gave her a smile of admiration then turned to Todd.

"Todd, turn off the TV in Laurie's room. We won't be long." Todd headed into the other room while Harry guided her out the door. She did look a little better as though moving around helped.

The trip to the store revived their spirits a little. Harry stopped to look in the window of Elegance Designer Apparel. They had ladies clothes that had flair. He plied her with garments she would probably never wear but insisting she try them on in the hopes that something would appeal to her, if not he threatened he would choose for her.

Finally she got into the swing of things as she tried on the outfits, some were rather risqué and he would eagerly shake his head yes and she would chuckle a bit then head back for another outfit. She kept trying on outfits until with Harry's bantering, there were four lined up on the rack by the counter.

They next headed for a shoe store. She would need something else other than the sandals she was wearing. Each time they made purchases, she would pull out her credit card. Harry would look at it and tell the store lady it had expired and trade his own credit card for the purchases. Laughing and winking at her.

Laurie was looking at him in amazement. He was fun, smiling so easily and she had to laugh despite herself. He was very polite and could charm her into agreeing with his choices.

The last thing they picked up was a suitcase which ended up as two. One was for her new clothes that he enfolded inside and a matching case for her incidentals and makeup. He did assent to her paying for her makeup, at her insistence. Harry had not had so much fun shopping in years. He was beginning to hope this friendship might have a future.

He even bought himself a new casual top and shorts which he insisted she help pick out for him, only being fair after pushing so much on her. He had to admit she had good taste although he pretended to be critical but accepting her choice because of her expressive reaction. He put his clothes in with hers in the suitcase.

Shopping over they headed back to the hotel with their purchases picking up bottled water and fruit on the way. Harry liked the idea of his clothes in with hers like a husband and wife. But his reasoning out loud had been, the case could hold everything for easier carrying. Laurie kept laughing but rescued the fruit from that same fate saying it would get bruised. He was pleased he had suggested the outing, and her laughter no doubt was soon to end, but for this moment in time it was what they both needed.

As they sauntered leisurely back to the hotel like they were normal tourists. Harry held her hand which he had taken while guiding her around a couple studying a map at a street corner. If the situation wasn't so tragic about the children, this could have been a happy memory of his trip.

CHAPTER ELEVEN

*U*pon entering the hotel room, Harry looked to Todd for a response to their arrival. Laurie had become quiet and reserved as soon as they stepped into the elevator, when the horrid memories snapped back intrusively. The carefree couple enjoying the shopping trip like normal tourists evaporated.

"Did Detective Reilly call?" Harry asked before Todd could say anything.

"Yes Dad, he did. They are definitely in Tallahassee. There is two explicit sightings from the pictures shown on TV of Jason, Bethany and Dennis. These two latest tips are from the same approximate area, as the other sighting he called about earlier." Todd spoke excitedly.

"The first sighting alleged they saw them visible in the car, but the second mentioned only Bethany. The reason the first couple noticed them was because Jason was writing 'help' with his finger on the window while stopped at a red-light. So the police are presuming the fact that the second sighting only mentioned Bethany, that Jason must have been restrained on the floor or on the seat. Perhaps Dennis caught him signalling other cars."

Laurie let out a strangled moan from her throat. *Surely Dennis wouldn't hurt Jason.*

"Todd, did they recognize the car as Dennis' or didn't he say?"

"Yes, they are in Dennis' Cavalier. He made the sighting sound hopeful. They have been breaking in frequently with news bulletins with their pictures and description since you left." Harry had hoped they had been found but this was something encouraging.

Laurie went into her room sinking onto the bed. The tears were coming in earnest now, partly in relief of the sightings and partly in sadness that they hadn't actually been apprehended. She needed the positive, that the police had her little ones in their possession. At least the area had been defined. Brave! Brave! Jason. Todd had such faith in him, knowing he would attract someone's attention to their plight and thank goodness he obviously had. She hoped Dennis had not hurt him as a result, her heart had a sinking feeling.

Harry walked over and sat down beside her on the bed and pulled her into his arms. She really broke down and began issuing loud sobs.

"I thought you would be relieved, that there were definite sightings" After her crying eased, he wondered if he gave her some aspirin would it ease her into a restful sleep. Only sleep would make the waiting bearable for her now, the ups and downs of the hunt telling on her physically.

Todd raced in. "Dad the news bulletin says another sighting has been made in the same area." Harry strode quickly to the phone. When his call was transferred to Reilly's office he spoke. "Mike Reilly here."

"Harry Cochrane. Is it true you have more concrete information?"

"Yes. We hope Dennis sees it and will be on the move again. We don't want him to go underground then we won't have any hopes of locating him. The last detection indicated that there was a woman with him. They described her as wearing a big floppy sun hat that hid her face. Unfortunately with no positive description, gives her the opportunity to move around freely, getting supplies and things."

"We have road blocks all over that area, as well as intense police patrols. The border police have stepped up procedures in that area of Georgia and also Alabama borders as well. The state troopers have Dennis' car description and licence number. The thing now is, we don't want him to switch cars again, so maybe we are reckless with our news bulletins. They are pulling in results of sightings, so we have to weigh that as a positive."

He took this opportunity for Mike to answer his question, regarding the time lag on the composite drawing. Reilly answered "Mrs.

McKnight was in no shape to think coherently before you arrived. I think your taking her to the hotel along with the sleep made a big difference in her answers and thoughts, besides the artist had to arrive from Daytona Beach." Harry accepted the explanation, because it was more or less what he had already surmised.

Reilly went on to say. "The FBI are now involved so there will be more TV coverage in the apprehension, should they be spotted. So far I have been able to dissuade them from questioning Mrs. McKnight again. By saying that there is probably nothing more that she could possibly reveal that she hasn't already told us."

Harry thanked him again for keeping them up to-date and hung up. He mentioned Reilly's comments to them.

"Todd, they are trying to persuade Dennis to move again. The continuous TV newscasts and road blocks everywhere are narrowing the net around them."

Laurie was watching him. The tears were evident on her face, but she was no longer openly crying. He had addressed Todd, with that express purpose in mind.

Harry went into the bathroom for the bottle of aspirin and some water. He wanted her relaxed, for bedtime and sleep, hoping the aspirin would remove some of the sorrow in its path. "Laurie, perhaps your new housecoat would be comfortable after your shower." Harry suggested as she swallowed the pills. He wanted her settled before Todd and he went to bed.

With Laurie obediently following his suggestion, he returned to his room to shower also. Upon departing the bathroom he looked at his son.

"Todd, how about a shower and your pyjamas too?"

Harry was dressed in fatigues of loose airy pants and a T-shirt. Unlike the demure nightgown and housecoat Laurie had bought.

He wanted to phone again, but he knew Mike would call knowing they were anxious so he cooled his impatience.

Todd was back out shortly. "That was speedy?"

"But Dad I've been sitting around all day, I am not really dirty."

"Sorry about missing out on Busch Gardens, Todd."

"I'm not. I would rather be here with Laurie and be here for Jason and Bethany's return. Besides I don't miss something I never had and

I sort of had my fill being at Disney World for so long."

"Thank you for understanding the situation so well." Harry ruffled his wet hair affectionately.

At that moment, Laurie strolled in noting the byplay of the two together with despondency. *Would she ever have her children back? Would she ever have them to love and hold?* It wasn't that she resented these two their closeness. She just wanted to share the same opportunity of ruffling Jason and Bethany's hair. She had noticed Harry included Todd in most of what he did, even consulting him on most matters.

"Look at Laurie, Todd. Doesn't she look pretty in her new attire?" His face mirrored his admiration. She stepped forward shyly. She felt odd in her housecoat in front of them, but not uncomfortable or intimidated. "Yes Laurie you look really nice." Todd said with a boyish grin. Then he looked up at his dad.

"She sure is pretty." Laurie came further into the room and curtsied and Harry smiled broadly. Todd's eyes sparkled. He did feel that he could love this woman as a mother. But it was out of the question at this time. Her mind was focused on her children's return, Todd felt sure.

"Do you feel better?" Harry asked with interest.

"Yes I do actually. This has been a rollercoaster day emotionally, of ups and downs." She ran her hands through her tawny wet hair letting the curls fall around her face. The damp curls were clinging to her neck. Her action was done unconsciously but his insides were churning watching the sexual act, that she was innocently unaware of.

Her eyes shifted to the TV when she noticed a news bulletin was coming on. All had been ignoring the television till then. Harry wanted to reach over and obliterate it but it was too late. There were the usual pictures of Bethany and Jason and their description. It switched to the composite drawing of Dennis which shocked Laurie, because now it looked even more true to life than when it was prepared this afternoon. It really was a positive picture of him. Dennis' full description plus the car's particulars were given. Listening, no mention was made of any woman accomplice. She wondered why not, perhaps because they didn't have a clear description of her.

She had mixed feelings as she watched the details play across the screen. To see the children's pictures and Dennis' together was disturbing but at the same time, knowing the police were putting out frequent bulletins asking for help in locating them was helping the police. The television went back to normal programming and she looked at Harry.

He was glad that she was taking the news bulletin so calmly. Perhaps the shower and aspirin combination was working. She came over to curl up on the chair with her feet pulled up under her.

Todd eyes went back to the TV, while Harry and Laurie discussed the day's events.

Harry was trying to point out his faith in Mike. "I think he is a very dedicated man, and he will leave no stones unturned." She needed to have her mind at rest, although she seemed too wired to sleep. Tomorrow could be another gruelling day. The thought that maybe she might lay awake; making the night longer with negative thinking bothered him.

"Laurie perhaps if I sat in your room with you while lying down, while we talk you will be more relaxed. Then maybe you will drift off to sleep?"

"I am rather exhausted, yes that might relax me." They headed towards her room. He stopped, "You go first and climb into bed, I want to get a drink of water." He was figuring this would alleviate some of her embarrassment. He soon followed her in. The pulled drapes made it a mellow glow from the lamp. Her curvy shape under the thin cover was revealing.

"Harry will you hold me the way you did earlier?" That was the last thing Harry wanted to do. His body was already reacting to her visible shape in bed, silhouetted under the covers. He could see her shoulders with the filmy turquoise straps, causing his mind to go off the deep end. "Of course." He stated pleasantly. He sat with his back to the headboard and his feet half off the bed and she settled into his chest like a homing pigeon.

He ran his hand over her hair settling for a few seconds at the nape of her neck caressing her. Then his hand lowered onto her back rubbing up and down in a light stroke. Her fragrance was invading his body. His senses were running rampant.

"Harry, I couldn't have survived the day without you and Todd with me." *I may not survive this.* He thought.

"Thank you." Laurie kissed his hand in gratitude. She had turned her head grazing him with her lips as his hand caressed her hair. This closeness was merciless enough without her lips coming into contact with his skin. "I was glad we were able to be here for you. Todd and I love Bethany and Jason. We couldn't imagine not being here to help."

He dropped a light kiss on her forehead. *And I am falling in love with you.* Now was not the time for declarations of this magnitude. She would probably be shocked and horrified. He went back to stroking her and Laurie's eyes closed.

Please go to sleep in a hurry. I am slowly burning here. Definitely another cold shower was coming up. But he kept caressing her back gently and even when her breathing changed, indicating she was sleeping, he continued stroking not being able to stop himself from touching her tenderly.

He was thankful now he didn't need to make conversation, because he couldn't have spoken without letting his yearning reflect in his voice. Finally he eased her down pulling the cover and blanket from the bottom of the bed up around her. He placed a loving kiss on her forehead and lithely left the room.

The shower was cold and long. He dressed only in his fatigue pants.

"Dad I thought you already had a shower?" Todd asked in horror, as a typical boy he avoided showers.

"Well I got stiff so I tried another shower to relax me. Lights out time Todd. Laurie is sleeping and we should be too." He flicked the television off, then checking on her once more, before turning off the light. He had left her bathroom light on with the door cracked open just a bit. Her body didn't appear to have moved.

He climbed into his bed not to sleep, but to lay with his arms under his head and wonder about his feelings. Can I keep up this platonic friendship without giving myself away? How would she respond if she knew? Only friends on the surface but wanting a deeper relationship with this woman, could he continue to hide his growing fondness for her? Laurie wasn't able to think about anything else other than her missing children, he rationalized. Dennis had betrayed her and her faith in men.

He slipped into sleep and was greeted by a smiling Laurie curled up in his arms. He tugged her more solidly against his body. She was so soft and sank into him like a soft pillow completely relaxing his body and mind, loving the feel of her pliant against his lean firm body.

His body twitched jerking him awake instead of Laurie, he was crushing a soft pillow in his arms. The blissful smile left his face, feeling a little foolish. He punched the pillow, pushing it under his head rolled over and went to sleep.

The ringing of the phone jolted him awake. Grabbing the phone he noted the daylight seeping between the curtains. "Hello."

"Good morning Harry, I have some good news for you. We have located Dennis' Cavalier and we have it under surveillance. His car is parked in a bush area near a trailer park. We aren't sure which unit he is in. A jogger spotted the car recognizing it from the bulletins. In his morning run, he had never seen a car parked in that area before, which made him notice the Cavalier." Harry was sitting upright with this news.

"What are the chances of locating him now?"

"It depends how well stocked they are whether they make a move or hole up for a few days. It is hard to say. We could go door to door but he might see us coming and skip out. The trailers are too close together making us visible ten trailers away. We don't want them stealing another car and lose our advantage."

"Yes I see what you mean. You want them to think they are comfortably hidden."

"Yes in fact the FBI is going to let it out that they have had a sighting in Pensacola so they will think the FBI are concentrating on that area, now they have access to a TV. I wanted to let you to know, so you will understand the switch in information and why."

"Thanks for letting us know." He hung up.

Todd was sitting up wide awake. He repeated what Reilly had said. Todd was grinning. "Dad, they will get them back for sure now."

"I hope so son, the sooner the better. At least, it is the most encouraging news so far. I wonder if Laurie's awake." Harry crept over to the adjoining door when he heard water running he knew she was.

He quickly headed for his bathroom grabbing his clothes on the way saying. "Laurie's awake so get your clothes on so we can have breakfast."

Todd scooted out of bed donning his clothes speedily and sat patiently waiting for them with a smug look on his face, the mention of breakfast and added incentive. He sat at the window watching the police cars around the police station on the corner to see if there was any action.

Another sunny day in Florida; Fort Lauderdale's streets were a bustle of people walking this way and that, with heavy traffic both ways. The morning interrupted with horns honking and the odd screech of brakes, Fort Lauderdale being a popular tourist place. Todd was busy watching the street happenings.

"Dad that looks like a good place for breakfast lots of people going in and out. It must be popular." Todd said pointing as Harry came back into the room. "With that much activity it must be good." He finished.

"All right that is where we will go when Laurie is ready." He turned his head as she entered the room.

"I see everyone is up and ready for a new day. Did I hear the phone when I was getting into the shower?" She asked. Thankfully she looked rested.

"Yes. I'll tell you all about it over breakfast. Todd has picked out the place across the street. His survey of the busy comings and goings indicates that it is the logical place. So let's check it out?" He seized her hand heading out the room their spirits higher after a good night's sleep and the early morning phone call.

As they stood waiting for the elevator Todd was observing Laurie and his father wishing they were both his parents. She would make a terrific mother. He quickly turned away so she wouldn't catch his longing look, ending his fantasy thoughts.

The elevator pinged, Todd looked expectantly for the doors to open. They went inside and were propelled to the lobby and the early morning activities already in progress. He raced to the automatic doors that swept away as if by magic. He stood part way controlling the door open for Laurie and his Dad. He glanced at them again thinking yes they would be the perfect parents.

The breakfast lived up to Todd's predictions, with the chosen king sized breakfast that he downed with relish. Laurie was happier today at the news that they were closing in on Dennis finally. Today the waiting, tomorrow can only be success. That was the way Harry was presenting it to her. Today's waiting would then, be worth it.

Laurie was wondering. *Were the children being treated well? Were they feeding them? Was Jason protecting Bethany like he always had or had they been kept separate? Why did Dennis want to steal them?* This she was having trouble with in particular because in all the time with Dennis, he had not shown any particular interest in her children.

The conversation of the launch had seemed to be nonchalantly introduced and it was Jason's avid interest that targeted the possibility of this trip. He had drawn Dennis' attention proudly to the groupings of planes and ships of his father's and his keen interest. Dennis picked up on Jason's desire to see the launch. Against Laurie's better judgement, she had given in noting the excitement illuminating Jason while Dennis was talking about the feasibility of the trip.

He had been the perfect gentleman on the way down and at night, having arranged separate rooms. He had not been pushy but slightly distant, but showed caring at the same time. He did not appear to be attentive to the children, leaving her in complete control of them until after the launch.

Things had changed, that is when he seemed to take over lifting Bethany and grabbing onto Jason.

Changing, she had noticed, after she had mentioned knowing Harry and the boy Todd, who stood with Jason and Bethany showing their joy of recognition. She had wanted to talk to them, mentioning this to him. Telling him how Harry had been so good with the kids and her when she got out of the hospital in Indiana.

Instead Dennis had rushed them out in a gruff manner and said they would wait to greet them outside the building. But when they arrived outside, he had whisked them away to the car instead, zooming out of the parking lot and away from the Cape.

She admonished herself, why hadn't she clued in that there was something erroneous going on. Dennis' behaviour was so different. Foolishly, she had made excuses, that there had been quite a crush of so many people leaving the viewing deck all at once.

Then when Dennis returned to their hotel, he left them to attend to some business. Not wondering about the sudden business, but just that she was more comfortable to be alone with the children.

At breakfast Dennis appeared to be all right but, in thinking back he had been kind of nervous and agitated wanting to be on the road. Of course, choosing the breakfast kept her occupied so she hadn't analyzed his behaviour. If only she had paid attention, could she have stopped the kidnapping from happening?

"Laurie where are you?" Harry asked trying to get her full attention for awhile but she had been deep in thought.

"Oh! I'm sorry Harry, I was just going over our trip here with Dennis. I missed the signals now that I think back. After I saw you and Todd, Dennis became agitated but he said it was because of the crush of the crowd. I didn't question his behaviour. Why didn't he want you and Todd around? Why didn't I realize? I was worried about getting separated from Bethany and Jason at the time so I missed the signals. Maybe if I had paid attention my children would be still with me now."

"Laurie it won't do any good to berate yourself. It did happen and we have to go on from there. Besides if you had made a fuss he might have injured you, if the intent of the trip was to kidnap the children."

"I only wish I had talked to you at the time, Laurie then maybe I could have picked up on his odd manner. Things might have been different but I didn't make a positive effort either. If we had, Todd and I could have helped you but I really think you couldn't have done it on your own without getting hurt in the process."

"Maybe you are right. Then matters would have been worse for the children if they knew he had manhandled me. That would weigh on their minds and add to their dilemma."

"Don't feel bad about trusting Dennis, as I thought he appeared like a caring man, when I first saw him with you." Giving his observation on the matter.

Todd conveyed his opinion. "Although Dad, I didn't like the way he grabbed up Bethany and dragged Jason away. That was when my opinion changed about him."

"Yes Todd, I noticed but thought it was his concern for the children in the crush of people." Harry paused. "Laurie let's get off this subject. It would have bothered me a great deal if you had been injured and Dennis had taken the two children anyways. Let's go back to the police station and we will inquire if there are any more new developments."

CHAPTER TWELVE

They walked the short distance to the police station. People were coming and going through the doors. The police station with its high level of movement and noise quickly surrounding them. Looking around Harry spied Gus.

"Gus, do you know where Mike Reilly is?"

"Yes, he is in one of the interrogation rooms. I will let him know that you are here." Reilly soon appeared, walking at a fast gait.

"I tried calling you but your room didn't answer." He paused then rubbed his neck as if he had bad news to impart. "They got away. We had a change of shift on the stake out, of Dennis' car and the officers were shooting the guff over by the patrol car, when they heard the car spin its wheels leaving. I have reamed them out for letting him get away but that is after the fact. At least Dennis is still in his car for now."

"We found the trailer unit used by Dennis. The park owner stated it was for overnight only. So I believe they are unaware we were so close. I know that isn't what you wanted to hear and neither did I. It is hindsight to say, I wished we had gone trailer by trailer. We didn't know the woman's description so she could have refused us entry and we would have been none the wiser. The park owner said he was suspicious but not sure as he dealt with the woman only." Mike was so remorseful Harry felt sorry for him but angry at the same time.

Laurie started to cry "My babies, my babies I'll never see them again." She swayed and Harry grabbed her before she fell.

"Bring her into my office." said Mike leading the way. "Gus, get a glass of water." He said in passing.

Laurie sank into the chair half falling over, her shoulders shaking in her grief. Harry held her in the chair trying to lend his strength. It was breaking his heart at this latest development for her. So close to success and then whipped away again.

Todd waited out in the corridor. He was angry that they had escaped. It hurt him to see Laurie so defeated. How much more could she take? It was over 24 hours now and they had escaped once again with her family.

Gus came into Mike's office with the water placing it in Laurie's hands. Harry helped her shaking hands hold the glass. She took a drink then choked on a sob. Harry talked her into more and her crying subsided. Mike told Gus to keep the FBI busy somehow.

"Harry, I am really sorry about this, you know that. We almost had them and we blew it." Mike said in disgust.

"I just wished it was over Mike, especially when you said the police had the car under surveillance. We can only hope now for another break. Hopefully someone will see the car and report them again to the police." Harry said optimistically.

"The surveillance crew really slipped up and missed their direction of departure. We have alerted Georgia and Alabama authorities that he is on the move. That's our position, until we get another sighting the route Dennis is travelling. I think you had better take Mrs. McKnight back to the hotel. Thank God she has you and Todd as I don't know what would have happened if you hadn't been here for her. Thank you Harry." Mike wondered again about their relationship. There was a definite chemistry going on between them.

The phone rang, so Harry took the opportunity to remove Laurie from the office. Some reporters were waiting for them on the steps, bombarding Laurie with questions. Harry tried to appease them. The trio finally reached the hotel only to find more reporters waiting there. A much sadder trio now entered the hotel than the three that had departed cheerfully for breakfast. The reporters weren't helping as they tried to slip by them. Laurie was back in her numb state moving along but unaware of her surroundings.

The rooms had been made up while they were away. Todd wanted to do something to help Laurie but not knowing how. Harry waved his head towards Laurie's room indicating for Todd to watch TV in there.

Laurie was sitting by the window staring into space not comprehending the movement beyond the window. No tears only numbness. Maybe this time she should have a tranquilizer or sleeping pill. Picking up the phone he asked to speak to the manager. When the manager came on the line Harry explained the situation. The manager knew, as a result of the reporters hanging around, who they were.

"Mrs. McKnight has just received bad news, and she is taking it pretty hard." Harry allotted.

"Did something bad happen to the children?" The manager asked quickly.

"No the police had them under surveillance, but the surveillance team wasn't observant enough, allowing them to get away again and disappear. Mrs. McKnight is taking it rather badly."

"What can I do for you?" The manager's voice full of concern.

"I think she needs a doctor to prescribe a sedative for her."

"I will arrange for one to come to your suite. Which room are you in?"

"We are in Rooms 312 & 314 mostly 314."

"He should be there soon. I will personally make the arrangement. Mr. Cochrane, I want to say on behalf of the hotel and myself, how sad we feel that this could happen. We are sorry your perception of Fort Lauderdale can be marred by this. On behalf of the hotel, we want you to know that your room rate will be minimal and all meals during your stay will be on the hotel. Don't hesitate to call, if there is any other way we can be of service."

"Why thank you and thank you for arranging the doctor's visit." Harry hung up with a slightly improved feeling, with the hotel manager's caring manner. He was going to wait to tell her of the hotel's generosity until her frame of mind had improved somewhat.

When the doctor arrived he was middle aged with a gentle manner about him. He obviously knew their plight because he made no inquiries about the children. The doctor just treated Laurie for her shock, giving her an injection and some pills for later. He indicated to Harry, the main thing was for her to drink lots of water or juice or perhaps some sweet tea if she will take it. Keep a light blanket over her as with shock there is a lowering of body temperature. He indicated her vital signs were normal.

"If she will take some food fine but don't press her to eat too much. I am sorry I can't help you more than that, but if she needs me any further don't hesitate to call." He was looking at Laurie sadly because he knew that things could become most unpleasant if the children weren't located.

The doctor informed Harry, as they stepped out into the hall. "Don't worry about my fee the hotel is taking care of it."

Harry went back into room to Laurie. He took her into her room and Todd quickly turned off the TV and put the chair back near the window. Harry said a quiet thanks to Todd. Todd knowing he could not help Laurie as much as he would like to left the room. Playing musical rooms without complaint was the only way he could help.

Harry made her drink some more water knowing the injection should put her to sleep shortly. He sat down beside her and pulled her into his protective arms and she came willingly.

She started murmuring sadly about her babies, the cuteness of the children's ways, the things that had made their life happy together. How bleak her future would be without them. Harry let her talk just listening with a breaking heart, holding her in his loving arms.

He knew now in his heart he really loved this woman but it definitely was not the time to let her know. Her mind wouldn't be ready to absorb his love. Even after Laurie drifted off to sleep, Harry continued to hold her not wanting to let her go, desiring so acutely to take away her hurt. Why were there distorted people in this world? Why did the police surveillance have to get muffed? Why couldn't they have stopped them before they slipped away? Laurie had just come around to being brave about the situation with his and Todd's help and then this setback occurred.

He knew he shouldn't but he kissed her lips then eased her down onto the bed and covered her with the blanket.

Upon entering his room he noted Todd was just staring out the window. There was a depressing silence in the room. Todd swung around as his father sat down across from him. "Dad, why didn't the police catch them? They had them. They had them trapped in the trailer park." Todd said angrily.

"I know Todd unfortunately they did escape and Detective Reilly feels very badly about the police slip up. The sad part is, they have no direction of their escape route or their ultimate destination."

"Dad, Jason is such a plucky kid. I still firmly believe that he will draw attention to them and he will keep trying no matter what."

Harry was looking at his son with admiration. "Todd, I want to thank you for all your consideration and your patience throughout this ordeal. It certainly isn't the vacation we planned. I think you have been a help to Laurie and your observations were a help to the police."

"Dad, it's okay. I love Laurie and I love Bethany and Jason too. I wish we were a family like the time Laurie stayed with us after the hospital. I used to pretend she was my mother. She even let me hug her once when the others were hugging her."

Harry was feeling so mellow listening to Todd speak of the family life he himself wished for also. "Todd I wished for a family life with them too. That last night when we were together at the restaurant, I had made up my mind fully intending making a home for them eventually. Laurie had known us for such a short time and her husband had only died three months earlier, so it was just too soon to mention it. But Laurie took the matter out of my hands by leaving Indiana. It just wasn't meant to be." His voice trailed off sadly. "Todd, will you be all right with Laurie if I go out and bring some juices and such. We still have some fruit if you want some." Harry just had to get out and do some walking to calm his nerves, the frustration of having the children almost, then Dennis' successful escape.

"Sure Dad I'll be fine. Besides I like the responsibility of looking out for Laurie because that is all I can do for her. I like being here for phone calls too. It makes me feel useful and helping the only way I can."

"Like you son, I hope Jason hangs in there and does keep trying to get people's attention but I am also afraid Dennis might hurt him this time. I will pick up some reading material and some games that we can use to pass the time. I want us to stay within reach of the phone. Thankfully the telephone enables me to screen the information before Laurie hears."

"Don't worry about me Dad. You don't have to entertain me. I just want to be here for you and Laurie." Harry opened his arms and Todd went into them with a boyish vigour.

Harry hugged his son tightly. This was unusual for them but both needing this closeness right now. He cleared the tears out of his voice before pulling away.

"I love you Todd and I don't know what I would ever do if someone took you away from me." He patted Todd's back affectionately then stepped back but not before Todd's words of. "I love you too Dad." Harry quickly left the room, flowing with emotion and dread for the next news if not favourable.

Todd peeked in at Laurie. He went in and stood quietly beside the bed. He wanted to touch her and tell her he cared; he wanted to take her hurt away. He whispered the only words he could. "I would be your son if you would let me. I think you would make a wonderful mother." Then he crept from the room. Laurie's quiet breathing continued.

The phone rang and Todd in passing, grabbed it quickly, cutting it off at the second ring hoping it didn't wake Laurie. "Hello."

"Hello Todd this is Detective Reilly. Is your dad around?"

"No, he went out to get drinks and reading material."

"Where's Mrs. McKnight?"

"The doctor came and gave her a sedative and she is sleeping in the other room."

"Good. I wanted to let your dad know we have another sighting and we are checking it out. Dennis is still in Florida according to this latest lead. Strange but, he is heading back our way. I have a feeling he still wants to go north, so he is backtracking. Anyways you can tell your dad we are still hopeful in locating him."

"Yes. I'll tell him as soon as he comes in. I hope you find them soon." Todd said fervently.

"I do too. I will give you an update as soon as I hear anything definite. I know this is hard on you and on Mrs. McKnight and your father but I will give it my best until this is resolved. We are still within the 48 hour period so I am thinking positive and I want you to do the same. Pass that information on to your father and I had better get back to work."

"Yes sir." Todd hung up with renewed hope. He turned on the TV in hopes of picking up more information but knowing at the same time he wouldn't or Detective Reilly would have already told him. The usual TV programs weren't holding his interest. His concern for Laurie, Bethany and Jason was uppermost in his mind. His ears perked up hearing a key turning in the lock. Harry walked in carrying two bags and a questioning look.

"Dad, Detective Reilly called. They appear to be heading back in this direction."

"When did he call?"

"About 15 minutes ago." The conversation had taken place in quiet voices.

"How is Laurie?"

"Last I checked she was still sleeping deeply. I just checked a few times." Todd said expressing his concern for her.

Harry replied. "Thanks for keeping things going here. I just needed to get some fresh air and walk off some of the tension. It took me longer than I expected because I wanted to get enough drinks and things for a few days. The less we have to go out until this is finished the better. I don't want to miss anymore of the Detective's calls. Also the reporters are still being persistent and a bit obnoxious." Harry reiterated.

"The manager is sending up ingredients for making sandwiches and a cooler with ice. The hotel is really trying to make our ordeal as pleasant as possible."

"That's good eating here is best. Detective Reilly said he thought possibly Dennis is still trying to get north. He had figured at first that logically their purpose was to lose themselves in the south but the latest sighting says otherwise."

The room service arrived with the cooler and a tray of sandwich ingredients. Todd dived in making a meat sandwich with cheese and tomato. He grabbed a V8 juice to drink. "Do you think they will catch them this time?"

"I don't know Todd, we can only hope so. Our best chance was, when they had him holed up in that trailer park. Let's hope the latest lead was genuine. I am going in to see if Laurie's awake."

Harry observed Laurie was lying on her side with her hand on the pillow cradling her head. He thought about touching her to wake her but thought better of it. Slowly he left the room.

"Sleep is the best medicine for her at this moment." Harry said quietly.

He too began to build a sandwich for something to do. "Today we wait until Detective Reilly calls with more positive news." His voice optimistic. They both settled down to eating without conversation.

. . .

The police had followed up on the latest lead with roadblocks but no vehicle of that description showed up. Had they changed direction again? Reilly was getting frustrated. He wanted this so badly to occur close by, so he could personally have the opportunity to grill Dennis. To berate him for kidnapping the children, before the FBI took over. He knew how impractical his thoughts were and changed to just wanting them caught. He was thankful to Gus for keeping the FBI busy.

The added worry now was the caller had mentioned Bethany and two adults only. Was it only Bethany that Dennis had wanted in the first place? Where was Jason? He had not mentioned this fact to Todd. There was hope that Jason was still with them but tied up on the seat or floor.

The police had gone over the trailer with a fine toothcomb hoping to find evidence of a direction or plans. No phone calls had been recorded by the trailer park owner. Nor had they found evidence that Jason was left in the area. The only thing they had found was the missing suitcase which was being shipped back to Fort Lauderdale. They would hold on to it temporarily as it might upset Mrs. McKnight more to know about the suitcase.

Reilly took another drink of coffee grimaced as it was cold. He wished he had a cigarette but he had quit smoking a year ago, but he still missed it. This type of manhunt was disconcerting to the nerves. He would give anything to get a decent sleep, but that would have to wait. He couldn't bring himself to leave until these kids were found. He had dozed in his chair a few times during the night, but that was all the sleep he had obtained since this started.

Reilly was thankful for the understanding of his wife. Grace had been vocally unhappy with his crazy hours, since his becoming a detective. They had even had a trial separation but she came back with the condition if he wasn't with the job he was hers solely. So he spent all his off duty time with Grace in order to keep their marriage on terra firma. He loved her so much, balancing the scale this way was not a hardship. He missed his buddy time with the guys, but she was more important to him. He couldn't lose her again.

Gus came in throwing a message on the desk. "Did you see that?"

"No what is it?" Reilly picked up the sheet of paper. It was a report of dismissal for the two police officers who had fouled up the surveillance.

"Did you order this?" Gus' manner was angry.

"No, I just gave the two officers a severe reprimand over the phone. Their superior must have ordered this. Apparently you feel this is a harsh action, is that it Gus?" Reilly wanted to let him vent his obvious feelings.

"Yes and no. Yes a little harsh but no because they should lose something for goofing up so badly, but dismissal is a bit ruthless." As though he had thought it over since entering the room, some of his intense anger had dissipated.

"I'm incline to agree, except we had them if those two had done their jobs right. Let's hope they have learned their lesson. Maybe in a week or so I'll go to bat for them and have the directive rescinded, but then maybe not if any harm befalls on those children." Reilly stated.

Gus got up from the chair. "You know I came in here ready to ream you out but now I have reconsidered. I guess I have to agree those two officers should be drummed out for failing to protect those children. I hope they are still okay?"

Gus' steps, as he left the office, were meek compared to the way he charged in. Reilly sat looking after him. He was a good chap, he cared about children too.

Then Reilly's mind went to Grace who hadn't been able to have children of her own. They had tried adopting but that fell through when Grace and he had separated and they hadn't talked about adopting since then. He wondered if it was too late. Perhaps it was time to approach the subject again with Grace. He picked up his cup and went looking for fresh coffee.

CHAPTER THIRTEEN

Laurie did surface an hour later looking rested. Her hair was still wet from her shower. Harry offered her something to eat. He had cautioned Todd not to mention the call from Reilly. He figured she was not capable of handling another win or lose situation. He wanted to protect her against any further anguish.

"I have been out to pick up drinks and we have the ingredients for meat sandwiches, if you would like some?" He wanted to occupy her rather than sitting waiting and waiting like they had been doing. He had always been a man of action but his role he knew at this moment was to be there for Laurie. He was beginning to feel like a caged animal. Today the waiting, was shrivelling up his insides. What would the ultimate end be for this drama? Would the children be recovered within hours or would it go on for days? He couldn't begin to think beyond days let alone months and years.

He intended to stay until the children were found no matter the length of time. God forbid if it did go into months or years. Could he talk Laurie into coming back to Indiana or would she insist on staying in South Carolina in the hopes they would somehow find their way home.

If she stayed in South Carolina could Todd and he relocate? What about his job could he open a branch office there if that was Laurie's decision, or would he just give up his partnership and start anew?

Harry knew he wanted to be part of Laurie's future and was willing to make it happen even if he had to relocate. He snapped out of his reverie when Laurie commented on the wide range of food in the cooler but not taking any.

Todd was looking at his father strangely. Laurie had been talking to his father and he hadn't responded. From the expression on his dad's face he was deep in thought. "Laurie, can I get you a drink?" Todd asked.

"A drink would be nice."

"Pop, iced tea or juice? Todd inquired.

"Some juice would be fine." Her voice was pleasant but there was a flatness to it despite Todd's gallantry. He placed a glass of V8 juice in front of her. "Thank you." Bringing the juice to her lips and sipping, she looked over the rim at Harry. *Why was he so quiet? Had something happened while I was asleep? I am so glad he was here for me. What would I have done if I had been alone?*

Laurie physically shuddered at the thought.

Harry quickly asked. "Are you all right Laurie?" Disturbed at her shudder.

"Yes I am okay, just shaking off the affects of the drugs." She lied.

"You should have something to eat. Todd could make a sandwich for you or maybe you would prefer some yogurt?"

"No, I'll just have the juice for now, maybe some yogurt later." *I can't eat till you tell me what's happened?* A question she didn't voice, not sure she really wanted the answer. Laurie sipped her juice still looking at him.

Todd was looking from one to the other. They were both staring deeply at each other. What was going on between them? Todd knew something but didn't comprehend what. He felt it was time to exit the room. He went into Laurie's room to watch TV after flicking off their own. Neither one noticing his leaving.

Harry broke the connection first saying. "Laurie, we need to make a decision in case the children aren't recovered soon."

Laurie's body physically flinched.

He wished he hadn't voiced that idea, although his thinking was they had better discuss this possibility while there was still some hope. If the hope was gone would her mind be able to function coherently?

"Laurie there is still hope. I am not inferring there isn't any, but if and this is a big IF we have to decide what our next options are? If they go out of state, then Detective Reilly can't control matters anymore. The FBI will take over. Would it be better to go back to South Carolina or could I talk you into coming back to Indiana with us?"

Harry paused wanting to know her reaction to what he had just suggested and let the possibilities sink in. He sat waiting for her answer, dreading the possibility that the children could be missing for weeks or months but not voicing that.

Laurie turned her head and gazed out the window. It was a bright sunny day. People were moving around enjoying themselves. *We should be taking the children to the beach. But the children weren't here!* Again her body shuddered.

"Laurie talk to me, what you are thinking? Please say something."

Her head swung back to Harry's face. Her eyes were brimming with tears.

"Harry, the children are gone." Laurie said flatly.

Not quite understanding her statement Harry said gently. "Yes Laurie but the police are still hoping to find them."

"But Harry what happens if they don't?"

"Well that is what I want to help you with. Will you go home or will you consider coming to Indiana with Todd and I?" Harry's voice was full of dread for her decision should it be South Carolina. "You know Laurie there is still hope as it hasn't been 48 hours yet. They are still in Florida, we have to deal with the 'what if' though? What if they don't recover them right away? We can't stay here indefinitely. We have to think about going home somewhere. My suggestion to you is come home with us. Todd and I will take care of you. We will keep up the search somehow." Harry paused to let this sink in.

"I don't think you should go back to South Carolina alone. The memories of the children will be too difficult to bear unless you have good friends and relatives for support? We really haven't discussed in detail your life in South Carolina and what it was like."

Laurie was still gazing at him intently not saying anything.

Harry was anxiously awaiting her decision. Why couldn't he have waited till there was no hope before broaching this subject? Then he knew the answer. Because she would be in no condition to be rational if he had waited. So he pushed on.

"Laurie, we have to think about this just in case. I want the children found as much as you do. But that might not happen so please think about what I am saying, okay?" Harry said gently.

"Yes Harry." But nothing more was forthcoming. She had gone back to sipping her juice and gazing out the window.

He doubted anything was registering in her mind. He didn't press her further. He was sorry now he had brought up the subject.

He rose to his feet and started pacing back and forth. He wanted to call Mike or Gus and yell at them for botching the surveillance. He just wanted to yell at someone in frustration. But there was no point and it probably would affect Laurie more. He finally dropped into a chair, his pacing ended.

Todd casually sauntered into the room. "Dad did you notice there is quite a bit of activity at the police station? They are jumping into the cars and speeding off."

Harry whipped around and glanced out the window hearing the sirens wailing as the cars were taking off, spinning their wheels in haste. Wouldn't it be great if it had something to do with the children? Then reality set in and his shoulders slumped a bit. Not likely. Dennis wouldn't come back here surely?

"Yes Todd, there does seem to be something going on. Maybe Reilly will let us in on it, when he calls next." He didn't add 'if he calls.'

Todd mumbling went back into Laurie's room his hopes dashed too. "Yes maybe he will." At that moment the phone rang. The voice indicated that it was Gus. "Mr. Cochrane, I just wanted to let you know, we had another sighting not too far from here. Mike and the others are going out to check it out. There was no stopping Mike. He wants this Dennis fellow real bad. So I will keep you posted as the information comes in. I can't believe they came back here?" Gus' voice was laced with wonderment.

"Well let's hope he did regardless of his reasoning." Harry's voice raised in excitement. There was no keeping this from Laurie. She was watching him too closely. This was the first sign of interest since yesterday's disappointment.

"Harry, tell me what's going on? Have they found the children? Tell me, please?" Laurie demanded her face was animated at last.

"No, they haven't found them but the latest sighting is close by in this area. Mike is out looking for Dennis. He wants him real bad Gus says." His voice was hope rejuvenated. Todd heard and leaped through the door. "Dad have they got them?"

"Not quite but soon according to Gus. They are back in the area. Mike seems to think he can find him but we will just have to wait and see." Harry sat down and squeezed Laurie's hands. "If anyone can find them it will be Mike. He is one determined guy. He is taking this very personally according to Gus."

"Harry, I don't want to hope again and then be shattered."

"I know honey but we have to put our faith in Mike, we have no other option."

"Yeah Laurie, Mike is super. If anyone can do it he will." Todd said with some hero worship in his voice. He wished he could join hands with Laurie and his dad. He wanted that connection too. He stood waiting but neither adult noticed his longing look.

The phone rang and broke the moment. Harry and Todd both dived for the phone. Harry whipped the receiver up so fast it flipped the base around.

"Yes Cochrane here." He yelled.

"Harry, we have the children. I'm bringing them back to the station. Meet us there. I want a doctor to check them over."

"Mike, thank you. How are they?"

"They seem to be okay considering the ordeal they have been through. Jason is real plucky like you said. Bethany's crying a lot but otherwise okay. Oh, I better mention, we also have Dennis too. He gave himself up, but there is no sign of his lady friend."

"Harry, I am telling you this because I want you to have Laurie in the interrogation room, where we first met without seeing Dennis yet. So go now before we get there. Tell her we want her there to greet the kids."

"Okay Mike, we will go over there now."

Harry whipped around as he replaced the receiver without looking.

"Laurie, Mike has the children. They are okay."

Jubilation was evident in his voice.

Laurie leaped from the chair into Harry's arms. He hugged her close. Todd said. "Dad that's great." Standing close, Harry hauled him into his embrace too so Todd was able to hug Laurie as well. They were three very happy individuals. Laurie was crying tears of joy this time. Harry stepped back sharing his wide grin. "We have to go over to the police station right away. Mike wants you there to greet the children when they arrive. He is arranging for a doctor to check them over. Come on my love, dry your eyes and let's go." His grin growing wider with each moment. Today the waiting was over. They had won.

Laurie was wiping her eyes and half laughing in response to his wide grin and Todd's yelp of hurray resounded loudly.

She flew into her room to grab her purse then wiped a cloth over her face. Taking the time to comb her hair and put some lipstick on so the children wouldn't be frightened at her distraught appearance, at the moment of their reunion.

Harry was by the door yelling in a laughing voice. "Laurie, come on you look beautiful." She covered the floor as though she had wings on her feet. He grabbed her and hugged her again and kissed her in his exuberance and whisked her out the door.

Todd had already pressed the down button for the elevator. The elevator pinged as they appeared.

Leaping inside in his excitement, Todd pushed the button engaging the elevator to descend to the main floor. Laurie and Harry had to jump quickly inside.

When they reached the lobby they nearly ran over a little lady standing waiting for the elevator in their haste. Apologies given hastily they headed for the entrance. Much happier than the trio that had entered these same doors, after this morning's disappointing trip to the police station.

The reporters took in their hastened steps. "Is there any news on the children? We heard sirens. Have they found them?" Harry pushed Laurie passed. "Yes"

But they didn't let the reporters detain them. The reporters leaped after them.

Ignoring the reporters. Gus was waiting for them near the main entrance. Barely greeting them, Gus rushed them inside and down the corridor to the interrogation room, Mike had indicated. "Hi Mrs. McKnight, good news at last!" He signalled them inside with his arm. "Mike wants you in here."

"Yes Gus, more than good news. We can't wait to see them." Harry replied. Laurie was still too overwhelmed and just smiled happily. They filed into the room. Laurie and Todd sat down but Harry remained near the door talking to Gus.

"Do you have any idea how long they will be?"

"They should be here in five or ten minutes no longer."

Harry enquired. "Do you know any of the details yet?"

"I am going to leave that to Mike to fill you in. He will want to tell you himself. It was really Mike that located them and he is pleased as punch. You do realize that Mike was taking this personally. He is that kind of guy. He hated having to sit around playing the waiting game these past two days."

"Yes so I surmised that from your phone call." The door opened and all eyes leaped towards it.

"Mommy! Mommy!" Bethany dashed towards her mother. Laurie swept her up into her arms hugging and kissing her. "My baby."

Jason stood in the doorway watching Bethany greeting her mother with Mike framed behind him. Jason's eyes swept to Harry. He walked quickly towards him. "Thank you for being there for my mom. Mike told me how you looked after her." He sounded so grown up. Harry just reached out and hugged him. "You're welcome Jason." Then Harry released him so he could greet his mother. Laurie was watching the byplay between Harry and Jason with devouring eyes. Her boy had grown up. Gone was her little boy.

"Hi Mom." Then his manner collapsed. He threw his arms around her and Bethany. The three were linked together in a tight embrace. Jason recovered first and spied Todd. "Hi." He released himself from his mother arms, straightening his posture to the matured boy that had first entered the room. Todd looped his arm over Jason's shoulder. "Hi Jason." His face showing his gratefulness that they were back.

Harry was shaking Mike's hand. "Thanks Mike. We are grateful for your continuous efforts of the last two days never wavering in your belief that this had to end this way."

"You don't know how pleased I was to see both of them safe and sound in that car. Dennis was bringing them back. The doctor should be here shortly to look them over. I have to go speak to Dennis to get his explanation. I just wanted to make the reunion happen immediately." Mike started backing away from the touching scene. "Thanks again." Harry shook his hand again, wanting to ask Mike about Dennis but he didn't want to cloud Laurie's reunion. The explanations would come later no doubt.

She was still hugging Bethany listening to Jason talking to Todd.

"I raised so many ruckuses every time they removed the gag and ropes I was tied with, till Dennis figured he had better bring us back."

"Way to go. I told dad and your mom, you would do that." Todd gave Jason a high five. He grinned proudly.

"Yes Jason you did splendidly." Gratitude was evident in Laurie's voice.

Harry walked over and placed his hand on Jason's shoulder. "You did a good job obviously, because he brought you both back to us." Jason grinned up at Harry.

"Yeah, Selma the lady that was with Dennis hated my behaviour so much she walked out on him this morning. It happened at a rest stop in a town near Gainesville, after arguing most of the way from Tallahassee. Between my behaviour and the police surveillance mentioned on TV, Selma wanted no part of the scheme anymore. She claimed the police where following us everywhere and they would never get away."

"Do you know why they abducted you?" Harry enquired.

"Selma said something about wanting kids. Bethany was okay, Selma liked her but I was not the type of kid she could handle. She made it plain to Dennis, I was unmanageable."

"Did they just want you for their children you mean? Was that their intention?" Amazed curiosity expressed in Harry's voice.

"Yes, Dennis said they had tried for ten years but had no success and they both really wanted kids. That was what they were fighting about. Selma made it clear; we were not her perception of ideal children for their family. Once she abandoned us, Dennis said he was bringing us back to our mother." Jason looked at Laurie with a devilish grin.

"Jason, I am so proud of you for making their lives miserable. You know that is the first time I have been glad you were obnoxiously troublesome." Laurie said fervently. His smile broaden, slightly pleased with himself.

Gus looked on with pleasure at the family scene unfolding before him, liking this impressive boy. They were interrupted with a knock on the door. Gus opened the door, the doctor had arrived.

It was the same doctor that attended Laurie in the hotel room. "Thank you for coming Dr. Johnson." Harry automatically said without comment of the same doctor's amazing appearance here.

The doctor smiled at Laurie. "I see you are a whole lot better now you have your children back. The police have told you I am here to examine the children, I hope?"

"Yes start with Jason. Bethany isn't ready to let go of me yet." Laurie's voice was quite strong now.

Jason stepped boldly up to the doctor. After what he had been through in the past thirty hours he had a right to act that way.

"Well son how are you feeling? Did they harm you in anyway?" Doctor Johnson was observing the boy waiting for a response.

"They treated us pretty good except when they tied me up and gagged me because I was trying to attract the attention of other cars. They fed us okay but I just kept being uncooperative till Selma didn't want me. That's why Dennis returned us." He ended proudly. He picked up Jason's wrist and noticed the burn marks but suspected rather than being too tight, that it would be because Jason had tried to remove them.

Lifting Jason's top the doctor used a stethoscope on his chest front and back. Next he felt his head and ran his hands over Jason's body lightly feeling for bruises while observing him for any reaction to his touch. He predicted Jason's obnoxious ways had indeed saved them.

"Congratulations for being such a grown up boy and protecting your sister in the only way you knew how." He shook Jason's hand.

Then he walked over to Bethany. She cowered against her mother.

"It's all right I won't hurt you. You can stay right on your mommy's knee." Laurie eased her top up so the doctor could check her back and front.

"Jason, were you ever separated from Bethany?" Dr. Johnson inquired.

"No."

"What about at night?"

"No, we slept together. Bethany wouldn't leave me. She just screamed if they tried to separate us."

"That's a good little lady. I think you are fine too." Completing his gentle examination of Bethany as best he could what with her clinging to her mother so tightly.

"Well Mrs. McKnight, you have both your children back and you are very lucky." The doctor's voice trailing off; leaving unsaid the fact that hundreds of missing children who were less fortunate. "Do you think you will need anything?"

"No not now doctor. Not now that I have my children back." She said emphatically.

"I thought so." He replied with a chuckle. "I had better get back to the office. I have patients waiting." Dr Johnson glanced back at the people gathered there. This family was back together in more ways than one if the look in both Harry and Todd's eyes meant what he felt it did. He smiled, leaving amongst their thankful goodbyes.

Gus said. "I'll go talk to Mike." He closed the door behind him.

"Jason, are you sure you are all right?"

"Yes Mom. Dennis didn't hurt us. In fact he was nicer to us than he had been in South Carolina. Even though I had to be tied up and made to stay on the floor. He kept apologizing while he tied the ropes, making sure they weren't too tight."

"I am so glad. I had visions of him mistreating you both. I am never going to let you out of my sight again. I'm sorry I brought Dennis into your lives." Jason went over to his mother and patted her arm.

"It's okay mom, we won't be separated again I'll see to it." Jason was back to his man of the house manner that his father entrusted him with.

Harry wanted to hug him and say that won't be necessary because his intent was to look after them all. But of course that was out of the question right now. Laurie was not ready to think about commitment or anybody else except her children.

CHAPTER FOURTEEN

Mike walked in. "Well how is everyone now?" He glanced around. He had a satisfied look on his face. A situation that had almost gone bad, reversed to a happy ending after all.

"Mommy that is the nice man that saved us." Bethany whispered pointing. "He took us away from the bad man."

Laurie hugged her tightly again. "I know darling. Thank you, Mike. I will never be able to repay you for bringing the children back to me."

Mike waved his hand as if it was just all part of his planned day's work. "I was only too glad to be involved in the end, picking up these two brave children to return them to you." Mike ruffled Jason's hair. "Here is the true hero in all this."

Jason smiled proudly.

Harry wanted to ask a few questions but he was letting Mike have his moment of seeing the family happily reunited. Harry wanted to go down the hall and grab Dennis and pelt him hard, for what he had put Laurie through. It was going to be a long time before she trusted another man in a relationship. He had to face the inevitable, as much as he wanted Laurie that wasn't the way it was going to be. Deep down the unhappy thought was creeping in. Their time together was diminishing. Harry felt sad about that.

Mike looked at Laurie. "I have to ask you if you are going to press charges against Dennis. Things have changed as far as the law is concerned since Dennis voluntarily brought the children back unharmed.

His statement is that he only borrowed them temporarily having every intention in returning them. He said he just wanted to show them to his wife, but certainly had no plans in keeping them long term."

"From experience this man had every intention of keeping the children but fortunately things changed because of Jason's obnoxious behaviour souring their supposed happy family to be." He paused to let that sink in for Laurie.

"As a detective of twelve years, in my opinion he broke an unforgivable law when he kidnapped the children. His intent was definitely there. I firmly believe this was preplanned by him and his wife, before you ever left South Carolina." Again Mike paused giving her time to absorb this information. "Have you any opinion on the subject?"

Laurie was staring at him trying to concentrate on all he was saying. She had naturally presumed that Dennis would be charged, not that the decision was up to her. She had mixed feelings. She hated Dennis for what he had put them through but was forgiving at the same time, because he had brought them back unharmed. The guilt was there for her too. She had put her children in harm's way, with a man she didn't know that well. So it was partly her fault? Could she persecute Dennis when she had more or less handed her children into his hands willingly. Laurie sat there looking intently at Mike.

"What are you thinking Mrs McKnight?" Mike asked kindly, knowing full well the trauma this woman had been through.

Laurie started to say. "I was. . ." She stopped cleared her throat. "I was guilty too, for placing my children willingly in his hands when I didn't really know Dennis that well."

"I had a feeling that was what you were thinking and it is a valid point, but you also have to take into consideration, that he had planned this prior to the trip and that makes it a premeditated crime. Using his charm to woo you into trusting him the way he did that was premeditated too. Think Mrs. McKnight, he was married, yet he deliberately was seeing you while posing as an unattached man."

"Yes that is my fault for being so trusting." Laurie stated lamely.

"I am going to leave you now. I want you to rethink what you are saying. We are going to book him on a stolen vehicle charge for the present. I need to keep him awhile longer before charging him with the children's crime but I would really like you to press charges against him for attempted kidnapping. I would like him to pay for what he put you and the children through. Will you do that? Will you really think it out? That is all I am asking of you. Being grateful for having the children back must not cloud your thinking. You should be still angry at Dennis." *I am.* He was seething inside at Dennis still.

"Okay I will think about it. Can we leave now?"

"Yes, I must request you stay in town for awhile longer until this is resolved." Mike looked at Harry meaningfully. Harry knew Mike was hoping he could influence Laurie into charging Dennis. If only Mike knew that she didn't know Harry that well either. He had skimmed over their relationship at introduction. What influence would he have now that Laurie wasn't dependent on him anymore?

She had a determined look. She had her children back grasping each by the hand, a statement she wasn't letting anyone have them again. She was anxious to leave the police station now, to squirrel them away in her safe protection.

Harry held out his hand to Mike and thanked him profusely for all his efforts. Mike studied him having the impression that he was devoted to Laurie but that Harry didn't think she shared the same feelings. Regardless he quietly said, "Convince Laurie, I want this guy off the streets. He shouldn't get off so lightly. This could have ended so differently if he had harmed the children or abandon them somewhere or even just disappeared with them."

Laurie had gone out of the door with the children with Todd following. Harry replied. "I really want him put away too. I just don't know if I can convince her." Harry finished sadly.

"Try, just try." Mike voice was resolute.

Harry nodded. Mike was left standing there staring after them. There was something about their link that didn't ring true, but he couldn't quite put his finger on it. He was usually good at sizing up situations but not these two.

He wanted Dennis booked and convicted but he could see Laurie was taking on the guilt herself. He fully intended charging Dennis with attempted kidnapping but Laurie's testimony would be more convincing if the charge came from her now that Dennis' statement was that he had never intended to keep the children. However, it was a fact that he had tied and gagged Jason which was a forceful act to submission. He could be charged. Laurie's valid claim of abduction would impact on the judge more, directing him toward a stiffer sentence.

Outside the police station, the reporters were bombarding them with multi questions. Harry gave them a brief statement 'how relieved they were that the children had been brought back safely' holding their interest while Laurie and the children continued on to the hotel.

. . .

Arriving back at the hotel Laurie used her own key directly to her room for the first time, saying she would see Harry and Todd later. "I need this time alone with Bethany and Jason." Harry said sure and Todd and he went to their respective suite.

Harry's eyes roved constantly to the adjoining door. The door was closed between the two rooms for the first time. He could not bring himself to open the door as he knew Laurie wanted it this way, with her present attitude of hugging her children to her, in a close knit family grouping, they had become since their return.

Harry felt bereaved. Todd and he were excluded as outsiders again. A role he did not want to accept and neither did Todd, by the disappointment and dejection showing on his face.

"Todd, we have to give Laurie time to get over all the emotional shock she has been through for these past two days. It was too much really for anyone to absorb. She will be okay when she accepts the kids are safe, and they will be with her for always now. We need to respect her wishes to be alone with Bethany and Jason. Do you want to go out and get some dinner?"

"No Dad, I want to be with Laurie, Bethany and Jason." Todd said slumping down in dejection.

"I know son so do I. But we can't. Do you want to go swimming or out for a walk? You have been cooped up for quite awhile now." Harry just knew he didn't want to be in that room with the closed adjoining door as a reminder of his hurt. He looked at Todd's stubborn face and continued.

"I know you want to wait here for the others but they might not want to join us." Harry reached for a drink. Should he offer some to the children? He went over to the adjoining door and knocked. Jason opened the door eagerly. "Yes?"

"Would you and Bethany like something to drink? We have lots here."

Jason looked back at his mother hopefully. Laurie must have nodded because he came forward. "Yes please. I am thirsty and probably Bethany is too."

Harry was rooting in the cooler. "Juice or pop?"

"Bethany should have juice." Jason stated all the while he was eyeing the pop.

"Would Bethany like orange or V8?"

"She likes orange juice."

"One orange juice coming up." Harry fetched out a bottle and loosened the lid before he handed it to Jason. "There are clean glasses in your bathroom."

Harry could see Jason was eyeing the pop so he said. "I have some V8 left but your mom will probably prefer that so I am afraid it is pop for you."

Jason said eagerly. "Pop is okay for me. Thank you."

Harry carried the juices while Jason flipped the clip on the pop can. He stopped at the door holding the juice out to Jason for Bethany.

"Come back and get the other juice for your mother." Jason looked at Harry strangely. Why was he being so distant?

"You can come in mom won't mind." Harry reluctantly followed Jason. Laurie and Bethany were sitting at the window. There were chairs but no table. Harry walked over to them holding out the V8 juice to Laurie. He looked beseechingly but Laurie's eyes were still on Bethany, her mumbled thanks leaving it at that.

Jason gave his sister her drink, then ran to the bathroom to get some glasses still clutching his pop tightly. The window sill was wide so Laurie balanced her drink there. Harry wanted this family scene so much but knew he wasn't to be included. He didn't have the right anymore. Laurie was looking very self sufficient now. He gave a quiet. "See you later." Leaving the room abruptly.

Todd was watching TV but he looked at his father hopefully but Harry shook his head, negativity showing on his face.

He glanced at the TV occasional but mostly he sat deep in thought. What would happen now? Would she go home by train or bus? Would she let Todd and he drive them home? Or was this how it was to end? Parting again.

Harry wanted them to be part of their life permanently. He recognized his own hopes, but what were her hopes? Laurie had a lot to think about. He couldn't accept that they could walk away from each other, discounting the past two days, when they had lived a hand in glove closeness.

He just couldn't walk away, not like he did the last time. They had been apart for over a year and in two days she had crept right back into his heart. Never to see them again, that was unthinkable for him and for Todd too. He had been in control for two days. Why was he acting this way? But he knew because to him, this was his lifetime in question. But Laurie's body language wouldn't let him in. He would try anyways; one last grasp at hope.

Harry again approached the adjoining closed door confidently. He knocked gingerly. Inside he recognized, he wanted to pound the door down. Jason again opened the door. "Hi?"

"Jason, Todd and I are going out for dinner. Will you ask your mom if she wishes to join us?" Harry invited warmly but his insides were churning.

"Mom, can we go to dinner with Todd and Harry?"

He heard Laurie making negative sounds. "Mom, please?" Jason begged.

"Okay Harry. Thank you for asking. We will be ready in a minute then we will come in to your room." Laurie's voice was brighter but it seemed to be a forced enthusiasm. Harry knew this wasn't going to be easy but he wasn't about to back off now that she had assented. He needed to see to their nourishment didn't he?

"Mike told me of a good family restaurant fairly close by. Todd and I could do with a walk after being cooped up. Are you game?"

Jason, who was bursting with energy wanted to be with Todd, shook his head yes. The decision was made. Laurie looked at Harry knowing her attitude was hurting him. "Of course I would love that."

He stepped back into his room giving Todd a thumbs up sign and a big grin. Todd shot his arm in the air. "Way to go Dad." Harry felt much better. He just hoped things would improve over dinner.

"Get ready Todd and be sure to wash your face as well as your hands." A typical parent comment. Harry glanced in the mirror running a comb through his wavy hair. Being so thick it never needed a lot of grooming. His face was carrying a rewarding smile. He wanted to give himself a thumbs up sign too but he realized he hadn't won yet. He hoped the reporters were gone. When they exited the hotel, there was one diehard still there ready to thrust a microphone in their faces. Harry disposed of him quickly.

Jason and Todd set the pace with Laurie and Harry walking behind them. Bethany was holding her mother's hand and wasn't letting go of her. Jason was telling Todd about his experiences. Todd curiously asked if he was scared. "No" Jason said then added. "Maybe just a little bit but once I saw my behaviour was bothering Selma, I really poured it on as I had a new purpose. I became really obnoxious instead." Harry and Laurie who had been listening broke out in low laughs then smiles, eyeing each other.

Jason's story continued. "With the realization my mom was left behind, I did not accept Dennis' gruff explanation of just going for a ride and to be quiet."

"That was when the terror set in as we sped away. Would we see our mom ever again? Then I saw Todd but I knew from his expression he didn't understand I was in trouble. Then I knew I had to turn my mind to a way to attract attention, to get over the terror. My behaviour was most upsetting to Selma when she joined us, especially when Dennis had the need to keep me gagged and tied up. Once when I was loose at the rest stop, although Dennis kept a firm hand on me ready to cover my mouth, I yelled 'help' and he whipped me up so fast covering my mouth and saying I was joking."

"This made Selma more nervous than ever. I was no longer scared or accepting the terror of not seeing my mom again, I just concentrated on being bad." Jason giggled in memory. Harry knew that Jason was a well adjusted boy for his age. It would be Bethany that might have nightmares over this misadventure.

Harry was listening intently to Jason's story. How could he convince Laurie to charge Dennis with kidnapping the children? That would be his mission and their relationship issue would have to be relegated to the future.

The restaurant's food was delicious and they all ate heartily. Todd had made himself the good humour man and had them all laughing during the meal. He told of the antics of a camping trip that had gone from bad to worse and became a terrible fiasco. Harry was proud of him for carrying it off so well figuring he was embellishing the story to keep them laughing. Harry was secretly forgiving him for the exaggerated truths, laughter being the best healer of tragedy.

Laurie was looking at Harry in a new light too. *Here was a man who had nothing to gain but had interrupted his holiday to be with her; her pillar of strength for two days. Why had she shut him out when they got back to the hotel? Harry had only been kind and caring to her. It must have been a slap in the face for him?*

Harry caught her staring at him. His face wreathed into a huge smile.

Is she feeling better? Does she want me to stick around or leave? What can she be thinking? She wasn't returning his smile.

Harry decided to bite the bullet. "Laurie, are you thinking what your next step will be, when the police say you can leave?"

"No not yet. I was thinking how nice you and Todd had been to give up your holiday, to stay here with me to be my support team. This sojourn in Fort Lauderdale was no vacation that's for sure. Thank you from the bottom of my heart and thank you Todd." Laurie was looking directly at Todd at the last part of her message of thanks.

Todd acknowledged. "That's all right Laurie. I wouldn't have enjoyed Busch Gardens knowing you were alone waiting for Bethany and Jason. After all I knew Jason was watching out for his sister, and you needed someone too. You did real good Jason." Thumping Jason on the back lightly.

Jason accepted it with an arrogant grin. "I knew I could do it but I just didn't know how long it would take. Thanks for being there for my mom." Looking from Todd to Harry.

They answered simultaneously. "I didn't mind."

Harry continued. "We are glad this ended so soon in a happy way." It went without saying Dennis and Selma could have kept them and disappeared or abandon them somewhere. It was just fortunate they had come out of this unscathed.

Laurie was still studying Harry. *Why does this man care so much about my family? Did the children form a special bond back in Indiana that she had been unaware of? Why is he able to make them respond so willingly to his goodness? Am I too negative a person? Why aren't I happier at the outcome?* She knew she was just holding onto the negativity and her guilt surrounding these two days. Two days of eternity.

"Laurie, are you ready to go?" Harry asked out of politeness. *Maybe she is going into shock the way she was staring off into space.*

"Oh! Yes I am ready." Quickly turning to the children knowing she had been caught absorbed in thought. "Well, you both ate well. You must have been really hungry." No one commented on Laurie's practically untouched plate.

"Yes mommy, I was really hungry. I didn't want the food Dennis gave us." Bethany excitedly added. "Harry is buying us an ice cream cone on the way back to the hotel. The place with lots of flavours and coloured cones, we passed on the way here."

Jason jumped up. "Yeah 47 flavours to choose from and double dip too."

Harry stood aside till all were standing letting them leave while he settled the check. Laurie tried to pay but Harry insisted it was from his inheritance and it was ill gotten gains in explanation trying to jest.

Laurie laughed. "That should be Todd's and your nest egg."

"Why would we need a nest egg when we have each other right Todd?" He was pleased Laurie laughed that was a start. "Yes Dad, anything you say." Todd replied grinning, many ice cream flavours dancing in his head.

The choices of ice cream took a long time deliberating the possibilities of two choices for a double dip but Jason and Todd ended up with three to hurry their decision. Todd's choices were the most colourful or yucky whichever way you looked at it. But Todd assured them the mixture tasted really good.

The trip back to the hotel was done in a much lighter vain. The uptight feeling had disappeared and so had all the reporters. Harry breathed a sigh of relief.

Later when the children were asleep and Todd was watching over them, Harry took Laurie downstairs for a drink. She had given Todd instructions to have them paged if there was a problem by calling the front desk. Harry wasn't ruling out that they might have nightmares although they both seemed in good spirits at dinner and after.

In the lounge bar there was a trio playing with a singer. The melodies were from yester year. Laurie sat down with an easy grace. Her body seemed more relaxed now. This was such a different woman from the face of devastation of yesterday morning, having seen her children whisked away in a racing car. The fearful face screwed up in screams plastered in that rear window, their frantic mother receding as they sped away. It was a lifetime ago. A lifetime, which Laurie would never want repeated.

Harry broke his thoughts to ask her preference in a drink?

"I'll have a Manhattan." She felt she needed something with a kick to it to help rid the last of her pent up feelings. He ordered a Scotch on the rocks although he would have preferred a beer. The drink order out of the way, Harry asked. "Laurie, I want to say how thankful that I was able to be here for you. It is nice being with your family once again. I missed you and the children when you disappeared from Indiana. Todd and I both did."

"My brother asked me to come to South Carolina and I thought I should go because I was at loose ends after my husband died." Laurie talked about their life in South Carolina with her brother omitting Dennis from her conversation.

Harry talked about Indiana, giving her brief glimpses of Todd and his life together updating her to the present.

CHAPTER FIFTEEN

arry felt the subject of Dennis could not be avoided any longer. He was on his second drink. Laurie was still nursing her first.

"Laurie, what are you going to do about Dennis? Mike needs you to charge him, to make the sentence stiff enough to meet the crime. Mike can only hold him on the lesser charge for a short time. Before you say anything, really think about this." Harry waited and then continued.

"I know you feel grateful to him for bringing the children back unharmed. But that does not negate the fact that he preplanned the kidnapping, with the idea that your children became Selma and his children permanently. The scenario could have been much worse if Jason hadn't figured out how to misbehave to aggravate them. What if Jason hadn't done that? Imagine if you hadn't got them back how you would feel." Harry paused taking a sip of his drink.

"You have to think about the immoral issue in this, the children being separated from you against their wishes. Imagine Jason being gagged and tied up. If he hadn't been a strong natured boy, he could have been traumatized by that. His behaviour saved Bethany from being too effected. She could have been frightened for a long time. Nightmares even. Dennis should not be able to get off lightly and you know his story is an outright lie. What if he tries this with other children? How will you feel then?"

Laurie finally responded after Harry's latest remark.

"I never thought of that." She paused taking a sip of her drink thinking about Dennis approaching another innocent victim. Recalling again Jason's screaming face speeding away. She had to put aside her guilt, in putting them in his reach.

"Yes, Dennis should be stopped. Especially from finding another victim. You were right. I was grateful to have my children back unharmed, so I had no intention of pressing charges. I just wanted this nightmare to go away, along with the memory. But now you have made me see things in a different light."

"Can I call Mike and tell him? He is waiting to hear from you."

"Yes Harry, you can call him."

He signalled for the hostess. He asked if it was possible to bring a telephone to the table. The hostess said 'yes, fortunately there is an outlet close by', and departed.

Laurie quickly said. "Harry, I don't want to go back there tonight."

"You don't have to. I am sure tomorrow morning will be soon enough. Mike will take care of everything in the meantime I am sure." Harry looked up as the hostess put a phone on the table, thanking her. Fortunately they had chosen a table a little apart which had been a wise choice for the more privacy needed to make the call. He dialled the well remembered number of the police station asking for Detective Reilly.

"Hello Mike." "Yes the children are fine. They ate a hearty meal and are asleep." "Yes, I know we were lucky. They don't appear to be traumatized by their ordeal but that is due to Jason's strong will."

"No, Laurie still is not completely over the upset. I have her with me now. We are having a drink in the lounge." "Yes she has made a decision. She wants to press charges of kidnapping." "Yes Mike." "We will be there first thing tomorrow morning to see you."

"It is time you went home. You deserve to relax after spending so much time on this case. My thanks again and Laurie's too. Goodnight." Harry set the phone down. "Well it is done. Mike wants you there first thing in the morning."

"Will I have to see Dennis?"

"No, you know him so you don't have to identify him from a lineup."

"That's good I don't think I could face him ever again."

"I'm sorry to say you will have to identify him in court, but it will be some time in the future before it comes to trial. When you go to the trial I promise Todd and I will be there with you."

"Harry you are such a good caring man. I'm sorry I shut you out when we got back to the hotel earlier. I don't know what came over me. You have been so super through this and I treated you so hurtfully. It is unforgivable of me." She finished forlornly.

"Laurie, I understand you were under so much strain, wanting to isolate yourself and the children with the relief of having them back. That is a natural reaction when they were taken away from you in that dreadful manner." Laurie was still looking forlorn.

"Someday this will be all behind you then you will be able to evaluate life differently. This will be relegated to the back of your mind. Eventually time will make the details recede. The only thing I want you to remember out of all this is the bravery of Jason. He is your true hero. Now shall we go back up to the rooms?"

. . .

The trip to the police station went without incident. Their feelings were calmer. The reporters were gone. The tragedy was over, the charges laid against Dennis for his devious purpose of kidnapping Bethany and Jason. The lucky part was that Dennis was decent enough to bring them back and turn himself in, which will no doubt go in his favour.

Mike advised that they stick around until the case came before the judge determining whether Dennis would be remanded into custody without bail. The judge wouldn't expect Laurie to say anything at that time, but the presence of the children and Laurie in court were important. This was a serious offence with such small children involved.

Mike thanked Laurie for following through on her decision. "When this was all over then you should put it behind you forever, and give the children the freedom to grow naturally without fear of these two days overshadowing their lives. You will feel the need to be a protective mother for the first little while, which is the natural inclination after a kidnapping." Mike noted that neither child seemed to be overstressed about their experience which was good. He knew this too would go in

Dennis' favour but regardless he wouldn't get off Scot-free. Hopefully it would be severe enough to deter him from ever trying this again.

Mike was shooing them out. "Now all of you out of here and enjoy Fort Lauderdale the way you should as a perfect vacation place. I will call and leave a message if I need you. Have fun and that is an order from someone who has lived here a long time."

They all headed out the door to the sunshine and freedom. Freedom to enjoy sightseeing without the anxiety of the past few days over-shadowing them. Anyone seeing them walking down the street would think this was a vacationing family not knowing the tragedy they had just dealt with, that had a marring effect on their lives.

The rest of the day was spent carefree at Hollywood Beach and in the discovery of Fort Lauderdale as a whole. When they got back to the hotel, they found out that the manager was arranging a special dinner for them in the restaurant. Harry had finally made Laurie aware of the caring hotel manager, Mr. Jenkins extending the hotel generosity to them. He was joining them at dinner at Laurie's request with his wife. The receding drama was allowing Laurie to want to include them in the celebration. Mr. Jenkins complied wanting them to have a better feeling towards Fort Lauderdale and its people.

The dinner was a huge success and festive. Mr and Mrs Jenkins took over as hosts with great enthusiasm wanting to make Laurie and the children feel really special. Jovially the kids accepted their friendliness. The Jenkins invited them to meet their daughter and son-in-law along with their grandchildren visiting them from Flint, Michigan. It was arranged for them to go there after dinner.

Mr. Jenkins had kept his family posted, as to the drama being played out in his hotel over the past two days. His family had prayed for the children's safe return and expressed their wanting to meet Laurie and the children.

After dinner, they all made the trek to the Jenkins' residence for drinks and cake topped with ice cream. Harry and Laurie knew that the Jenkins were special people, showing them that even bad experiences could eventually have a positive aspect. They would both remember the generosity and kindness of this family. The good feelings had prevailed during the whole evening. Todd was happy to have the companionship of Bethany and Jason once again. It was as though they had never been apart. Even playing with the visiting grandchildren had been fun.

Later when they were going back to the hotel, Harry was happy that Laurie was more comfortable with him too. Her attitude after the children were returned forgotten. He was so thankful Jason and Bethany were showing no ill effects of their ordeal. The time was drawing near for some decision about going home.

Laurie wanted to put it off but her job was waiting for her. She had phoned for an extension of time without success. But the big decision was about Harry and Todd.

Laurie thought maybe she wanted to stay part of their lives. Why had she moved to South Carolina? It was so far away from them. It seemed like a good decision at that time when Jack and Betty had encouraged her to leave Indiana. The weather was warmer and it would be a place to start anew at her brother's enticement after losing her husband.

Her job wasn't inspiring but did pay the bills. Their house was not as cute as the place in Indiana but was clean and liveable. The children had found some new friends there. She wondered if her experience with Dennis would cloud going back to South Carolina having met him there.

Harry was right, she would have to re-evaluate her life, making sure she could give the children the assurance of a stable lifestyle. *Where would she go otherwise? Back to Indiana and her memories there? Should she move to somewhere else entirely?* All her life Laurie had moved because her parents were always looking for greener pastures which they never found. Was she going the same route?

Harry knew Laurie was deep in thought about her situation. He was wishing she would consult with him. He wanted to know the way her thoughts were heading in her decision, but essentially not wanting to hear it might be goodbye again.

Harry having important commitments, meant his presence was required in a week's time in the office. *Could he relocate to South Carolina? He didn't want to lose Laurie and the children again.*

The last time, he and Todd had been so lonely, after they disappeared out of their lives. He had formed a new relationship with Denise but he knew it hadn't been a lasting one, particularly now since meeting Laurie again. She was very different, causing him to feel, he was whole around her. To be part of a family again would be perfect. Todd wanted that too. He had come alive in the company of Bethany and Jason. Harry also caught Todd looking at Laurie with longing looks when she was touching them. His son wanted to be mothered again, his own mother leaving him too soon.

Harry wasn't looking forward to having to deal with Todd if this petered out at Laurie's insistence. The doubts kept invading his mind.

She had never shown an interest in him as a man, just a companion to share her troubles, but that was no longer good enough. He was a man with feelings, couldn't she recognize that he wanted her in his life. The love he wanted to give Laurie was in his heart, waiting to be shared with her.

She was staring at Harry as the elevator rose to their floor. It was as though she was memorizing his face. *Did she really not know him? Know, that he only wanted to love her?* Harry wondered.

"Laurie, are you going out tomorrow anywhere or do you want to plan a day sightseeing or go to the beach?" Harry asked breaking the silence between them that had lasted too long.

"Harry, I think I should have a day alone to think. Would you mind taking the children for the day? I trust you with them, you have shown me that. I have decided to talk to Mike about my situation. He is a man who has a reassurance about him. There are some legal things I have to consult him about and I think he is the person to help me."

"All right, I will not push you for details and yes I would love to take the children for an outing tomorrow." Harry felt bleak inside but his voice was jovial, not wanting her to know his true feelings at the sadness. Her concerns might include him.

Todd and Harry entered their room with trepidation. Todd had picked up Harry's vibes of foreboding. Would they never see Laurie, Bethany and Jason anymore? The father and son were watching TV both afraid to express their fears out loud. Both were to have a restless night's sleep.

Laurie showed evidence of her sleepless night when they met

together for breakfast in the downstairs dining room. The waitress
knew them now, greeting them and serving them with a personal
touch. Harry was glad the children were not picking up on the under-
current between Laurie and he.

After breakfast, she went up to the room with the children getting
them ready for their day's outing with Todd and Harry. Opening the
adjoining door she kissed them goodbye and told them to be good, then
she proceeded to the door. He watched her walk to the elevator. He
now knew from her body language that he would be part of the topic
with Mike. Why didn't he speak up? It was because of her experience
with Dennis that he hesitated.

Harry took the kids to the underwater marina where the fish were
plentiful and the dangerous species were confined. They were exclaiming at the squid with his many tentacles waving around. Another
aquarium held dolphins that leaped and caroused with such antics
the children were laughing in delight.

Harry took them to Checker's for hamburgers enjoying their banter
during the meal. It was decided, the afternoon would be spent at the
hotel pool teaching Jason and Bethany how to swim. Their mother
wasn't a lover of deep water so swimming was seldom an opportunity
Jason said. Harry felt sure he could change that, if they stayed together.

Why did he want this woman in his life when he knew she was shying
away from him? Was her attitude only because of her ill-fated relationship to Dennis? Could she be planning with Mike for her trip home? Was
this goodbye again? But I just know I want to be with her. "No! I will
have it out with her when she gets back." Harry muttered to himself.

The pool was big and the children were frolicking about. Harry
was watching Bethany while Todd who was an excellent swimmer
was teaching Jason. Todd really loved the water having spent a lot of
time in the lake at home.

Jason being very determined soon caught on. He was quite buoyant
and flexible so he was a natural swimmer and his efforts showed it.
Bethany was a little braver now. She was dipping her face in the water
holding her nose. After a few times a smile appeared and she wasn't
treating it as a death sentence which was her first reaction to Harry's
suggestion. Todd now had Jason swimming laps with him. Jason was

getting stronger each lap. Todd was pacing him slowly wanting him to get practice and not feel it was a race.

Todd was easily bonding with both children again. Jason partnered Todd in all he did, and Bethany followed Todd around like he was her big brother. What could he do to make this up to Todd when they were gone? Harry knew he was the problem with Laurie not Todd. He just had to have it out with her for himself as well.

He called a halt to the water sports because the sun was too intense. He ushered them out into the shade. Jason was asking Todd to teach him diving next. He figured he had the swimming mastered. He was anxious to learn everything and figured Todd was just the person to teach him.

They sat around discussing Disney World as Laurie had taken them there last year. A shadow was coming into view of Harry's left eye. He turned and there was Laurie walking towards them. She had on a bathing suit the colour of coral. She walked with an easy pace swinging her hips ever so slightly. He studied her smiling face but Harry could see it wasn't quite reaching her eyes. Later probably, when the children weren't around, he knew the axe would fall he felt that underlying feeling, their future relationship was in jeopardy.

"Mom I can swim." Jason was jumping up and down in excitement. "Do you want to see me?"

"Mommy, I can put my face under water." said Bethany not to be out done by her brother.

"Of course I want to see you both." The children headed for the pool. Harry stayed seated giving Laurie the space he knew she wanted. She got in the pool with Bethany watching her dip her face a few times, praising her when she did. Jason and Todd were swimming laps again. Laurie was pleased at their progress under Todd and Harry's tutelage. She knew she lacked in giving her children water skills because of her own phobia.

"Mom, come and swim with us?" Jason yelled.

"It's okay I will stay here with Bethany."

Harry wanted to get in the water, to help her learn to swim. He wanted her to love the water the way he and Todd did. It was obvious that Bethany and Jason were enjoying themselves. It would be a shame for them to go home, to never fully develop their water skills. Jason was a natural water person. Soon he would be as proficient as Todd given the opportunity.

But that decision was Laurie's. She was helping Bethany to float and keeping an eye on the swimmers. She was waist deep and with the swaying of the water looked like a beguiling mermaid. Harry wanted her more than ever.

He finally called a halt suggesting they were getting too much sun. Laurie sent him an appreciative smile then helped Bethany out. The boys quickly obeyed splashing their way up the steps. Jason showed his reluctance on his face only.

After Todd and Harry were dressed they headed out to see some more of Fort Lauderdale. Harry was giving Laurie her time with the children. When they were away from the hotel, Todd asked. "Dad, why didn't we bring Jason and Bethany?"

"Because Laurie needs time alone with them."

"Are we leaving soon?"

"I really don't know. Perhaps Laurie will tell me her plans tonight when we get back." Harry was chiding himself for not telling Laurie how he felt about her. Also not telling her how much Todd and he needed her and the children to integrate in their life, as a family.

"Dad, I get the feeling that Laurie is going to disappear again like last time. Granted last time we hardly knew them but this time after these past few days I feel we have known them forever. Do you feel that way?"

"Yes Todd I do. I want to keep them in our lives too, but we have to face the fact that they live in South Carolina and we live in Indiana. Two days driving time apart. We are established in Indiana. Laurie is looking for a comfort zone which being near her brother and sister-in-law gives her. So how do we resolve that? I am open to any suggestions."

Todd looked at his father. Here was a man who spent his time doing for others and never seemed to ask for much for himself. Todd knew he had tried female companionship at home without success. The feelings and behaviour with Laurie was evident, he loved this lady. Why didn't he tell her? Todd thought his father was very nice looking, clean cut kind of guy. He and Harry were closer since Jason and Bethany came into their lives.

"Dad, I want Laurie, Jason and Bethany to be a family with us."

"Todd, the choice isn't ours to make. Laurie has to want the same thing. I want to be a family too. Heck, I would even relocate if she just would say yes. The situation with Dennis didn't help matters. Laurie has really clammed up since the children have returned."

"I noticed that too. Why don't you tell Laurie how we feel?" Todd asked sadly.

"I intend to when we get back. However Todd, we have to be prepared to leave here without them. I have been delaying telling you this. Laurie's visit to Mike may be for him to help her return home. I am just guessing but I fervently hope I am wrong." They had been driving around aimlessly not really taking in the sights. At least they had each other, Harry was thankful for that.

He pulled Todd into a one arm hug letting him know his feelings of love for him. He was a grown boy now. Even so Todd was thankful for the closeness even though it lasted only for a moment. They were stopped at Lauderdale-by-the-Sea Beach. There were numerous high school and college students throwing Frisbees. They strolled onto the jetty, bordering the beach making it private with the water a little choppy slurping at the pylons. But neither was really interested in the fact that the water wasn't exactly a swimmers beach but rather a surfer's delight. They finally gave up the pretence of sightseeing after an hour, driving back to the hotel.

Mr. Jenkins waylaid them with a message. "This was given to me by Mrs. McKnight for you. I promised her I would see you received it as soon as you came in. She came to say goodbye, and thank me for the stay." The hotel manager still wondered about the relationship between these two families. He felt there was another story here. Harry bravely hid the hurt.

He thanked him and headed for the elevator. Knowing maybe Laurie's escape was coming didn't stop the hurt however. He waited till they got to their room before opening the message. The emptiness hit him like a blast. The silent adjoining room. Laurie had disappeared out of their lives for a second time. Was there any point going after them?

The note was brief.

CHAPTER SIXTEEN

*H*arry and Todd

Thank you for being there for me when I needed your support. Mike has arranged to get me home. Sorry we left so suddenly.

The experience the last few days has taken quite a toll on me. I wanted to go home quickly, to gain some normalcy for myself and the children.

Thanks again.

Laurie

Harry wanted to cry. He didn't say anything just handed the letter to Todd. His throat had closed. Walking to the window he stood looking out. A plane was in full view in the bright sky. *Was she on it?* The scene at the pool with Laurie standing in the water and the children frolicking around her invaded Harry's memory, their last real memory together. This woman had crept into his heart and was still camped there.

Todd drew his attention because he was crying openly. Todd who was so grown up for a boy of eleven but still young enough to cry. Harry turned and took him into his arms letting him cry it out sharing his sorrow. Father and son were devastated. Such an anticlimax to such intense drama of the last few days making it seem like forever. Now their sudden loss of the family they both had come to love. They stood like that for awhile till Todd pulled back. "Dad I didn't even get to say goodbye to Jason and Bethany." His voice so full of hurt.

"I know but Laurie is having a hard time too right now, and we have to be understanding. After all we have only known them for such a short time. But each time has been so dramatic that it feels like a lifetime. I'm sorry I didn't get to tell Laurie how we felt about them. I certainly intended to before she left but a relationship is probably the last thing she would consider right now."

Todd wiped his eyes and sniffed that touched Harry so much. The answer was to leave here quickly.

"Where do you want to go Tampa or home?"

"Home, Dad. I never want to see Florida again." A normal response to his deep hurt, Harry knew. It was going to take longer this time for them both to get over the pain. The best way was to go home speedily, to resume their own life they had left behind.

"Todd if we leave right now we could maybe get a flight out of Orlando. But I do think I should call in on Mike first and say goodbye. After we check out of here, we will go to the police station in the hopes that he is there."

"Okay, I would like to say goodbye too. Mike was an all right guy." Todd tried to put some enthusiasm in his voice. The boy was trying to mask his hurt.

Suitcases packed and the room glanced over one last time, both remembering the drama that had been played out in these two rooms in the past 56 hours and he couldn't believe they were parting alone.

They checked out and said their goodbyes to Mr. Jenkins. Thanking him for his many kindnesses. The two voyagers leaving the hotel for the last time.

Mr. Jenkins had been touched by the two families and the plight which ended happily with the recovery of the children. He believed they were disappointed in Mrs. McKnight's decision to leave without seeing them.

When Harry and Todd arrived at the police station, Mike was available and he came to his office at once. Shutting the door, he looked closely at the two sitting there, a definite sign of defeat in both of them. "Well it is all over. Dennis was arraigned before the judge and bail was set." Mike didn't enlarge on pushing forward of the court appearance to facilitate Laurie's escape. "What are you two guys going to do now? Are you going to Tampa where you originally intended?"

"No, Todd and I are heading home. We have had enough excitement so we are anxious to get home and pick up our lives again."

"I am sorry to hear that, you would have enjoyed Busch Gardens. Todd, you were great throughout this and if I had a son I would want him to be just like you. I am glad I met you and your father."

"Thanks Mike. I am glad I was of some help with the investigation. Most police officers would have said I was too young to have any reliable input."

"Not at all, your input was a great help for sure. I am just glad it had a happy conclusion to a drama that could have been a tragedy. Harry, thanks for helping with Mrs. McKnight. It made my work a lot easier not having to deal too closely with the grieving mother during the kidnapping, letting me get on with the police work. It was a story that ended well except for you two I feel. Mrs. McKnight explained your relationship which I had thought was odd from the beginning. Even though you were strangers, you had a special ingredient in both of you that most couples never attain in a lifetime. I feel that you are the ones who came out scathed. I did try talking her out of leaving the way she did."

Harry shifted uncomfortably in his chair. Quickly standing up he held out his hand not wanting to express his disappointment in Laurie's decision and make Mike feel bad for helping her escape. "Todd and I had better be hitting the road if we want to make Orlando. We will return the car and get a flight home. Thank you Mike, for the recovery of Jason and Bethany that is the happiness in this."

Mike shook his hand firmly and walked them to their car. He saluted them as they drove away. Another case closed but not forgotten, he doubted he would see them at the trial.

Todd and Harry left Fort Lauderdale for highway 528 to reach Orlando and home.

. . .

Orlando airport signs were appearing. "Todd, I really think we should go to Busch Gardens as we may never get to Florida again." Todd's first reaction was no way but in the end he was inclined to agree.

"All right Dad, we can stop there tomorrow or maybe go for dinner there now and hit the rides tonight." Todd was vaguely showing interest now.

"After the evening at Busch Gardens, we can head for the Gulf Coast and a motel there. Perhaps have an early morning swim then Tampa Airport and home. How does that sound?" Harry said getting into the spirit of things, returning to Todd's and his natural existence together.

"That way, we will have swam in the water off both coasts. That will be neat to tell my friends." Todd exclaimed.

"While we are in the area maybe we should take in a ball game. Who's your favourite team Todd?"

"Detroit and Toronto Blue Jays wouldn't it be neat if they were playing each other." Todd was getting excited.

"We will look into that when we get there." They had to pick up their lives. Now that Laurie and the children were gone, their own lives were on the line. How they handled this now, was a way to handle their future.

The atmosphere in the car did a complete turnabout and they continued with some expectation that they thought they had lost.

When they reached Disney World they both realized how much had happened in their lives since being there. The Disney World scene, seemed like an irrelevant period in time now. The memories of Fort Lauderdale and the drama played there overshadowing them for a moment. But the expectations ahead soon prevailed.

The rides were all they needed to get the exhilaration going. Enjoying Busch Gardens so much they didn't have time to attend a baseball game. The evening flew by and they headed for St. Petersburg and their motel on the coast.

They found a motel on the water and wandered the beach in the moonlight, skipping stones on the water and walking in the surf with their bare feet. Todd noticed that the reason the sand sounded crunchy under their feet, there were millions of little shells mixed in the sand. The day had ended in an upbeat note after all.

The next day they arranged a flight home. After their early morning swim, they were ready now to face the trip to Indiana.

· · ·

Todd and Harry settled back into their routine now they were back in Radford Falls. Todd had settled in faster than Harry. Having his friends to bike race and trail blaze with after the day's school curriculum. The odd time Harry would catch him looking off into space. Harry was sure his thoughts were with Jason, Bethany and Laurie.

Marvin, Harry's partner and friend was worried about him. Since Florida he had lost some degree of interest in the business. He worked harder and longer but he had lost some of the spark that gave him the edge in his profession. He was doing more assignments travelling out of town, as though variation was desirable.

Marvin had tried to invite him out on a double date, providing a date for him now that he wasn't seeing Denise anymore. After two dates that fell through, Marvin invited him to barbeques but Harry seemed to talk to the guys only not the single ladies.

Louise and he were ready to throw in the towel. A few social functions were not going to change whatever happened to Harry in Florida. He was very evasive about his time spent there, other than Disney World and visiting the Grandparents. Marvin was positive they had done more than that. Todd had mentioned Fort Lauderdale but had clammed up at a look from Harry.

Harry and Todd were doing two day hiking trips. Todd was getting quite proficient at it. Harry did hone up on some of his skills during these trips. But he just went along mainly to provide a new interest for Todd.

Denise kept calling. She invited him to a couple of dinners she hosted. Harry went to the first one but refused the second one. When he had gone the first time, he found he was only going through the motions. He realized as the evening progressed, he no longer felt comfortable with her-in-crowd.

He only sat amongst Denise's friends wishing Laurie was there with him. His thoughts were bombarded with her. She had disappeared as though those three days had never been. Todd kept looking for a message from Jason but none arrived. He would have written but he didn't know where they were in South Carolina. Harry tried to phone but Laurie must have an unlisted number.

The evening had finally ended. He thanked Denise and apologized when she teased him about his being so reserved now.

End of the Denise chapter in his life.

. . .

Harry buried himself in his work bringing it home evenings. The only break was the occasional three day outings with Todd now that summer was here. Todd spent a lot of time with his friend Bobby at his cottage on the lake not too far from town. Bobby's parents were happy to have Todd there to keep their son company. But that made things lonelier for Harry. Occasionally they invited Harry to join them. Todd was happy to be included in a family atmosphere with his friend and his parents. The heartbreak over the missing family was receding for Todd.

Harry's out of town work increased now that Todd was away so much. His designs were diverse. He had developed a new style that he was promoting. His evenings at home were listening to music while working or else out with the guys now and then. Never seeming to want or need female companionship. Sarah popped into his mind occasionally and more often Laurie, but he quickly relegated that back into memory.

The summer passed and the winter came and Todd and he settled into a simple routine. When Harry wasn't away travelling they were out snowboarding. Once Spring arrived it developed into wilderness camping again.

One day they were asked to take part in a survival wilderness camping trip in South Dakota with some of the members of the local wilderness group. Harry feeling guilty about all of his out of town work encouraged Todd to go with them.

The trip was planned for the end of June which arrived quickly. Todd was doing well in school. His final exams were only one subject, Science. All the others he had aced, so he would be out early this year.

The Wilderness Adventurers set out on the following Saturday, with great expectations. There were eight going from their wilderness group, some for two weeks some for one. Harry had committed to two weeks. Bobby and his Dad were going for one. Harry had offered to keep Bobby for the second week but Bobby wasn't as keen as Todd for the wilderness activity.

Arriving at camp there was the usual enthusiasm and lots of participants, because the groups were from all over the States. The instructors had devised three courses, regular, hard and the impossible. The last was a tongue in cheek comment meaning only for the hardy and devout wilderness trekkers.

Harry wanted the 'hard course' but Todd wanted 'the impossible.' Later Harry had a discussion with the instructor Jim expressing his concerns. Jim said he had personally spoken with Todd as to his abilities and thought he was capable of doing 'the impossible' course.

Todd may be up to the challenge but Harry didn't think he was, but he was determined not to let Todd down. Bobby and his father were taking the 'hard course' and Harry was wishing he could join them. Todd would not be deterred from his decision even when Bobby wouldn't accompany them.

• • •

In the chain of seven hikers Harry was dead last. Todd was in front with the instructor, with Todd's avid attitude. As the trek progressed Harry thought this was carrying fatherhood a bit too far. He enjoyed the outdoors and the wilderness trips at home but this was rugged country. Then Harry admonished himself and picked up the pace determined to enjoy this adventure. Exhausted he fell into his bedroll that night nursing a few aches and sore feet.

The second day he slipped and fell down a small incline. The rescue entailed encircling his waist with a rope and being dragged up. Todd kept yelling down words of encouragement. The instructor advised that Harry shouldn't be last so he ended up with Todd at the front of the hikers. He was just thankful the only thing he hurt was his dignity, and kept the fright bottled up inside. It was difficult but he managed to keep up. That night bedroll time was earlier for him and his aches were encroached with more pain.

The next day things went better as the area they were in was relevantly easier to transgress, which bolstered Harry's spirit. Todd was in his glory keeping up with the instructor Jim Coles. Jim was amazed at Todd's natural ability taking the rough terrain and the uphill climbs in his stride in the day's progression.

Harry wished Sarah could have known that they had made such a boy as Todd. He was so proud of him. Harry's steps quickened for a few seconds at the thought. However, he was soon back to plodding along hiding his own feelings inside, slipping further back than he should. This course was beyond him at times, he was not in the best of shape, what with spending all his time working. But he was determined not to give in for Todd's sake. The course was geared to end the trek back at the same location as the other courses, so all of them would be together for the last night of the first week.

Just as Harry was getting into his stride the week was over and they met up with Bobby and his father at the base camp. Todd was happy to see his friend and divulged his experiences, which they continued chattering about at the bonfire that night. There were recognition awards. Todd won the Best Achiever's Award of their group. Harry won the Most Persistent Award for his stamina in trying to keep up with the others which he accepted in the spirit it was given. Todd's, 'Way to go Dad!' brought smiles and laughter from many.

Sitting around the fire that night a discussion came up about the second week of their continuing. Todd opting to do the 'hard course' versus the 'regular course' Harry wanted. Not that the regular course was a breeze either, Jim said. Harry wasn't too sure about his durability but he was determined to keep up with Todd and his preference.

Bobby opted to go home with his Dad. Harry and Todd set out for the second week. The 'hard course' was much easier. Harry felt he was a seasoned Wilderness Survivor finding the 'hard course' almost a breeze. Jim Coles and Todd had formed a camaraderie carried over from the first week. Harry was comfortable with the group that stayed and the week flew by without mishap. When they were leaving for home, Jim Coles made a point of letting Harry know how impressed he was with Todd. Harry was really proud of Todd too.

Homeward bound, they had been sailing along quite speedily for a Friday. Traffic wasn't that dense so moving along swiftly was effortless. They should be home in good time Harry was thinking, having started out so early. Suddenly the traffic started getting heavy as they neared the out skirts of South Dakota. They were slowed to a crawl, barely creeping along.

When they finally could see some action up ahead they found out that, apparently traffic was being waylaid by a fire area. The sun had disappeared into the darkening clouds of smoke. The highway patrol were rerouting, while also asking for volunteers to help with road blocks and dig trenches to contain the spreading of the forest fire.

Todd and Harry offered their services. Although Todd was on the young side, they said he could help digging trenches, they stuck to it until they were approached by the Fire Chief to aid a few of his men in clearing a town in the path of the approaching fire. They both were covered in sweat and dirt their lungs sore from the smoke blowing in their direction. They started out in a truck with four other men and one firefighter. Todd was thankful for the break, to consume water for his parched throat and splash water on his face.

They drove through dense smoke passing two teams of firefighters extinguishing spot-fires and creating a fuel-free cutline hoping to dissuade the fire from reaching the town, using chainsaws and pulaskis (a head that is an axe and adze) while others manned shovels. They worked diligently in waves keeping a good ten feet apart. The sawyers, the men felling the trees. The swampers who were there to clean the felled trees and branches, along with the diggers hoping to starve the unquenchable fire of its fuel, all working together as a team.

The main fire storm was up the valley more but leaping in their direction with whirling winds, aiding its furious hunger to consume more. Also burning embers seemed to be carrying for miles leaping around swirling on the wind igniting more areas heading in the direction of town. Evacuation was imperative now.

When they got into the town of Melville they were to work in two's going door to door telling the people to leave, and ask if they needed aid. The firefighter set up a command post at the truck in the town centre. He announced, if they found anyone needing special assistance due to illness or disability one of them was to come back and he would let command know. They will arrange transportation vehicles or ambulance when possible. After their instructions, they spread out to their designated areas.

Harry and Todd had a large seven block area. Everyone they had called on was cooperating. Most had been following the news reports on their radios expecting the evacuation. They were in the process of packing their cars, when Todd and he paced by. Todd was good at directions of the planned escape route to Eugene which he relayed quickly.

They had arrived at the last street when Harry spied a woman in a driveway packing a car. Then he noticed two children walking to the car. Harry did a double take they looked like Bethany and Jason carrying bags. Then his eyes swivelled back to the woman for a closer look. It was Laurie.

They worked their way up towards Laurie at mid block. "Laurie, do you have any more things to get?" Laurie whipped around at her name.

"Harry. What are you doing here?"

"Helping with the fire naturally. What are you doing here?"

"We were here visiting my brother for a week but he is off helping to contain the fire. Betty his wife is inside. As she is pregnant, I am trying to pack the more important things in the cars. She is putting things in the root cellar hoping the cellar will escape the fire to save extra things that way."

Jason and Bethany were greeting Todd. They were happy to see each other.

"Laurie, we have to complete the rest of the block then we will be back to help you. Wait for us." Harry and Todd continued running from house to house but most were just leaving or had already left. They headed back towards Laurie.

CHAPTER SEVENTEEN

*L*aurie was at the station wagon in front of her car. It looked like she was trying to pack them both when Harry and Todd arrived back. Because of the urgency of the situation neither took time to socialize.

"Why take two cars?" Harry asked.

"Betty wants to save as much as she can. She will be driving the station wagon." Calling to Jason to get into the car, Laurie was belting Bethany in.

"I will drive Betty and you can follow us. How far along is Betty?" Harry enquired as he glanced towards the house.

"She has another couple of months before the baby is born."

"Good. You back out and wait, I'll get Betty. Is there anything else?"

"I think Betty has another case and some boxes."

"Todd you come with me. Jason, get in the car with Bethany. We will be right back." Harry and Todd headed inside. There was a woman carrying a small ornate table towards the door that Harry assumed was the root cellar, Laurie had mentioned.

"Betty, you don't have time for this just get to the car. We are friends of Laurie's and you have to leave right now."

Betty wasn't about to be deterred from her mission of saving the little table continuing toward the cellar door.

"Betty that table will probably fit in the car. I'll take the table and you carry the suitcase Todd. Along with the table I'll take one of the boxes and Betty you take the smaller one. Do you have your purse?"

"Oh my purse." Betty turned back to the kitchen quickly, tripping over the box she had previously bypassed. Falling down heavily she hit her stomach on the doorjamb and her head took a whack as she fell. Harry dropped the table and ran to pick her up. "Are you okay?"

She nodded yes but she seemed a little dazed. "Just give me a minute."

"I will have to help you because we need to go." He lifted her carefully.

"Todd, grab her purse I can see it on the kitchen table." Harry was helping Betty to the front door. He assisted her into the passenger side of the front seat, and fastened her seatbelt loosely as possible under her protruding stomach. Then he headed back to grab the table and boxes. Todd had passed him with the suitcase and the purse slung over his arm.

As Harry was getting into the car two men ran up to him.

"You better hurry the fire is closing in faster than they expected."

"I am going to drive this woman out of here. Can you tell the fire-fighter at the truck on main street where my son and I are?"

"Okay but get these two cars moving before the road gets cut off."

After buckling himself in Harry backed up quickly and headed out. Laurie was right on his tail. "Betty, are you feeling all right?" He didn't like the way she was holding her stomach.

"I feel a bit dazed from hitting my head, and my stomach hurts."

"Yes, you did hit the doorjamb pretty hard. Do you think your head is just bruised?"

"No, I think it is more painful than that." Her voice sounded confused.

"Take deep breathes and we will find someone to look at you."

They drove back to Main Street stopping at the truck and the firefighter waiting there to give directions and assistance.

"This woman had a nasty fall and hit her head and stomach. She is seven months pregnant. Is there somewhere I can take her to be checked?"

"When you get to the main road outside of town follow that for five miles then there is a road to the left. It will take you away from the fire. You will come to the town of Eugene for the evacuees but keep going and it is the next town past that. There is a small hospital there in Merritt. I will radio ahead so they will be expecting you."

Harry took off driving fast. The car ate up the miles in his urgency even though the smoke was dense and they could see flames leaping through the trees in the distance. He kept glancing behind to make sure Laurie was keeping up.

Smoke was causing very poor visibility. Harry was getting concerned about missing the road. Had they gone too far?

"Todd, keep watch for the road, we should be there soon I have gone about five miles." He had no sooner said that when Todd sang out.

"Just ahead Dad." Harry swung the wheel and they entered the road. He thought there should be others in front of him but there was no one ahead. Did they take that long to get Betty and her belongings into the car?

The smoke didn't seem to be as dense as they drove down the road away from the fire. They finally came to the town of Eugene that was the destination of their evacuee directive. There seemed to be cars and people milling around everywhere. No longer a sleepy town, but then an invasion of evacuees could do that.

They soon left the town of Eugene behind. He was still travelling at a good rate of speed and Laurie was hot on his tail. He was still concerned over Betty's obvious discomfort. "Betty, talk to me. Tell me your husband's name."

"His name is Jack. Some men came and got him to help with the fire. I didn't want him to go. Jack will worry about me if he doesn't know about the town evacuation."

"How is your head feeling? Does it hurt still?"

"Yes a little. I must have whacked it harder than I thought. My stomach hit first and I was worried about the baby." Betty was trying to play down her hurt.

"We should be at the hospital soon. They will be expecting us. The firefighters will pass the word on, that your town has been evacuated to your husband. I am sure he will ask when he has the chance, as he probably knows which direction the fire is travelling."

"Todd, can you reach the pillow I saw in the seat behind you."

"Got it." Sang out Todd lifting the pillow towards the front seat.

"Put it beside Betty's head against the window. Betty, lean into it and try to relax." Betty did so gratefully easing her aching head.

"Todd, start watching for signs. We are coming to the town of Merritt and hospitals are usually clearly marked." They drove for five minutes when Harry saw the H sign and Todd yelled at the same time. "There it is and the arrow is pointing left."

Harry turned at the next intersection, seeing a big building about three blocks away. The car soon ate up the distance, quickly taking the first entrance to Emergency. It was evident that they were expecting them, as Harry stopped the double doors opened and a gurney appeared with a nurse and two doctors. Harry leaped out, but one of the doctor's was already helping Betty out. The doctor picked her up and laid her on the gurney whipping it inside, while the other doctor asked Harry for details.

He explained briefly that Betty had fallen against a doorjamb rather heavily hitting first her stomach then her head.

"How many months pregnant is she?"

"Seven months and she was exposed to a fair amount of the smoke from the forest fire too." The doctor hurried off following the direction of the gurney.

Harry went back to Laurie's open window of the car. "What happened to Betty?" Laurie looked anxious.

"She fell and hit her head and stomach. They are checking her over. She was talking coherently during the drive but she is slightly dazed."

"I wondered when you bypassed Eugene and your excessive speed during the dense smoky condition of the road. I will be in as soon as I park the car."

"I'll have to move the station wagon too." Harry went back to the car. "Hop out Todd you might as well wait here." Todd jumped out slamming the door as Harry drove off.

Laurie and the kids reached Todd before Harry.

On entering emergency, a nurse approached Laurie asking her to help fill out forms for Betty. Todd directed Bethany and Jason to seats nearby all three chattering eagerly. Harry wasn't far behind them. The forms completed Laurie walked over to him.

"Hello Harry. I was so surprised to see you. You seem to come to my rescue every time I need you. How do you manage that?" Her voice held amazement.

"Todd and I came from two weeks at a wilderness camp in South Dakota. We were on our way home when we were asked to volunteer fighting the fire. We dug some ditches first then they commandeered us to help with the evacuation of Melville.

"We were amazed to see you here. I spied Jason and Bethany first. Then I recognized you. I am glad we were here to help you."

"Harry, I owe you an apology for running out on you in Florida. My head was all mixed up wanting only to go home to normalcy. We got part way home and the full ramification of what my escaping must have done to you hit me. But it was too late when I called the hotel. Mr. Jenkins said you had already left. So I thought maybe you had wanted it that way too."

"Laurie, Todd and I will always be there for you if we can. We want to be with you and the children. I am glad we were directed here now."

"Thank you Harry. I promise I won't run away this time. What happened to Betty?"

"She tripped over a box in the hall with the momentum of falling she hit the doorjamb with her stomach, then continued to the floor hitting her head with a whack. She took quite a jolt, that was why I brought her to the hospital."

"I sure hope Betty and the baby are okay." Her attention was drawn to the children's excited voices.

The three children were catching up on their separate lives these past many months since they saw each other last, and the excitement of the fire. Laurie and Harry stood watching their animation reminiscing about Florida and since. *If only she could communicate as freely with him.* Harry was thinking when Laurie said. "Harry, I want to tell you about the trial. I almost called you to come down. Dennis was most repentant but the judge gave him two years plus a day. He took it badly collapsing in tears. I almost went to him but the prosecutor held onto me as they took him away. Harry it was awful." She gave a little shudder.

"The judge felt he needed to dwell on his wrongful act for what he had put me and the children through. His lawyer pleaded leniency because he brought them back unharmed and turned himself in. The judge said he should get five years so two years was leniency enough in his opinion."

"Why didn't you call me I told you I would be there for you?"

"I know Harry but after running out on you I didn't feel I had that right."

The doctor was approaching drawing their attention back to the present.

"Hello, I am Dr. Cameron. The patient is okay. The baby has a strong heartbeat. We've given her a Tylenol for the headache. Otherwise she can leave as soon as she is dressed. Do you have some place nearby to go?"

"No, we are evacuees. I guess we are supposed to be billeted in Eugene."

"There is a motel down the street. I would prefer she stay close by the hospital just in case there is a problem that we were unable to detect. I think we should err on the side of caution here. I will give them a call that you are coming. Are you her husband?"

"No, her husband is out fighting the forest fire. He doesn't know she is here except he probably has heard she was evacuated." Harry replied.

"Perhaps we should call Emergency Control and let them know where you are. What is her full name?"

"Betty Wilson and her husband's name is Jack." Laurie supplied. "Jack is my brother."

"I'll get someone right on to it. I'm sure her husband will want to know where she is, as well as the rest of you." Dr. Cameron alleged.

"Thank you, doctor. You're sure Betty and the baby are okay?"

"Yes, I'm sure. However if she has any problems bring her back right away." The doctor walked away to make arrangements for the call to Control Centre and the motel.

A nurse was wheeling Betty down the hall towards them. She had an elated reassuring smile on her face. "Everything is okay. I wish I could let Jack know where I am."

"Dr. Cameron is making arrangements for someone to phone the Emergency Control to let Jack know you are staying here in town. Can you walk?" Laurie asked looking inquiringly at the nurse.

"Yes, she can walk but just be careful till that head clears." The nurse said helping Betty out of the chair at the emergency door.

Harry took her arm and Laurie called to the children and they headed for the cars in the parking lot. Harry had snagged a spot quite close to the Emergency door.

When they were established in the motel, Harry had a shower to get rid of the smoke and grime wishing he had some clean clothes. He was slowly recovering from the shock of finding Laurie and the kids again. Fate had once again drawn them together.

While Todd had his shower, Harry thought about Laurie. He analyzed his feelings and found his wanting Laurie hadn't changed. This time he was going to be more outspoken and insist they try for a future together. She would not walk away again. He could not depend on being her saviour, showing up each and every time she was in the path of trouble. Somehow his life and Laurie's kept being directed towards each other. Three times now in fact. Could they always be there when needed? Harry doubted it.

His intention was getting her alone to let her know his mindset. Seeing her again strengthened his need for her in his life. At the hospital, just standing close to her made him aware of that. She was not walking away this time without a very good reason. He knew now why he could never settle into a full relationship with Denise.

Todd was jubilant when he walked out from his shower.

"Dad, wasn't it wonderful to find Bethany, Jason and Laurie again. Jason asked his mother to contact me so many times but she never did. I would really like Laurie for a mother and be brother to Bethany and Jason. You want that too don't you Dad?" Todd studied his father's face anxiously. Harry was amazed that Todd was mirroring his same thoughts so soon. Could it be possible the children have voiced their wants too? Why could Laurie not see it?

"Yes Todd, I was just sitting here thinking it was time to tell Laurie how I feel about her. Unless I can successfully convince her, she may walk away once again. We have never once corresponded, so it is over a year again, since we saw them last. It may be difficult to convince her unless she is over her unpleasant experience with Dennis."

"But Dad, I can see you really care for her every time you look at her. You seem more alive around her whereas at home you seem to just exist."

"Todd that is so true. Well this time I am going to woo her until she gives in. No escape this time if I can help it." He ended arrogantly.

"Dad, Laurie always lights up around you too I have seen it. Possibly she is just waiting for you to say something and you never have. You have to put the move on her."

"The move? Is that what they call it these days?" Harry chuckled.

"Dad, just do it and call it what you want but I want them in our lives."

"So do I son. So do I."

There was a knock on the door. Todd hurriedly opened the door to see Jason there. "Mom wonders if you want to go somewhere to eat. We are hungry and Aunt Betty is feeding two." Jason asked hopefully as though his last comment cinched it.

"Well we can't keep Aunt Betty waiting now, can we? Coming Todd?" This was an empty question as the two boys scooted out the door.

Laurie was just exiting her room and she smiled in his direction. She had made use of her suitcases with her, because she had changed her outfit. Her smile was stunning. Harry grinning in return, then he looked to Betty. She was standing near the car parked in front of their room.

"How are you feeling Betty?" Harry inquired.

"Fine, much better than I thought I would. My headache has lifted." Her smile was striking.

"That's good it will be better without using medication for the baby's sake, I'm sure." Harry transferred his gaze to Laurie. "How about you Laurie, how are you bearing up?"

"Better now that I have had a shower. I felt so grimy around the fire. How do you know when I need you? You always seem to materialize like a genie?" Laurie's voice held astonishment.

"It isn't easy to be a Sir Galahad but really I have to confess it is mere coincidence each time." His smile was prolific. "Shall we all go in the station wagon or would you rather walk? I didn't really look for restaurants on our way here."

"Walk I think. The restaurant is six places down from here. Jason found out from the manager." Laurie alleged.

"We walk then." Holding out both his arms gallantly to both women to latch onto him, the children were already running ahead.

The cafe was small and cheerfully decorated. Several of the tables were occupied. A young girl appeared after they were seated at a large circular center table, she stood poised with pen and pad.

"Hi folks. My name is Cindy. Are you from out of town?"

"Yes, we are from Melville. We were evacuated because of the forest fire. We are staying at the motel." Laurie explained.

"Gee that's too bad. I hear the forest fire is really bad near Melville. Well I have to tell you the food is really first class here. Maddy sure loves to cook up a storm. Are you ready to order or do you want more time?"

"A little more time please but I would like coffee. How about you Laurie and Betty?"

"I'll have iced tea and milk for the children." Laurie sent an enquiring look to Todd. He nodded okay. Betty confirmed she would like iced tea too.

Cindy arrived back quickly with their drinks.

The surrounding cooking aromas were making them feel really hungry. Everyone was verbalizing their wants, as the waitress took their orders. Then she mentioned that Maddy, the owner said the lunches were on her. "She thinks it must be difficult having to be removed from your home."

"Yes it is and it is certainly nice of her." Laurie said. The waitress left on that note.

"Well Bethany and Jason how have you been?" Harry queried.

They both talked at once tripping over each other's sentences in their eagerness. Harry had a big smile on his face. He had missed them very much.

"How have you been, Laurie?"

"I've been good now the trial is behind me. Nothing spectacular has happened to me. We only decided to come here on the spur of the moment. It's good being here for Betty's sake, what with the fire and

Jack called away to help out."

"I'm glad you were here. I don't think I could have gotten out of there alone." Betty gave them a relieved smile. "Besides Laurie it has been too long since Jack and I moved. We miss you and the kids."

"I'll second that, it has been too long since we were together too. We missed them, didn't we Todd?" Harry put in shifting his eyes to Laurie.

"Yes Dad, I have missed this knucklehead." Giving Jason a loving jab on his arm.

So Laurie doesn't live near her brother anymore. Maybe that will work in his favour.

"Laurie are you still working?"

"Yes I haven't come into any riches so I still have to work."

"How is the job going? Still working at the same place?" Harry asked.

"No they closed down and moved to Georgia. I am working for a real estate firm now. How about you, still in the same office? Architect wasn't it?" Doubt in her voice. Pretending she couldn't remember but she remembered every little detail about him clearly. This caring man she had relied on in the past but never asked anything for himself.

"Yes, still the same office except I have been doing more out of town work in the past year. It makes more of a challenge."

"Betty, Harry has come to my rescue a few times now. I should call him my knight in shining armour. He seems to show up when I need him most. Harry once took the children in while I was in the hospital. Then he was with me in Florida with that bad experience of the children being kidnapped. Much to my surprise here he is once again."

"Betty is something wrong?" Harry noted she seemed uncomfortable.

"No just the after affects of the bump on the stomach I guess." Her hand rubbing in circles on her tummy gently.

The arrival of food caused a stir, so Betty's comment went unnoticed.

The appetites were hearty so the food vanished quickly and the dessert menu was discussed. After lunch was finished they gave their thanks to Maddy and departed amongst well wishes from the staff. The children were happily frolicking about as they made their escape through the door. To release some energy, they decided to walk around town a bit.

After the smoke this morning, the air was clean and refreshing. Merritt was a larger town then Melville with a few modern buildings, more stores and a big park. But it still had a small town atmosphere which Harry liked.

CHAPTER EIGHTEEN

*B*ethany was talking to her Aunt Betty ahead of Laurie and Harry. The two boys were well out in front. Laurie looked at Harry slyly.

"Harry, are you ever going to ask me how I am doing in my love life?"

"No, I have been afraid to ask. But how is your love life going?"

"Terrible. I haven't met anyone since Dennis and maybe that's my fault after Dennis' behaviour." *Now why ever had she asked that? She usually wasn't forward like that. Had it just popped out by mistake?*

"That is understandable. Aren't you going to ask about my love life?" Coy was not in Harry's makeup but he tried.

Laurie laughed. "How is your love life?" She definitely seemed more outgoing he thought.

"Terrible and I didn't have a bad experience like you for an excuse. That is all the confessions you are getting out of me. Still liking South Carolina?"

"It is different since Jack and Betty left. I have been seriously thinking of relocating somewhere else." His heart speeded up.

"Have you considered coming back to Indiana? Or are you looking towards another State?"

"It is a passing thought, but no particular place comes to mind."

Harry helped Laurie by grasping her hand when she half tripped on the raised sidewalk. "Careful, the sidewalk's uneven here."

"Do you know what arrangements were made with Jack if you all were evacuated?" He asked.

"Jack knew if it became necessary, we would be sent to Eugene. When the fire's rampage was impeded, maybe then he could get some free time to look for us in Eugene." Laurie replied.

"I hope the Emergency Control gets word to Jack telling him we are in Merritt. I imagine it depends if it is near the main command post area, when he comes in to get relief from the fire with much needed food and rest." Harry supplied.

"We should stay here now that we have sent Jack word that this is where we are even if Betty is feeling alright." Laurie reasoned

"I agree we should stay here. Eugene looked pretty full of evacuees needing some type of accommodation. Most people prefer to stay close to their home town, because when they get the all clear they want to get home quickly. The concern for their homes is most paramount in their minds." Harry expounded.

They had walked for a few blocks when Betty said she wanted to go back to the motel. Laurie and Harry thought she was concerned that Jack might be looking for her. So they made a loop heading in the general direction of the motel.

When they got back to the motel the manager offered them games for the children. Betty suggested Laurie and Harry continue walking while she refereed the games. They looked at each other for consent, then left with thanks to Betty's proposal. Laurie felt confident that Betty was capable of handling the children once they were playing games. Harry and Laurie headed on another path. They came across an old-time saloon, grinned at each other then turned in.

The decor inside would compliment any movie set for lavishness and authentic realism, spittoons and all. The dancehall girl attire on the waitresses was not surprising. There was hearty laughter and camaraderie with a background of tinkling piano music.

It wasn't long before they were included into another table with two local couples that had dropped in for some fun. They were treating Harry and Laurie like they were married and he was not about to correct them. A round of drinks arrived at the table and the two couples were expounding on the virtues of Merritt. Asking Harry when he was going to move the family there?

Laurie blushed at the mistake of their omission; it was too late to fill these people in on their status. Harry was grinning in pleasure visualizing Laurie as his wife letting the conversation flow around them.

Walking back to the motel later Laurie asked the plans for dinner. Harry suggested the kids choose knowing they had passed several places on their earlier walk. She suggested a late dinner because of the late lunch.

Opening the door to Laurie's room Harry found the children playing and Betty lying down. Laurie asked. "Are you okay Betty?"

Jason piped up. "She has been having pains ever since you left."

Concerned Laurie walked to the bed. "Are you having labour pains?"

"I don't think so I just think it is a result of the hitting the doorjamb. I just thought I would rest awhile." Betty said weakly.

"You rest and we will take the children to the park we saw earlier. They need to let off some steam. Your rest will be peaceful then. You're positive that it isn't labour pains? Do you think we should contact Dr. Cameron?"

"No, I am sure it isn't that bad. It just hurts a bit." Betty played down the pain although she was worried about the baby.

Todd and Jason were putting the game back in the box. Trying to outdo each other to see who could put the most pieces away in their haste.

Harry was pleased Laurie had automatically included Todd and him. Maybe things would be different this time around.

When they got to the park, Jason and Todd shared the responsibility of Bethany on the swings and the slides. They used some of their excess energy climbing the monkey bars. Laurie and Harry looked on like proud parents.

"Laurie, do you think we could spend some time together after the ruffians go to bed?" He was laughing at the boys antics trying to compete against each other while Bethany giggled too.

"Probably it could be arranged provided Betty is feeling better. I'm worried about her." Laurie replied her gaze flowed over the children now playing tag.

"Well of course, it would be subject to Betty's feeling better."

They sat talking about different aspects of their lives since they last saw each other. While Laurie was content to just sit there and talk she also felt a niggling feeling to check on Betty and expressed her feelings to Harry.

Arriving back at the motel room door, Laurie ordered. "Everyone wash your hands then you can choose the restaurant for dinner."

Opening the door, she realized immediately, that there was something wrong with Betty. She was still lying down but her clothes were different and she had changed to another bed and her bed had been stripped. "The girl is bringing clean bedding." She explained.

"What happened were you sick?"

"No my water broke. My baby has decided to be born I think. I didn't know how to find you so I just told the girl I had an accident. Oh Laurie it is too soon." Betty finished worriedly.

"Good heavens, why didn't you ask for an ambulance?" Laurie fearfully asked looking to Harry.

"Todd, you and Jason transfer the things out of the station wagon into our room so we all can go to the hospital together. Betty, it is time for another journey to the hospital." Harry was ushering everyone around so that he could help Betty into the car. Her discomfort was obvious, a matter for grave concern.

No one complained as they just sped around clearing the car and Laurie packing a small suitcase. Bethany was responsible for carrying Betty's purse.

Harry handed the boys keys, to lock their respective rooms. He eased Betty up off the bed with Laurie's help. Betty was eased into the front seat but they did not bother to strap her in as she was holding her stomach protectively. The children had leaped in the back with Laurie.

Thank heavens they had stayed close to the hospital. Betty doubled over as a spasm hit her while cradling her precious burden protectively. Expressing her concern that it was too soon for the baby to be born, in a pain filled trembling voice. When they pulled into emergency Laurie ran in to alert the staff and get a wheelchair.

Harry helped Betty out of the car but she was leaning heavily on him.

Dr. Cameron was just leaving for the day when he spotted the activity over near the station wagon. He came over as Betty was eased into the wheelchair.

"What seems to be the problem?" Recognizing Betty instantly.

"She is going to have a baby." Bethany announced proudly.

Laurie expressed her concern. "Betty seems to be in a lot of pain more than normal at this stage for a first baby and her water broke."

"I had better come and have a look." He issued orders as soon as he hit the doors to a nurse adding. "And get someone to phone my wife, I'll be delayed."

Harry parked the car. Arriving inside he saw the children were occupying the same seats of the morning but no Laurie.

"Dad, Laurie went to be with Aunt Betty. She was holding on to Laurie and didn't want to let go." Todd stated with a troubled voice.

Harry sat down with the children. Laurie joined them after a short while.

"They think Betty might have some internal bleeding so they are going to have to take the baby by caesarean section, that fall must have caused more damage than they suspected."

"Harry, do you think you could find out how to contact Jack. I think he should be here." Laurie's face reflected her concern.

Harry headed for the nursing station without delay. He asked to use their phone and also for the emergency number for the fire department. Harry called and explained that he was trying to reach a Jack Wilson. He was not a firefighter but he was fighting the forest fire near Melville. The operation officer connected him to the duty officer at Emergency Command station near the fire site.

"This is Harry Cochrane. I am trying to contact Jack Wilson. He is not a firefighter but he is helping somewhere with the forest fire crew. His wife had a fall and as a result is having a baby that might also entail medical problems. I feel he should be here at the hospital in Merritt with his wife, if at all possible."

The duty officer felt that was pretty much an impossible task, as the fire crews were spread out over a two mile radius. "The only hope is that he is due in for a break and some food. If not I doubt he will get the message till sometime during the night. But I will past this on to the line camp. What is her name and where is she?"

"Her name is Betty Wilson. She is in the hospital in Merritt. She is having a baby by caesarean delivery because they suspect internal bleeding from a fall. We think if at all possible her husband should be here. How are things there?"

"We will do everything possible to find him and pass this information along but no promises. We have deployed men into a wider area as the wind has changed and the fire is now entering a younger forest and the ground fires in the duff and moss of the forest floor are climbing preheated trees that are exploding into flames like a candle, igniting dry tree tops. They are going to be busy so I don't hold much hope of finding him."

"Well thanks for your help anyway. I realized before I called it might be futile but I had to try." Harry went back to Laurie to relate the phone conversation. She accepted the impossibility of finding Jack but at least they had tried.

"Mom, will Aunt Betty's baby be okay?" Jason inquired observing his mother's agitation.

"We must pray that the baby will be safe, that is why they are operating rather than waiting for the natural birthing of labour pains."

"Do you know what caused her to be sick mommy?" Bethany asked.

"Aunt Betty fell and hit her stomach and she is having two kinds of pain. We hope by operating it will be easier on her and the baby will arrive safely. Do you children want to go with Harry for dinner? We promised you could pick the eating place." Food was the last thing Laurie wanted.

"No. We want to stay with Aunt Betty." Jason replied.

"It will be awhile yet and the time will pass faster if you eat."

"But Mom we are worried about Aunt Betty." Jason's face held concern.

"I know and so am I, but I'll wait here in case Uncle Jack comes otherwise I would have come with you too." Laurie rubbed Jason's arm in sympathy.

She didn't want the children witnessing her distress which she was finding hard to contain. They finally consented but only to the A & W which was the closes eatery. She asked Harry to bring her back a drink.

The A & W visit was less than jovial. The drama being played out back at the hospital was over-shadowing their usual chatter. The talking was sparse and eating was prevalent so the burgers vanished quickly. Then they were rapidly heading back to the hospital.

"Any news?" As they swiftly approached Laurie.

"Not yet. She is still in the Operating Room. No word from Jack either."

A voice came at them. "Hi Laurie." Harry's look was drawn towards a man hurrying toward them with worry written all over his face. "How is Betty?"

Laurie hugged him even though he was dark as coal and smelling of smoke. "Jack, am I glad to see you. Nothing yet she is still in the OR." When the man stepped back the fatigue and grime was evident in his face, his hands and clothing, making it obvious he had come directly from the fire line in haste.

"Dr. Cameron was just leaving for home when we arrived but he stayed to help Betty. She has been in the OR for quite awhile. We should be hearing soon."

"How did it happen? What about this internal bleeding? The baby wasn't due yet." His voice held anxiety.

"When we were leaving the house, Betty went back to get her purse and tripped over a box throwing her into the doorjamb heavily, with her stomach taking the brunt of it. Continuing to fall Betty then hit her head. We came directly here but the only thing that showed was a nasty headache. So they released her asking us to stay nearby. Then later she developed pains which kept getting more severe and her water broke so we knew the baby was coming."

"But the baby isn't due for two months." Disbelieve in his voice.

"She was visibly in more pain than just normal labour so they checked her out as soon as we got here. Determining the possibility of internal bleeding, from the contact with the door jamb during the fall, so that probably brought on the baby Dr. Cameron said."

"I think I'll go clean off some of this grime." Jack wanting to be alone to gather his thoughts. "I don't want to frighten Betty or the baby. Jason come and get me if the doctor comes with news of Aunt Betty or the baby." said Jack. Turning away he noticed a nurse approaching pushing an incubator.

"This is baby boy Wilson. He is very tiny and will be in an incubator for awhile but I will let you peek at his face." The nurse said kindly knowing these people were very concerned. They all crowded around. The nurse assumed the grubby black smoky man must be the baby's father summoned from the forest fire.

The nurse pushed the blanket away to reveal more of the baby's face. The baby was a miniature doll. Jack's smiling white teeth broke the mask of his black face. Harry and Laurie were in awe and the children were making whispering squeals at the size of the miniscule baby. The moment of awe was broken. The showing over in seconds, the nurse had recovered the precious bundle to be whisked away to the nursery.

"How is my wife?" Jack asked anxiously.

"I'm sorry I don't know. They are still working on her. I have to get the baby to the nursery right away. He needs to be hooked up to provide extra warmth in the incubator till he gets stronger." She glided away in a hurry.

"Congratulations Daddy." Laurie was hugging her brother and Jack had tears making rivers on his black cheeks. Laurie was ignoring the grime just hugging her brother in his astonishment and the emotion of the moment.

Jack was thinking that wee little bundle was his son. He was going to be afraid to touch him with his huge hands. "But... but he was so tiny?"

"He will soon grow and become a strapping lad like his father." Laurie cajoled Jack. "You will soon be taking him home." No one wanted to voice, if they even had a home to go back to.

Laurie uttered finally. "We heard the wind changed, does that mean the town was saved? Did you hear?" It was out in the open and they were waiting for Jack to respond to Laurie's question.

"Yes the wind changed, at present the fire has moved direction to an area of young forest growth. We hope that means they can stop the fire on the outskirts of town. That is what they are concentrating on now. The main objective is a backfire which is set strategically to burn towards the fire robbing it of new fuel and stop it in its tracks on its path towards Melville. That was what they were working on when I left. But the wind conditions have a lot to do with its success. They seemed to think it should work. Besides they really have no other choice, it was that or lose the town."

"We'll keep our fingers crossed and pray for their success." Harry said encouragingly.

The news sort of deflated their elation over the newborn. That tiny baby who would be fighting to survive the 36 hours when preemies statically had their hardest time toward survival, versus the success of the firefighters fight against nature with the backfire where the baby's future home was in question. This message was written on everyone's face.

The doctor was watching the group as he walked towards them. He surmised the fire grimy man must be Betty's husband. They all seemed to be very serious so the man must be imparting sad news on the fire's condition, from the seriousness in his expression as he talked. Well the news he was about to impart should perk them up. Jason spied him and pointed. "Look."

Dr. Cameron's sudden appearance, called them all back to their present, showing concern for Betty.

Dr. Cameron stopped before the group. "Mrs. Wilson I am proud to say came through satisfactorily. We found the problem after we delivered the baby. We have stopped the bleeding and she should recover soon but it will mean extra time in the hospital until she is well enough to leave."

"The baby is a different matter. I am afraid that brave young man has a hard time ahead of him to survive. We should know in a couple of days. He is fully developed but seems to be having some problem breathing, but that is sometimes normal for preemies. It would have been better if he had a couple of weeks longer before delivery."

"But that isn't the case, so we will do our best to help him in any way that is necessary. I will be doing some tests on the baby. My feeling is the baby is fully developed." He continued quickly. "It may be a long stay as I would like to see him gain at least two pounds before leaving the hospital. He is only three and a half pounds now."

"Three and a half pounds wow!" Jason said in wonder. He remembered getting on the scale and being 75 lbs last week.

Dr. Cameron smiled at Jason then turned to the father and held out his hand. "Congratulations." Jack was franticly wiping his hands on his grimy pants before touching the white hand offered to him.

But his pants were all grimy too so that didn't make much difference. "It's okay." Grabbing Jack's hand laughing. "I am finished for the day."

"Thank you Dr. Cameron. Can I see my wife now?"

"She is in recovery exhausted from the labour and the extended operation. I see no reason why you can't see her for a few minutes. But I might suggest you wash off some of the grime. I doubt she could recognize you in her drugged state looking like that." His smile held humour at the blackness of the man's face. "By the way how is the fire effort going when you left?"

"Hopeful, if the backfire works. That should stop it from reaching the town of Melville and that is their expectation."

Dr. Cameron was glad the man had some encouraging news. He felt the young man needed it. "Well I better be getting home my wife has been holding dinner."

They all chorused 'thank you'. Jack quickly loped off to the washroom.

CHAPTER NINETEEN

Jack returned looking more like the proud father he was. He had removed his shirt and exposed the T-shirt below which wasn't quite so grimy. Now Harry could see the resemblance between Laurie and Jack. He was younger than his sister, Harry observed.

Jack was approaching them with a wide smile. After the day's events he had come to grips with the fact that he had a son and Betty was going to be fine, and that was what he was holding onto. His smile projected his pleasure. When Jack reached them he hugged Laurie again and said how happy he was. She hugged him back congratulating him once more on the successful outcome of a new son.

Harry observed the brother and sister, realizing their closeness had enticed her to South Carolina. But Jack wasn't living there anymore and Laurie had been having thoughts of moving. Could this be the opportunity he needed? He had planned on speaking to her tonight, but with the emergency trip to the hospital, he would probably lose that opportunity.

Jack kissed her and pulled back. He looked at Harry questioningly.

"Oh Jack, this is Harry Cochrane, a friend that has been an immense help to me on a couple of occasions over the years and appeared out of the blue again." The two men shook hands sizing each other up. "I have heard about you from Laurie and the kids, and this must be the famous Todd, Jason talks about." Shaking hands with Todd "Nice to meet you." Without stopping for a breath he continued. "I'll go in to see

Betty now, and then I would like another peek at my son." Finishing proudly on an upbeat note Jack turned away.

"We'll wait here for you." Laurie said. Jack raced down the hall to his wife. Harry was noticing the children were getting restless. He suggested taking them out for a breath of fresh air. "I'll let the nurse know where we are, so she can let Jack know if he comes back before us."

The children were whooping and scampering around the lawn in glee as though the cage door has been sprung and they were free. Laurie and Harry stood watching them with shared smiles.

"Laurie, this isn't the plans I had for tonight. I had another location in mind, but I would like to say some of the thoughts I originally intended expressing."

Harry took a deep breath.

"Laurie, we have been brought together under unusually circumstances three times and I think that contributes to triple the knowing time. These occurrences we have shared were unusual, producing a closeness that most couples never attain. I know I want you in my life and I don't mean just on difficult occasions. I want to share some of your good times. We know we will survive under the bad, so don't you think we should share some good times now?" Harry tone was persuading.

"But how can we do that? We live too far apart." Laurie exclaimed.

"You said you where thinking of relocating now that Jack and Betty have moved. So why can't you come back to Indiana?" Harry said hopefully. He rushed on. "I feel I have a special bond with you and the children. Also I feel Bethany and Jason really have a good relationship with Todd. So the children won't be any problem." He trailed off.

"Harry, I said I was thinking about moving but I haven't set any time." She said to give herself time to digest what he was suggesting.

"Laurie, every time you walk out of my life I seem to die a little. I never can go back to my life as it was. We can't keep expecting fate to throw us together, besides how many more tragedies do you want in your life? If something happens again I may not be there, and I want to be there for you always." Harry said earnestly.

"Harry, I have been so thankful each time you were there for me.

I do like you and Todd a lot. But I don't know if I could ever go back to Indiana again." She paused feeling unkind.

"If we could get together somehow, I know we could make a good pair. I feel that this is something we should try, a long term relationship. Why won't you give us a chance?"

"Harry, I have never thought of you in that light but only as a friend. Please understand that I do well on my own, and I have to consider the children and what's best for them."

"Laurie, can I approach the children on this? Would that convince you?"

He was willing to try anything at this stage. He didn't want her out and out 'NO'.

"Harry, the children aren't old enough to make decisions like that."

Just then the door opened and Jack came out. "How is Betty?" Laurie asked.

"She seems fine and in good spirits but very tired. The little guy looks stronger but it was sad to see him with wires on his tiny body, hooked up to machines." Jack paused shook his head, and continued as if to remove the image from his memory. "Well I have to get back to the forest fire. I promised I would go back to help out on the fire-line still. I know I am badly needed there."

Harry asked. "Can you give me a lift I left my car back there?"

"Sure, will you be alright with one car if I take my station wagon Laurie? Betty said they were keeping her in for a few days. I may be back before then."

"Yes, we'll be fine with my car."

"Todd, do you want to stay here or come back with me?" Harry asked giving him the opportunity to decide.

"Dad, can I stay with Jason and Bethany? I would really prefer that."

"Sure that's fine. I was giving you the choice." Swinging to Laurie he asked. "You don't mind Laurie do you, I should be back soon after I pick up my car."

"That is fine with me, Harry." Laurie noting the expression on her children's faces of pleading looks for yes.

After Jack and Harry left, Laurie was collecting the children to travel the short walking distance back to the motel, feeling a little guilt, niggling at her that she had only thought of Harry as a friend, and now the fact that he seemed to be expecting more.

. . .

When the two men got closer to the fire area it was very evident that the raging fire was still out of control. The area where Harry had left his car was blocked off by flames devouring trees. They drove further to an area of activity. The firefighters were getting ready for shift changing. Harry watched as the bleary eyed smoke eaters were tumbling out of sleeping tents; too few hours of sleep but answering the necessary call. Walking toward the eating tent the firefighters needed to fuel their bodies, so they could fight the fight. Harry felt guilty that he wasn't helping. Jack inquired where he was to report. He was told the sector adjacent to the tower. Men were desperately needed there. Harry offered his services as the concern in the man's voice hit him, that area wasn't all that far from the town.

Before going off with Jack, Harry asked if it would be possible to let Laurie and his son know he wouldn't be back right away after all. He gave Laurie's name and the location of the motel in Merritt.

"We really appreciate your services so I will arrange for her to be informed." After picking up protection gear Harry and Jack took off in a truck with six other men. The smoke was coming at them causing a choking feeling. The six bone weary and tired blacken men looked like Jack when he had first arrived at the hospital smoky and grimy.

Jack and Harry's conversation on the drive was about Harry's involvement in Laurie's life. How the children originally arrived on his doorstep. How he convinced his sister to let them stay. Laurie joining them from the hospital, Jack was unaware of that part. But Jack did notice the inflection in Harry's voice was very tender particularly when he mentioned his sister. The children seemed to be important to him too, in his dramatization of past events.

Then Harry mentioned the proceedings during the period of the kidnapping. The details Harry imparted were far more extensive than Laurie had given him. Jack liked Harry and felt it was odd that his sister had left him so abruptly in Fort Lauderdale without so much as a goodbye. Harry's voice had been regretful about Laurie's method of leaving.

Evidently, she had down played Harry's role in that period of the abduction when relating the details to him. Did she not like this man as a man? Harry and Todd seemed so friendly and caring to him. The tone in this man's voice showed he definitely cared about her.

But Jack had to ask. "Harry, how do you feel about my sister?"

"Plain and simple I love her very much, and I want to marry her. I love the children too."

"Why haven't you discussed it with Laurie? Why haven't you expressed your love for her?" Jack enquired.

"I tried while you were in with Betty but she said she didn't think of me in that manner. She appreciated me but romance didn't enter into the equation."

"Are you going to accept that?"

"I don't seem to be able to reach her. I doubt our paths will keep crossing. The odds that it happened three times are rare enough. All I know is after being with her, I lose some of the quality of my life, when we separate each time. I miss her so much and Todd feels the same too. He gets quieter and not so open for the longest time after. He is a lonely boy without his mother to start with. I have watched him around Laurie and he always seems to get a glow just being near her."

"Why don't you ask the children maybe they will aid you in bringing Laurie to her senses." Jack knew Jason could be pragmatic in helping.

"I did suggest that to Laurie but she refused me, saying they weren't old enough for that kind of a decision. I don't know what more I can do other than try romancing her but that is rather difficult with the unsettling conditions of our reunions and the distance between our homes."

"When I saw you all together outside the hospital the thought occurred to me how well you all looked together. Your interaction was more than just friends. After all, I have an interest in this too. I hated the idea of leaving Laurie in South Carolina when I moved here. The transfer was too beneficial to Betty and myself to refuse. I think Laurie cares about you, but just hasn't faced up to it. Because of the brief periods you have been together, and the Dennis' situation didn't help. My suggestion is just keep trying."

"Thanks for your approval. Laurie is a hard woman to convince. But convince her I will." Harry alleged with conviction.

As the truck stopped Harry came out of his reverie of the conversation with Jack. The next thing he knew he was in the thick of the roaring fire. The fire had leaped the trenches that he and Todd had built earlier. The young forest with its slimmer trunks, and close proximity, causing the spread of the fire, tripping from tree to tree speedily. So the backfire hadn't worked the way they hoped. The fire had gone sideways as well as forward, but the backfire at least saved the town. Harry and Jack ascertained this on their arrival.

The hungry flames were dancing ever upward, driving the hot air down towards them. The air was scalding hot and becoming unbearable. If they didn't get this fire under control soon they would have to retreat. Harry's face was burning with the heat and his throat felt dry and sore. Smoke and burning fragments reigning around them making them leap for safer ground. The wind was picking up and the fire seemed to be changing direction.

Harry, although inexperienced, knew a decision needed to be made soon. How much longer could they keep this up? They had not been successful in starving the greedy fire, with their efforts of downing the snags and hitting the hotspots while cutting, beating, hacking and sweating.

The call came to retreat. The men did not hesitate; they knew things were beyond them. Fire was all over, above them and around them feeding on the young saplings and brush. The trees consumed by the greedy fierce inferno. The explosions of the trees in the background aided by the wind made them thankful for their escape.

They were directed to another area to set up a line of resistance from that direction. Harry managed to get a drink to relieve his parched throat. Their new task was trying to put out the fire-spots. Time lost all meaning and yet they fought on. Harry wondered if they were making any headway.

Darkness was not a factor because the forest fire's glow in the night was bright. Exhausted they were brought in for a little break and some sleep.

When they arose with the dawn of a new day, there was more bad news. Activity in the camp was at a high with this new happening. Now the fire was encroaching on a new area, which held several camping facilities making a new worry. The campers had been asked to be ready to leave, but the fire aided by the swirling wind had leaped upon them before the evacuation had been completed. Several of the firefighters were piling into trucks to head for the camp area.

Jack and Harry were assigned burdensome shoulder packs with heavy tanks of water. Their job was to get to a new area, the outskirts of where they had been working last night and stop the fire from progressing, by putting out the wind carried ashes, and stop them from starting new ground fires, on the overly dry forest floor. Since there had been no rain in this area for over a month, the forest floor was edible tinder. Others were in the area trying to clear a saw line to starve the beast.

They were making good headway annihilating the hot burning embers of falling ash and hotspots, working independently but within shouting distance of each other.

Noting that the area, that he was working in seemed to be like a meadow, as he worked he was getting further away from the trees. Harry felt victory was soon to be his. He had been intently concentrating on controlling some ashes that had built into a sizeable ground fire. Dousing the fire, that burnt in a wide circular fashion like a ring.

Suddenly, he was falling, speedily into open space. It was a matter of seconds that felt like hours, in his terror of helplessness. Groping at air, Harry tried to locate a tuft of shrub or a branch or an outcropping of rock hoping to break his fall, trying to twist in his frantic need to reach something solid to hang on to, as he pummelled down a cliff face.

Instead his head encountered a jagged protruding rock, ripping at him and at his body's passing. His hard hat forced forward by the jagged rock, but held on by the tightening strap under his chin. He finally landed encased under a huge bush against the cliff base. He tried to assess his condition. His right arm was in a precarious position as well as his left leg. His head that had connected with a sharp jutting rock was making him feel very nauseous and lightheaded.

The moment he tried to move his leg he knew he was in trouble.

Added to his dilemma he was pinned sideways under the bush at the cliff base. He tried yelling but that hurt his already aching head intensely. He tried moving in desperation only to have blackness consume the pain.

Jack had been concentrating on his own area to the right of where Harry was working. They were working their way toward each other until Jack had seen some small shrub fires to his left so he skilfully put them out first, then headed back towards where he thought Harry should be. The fire that Harry had almost eradicated was now building momentum.

Jack assumed Harry had run out of water, leaving to refill his tank from the vat back at the truck. Jack worked on the fire until he too ran out of water.

Arriving back at the truck, Jack looked around but couldn't see Harry. Maybe he hadn't come back for water. Jack felt the last spot he had been dousing should have been Harry's location. Maybe he had been on the other side of the rim of fire. Why had he not seen him? He was thinking Harry should be out of water as well. He knew others were working in the same general area.

So when a couple of the guys came towards him to refill their tanks Jack asked them if they had seen Harry and described him. They both said no. Jack headed back towards the area where Harry had been working, still no sign of him. Another two men, he recognized as men that had been on the same truck on the way here, were walking towards him.

Jack asked them if they had seen Harry. Again he described him. They said they remembered him from the ride but they hadn't seen him. They said they would refill their tanks with water and then come back to Jack and Harry's assigned area. Their own assigned area was secured they said. The ashes weren't flowing in that direction anymore so they were willing to help Jack and Harry, seeing the glowing fire through the trees.

Jack trekked back to the area that Harry had been fighting the ring of fire. He called a few times for him as he attacked the circling flames.

He still couldn't see him but he was making headway putting out the fire. With the temporary absence of wind, the fire seemed stationary, having spread only a short distance from when he had last observed it. The other two men reappeared, each attacking it from another direction until they were working towards Jack. The three soon had put out the ring of fire, but still no Harry. Jack explained, Harry had to be nearby somewhere.

They walked in the general direction of where Jack had seen Harry toiling last. They could see where the spot-fires had been sprayed and arrested before they became ground fires. Harry must have soaked them. So they went back to the ring of fire that they had last extinguished, which they now felt was where Harry most likely had been, but no Harry. They started calling but Harry never answered. They decided to split up but they still couldn't find him. Jack now noticed the burnt area fringed near a cliff edge which he had previously discounted. Now he wasn't so sure. He went over to the cliff, but he couldn't see anyone. So he called to the other two men.

"Over here." Jack waved his arms. They came running. He pointed out the small patches of dead debris knowing Harry must have been near there.

"Look over the cliff and see if you can see anything." They all cautiously peered over the cliff positioned a considerable distant apart; shaking their heads negatively at each other.

One of the men suggested "You go that way and I'll walk this way. What is your name?"

"Jack."

"Well Jack, you two look out for any other spot-fires he may have put out and if they are near the cliff look over at that point. Yell if either of you find anything. By the way I am Steve and this is Bert."

The three men searched but didn't find anything. They convened together back at the fringe of ashes on the cliff edge to decide what to do next. Jack said. "Harry must have fallen over the cliff here but I couldn't see him down there."

"I looked all along the burned area and Bert covered the other way and neither of us saw anything. Let's try calling. One person yell then everyone listen. We'll stand about fifteen feet apart. Bert you call first than wait a few minutes then Jack you call then we'll wait few minutes then I will call."

They fanned out and they listened after each call. Nothing was heard from below. "This area is pretty well secured from further breakouts of fire." Steve said. "So I'll send the other two men working nearby back here just in case you need them. We seemed to have this area pretty secure now. I will take the truck back and get help. Keep calling maybe he passed out from the fall and will recover enough to yell back eventually. Okay?"

Jack and Bert kept calling periodically. Jack wished he had binoculars. They really didn't know for sure the location he went over the cliff. The only hint was the burnt area that had definitely been partially put out by Harry where Jack was standing.

Harry wouldn't have wandered off surely. Where could he be? Jack yelled again and listened. The two other men arrived, that Jack had first asked if they had seen Harry. They said "Our area seems to be secured and there are no more ashes floating in this direction. This is Ralph and I am Norman. Have you found the missing man?"

"I am Jack and this is Bert. Harry, my friend is around here somewhere but I can't find him. We are assuming he fell over the cliff, but we can't see anything down there that resembles him. One of the fellows has gone for help." The two men looked over hoping to see Harry below.

"Do you see anything?" asked Jack. The two men said 'no' then the men started walking away from him in separate directions calling periodically then Bert, Ralph and Norman came back.

"Why do you think he went over at this spot?"

"Because the area has been charred and it is closest to the cliff. There are more burnt areas around here as you can see but this is the only one close to the cliff edge. If he was walking backwards, logically he might not have realized he was so close the cliff edge." They called some more but no answer was heard only the breathing of the men.

CHAPTER TWENTY

*E*ventually they saw the truck heading towards them. Steve was in the cab and there were four men on the back. They hopped off. One of the men named Melvin said he was a rock climber. He said he would be willing to go down. They had brought long ropes with them. Jack's anxious looks must have made them realize Harry had not been found.

Bert said "I'm not a rock climber but I have been on survival courses. On those courses, you rappel up and down ropes. I would be willing to go too. They got busy and tied the ropes to the back of the truck then dropped them over the cliff. Bert and the rock climber went over the cliff rappelling themselves off the jagged rock face with their feet, to the valley below. Meanwhile the other men fanned out calling for Harry.

When the two climbers landed, they each walked in different directions but they came up empty. When they met back at the ropes, they discussed the situation. "Jack feels that this is where he went over. We have searched and found nothing. What do you think?" Bert asked.

"We'll try again only this time call out at intervals and then listen." Melvin suggested.

The men up above had spread out again looking too. Jack stayed at the cliff rim. Where could Harry be? He just can't vanish into midair? What would he tell Laurie and Todd? They will be devastated and so will Jason and Bethany.

Down below, Bert and Melvin called and listened at intervals. Straining to hear a cry or moan. Again they met back at the ropes. "What now?" Melvin asked. "Is it possible he left without telling anybody?"

"Jack was pretty certain that wasn't a possibility. He is convinced Harry went over the cliff. The only solution is to check out the bushes. Somehow he may have gone down behind one or rolled under." Bert's eyes went instantly to the huge bush at the base of the cliff near the ropes but it appeared to be growing out of the cliff and undisturbed. He couldn't possibly be in there.

The two men checked systemically searching each bush around the area. Bert came back towards the rope again only this time he noticed the growing bush at the base of the cliff, from this angle, seemed to have broken foliage. He ran to the bush while yelling for Melvin. He dropped to his knees. He saw something but he wasn't sure what. Melvin was coming on the run.

"Can you pull back some of the branches so I can see in behind?"

"Bert that's impossible he can't be in there it is too tight against the cliff."

"Melvin look here, see these broken pieces, he has to be here."

Melvin and Bert pulled the bush away from the cliff. Bert looked under and there was a boot. "He is here. He must be unconscious. Now we just have to get him out. He must be badly hurt."

Melvin alleged. "We'll need a chainsaw. Call up to Jack for one. I'll try to manoeuvre under to see if he is all right. I can't believe that bush was able to swallow him so completely that we didn't notice it."

Up above the other men had returned saying no luck.

Jack's heart fell when a yell came up from below. Bert yelled. "We found him but he is unconscious. Send down a chainsaw."

Jack exclaimed peering over the cliff. "They have found him; looks like they are looking down behind that big bush at the base of the cliff to our left. Pull up one of the ropes and we'll send down a chainsaw."

The men leaped into action pulling up the rope while another positioned the chainsaw to be attached. They were quickly easing it down the cliff. Ralph who was an expert at knots had secured it well.

"Sounds like Harry must be seriously injured if he didn't answer

so we will have to rig a seat to remove him from down there."
Norman explained.

"That won't work. He will be bounced around too much against the
cliff which is quite jagged in places. We are going to need a stretcher."

"But we need the truck to secure the ropes. I can't believe with all
the forest around us this happened in a meadow area with no trees."
Norman declared shaking his head.

Jack suggested. "We've sent down the saw, so we can pull up the
ropes. Somebody take off with the truck. We need a stretcher and
some medical help. The rest of us will just have to hold the ropes if
they need to come up sooner."

Norman offered to take the truck to get the needed medical help.
Steve offered to go down to help below before the ropes were removed.
Jack looked around for the nearest tree in proximity to the cliff. The
only ones he saw were spindly, partially burned and wouldn't hold
a man's weight. All he could think of was that Harry needed help
right away.

Jack yelled "I want this truck out of here now." The ropes were
released, Norman started off just as voices from below yelled up that
splints were needed for a broken leg. As the truck sped pass Ralph he
yelled to Norman to bring splints.

"Steve if you want to go down we will hold the ropes. But I really
think we should wait for the truck to bring the stretcher."

Jack went back to the cliff. Looking down, he could see they had
cut most of the bush away. He could see Harry's injured body.

Melvin yelled up. "He has a broken arm too. He is fading in and
out of consciousness and is in a lot of pain." Steve said he had some
medical knowledge and he insisted on getting down there to help.
Three guys grabbed the rope to lower him down the cliff.

Bert and Melvin had managed to clear the bush enough so that
Harry was completely visible. The two men didn't want to move him
until he received profession help. Steve dropped down on his knees
beside Harry. His eyes were open but dazed. "Harry do you feel like
you have injured your back or head?"

Harry's reply was weak. "I have a terrific headache so I must have
hit my head a thwack on the way down. My back feels all right. It's

my left leg and my right arm that hurt the most." His voice trailed off as another wave of nausea set in.

Steve didn't like the position of his leg. The weird angle meant more than one broken bone. He went around the bush to get a better look at his leg. He gently ran his hands along the leg. He could feel the bone below his knee was broken and sticking out his skin. He cut the pant leg to expose the break. Steve could clearly see the bone protruding but the skin wasn't broken. He eased his hands over Harry's right arm, as best he could the way he was lying. It was broken just above the wrist.

Going back around the bush, he thought he would feel for damage if any to his head. He kept his fingers going lower to his neck. Easing his hand under Harry's neck it was liquidity. His hand was covered in blood when he gently removed it. Harry's helmet was at a precarious angle Steve noted. He debated leaving the helmet on to help protect the wound, which appeared to start under the helmet edge down into the neck, but thought better of it.

Steve took off his shirt and removed his t-shirt tearing it into strips. Tying the strip around Harry's head, then folded another wider piece into a pad and slipped that under the band for a pressure bandage.

Next he tried to move the leg, hampered by the bush, it was difficult. Even with Steve's gingerly movements it had still been too much for Harry who fainted again, letting the blackness immobilize the pain.

The truck was a long time returning. Jack was frantic. His agitation was driving the others crazy. When the truck finally arrived Jack ran over grabbing the door open before Norman could come to a full stop. "Were the hell were you?" Which was unlike Jack under normal conditions.

Norman spoke with concern. "I couldn't find a medical person. There was a bad situation over at Nelson RV Campgrounds. Several people were trapped by the fire and there were serious casualties, so all the medical help were sent over there. The ambulances are transporting the worst cases to Merritt hospital. I did get a stretcher and a doctor happened to arrive just as I was leaving." He indicated the man who had jumped out when the truck stopped. "They are trying to find a helicopter to come and help with the evacuation, as I explained that it was a pretty serrated cliff face."

"We are not waiting around. We will manage somehow." Jack was very positive about that. The men were already unloading the stretcher and supplies that would be needed. Norman backed the truck up to the cliff edge and Ralph quickly secured the ropes to the truck.

A couple of men were helping to ease the doctor down while others were tying his medical bag to a rope and lowering it. Upon release of the ropes they were quickly brought up so splints could be sent down.

"The best thing we can do with the stretcher is tie it at both ends and then if we keep it level and bring the two ropes up simultaneously it shouldn't bump too much, hopefully." Jack theorized.

Everyone was working as a team. Tying ropes moving supplies around, easing them down the cliff. Ralph was the one anchoring the ropes securely on the stretcher. Rather than just waiting around, the men practised with the empty stretcher lowering the ropes and pulling it up as levelly as possible. Moving around to find an area where it would snag the least on the jutting rock face. The truck was repositioned, the men were working more from the need to be helpful rather than necessity.

Down below the doctor had examined Harry. He stabilized the arm with a splint. The leg wasn't as easy. He had Steve help him straighten the leg a bit so he could splint it also. Thankfully Harry was still unconscious. The doctor complimented Steve for his efforts to help Harry with the pressure bandage. Melvin and Bert were observing the efforts at precision teamwork of the men trying to synchronize the lowering and raising of the stretcher over the jagged rock face with less snares to hamper the stretchers ascent.

When the stretcher finally arrived at the base of the cliff they settled it on the ground, thankful the ropes were long enough. Taking a blanket they went over to Harry. The doctor had stabilized him as best he could under these precarious conditions as he was still embedded behind the bush. Melvin and Bert had cleared as much as they could without harming him. Steve had put his shirt over Harry's face to protect him from flying debris, as they cut more bush away to ease his removal. The water tank had been partially ripped off him in the fall. Steve cut the other strap of the water tank to release Harry for transportation.

The two men laid the blanket close to the bush as they were able. They tried to pick up Harry, the small space making it almost impossible to grip him. He yelled out in pain as unconsciousness left him. They stopped immediately lowering him again. The doctor reached for his bag and gave Harry an injection for the pain, asking Harry how his head felt. While they waited for the shot to take him into semi-oblivion the men discussed the best strategy to lift him out into the open.

Melvin suggested. "I'll lift his shoulders two of you try to move his legs. I will move towards you. When we get clear of the bush we will try for a better hold." He bent over. "One Two Lift."

The men lifted in sync to Harry's audible groan of pain. The doctor was ready to stabilize the upper body with Melvin once they were clear of the bush. They lifted him clear and lowered his body onto the blanket in unison."

Then they each took a corner of the blanket, carrying it like a sling around his body, lifting Harry onto the stretcher at Melvin's signal. Strapping him in securely to the sounds of Harry's moan as he was still semi-conscious. They signalled for the stretcher to be hauled up.

They all held their breaths at the stretcher's ascent. It swung precariously as the men started hauling him up. The added weigh made it more difficult than when they had been practicing as they surmised it might. There were two men on each rope and Jack was giving the signals of keeping the stretcher coming smoothly and slowly by looking over the side of the cliff watching its progress.

Part way up the stretcher snagged on a jutting rock; Jack directed the men to ease the stretcher sideways to the left for two feet. At first it was anchored solidly on the protruding rock and refused to budge. Then they gave the one end a bit of a jerk, it tipped precariously. The watching men below all flexing muscles as if to catch it. Then the stretcher righted itself as it slowly swung sideways. The men were sweating as they eased the stretcher upwards again gradually. When the stretcher reached the top, they quickly disengaged the ropes to throw them down to the men waiting below.

Jack was already bending over Harry. "How are you doing? You gave us quite a scare." Harry gave a weak grin barely conscious. "Nothing to it." he said weakly. A deceptive statement that was for sure; thankfully the injection had deadened most of the pain.

The men were busy hauling up the medical bag, the chainsaw and the men from below, while the stretcher was being secured in the back of the truck. When all was secured at the top of the cliff, they untied the ropes for the final time.

They knew there wouldn't be room for everyone. The ones doing the hauling elected to stay behind and rest before trekking out. They had hauled four men and the stretcher up in double time for expedience sake.

The truck took off with three in the cab and Jack, Steve and the doctor with Harry in the back. Jack had taken responsibility for Harry as though he was family. He told antidotes about Laurie, hoping to occupy Harry's mind, while he hovered on the brink of unconsciousness. He was telling little tales of the younger Laurie growing up, the tricks they played on each other; as the younger brother being harassed by the older sister. And when Laurie had an admirer over his insisting on the right to share the living room. Jack's exaggerated humour made them laugh even Harry tried to crack a smile at one point before he let the black fade in with the jolting of the truck over the uneven ground

When they arrived at base camp Bert, Melvin, and Steve jumped off to be reassigned to the fire. The truck with Norman driving continued on speedily to Merritt.

Arriving at the hospital in Merritt, the doctor bustled Harry inside to be x-rayed. Jack felt the responsibility shift from his shoulders. He thanked Norman for all his help knowing he was anxious to get back to the fire line. Hurriedly, he entered the hospital only to be spotted by Bethany and Jason.

"Uncle Jack, what are you doing here?" Leaping towards him.

"Hi kids, is your mom with Aunt Betty?"

"Yes. We got to see Baby Anthony through the window." Bethany said excitedly.

"Baby Anthony?" Jack queried ardently.

"Yes everyone calls him that. Aunt Betty told us his real name was Anthony Stewart Wilson." Bethany said proudly. "I didn't know your middle name was Anthony." Jason exclaimed.

"Anthony Stewart Wilson is quite the handle for such a little guy that I saw so briefly." Jack voice replied.

"Uncle Jack, we can hardly see you with all that black." Bethany was staring up at him.

"Well I intend to remedy that right now. Grime and smoke are part and parcel of what fighting fires is all about." Heading down the hall to the washroom, an act that was becoming a habit it seemed. He wished he had a change of clothes. He felt so sweaty and was quite smelly he was sure. None the less, this was the best he could do he thought, looking in the mirror.

Jack was anxious to visit Anthony and Betty. On his way back to the kids he stopped the nurse coming his way to ask after Baby Anthony. The nurse said "The baby seemed to be responding nicely. The Merritt hospital staff has taken Baby Anthony to heart, and bulletins were being passed out regularly hoping the baby would beat the unfavourable odds. Your wife is doing fine too."

He didn't expect any news on Harry yet so he continued quickly back to the children. He saw Laurie with them. "Jack? The children said you were here. Are you finished at the fire?"

"No Laurie. I have some bad news."

"Harry?" Laurie felt her body sway. She just knew it had to be about him.

"Yes. Harry fell over a cliff while fighting some spot-fires and we just brought him in." Laurie's face took on a stricken look and her heart catapulted to her stomach.

"How bad is he? Tell me?" Laurie was devastated and a bit shocked at her intense reaction. Why did she feel so distraught? Harry had always been her stabilizer so she couldn't imagine him injured in any way.

"Harry is going to be okay. I'm sure. But he has a broken arm and leg and a head injury. He was in a lot of pain when we brought him in." Jack took his sister in his arms as she seemed to be pole-axed by the news. The tears sprang to Laurie's eyes.

A gasp came from behind them. "My dad is hurt?" The shocked voice was Todd's. Todd had arrived with some drinks in his hands.

The couple whipped around. In Jack's effort to console Laurie he had forgotten Todd.

"Yes Todd. He fell over a cliff. They have him inside OR attending to him."

"That was my dad I saw wheeled in?"

"Yes Todd. I didn't know you were here or I would have prepared you."

"I went to get drinks for Jason and Bethany. They were all right, while I was gone?" Todd asked as if he had shirked his duty.

"Todd it's okay, Bethany and Jason are fine on their own here and your dad will be okay too." Jack's voice was firm as though nothing could possibly be otherwise.

Laurie went over to Todd and hugged him. He looked up into her face. "Do you really think he will be okay Laurie?" Noting her tears.

"Todd, I hope so. The doctors are very capable here, look what they did for Betty and the baby." She said reassuringly as much for herself as Todd.

"How long ago did you arrive?" Laurie asked Jack.

"Time enough to wash my face and hands then speak to the nurse about Betty and Anthony. I hear Betty announced the baby's name as Anthony Stewart. We had a discussion on names but I hadn't realized any name had been carved in stone."

"Betty wanted the baby to have a name, she felt rather strongly about that." Laurie was pulling herself together but she still held onto Todd.

Jack continued watching the two embracing tightly. "It is too soon for any positive information on Harry. I was worried because it took us so long to find him. He was down in that ravine a long time, before we were able to get him out and bring him here. The guys that helped were amazing. They were the ones that made the rescue happen. We had eight guys looking for him besides me. It took us a long time because he was hidden under a bush at the base of the cliff."

"I am not telling you this to upset you but as an expression of the fear I felt for him. It ended finally when we arrived here. We did find him and that's what counts." The anxiety and the sick feeling was still within him, due to the difficulties in rescuing Harry. Needing to be on his own for awhile to regain his composure, after the intense drama experienced, he asked, "Do you mind if I go see Betty now?"

"I'm sorry Jack. Of course, Betty is doing fine and we have good reports on Anthony but I'll let Betty tell you. We'll wait here for you."

Jack gave a wave at the kids as he zoomed pass them. Laurie reassured Todd. "Jack gave the impression that your Dad would be okay and I trust his judgement. He is in good hands here."

Whenever she thought of Harry's broken body embedded behind that bush against the cliff, her insides shuddered. Poor Harry, he had always been there for her. She felt lost without his support.

Harry had always been a gentleman with her, never stepped out of bounds. Never touching except when she needed consoling. His only wish was to have her back in Indiana to share some good times but she had refused him. Now she was sorry she had told him she wouldn't go back there.

Todd was over the shock but he didn't want to break the connection with Laurie and her mothering. He had difficulties now, remembering his own mother. Since he had known Laurie, it was her face that came to mind when they were apart not his mother's. He wanted them as his family. They both tightened their grip on each other before their bodies parted.

Laurie was letting it sink in at last that she did love Harry. She wished now that she had said she would be willing to return to Indiana. Was it too late? What if he doesn't ask me again? What then?

Before she could think any further she saw a doctor coming to the nursing station. Her first thought was that it had to be about Harry. She strode over towards them. "Excuse me did you just take care of the man with a broken leg and arm?"

"Yes, are you the next of kin?"

"No but I am a very good friend of the patient. I am presently looking after his son. Why, is there something the matter?"

"He keeps asking for Laurie so I figure that she must be his wife."

CHAPTER TWENTY-ONE

"No. I am Laurie but not his wife. My brother Jack brought him into the hospital. Is he all right?" Worry in her voice.

"I was hoping to talk to his wife. However, if you are Laurie and looking after his son I guess it will be okay to discuss things with you. The bones will heal but his head injury seems to be causing a little confusion and disorientation. We don't know at this point how serious it is going to be." Dr. Connolly said. Laurie knew now, there was a real worry about his condition.

"What about the broken arm and leg?"

"Well the leg will take a long time to heal as I had to put a plate in it because of the type of fracture. He will be in a cast for awhile. Although the arm is badly broken, I was able to repair it. The head injury is the worry. When he recovers from the anaesthetic, there is a possibility of memory loss or black outs, which happens quite often in this type of head injury. He may have memory loss for a week, a month or even longer, or he could recover it in a few days." Dr. Connolly paused.

"He seems to really want to talk to Laurie the way he is calling for her, I suggest that I take you to see him. He seems agitated about something and you may be able to ease his mind. He needs to let the drugs alleviate his pain."

"His son, Todd is here, right over there. Do you think you could speak to him?"

The doctor and Laurie were heading towards Todd. "Yes that may be wise."

"Todd, I am Dr. Connolly. I operated on your father. He is in recovery. We had to heavily sedate him to repair the fractures. His arm was easier to fix than his leg. We put a plate in his left leg. The real worry is his head injury. He seems to be experiencing some confusion. Your father doesn't seem to know about his fall and the fire. We don't know, at this point, how serious his memory loss will be. So you have to be understanding for the next few days. Can I count on you for that?" He had reached out for Todd's shoulder and he exerted a slight pressure of concern to the boy. Looking up at the doctor Todd asked in a questioning voice. "Will my Dad ever be the same as he was before this happened?"

"By all means, I just meant he might have a memory lapse of details and your dad's concentration may be off for a few days. I don't believe it will be permanent or long term. Anything else you want to know?"

"Yes, when can I see him?" Todd said matter of factually.

"Well son, you can have a few minutes, but I would like to have Laurie see him first as he has been calling for her. So maybe you can stay here with these children till she returns." Turning to Laurie. "I assume the two children belong to you?"

"Yes this is Bethany and Jason." Laurie introduced them.

"Will you keep Todd company till your mother gets back, can I trust you to do that?" Jason and Bethany both solemnly nodded their heads yes.

"Good. We'll be returning shortly Todd." Dr. Connolly led her away.

When they reached the recovery room Dr. Connolly let Laurie precede him into the room. She quickly located Harry. They must have cleaned him up because there was no evidence of telltale grime like Jack had when he arrived.

"Harry?" Laurie said breathlessly.

"Look who I found. The Laurie you keep calling for I presume." Doctor Connolly said grinning. "Now you treat her good or I will whisk her away." He said jokingly.

Harry had his eyes closed but they flew open. "Laurie what are you doing here?" He studied her for a minute. Harry's raspy voice changed. "Laurie, I need you to find Todd and look after him until I get better." She was shocked. His voice was so impersonal and cold.

She felt she had been hit by a thunderbolt rendering her dumb. This was not the Harry that had begged her last night to go back to Indiana. The caring man that had stood by her during all her troubles. This man acted more like a stranger.

Dr. Connolly recognized what was happening by Laurie's expression. He gave Laurie a meaningful look. Then shook his head, as if to say 'no don't say anything'. Laurie looked back at Harry.

"Of course I will see to Todd while you are laid up. Todd is here, he wants to see you. I will send him in." Laurie stumbled to the door the tears welling in her eyes. At last she had recognized her feelings and now Harry acted as an acquaintance, nothing more. In each of the occasions they had been together Harry had always been a comfort to her not this stranger. How could she accept this now that she had finally realized she loved this man? She tried to contain her tears for Todd's sake.

"Laurie, wait I want to talk to you?" Dr. Connolly was hastening after her his stethoscope swinging. He yanked it from his neck and shoved it into his pocket. "Laurie, remember what I said before you went in to see Harry. He might be having memory problems. I could see you were hurt by his unfriendly manner. But I did warn you this might happen. I definitely think it will be short term."

Laurie tried desperately to keep the tears out of her voice. "But I don't understand. You said Harry was asking for me. How did he know I was here if he doesn't remember?"

"It was probable the anaesthetic caused him to call out for you. Many people say strange things, or ask for loved ones, or acquaintances while under the influence of anaesthetic. When I brought you in, he did question why you were here, then he just accepted it. In his mind he must have known that his son needed someone to look out for him so he asked you. Perhaps when Todd is finished seeing his dad you might leave and come back tomorrow. Maybe by then his mind may well be recovered."

"Yes, I will take them back to the motel. We were evacuated from the forest fire's path so we are staying here in Merritt."

"I'm sorry to hear that, but I didn't realize we had any evacuees in town." Dr. Connolly said puzzled.

"My sister-in-law is here in the hospital. She just had a premature baby caused by a fall with internal bleeding as well, which they operated on so we are staying in town."

"You mean Baby Anthony's mother?"

"Yes that is the one."

"I'm glad the baby is doing well and I hear the mother is too. This must be like a double whammy of concerns caused by the forest fire. I understand that was where Harry got hurt."

"Yes. We certainly didn't expect all this when we were told to evacuate. We're facing the possibility of my brother Jack and his wife losing their home, the sudden unexpected arrival of the baby and now Harry. Maybe tomorrow will be better." Just then Jack called to Laurie. He was hurrying over to them.

"Dr. Connolly, this is my brother, Jack Wilson, Baby Anthony's proud papa."

The doctor held out his hand. "Congratulations, that baby has won the hearts of all the staff here. I hope you don't mind the hospital staff has dubbed him Baby Anthony. He seems to be progressing nicely. He is putting up quite a fight like his brave father fighting the forest fires. I hear you are one of the ones that brought in Harry. The story I received was, you were instrumental in his rescue." Dr. Connolly noted the fatigue that was showing in this man's face, along with the red rimmed eyes and the smoky odour his clothes was permeating.

"Well it wasn't just me. There were many others involved in the actual rescue. It was certainly amazing the way they all worked as a team to save him." Jack appreciated their help, realizing that it could have been much worse without them. "But I am pleased to hear my son is holding his own in the uphill fight to survive. He does look like a fighter, doesn't he?" Jack said proudly with a big grin.

Turning to Laurie, Jack continued the grin which had even broadened. "I was just in to see him. Laurie, it makes me so proud that he is my son." Jack finished emotionally. Laurie gave him a hug.

"We better get back to Todd. I told him I would be right back. He wants to go in to see his father." Dr. Connolly said as their steps placed them back in the waiting room. "Todd, you can come in now." Todd jumped up and raced towards the doctor fear written all over his face with concern for his father.

"Remember Todd, I told you about your father's memory being affected by his injuries. So he may perhaps say odd things or maybe not. We don't know the full extent of the situation just yet. I just want you to be aware of his condition just in case." Todd walked into the recovery room. His father had his eyes closed.

Todd stood watching his father closely. It was a natural reaction as his hand reached out to touch him. To feel that his dad's hand was warm and responsive to his touch. His father's eyes popped open.

"Todd, how are you?" Harry asked in a rasping whisper the after effects of the anaesthetic. "I'm going to have to ask you to stay with Laurie for a few days. Do you think you can manage that till I can come home with you?" Todd looked at him oddly but kept a straight face.

"Yes Dad, I like staying with Laurie, Bethany and Jason. Last night Laurie let Jason and me stay in our motel room by ourselves." He quickly added. "But we didn't stay awake too late."

"How odd? How come you were with. . ." Puzzlement in Harry's voice as it trailed off. Then he closed his eyes and seemed to drift off into sleep. Dr. Connolly steered Todd out of the room.

"Are you okay Todd?"

"Yes. . . maybe it is the drugs that make him seem strange? Do you think that? Couldn't that cause his memory problem?" Todd asked hopefully.

"Possibly Todd, but I think it has more to do with his head injury, after all, he has quite a nasty gash on the back of his head, only time will tell. I have to leave you now so can you find your way back to Laurie and the others?"

"Yes sir." Todd headed back to the waiting room. Jack was hugging Laurie. Todd could see she had been crying. Laurie had just told Jack that Harry had treated her like a distant acquaintance and how upset she was because at last she had realized she loved him. Jack tried to reassure her that Harry had told him he loved her too. She was sceptical. He was assuring her that when Harry recovered his memory, he would remember his feelings.

When Laurie saw Todd approaching, she stepped away from Jack to pull herself together. Laurie walked towards Todd. "How is he?"

"Oh Laurie, he is talking so strangely. He is talking like the fire never happened." Todd voice broke and Laurie opened her arms to him Todd went willingly. "Laurie, he sounded so funny saying things like it was odd that I stayed with you last night. Dad obviously didn't remember we were staying at the same motel together. It was sure strange"

"Todd, we just have to accept what Dr. Connolly suggested, being patient over the next few days, which his mind needs to heal. His head injury is what is making your father seem like a different person. He did injure his head severely on the jagged rock face of the cliff, that is probably what is causing his memory lapse."

She gave Todd an extra firm hug and rested her head on his, to let him know that she was just as disturbed as he, at the change in his father.

"Now let's gather up the others and head back to the motel. Everyone must really be hungry by now. How about you Todd?" He was still young enough that the thoughts of food could distract him.

"Yes, I am." Todd turned towards Bethany and Jason.

"How is your Dad, Todd?" Jason inquired as Todd and Laurie joined them.

"He is sleeping but he talked to me so he must be okay." Not wanting to voice his concerns openly.

"Mommy, when are we going for something to eat? I'm hungry." Bethany whined. She was tired of waiting around in a hospital where you just had to be quiet and just sit.

"Right now that is our first priority. How about you Jack?" Laurie had put on a smile for the children's benefit sounding cheerful. Inside she was still wounded at Harry's attitude towards her.

"Yes, let's get this show on the road. Is there a good restaurant that you are aware of near here? Lots of good wholesome food is what I need. The food back at camp taste like smoke. Talking about smoke, Betty was chiding me about the smoky smell I was exuding. I wish I had a complete change of clothes." Jack was feeling grimy still. Wanting a shower but not wanting to hold them back from eating.

"There are some clothes back at the motel. Betty packed them just in case you could be with us. There is a restaurant that is near the motel. The food is scrumptious. The cook is a wonder."

"Yeah." Piped up the young voices.

"The children can play a bit when we get back to the motel. They need to expel their energy before they eat so you will have time for a shower and a change of clothes." Laurie knew that Jack would feel bad about the delay.

They all piled into Laurie's car. Jack directed the car towards the motel, which promised a shower and fresh clothing, his prime concern at this particular moment.

Maddy greeted them herself. Seating them in a roomy booth, she asked about Baby Anthony. Apparently Baby Anthony's early arrival had made the local news mentioning Betty and her preemie son as casualties of the forest fire situation near Melville, that had ended happily with the birth.

"Maddy, this is my brother, Jack. He is the baby's father." Laurie declared.

Jack acknowledged Maddy's question. "The baby is coming along better than expected. He is giving it a good fight." Jack finished proudly.

"I am pleased to hear he is doing so well. Now folks what can I cook for you? Are you hungry because I love cooking up a storm? I better get back to the kitchen. Lorraine will come and give you menus." Maddy hurried away like a rush of wind before anyone had an opportunity to reply to anything she had said.

"Mommy, how can someone cook up a storm?" asked Bethany.

"That just means she enjoys cooking lots of food for people." Laurie smiled at her daughter.

A girl approached their table carrying menus. "Hi, how are you? My name is Lorraine." Handing out menus all round. "I'll be back to take your order when you have decided. I will just give you a moment to browse." She darted off before anyone could say anything.

The menus were instantly scrutinized and choices made. They gave their order to the waitress upon her return.

"Laurie, I don't feel I can go back to fight the fire anymore; first the drama over Betty and Anthony, then the dread of not being able to find Harry, and finally the rescue after we found him. I somehow felt responsible for Harry because I took him back with me. It has just sapped all my energy. I feel I have nothing left to give anymore. Do you think that is cowardly of me?"

"No Jack. What you have been through in these last four days is more than most men have to endure. Worrying about us the two days before we were evacuated, were bad enough without the added worry over Betty and Harry as well. I'm sure they wouldn't even imagine you would return."

"But Harry's and my car are still there. I have to go back." Jack realized.

"Jack, we can go back in a couple of days to get them but not right now. We have my car here. We need you with us. I feel really drained too. I need your moral support to get through this latest occurrence with Harry. Betty needs your support with Anthony until he is more stable. Besides if you go back for your car you will feel obligated to fight the fire again. You know you will."

Lorraine showed up with their dinners. Laurie supervised the kids as they salt and peppered their food and made sure their napkins were close at hand.

Jack took the time to savour Laurie's words and the die was cast. He was going to take a couple of days to be with his wife and son. The more he thought about it, he felt the burden of his responsibility of the fire had been lifted from his shoulders. He knew his duty was to his family now and always.

Jack started eating with a lighter heart and a deeper hunger. He smiled as he looked around at his family and Todd, satisfaction showing on his face.

If only she could solve her problems that easily. She dreaded the next few days. *What if he didn't get better? Had she missed out on the opportunity of sharing some good times with Harry?* Laurie played with her food rather than enjoying it.

Jack and the children were keeping up a lively conversation. He had always loved to joke with them. He gave Todd an equal share in the bantering. He liked this boy of Harry's. He hoped Harry would have a complete recovery. It would be hard for Todd until his dad got better.

There was still some time to wait for Betty, Anthony and Harry to recover before this family could enjoy complete happiness. The fire is always the victor claiming its victims as it's vortex of flames races through the forest and peoples' lives in its path.

CHAPTER TWENTY-TWO

*A*fter their meal, the hospital drew them back, as their thoughts were with their loved ones residing within its walls and not wanting to be anywhere else. The nursing station attracted them at once. Answers to their concerns would be best dealt with there. The nurse recognized them with a big smile. She had good news for them.

"Baby Anthony is gaining weight. He has gained half a pound which is encouraging. Betty was able to walk down to the nursery to feed him instead of pumping the milk like she has been doing. The baby was allowed out of the incubator only long enough to feed him. The doctor thought it would be best for both of them." The nurse's voice was full of pleasure being able to impart this message about Anthony.

"The second good news is that Mr. Cochrane is more wakeful and he seems less agitated now as though he is more comfortable. We have moved him to room 202." Her smile was encompassing the children too. "Mr. Cochrane can have one visitor at a time but only for five minute intervals with a half hour in between. He is having intense headaches, so we want to keep his visits to a minimum, for the first little while."

Todd being anxious was the first to go up to see his father. He approached the room quietly. He stood at the door peering in. His father was in a raised position elevated by the bed's mechanism. His eyes were closed. He crept forward not wanting to disturb him but Harry must have sensed his presence, because his lids slowly ascended into awareness.

"Hi Todd." Harry's voice was sleepy sounding like he was sedated.

"Hi Dad. How are you feeling?"

"A little bit better since you were in last. Are Laurie and the children here with you?" Harry was sounding doubtful that Laurie could still be here, although she had agreed to look after Todd.

"Yes, Jack brought us."

"Jack?"

"Yes Laurie's brother."

"I would like to meet him."

"Dad, you know Jack. You met him before and worked with him at the forest fire. The fire was where you were hurt." Todd imparted with great concern.

"Yes I'm sorry. . . uh. . . they told me that was how come I was injured and brought here. Exactly where is here? They only gave me details about being injured while helping put out a forest fire near Melville."

Todd's heart sank. This was worse than when he had visited his father before. He squared his shoulders remembering Dr. Connolly's talk about his Dad's memory and lack of concentration, then he plunged into an explanation.

"We are in Merritt. Laurie and the children were visiting her brother Jack and Betty in Melville a town near the forest fire. We were heading home from a Wilderness Adventure trip in South Dakota and the state troopers requested our assistance in helping to fight the forest fire." Todd paused but his dad was still looking puzzled.

"We were instructed to tell people to leave their homes in Melville as the town had to be evacuated, because the fire was heading that way. That was when we came across Laurie, Bethany and Jason. We are here in Merritt because Betty, Jack's wife had a baby and you are here in the hospital because you fell over a cliff, when you went back with Jack to help fight the forest fire." He paused again hoping that his dad would remember the things that he was mentioning. Todd didn't know how to express to his father the worry he had about his loss of memory.

Harry took in willingly all that Todd was saying in the hopes that the fog would lift in his mind. Nothing was making sense, and he could hear the worry in his son's voice, that something wasn't right. All of this was news to him. The last memory he had was the plans for the Wilderness Adventure, and now Todd was saying it was over and a few days thrown in, that he couldn't account for. Harry could see Todd was upset but he felt helpless because he couldn't remember and the headache was becoming excruciating.

"You know Todd when you are injured strange things occur and that must be what is happening to me now." Harry gave himself a shot of painkiller to ease the throbbing before he continued slowly. "There is no other explanation for the time lapse." Harry was having trouble hiding the persistent pain which Todd could see plainly on his father's face.

"Dad, my five minutes is up. I have to go but Jack is coming in to see you in half an hour. Maybe if you talk this over with him, his explanation may make things much clearer for you." Todd had such hope in his voice. Maybe he was just too young to help his father comprehend the missing time.

"Okay but tell him to give me time to close my eyes and get rid of this headache. I love you, Todd." Harry wanted to give into the darkness that was seeping towards his mind.

"I love you too, Dad." Todd reached over the bed and hugged him gingerly so as not to hurt him. But Harry closed his good arm around his son and clung to him. He finally released him. They both had tears in their eyes. Todd being scared at his father's inability to remember their time together these past few weeks. Harry, because he couldn't recall a space of time in his life. Why couldn't he remember? Was there something important that had happened during that time? Something was needling the back of his mind but he couldn't figure out what it was. The pain was becoming overpowering.

"Bye Dad. I will be back tomorrow."

"Bye Todd, please do and maybe by then I will remember the missing time." Harry knew Todd was frightened at his behaviour. He wanted to ask, is there something I should know, but he couldn't bring himself to ask about the unknown. His head and his injuries were throbbing too much. He gave the button on his IV a push to medicate the pain again, to let him slip into oblivion where the pain was dispersed.

Todd left with a lift of his hand, but his father had already closed his eyes.

His feet lagged not wanting to join the others. He needed a little time to take in his conversation with his father. How could someone lose almost three weeks of events of current happenings? Could he believe Dr. Connolly that his father would recover? Will it be more harmful if I talk about the time he lost, or will I speed up the recovery of his memory? Todd's mind kept circling.

When he joined the others they could see he was upset. He went to Laurie like a homing pigeon. "Laurie, Dad can't remember coming to South Dakota at all. He doesn't recall the wilderness trip or the forest fire. He doesn't remember meeting Jack and Betty." Todd let the tears flow now.

"I know Todd. These next few days are going to be hard on all of us. Remember what the doctor said he probably would have memory problems for a few days."

"Laurie, he looks so defeated. I have never seen my dad like this before. He has always been so powerful in every way. To see his leg and arm in a cast along with bandages on his head makes him look so helpless."

"I know Todd, it breaks my heart to see him this way too." Laurie looked over his head at Jack for help.

"Todd, we were just going down to see the baby. Maybe the nurse will let us closer this time." Jack was hoping to distract the boy knowing that only time and care would help his father.

Todd eased back from Laurie. "Do you really think we could?" He raised his arm wiping his eyes dry on his sleeve like a typical boy.

"Why don't you and Jack go? Perhaps then the nurse will let you have a closer look." Laurie was thankful for Jack's suggestion. She continued with some other news that she wanted to tell them.

"Do you know we have the opportunity to see some special event to raise money for the fire victims, who lost most of their homes and belongings? The nurse told me part of Melville did get burned apparently before they could divert it. Just four houses on the out skirts of town. They want us to attend as their guest of honour. The nurse had a call from the Mayor. She was to pass on the message to us, because he was sure we would want to be there. Plus the Mayor was letting the staff of the hospital know about the special event. I spoke with him briefly. Now Todd you go with Jack and I will take Bethany and Jason in to see Betty."

Jack took Todd by the shoulder gave him a squeeze then said. "Come on, let's go see this son of mine. He is a real scrapper and he should be almost ready to solo without that incubator."

Todd went willingly. He had never seen anything as miniature as Anthony before. He didn't want to ever hold him but he just wanted to admire this little baby.

The nurse did invite them in closer this time. Some of the wires had been removed so he looked less frightening to him. He was given a glove to put on so he could touch the baby by putting his arm through a hole in the plastic incubator. To touch this squirming helpless son was a incredible experience.

Jack needed this connection to this tiny form of life who was quickly invading his heart. His son! He rubbed the tip of his finger ever so gently against Anthony's cheek then down his arm that was flailing a bit at his touch.

Todd looked on with awe. The way the baby had seemed to have grown, since he had first seen him from way back behind the window. He wondered what it would be like to touch him like Jack was doing, to have that connection with this newborn.

The nurse signalled that their time was up. Jack gave the baby one last pat on his cheek like he was kissing him. His broad grin was 'thank you' enough for the nurse.

"Come on Todd, we can go see Betty now."

"Anthony is so tiny. It is like he is hardly there." Todd said in wonder.

"He is tiny but he is definitely all there." Jack replied proudly.

Betty was sitting brightly in a chair with a pretty dainty nightie and housecoat in a brocade pattern, that Jack had picked out for her in anticipation of her eventual trip to the hospital. Seeing how pretty she looked sitting there, he was happy with his purchase.

In fact, Betty was looking so well she would be able to leave soon. She had been telling Laurie, when they entered the room, that she didn't want to leave until Anthony was able to leave too.

Jason was asking about their little cousin and Betty was supplying the answers. Jack and Todd joined in the conversation. Todd with awe in his voice.

Laurie seemed to have removed herself from the scene. She moved to gaze out the window. But her mind was with the man in 202. Harry was her special concern right now. She couldn't believe she had refused his offer of a closer relationship so blatantly. When now she realized she loved him, needing to be near him. To see him daily was all she wanted now.

. . .

Harry was just dozing. His troubled mind would not let him escape into the oblivion that he longed for. *Why was he not able to remember the events of the past two weeks or so?*

Todd had said they had completed the Wilderness Trip which was supposed to be two weeks in duration. Gone! How is that possible? If only my head wasn't hurting so much. Please let me go to sleep? No, I want answers but it hurts. It is too soon for medication.

Why can't I remember? What is Laurie doing here? Last thing he remembered she was in South Carolina. Do I really know Jack and Betty? Todd says I do. Oh my head, my leg and my arm I don't know which hurts worse. I just have to take more medication. I have to quit worrying about the time I am missing. Harry reached for the button and hopefully oblivion. Why can't I remember? Is Laurie back in my life? Have we perhaps changed in our relationship? No, Laurie will just leave. She always does. She always does . . .

. . .

A noise in the room caused Harry to open his eyes. There was a man standing there but he didn't recognize him. He didn't look like a doctor.

"Hello Harry. How are you feeling?"

This man sounded like he knew him. *Todd said there was a forest fire. Laurie, Jason and Bethany were here. Laurie was visiting her brother*

Jack and Betty. Is this man Jack? Why couldn't he remember? Harry kept staring at the man. His head was hurting more every time he delved into his memory. The man was looking uncomfortable.

"My head has cloudiness. I can't seem to clear it. My son says I have lost some time." *He didn't want to say memory. That sounded too permanent.* "My arm gives me more discomfort than my leg. Do I know you?" Harry finally asked the question in a puzzled voice.

"Yes Harry you do. I am Laurie's brother Jack. I was with you when you were injured. You fell over a cliff. I was not beside you but in the general vicinity. We had a terrible time finding you. You were down behind a dense bush smack up against the cliff face. We had quite a time getting you out of there, once we located you. Norman and I brought you into the hospital."

"Norman? Do I know him?"

"No but there were several men helping me to rescue you. We managed to get you out much faster than waiting for a helicopter. It was something to see, the way they worked so hard to remove you." Jack's voice held such pride in the men he was talking about. Harry's head was tightening in pain like a steel band was binding it. *Why couldn't he remember?*

"Thank you and to all the other men that helped me. Was I unconscious when they brought me up? Is that why I can't remember?" Harry asked.

"Part of the time you were out of it but you came to enough to make one response." Jack was hoping his explanation was helping him.

"I can't remember. I know I have frightened my son with my lapse in memory. I am sorry. . . you are a complete stranger to me. Has Laurie introduced us? You are Jack, Laurie's brother that Todd talked about? You must have been introduced to me if I fought the fire with you." His head was hurting so much, he could hardly think what he was saying.

"Yes, and it was my wife, Betty that you brought into the hospital. She had a baby and internal injuries."

"Betty? Baby? Injuries?" Harry's face was showing the results of the pain he was enduring in his attempts to remove the cloudiness from his mind.

Jack could see the deep pain engraved on his face. Would it be wise to stop or keep on trying to help him remember? He was out of his element here.

The pain was just too much so Harry reached for the button that was becoming his lifeline. Jack reached over and helped him push the button.

Jack let his hand reach out to Harry's shoulder. Giving him a comforting squeeze he said. "Give yourself time, Harry. The doctor says you will be all right in a few days. Your mind will clear. I just wanted to see for myself that you were okay." Jack applied another gentle squeeze. "We were some worried about you for a while, out there at the fire. Finding you was quite a challenge, and a further challenge to haul you up with so many injuries. You rest now. Let the medication help you. It is the best thing for you at the moment."

Harry's eyes closed and he appeared to be giving into the need for sleep. Then his eyes popped open. "Was the baby a boy or a girl?"

Jack chuckled. "Anthony Stewart Wilson quite a mouth full for a four pound preemie."

"Congratulations. How is your wife?"

"She is fine now thanks to you. You took care of her when she fell. Her fall caused internal injuries and then the baby came prematurely."

"I'm sorry I can't remember, Jack." The pain was invading his head so much that it felt like it would explode. *Why wouldn't the painkiller work? He needed his lifeline before his head was no more.* Harry's eyes were closed but Jack knew he wasn't sleeping. The pain etched on his face was too much in evidence.

"Don't sweat it Harry. It will come back to you. Dr. Connolly assured us of that. I'll get going Harry, take care. It probably would be best if you leave it for now. Don't push yourself to remember." Jack turned away. It was making him feel inadequate not being able to take away the pain and the fog in Harry's mind. Jack wanted to take some of the pain into himself after all he was partly responsible for Harry being involved in the fire that caused his fall.

Harry's voice came racked in pain and barely audible. "Jack will you tell Laurie how much I appreciate her looking after Todd?"

Jack turned back. "Okay Harry but you can tell her yourself soon, she is coming in next. You can have visitors for 5 minutes every half hour." He thought this might cheer Harry.

"Jack, tell her my thanks, but she won't have to bother to see me." His voice was slurring off but Jack could still hear the impersonal sound in Harry's voice. Laurie was going to be devastated. The message wasn't what she was hoping for. Jack wondered if he should see Dr. Connolly or if he was even around still. Not that the doctor could change anything with his memory.

Jack just wanted reassurance Harry would regain his memory soon. It was sad when you worked so hard to save someone's life, creating a kinship, and he is completely unaware you exist. He wanted more than ever to take away the pain and cloudiness. He said helplessly. "Well I'll be going Harry."

CHAPTER TWENTY-THREE

Jack stopped at the nurse's station to tell her how much pain Harry was in and asked for Dr. Connolly. The nurse said she would try to page him.

He couldn't go back to Laurie and hurt her with Harry's message. He just couldn't. He felt sick about it. He wanted to take the coward's way out and go in to see Betty but he also wanted to talk to Dr. Connolly.

He walked to the huddled group waiting expectantly. Laurie was looking at him beseechingly. The worried look on her face was showing her trepidation.

Jack's delay in saying anything caused Laurie to ask. "How is he, Jack?" The anxiety in her voice was a reflection of his bleak face.

"Not so good. His loss of memory is causing excruciating headaches so I don't think you should go in to see him. Let him rest and let the medication heal him. He is trying too hard to remember, when people talk to him. I think you should forego your visit, until he is a bit better." The look on Laurie's face was inconsolable.

"But Jack, I want to see him. You know that." Laurie's shocked voice held the tears she was trying to keep hidden.

"Harry is in too much pain right now to see anyone. Please Laurie, give him a chance to let the medication do its healing? Here comes Dr. Connolly. I need to talk to him."

Jack rushed towards him to forestall him from reaching Laurie.

"Can I help you?" Dr. Connolly inquired.

"Yes, I was just in to see Harry. He knows nothing about the forest fire or being in South Dakota? He doesn't remember about my wife having a baby or the wilderness trip in the past two weeks. He has lost eighteen days." Jack voice was escalating with worry.

"I was afraid of that. Well I am still hoping it will come back within the next few days. I mentioned this before. I have seen cases where this happens, but it does come back. However, it is possible that Harry's memory loss is more severe than we anticipated. I wish I could reassure you further than that, but it is more a case of a waiting game. The mind will heal but Harry is dealing with a lot of pain and his mind may not be able to cope with it right now."

"It is worse than you think. My sister and he had almost come to an understanding for a permanent relationship, and now he doesn't remember and treats her like a distant friend. He doesn't want to see her even. Laurie is taking it pretty hard."

"Did they have that type of a relationship before the forest fire?"

"Well no not exactly if you know what I mean? They missed each other when they were apart, but they hadn't actually recognized their feelings for each other till the forest fire threw them together again. Laurie will be devastated, if I tell her that Harry doesn't want to see her. I managed to put her off saying he was in too much pain but what about tomorrow? She won't keep accepting the excuse then?" Jack voice reflected his qualms for his sister.

"I know Jack but we have no choice. These things happen. The body is a wonderful entity but it also knows when it needs to heal itself. This memory loss may be a way of blocking out incidents that possibly are too much for his mind to accept, such as severe pain or the trauma of falling without end. We don't know at what point he was rendered unconscious. We can only hope it won't be too long, before he completely regains his memory. Sometimes the brain stops the process of accumulating memories during brain injuries. The last clear memories can be days, weeks or even a year before. The body has its own time-clock when these things happen. It will cure itself when it is ready. The mind is a fragile thing. It is best if it comes back naturally." Dr. Connolly paused.

"Unfortunately you have to be the one to break this to Laurie. She needs to know the truth. It would be upsetting to Harry for her to go in there the way things stand right now." Dr. Connolly's voice held remorse and sympathy for Laurie.

"Thank you for seeing me." Jack turned and walked towards his sister.

Laurie was suspended as if frozen in time; knowing full well that Jack's explanation had not rung true.

What could he tell her to make it less demoralizing? Jack hated to hurt her, particularly now when at last, she had recognized her love for Harry. How could he tell her Harry didn't want to see her? Jack wanted to run the other way, but her expression drew him towards her. He couldn't leave her like this.

"Jack, what did the doctor say? Harry is okay isn't he? What aren't you telling me?" Laurie asked with shrinking feeling knowing Jack was holding something back.

This was the cruellest thing he had ever done but he had no choice. Laurie had to be told right now.

"Laurie, Todd told you Harry has no memory of the last eighteen days. Well he seems to have lost sight of his feelings for you too. He doesn't want . . ."

"Doesn't want what?"

"I'm sorry Laurie to have to be the one to tell you . . . Harry doesn't want to see you. He doesn't think it is necessary. He just wanted me to pass on his thanks for looking after Todd." Jack grabbed her as her knees caved in and she would have fallen to the floor a keening noise seeping out of her mouth.

"How can that be? You told me that Harry told you he loved me when you were driving back to the forest fire." Laurie's face was drained of all colour. The shock written on her face was tearing Jack apart.

"Laurie, Harry told me he loved you and he meant it. I am very sure about that. This is only a temporary lapse of memory. Harry will remember he loves you. We just don't know how long it will take for his mind to accept the time he lost. Dr. Connolly is positive he will regain his memory. Laurie, I wish I could say otherwise but that is the way it is for now."

Laurie looked like she wanted to go scream 'No, No', to Harry. Jack tightened his grip. She was struggling but he held on, she stopped flailing around and sunk against him crying. She was slumming in defeat.

"Sometimes we have to accept the bad before the good can come into place, but it will come, just like Harry's memory will come back. In the meantime we just have to take it one day at a time. Todd needs you to help him. He is only a child and is frightened by all this."

Laurie back stiffened at last. "You said Harry told you he loved me."

"Yes he told me when we were driving back to the fire. He intended to win you over when he got back."

"I love Harry too. I wonder why I didn't recognize that sooner. He asked me to go back to Indiana so we could spend some enjoyable time together. I wouldn't give him the answer he wanted. Oh Jack, if he asked me now I would say yes. But now it is too late."

"It is never too late. You will get a chance in the future to tell him I know you will. In the meantime. Todd needs your support while we wait." Jack held her at arm's length. "Come on, where is that brave sister of mine that use to look out for her little brother? Dry your eyes and let's get the kids and go back to the motel. Our prayers tonight will be for Harry's speedy recovery." Jack grinned at her trying to boaster her moral.

Laurie wiped her tears on the handkerchief Jack pressed into her hand. She said in a firm voice. "Let's go get the children. We can pick up ice cream on the way back to the motel." Todd really loved ice cream she knew.

There was deep sadness in them but their thoughts held hopes of a happier tomorrow.

· · ·

The next day which was Sunday was the day of the commemoration for the burned-out victims. Laurie and the children's names had accompanied the notice in the local paper depicting the fundraiser benefit for the burned-out victims, mentioning that they were staying in town. There was also a good news update on Baby Anthony's fight for survival.

She had bought new outfits for everyone so they would look good. They had spent the morning shopping for them. Jack had gone to the hospital to see Betty and the baby. Laurie had begged off saying the shopping spree was a priority, and the children needed a break from the hospital. Besides the new clothes she hoped would give everyone a lift they badly needed. The stores all insisted on giving them discounts on everything they purchased.

Laurie was amazed at the generosity of these people, who were so kind and caring for others. She wanted to be a part of this community. Maybe they should all move here including Todd and Harry, remembering the couple that had tried to persuade them of this very same thing in the saloon. They could all start over together.

The thought was one she couldn't shake all day, as the people made such a fuss over the children and her. Even Jack came into special attention, when they presented a new wardrobe for Baby Anthony which also included a car seat, stroller and cradle. He had tears in his eyes, the way these people had taken his son into their hearts. The populace figured that the new preemie needed their gifts, in case Baby Anthony's unexpected arrival wouldn't have given the couple time to prepare; a further display of this community's generosity.

When Jack in his thank you speech said their home was intact so they weren't part of the burned-out victims, but he would accept these gifts on his son's behalf. He mentioned with sadness, the lives lost at the Nelson's RV Campgrounds and other casualties he knew about.

Next Todd was called upon to accept on his father's behalf, the acknowledgement of the Town of Merritt of his father's bravery, disregarding his own safety during the course of his duties in fighting the fire, and as a result Harry Cochrane, his Dad, had become one of the casualties of the forest fire. Todd was speechless as the Mayor presented the large gold key to the town and a certificate honouring his father. Todd had to stand with his hand engulfed in Mayor Davidson's hand while their picture was taken. He was so in awe of the situation he forgot to smile.

The Mayor requested that Bethany and Jason join Todd on stage. The Mayor presented them with passes to the swimming pool as a welcome to the community. The three taking each other's hands bowed to the crowd in thanks. Laurie and Jack standing watching were beaming broadly at the children.

The bright flashes were going off consistently as they were told to hold up their passes. The children noted then that their individual names were on their passes in bold letters. The Mayor closed the ceremonies with a special thank you for the generosity of the community for the burned-out victims. Saying, there are donation jars located all around the grounds as well as boxes for the clothes and furnishings, that were being donated as well. The park also contained games of chance and contests with all proceeds going in with the donations to the fire victims.

The big day ended with a BBQ and Corn Roast which drew the hungry, with smells of charcoal and roasting meat flowing in the air. The abundant desserts were a showing of the community's wonderful culinary art. The City Park and Community Centre were a mass of people enjoying the fair. The community was unified, in the caring for the fire victims, filling the centre and spilling outside to the tables there. Laurie, Jack and the children preferred to be out of doors enjoying their picnic dinner. Ladies kept coming with trays of food and desserts for them, taking the opportunity to chat.

The donation tally was announced after dessert. The community had dipped deeply into their pockets and the burned-out families would have a fresh start in replacing their lost belongings.

Laurie had put her worries of Harry on hold. She was very appreciative of the generosity of this community and spoke her gratitude in her conversation with them. She wished that Betty and Harry had had the chance to be part of the feeling oozing from these warm hearted townspeople. Then her problem slipped back unwanted when she thought, if only Harry had his memory back, it would be a perfect day.

Mayor Davidson interrupted her thoughts when he announced, over the loud speaker, that the fire was contained at last and all that was left was the mop up of the smouldering ground to assure that there were no more outbreaks. The crowd cheered ecstatically. The noise resounded all around the park in waves almost. It was a fitting end to the day.

Eventually, Laurie indicated it was time to leave, saying many heartfelt goodbyes to many of the folks that came to wave them off, as they left the park to head back to the motel.

. . .

Laurie had been invited to take in the happenings at the local theatre that night. She had been informed it was to be a funny children's program, the kids might enjoy. Jack was going to the hospital to see Betty and Anthony. He wanted to give Betty the news of the day's events. Laurie knew she was avoiding the hospital but she couldn't help herself. She knew she couldn't be there and not see Harry. It would just hurt too much.

Todd was torn. He wanted to see his dad and tell him about the gold key and the certificate of bravery but he also wanted to go to the theatre with Bethany and Jason. Jack convinced Todd that he could see his dad tomorrow, the delay could hopefully give him extra time to recover his memory. Todd accepted Jack's philosophy to go to the theatre instead of the hospital.

The program which was geared to kids was also entertaining for the adults. Laurie and the children, in their laughter, shed some of their anxieties which uplifted their mood. They talked animatedly all the way back to the motel. Laurie was watching them with amusement.

When the children had received their awards, Laurie had wanted to jump up on the stage to give her special thanks, for the many hours they sat waiting quietly. That is what the award truly should be, being supportive in their quiet behaviour. Her heart was bursting with pride when thoughts of Harry invaded her mind. If only he would recover his memory and his need of her, then her happiness would be complete.

Later when Laurie was in bed trying to sleep her mind was floating. The events of today had filled her heart except for the corner she saved for Harry, that he wasn't even aware of. Why had she not realized her feelings when he asked her to go back to Indiana? He only wanted them to share some good times together.

Now all she wanted to do was dash to the hospital, to be with him, while his body healed in sleep. But not when he awoke, and looked at her with distant but kindly eyes of an acquaintance. Her heart would break all over again. She knew it was because of her abrupt departure in Florida. Regardless, she was going to see him tomorrow. Not seeing him was agony too. She knew she just had to accept the estrangement but see him she must. Finally with this resolve she slipped into sleep.

· · ·

Jack was sleeping in Todd's motel room. When they awoke Todd's mind went to his dad. His face held a look of apprehension.

"Will my father feel better today, enough to recognize the missing time?" His voice was watery and anxious. Jack was viewing the boy so mature in his ways but still a young boy. His sympathy went out to him, wanting to console him.

"The way the doctor explained the condition to me was that the body and mind have their own schedule of healing. When the agenda is met, he will return to normal. Time is of the essence here but we just don't know how much time." Jack continued feeling his way to help.

"We don't know what may trigger the response he needs to remember, but the doctor was quite confident that he will recover. The only thing we can do to aid the process is to visit him mentioning the past weeks, but if he seems agitated or frustrated stop. There is no magic antidote but just time. I know you are frightened and I can understand that but the mind lapse will resolve itself. Will that help you to view things easier?"

"Yes, I will keep in mind what you have said. I want him to recover. I want my Dad back fully. We should be getting in touch with my Dad's office about our delay. Marvin, his partner will be wondering what happened to him."

"Todd, we will call him today. I think we should go to the hospital to get the latest information on his condition first, before we call." Todd accepted Jack's explanation.

"I am glad the forest fire is finally out. You will be able to return to your home soon won't you?"

"Soon but I think we should wait till the smoke clears and there is no chance of flare-up before I expose Betty and Anthony to the air around our home. The smoke will stay for awhile, unless there is a strong wind sending it in the opposite direction. The house is bound to need a lot of airing too." Jack was drawn to this young boy with his mature outlook.

"Do you think you would like a change of scene? You could come with me to get my car. A fellow at the activities yesterday offered to drive me. Maybe Bethany and Jason would like to come too. Then we can check on the house and neighbours while we are there. Would you like to join me?"

"Yes" Todd said eagerly. "I'll go tell Jason if he is awake and invite him for you okay?" Jack chuckled at the change in the boy so quickly, the result of being young.

"Fine son, you do that while I shower and shave."

Todd whizzed out the door, dashing to the next motel room. He knocked lightly in case slumbering was being enjoyed by someone inside. Jason came to the door looking sleepy-eyed. He perked up when he saw Todd.

"Do you want to go with your Uncle Jack and me to get his car from the fire area?"

"Yes that will be neat." He answered excitedly. "I will have to ask my mom first." He ended with hope evident in his voice.

"What is it Jason?" Laurie's voice was getting closer as she appeared behind Jason in her housecoat.

"Mom, Todd and Uncle Jack want me to go with them to pick up Uncle Jack's car. Can I go? Pleaseeee?" Jason's eyes and speech was so beseeching.

"Bethany is invited too." Todd added quickly noticing Bethany pressing her way into the doorway too.

"Where?" Bethany had been so anxious to see Todd that she had not paid attention to the talking.

"The fire area, to pickup Uncle Jack's car and we will check on the house while we are there." Todd replied.

"Not really. I will stay here with mommy. It is too smoky there and it makes me cough." Even though she liked tagging along coughing wasn't fun.

"Mom, can I go still?" Jason glared at his sister for putting up proposed problems.

"All right, the fire is out so it should be safe enough. You can go but stick real close to your Uncle Jack and do whatever he tells you." Jason let out a resounding yippee racing inside to get dressed. Laurie yelled after him. "Not your new clothes." They were piled over a chair which he was heading for in his haste to get dressed.

"Todd would you like to come in?"

"No thanks. I will go back and tell Jack, Jason is coming. He is shaving."

"Fine, you do that and we will get ready for the day. Come Bethany." Todd hurried back to his motel room. Laurie shut the door. She would take Bethany with her to the hospital. Surely Harry wouldn't order her out of his room if she was with her. She would have to accept the distant attitude but she just had to see him. She hoped the nurse would let Bethany in with her.

They saw Jason, Todd and Jack off with Curtis, the man who had offered to drive them, when he arrived in his jeep.

She helped Bethany into the car for the trip to the hospital. She would stop for a quick bite at McDonalds not wanting to take the time for a more leisurely breakfast. So what if it wasn't the most nutritious way, but it was fast. Time was of the essence. She was impatient to see Harry; Betty and the baby. She added guiltily.

CHAPTER TWENTY-FOUR

*A*fter MckyD's (as Jason loved to call it) Laurie arrived at the hospital. She had been bolstering her courage to enter Harry's domain but her bravery failed when she was outside his room. Retracing her steps to the other wing she entered Betty's room instead.

"Betty, Harry doesn't want to see me." Laurie wailed without even greeting her. "He doesn't remember these past three weeks. And most of all, the memory of how close we have become since his arrival here. He isn't the Harry that always supported me." She stopped her voice catching in the tears that were rising behind her eyes.

"Laurie, things may be different today. Jack told me all about this yesterday. He said he spoke to the doctor and he was positive that Harry would recover. You might even help trigger his memory with your presence today. Now go in and see him and I will take Bethany to see Anthony."

"But I was going to take Bethany in with me." Not giving Betty an explanation of her reasoning.

But Betty already guessed. "No hiding behind your daughter. You have to do this alone. Try talking as though nothing untoward has happened. Be friendly. Be nonchalant. You can handle that can't you? Your breezy manner may just carry it off and then see how he reacts. You can always abandon that approach you know." Betty was hoping for Laurie's sake this wouldn't be necessary.

Laurie headed off with a troubled look. She walked briskly from the elevator until she was ten feet from the door then the trepidation set in. After a few lagging steps, she straighten her back and breezily floated into the room with a warm, "Good morning Harry" She marched firmly over to the bed bending over to plant a kiss on his lips before he could protest. She realized then that they had never kissed each other in such a friendly fashion that she could remember. Oh well she would carry this off, saying brightly to his look of amazement.

"How are you this morning? Did you sleep well? How is your leg and arm feeling? Less painful I hope. Can you feel your fingers and toes? Is your head feeling better?" Laurie prattled on. "Are you feeling better? Has the pain lessened?" She kept up a running chatter like a wound up talking doll spieling her repertoire.

Harry laid there staring at her with his mouth open in shock. Had Laurie gone mad? Laurie, his dainty needing my protection person. She had never been this overpowering woman type, especially in Florida. What in the world had come over her?

"Hello Laurie." Harry said very quietly and with some hesitation. "I am feeling a bit better. My headaches are bad but the pain in my leg has lessened but not my arm." Harry was glancing around as though looking for a lifeline. "Where is Todd? How is he?"

Laurie swallowed noting the distance still in his voice although it also held puzzlement, because of her behaviour she was sure. "Todd is fine. He went with Jason and Jack to get the station wagon he left at the forest fire area. Good news the fire is out at last. We will be able to return home soon. The house survived, thank goodness. There were a few that weren't so lucky before the fire turned, the rest were saved with the change in wind direction. Jack was thankful it was over. He didn't want to go back there although he felt it was his duty."

"The forest fire. . . Jack and Todd both mentioned it, saying that it caused my injuries." Harry hesitated then went on. "I just don't remember any of it. When I try to remember I get a violent headache and have to give up." Laurie went silent. What could she say now?

"How are the children? Are you going to be staying here for awhile longer with Jack and . . . Betty?"

Laurie silently pleaded. *'Please don't do this to me?'*

"I had planned going home on Wednesday to South Carolina, but now that this has happened I think Betty will need me here for awhile longer. I phoned to let my boss know."

"And the children?" Harry was fumbling to think of something to say, which you do with strangers that you don't know that well. *Then a flash came in his mind of kissing Laurie in a hotel room somewhere but it was gone so fast. It must have been in Florida.* His face went red remembering. Laurie was unaware of his flashback because she had closed her eyes. *But. . . Laurie had left him there without a goodbye.*

Bringing his thoughts back to her, she was saying. "Jason is fine. He is with Todd and Jack getting the car." She was repeating herself unnecessarily her mind running amuck. "Bethany is fine too. She is visiting with Betty and Anthony."

Harry remembered Jack mentioning his son's unexpected birth. Jack had said his wife had a baby prematurely as a result of a fall. Puzzlement etched in his mind, as he found it hard to believe he had been the one to bring her to the hospital like Jack had proclaimed. He must of voiced his thought because Laurie replied.

"Harry, you were there at the house when we were evacuating. You helped us pack the cars to get away from town. You even drove Betty here to the hospital in Merritt, to have her checked out because she had fallen and hit her stomach and her head." Pausing waiting for some acknowledgement and when none came, she continued.

"We spent the day together. Going to a saloon in town in the afternoon for a drink where we met two lovely couples, that were trying to talk us into moving to Merritt. When we went back to the motel to get ready for dinner, we found Betty's water had broken and the baby was on the way. She had internal bleeding so they had to take the baby by caesarean section. Anthony was only three and a half pounds. The nurse came and showed us Jack's son. He was a miniature of a baby, your heart went out to him. All of us felt like that, even the hospital staff has taken Baby Anthony into their hearts as has the whole town thanks to the news media."

"Betty pulled through the operation. Jack and she are elated about their newborn son. Anthony has gained half a pound. We are hoping he will be released soon but he has to be at least five pounds." Harry had his eyes closed, but she was pretty sure he wasn't asleep because his breathing was normal.

"Did I tell you their home is fine? I am glad for them. It would be too devastating if they had lost their house." Laurie rushed on. "There were some that were consumed by the fire at the edge of town. Yesterday, the Town of Merritt had a special gala to raise money for the fire victims. Quite a bit of money was raised. They even supplied a wardrobe for tiny Baby Anthony along with a car seat, a stroller and a cradle. They even awarded a key and a certificate of honour to you for your dedication at the fire. Todd accepted it on your behalf." Laurie rambled on.

"The local news is full of the baby and your exploits and the unfortunate deaths of the people at the RV camp that was partially destroyed."

Laurie voice faded away. Harry was not responding to her monolog. The silence hung over them. He finally opened his eyes. "I am sorry. I just don't remember any of what you are telling me. I tried concentrating while you were talking but nothing came to me as being familiar. The last thing I can recall is setting out for our Wilderness Adventure. Why did I lose everything after leaving home?"

"Dr. Connolly thinks that it happened during your awful fall over the cliff, by the traumatic blow when you hit your head on the jagged rock-face, or possibly it was the fear while helplessly free falling through space, caused the memory lapse. You were in pretty bad condition by the time they found you, and hauled you up the cliff. I am sure the doctor has gone over your injuries with you since you came out of the anaesthetic. As a result, if you are right handed, you won't be able to take up your career for a long while."

"You know me well enough that I am right handed." His voice took on the remote sound again. "How have you been? How did the trial go? Was it too unpleasant seeing Dennis again?"

Laurie drew in a quick breath. It took her a moment to gather her wits about her. Then she let the air out with a sigh of hopelessness. She remembered how she walked out on him. *No wonder he was being so cool to her, if that was his last memory of me, if these last weeks were wiped out.*

At last she understood, it must be his last memory of her was her walking out on Todd and him without saying goodbye. Harry wouldn't know that he had forgiven her and accepted her explanation as to why she had left Florida so hurriedly. He had seemed so happy to see her again in Melville.

Laurie felt she had to continue talking. "The trial went well for me but not for Dennis. He was convicted and sentenced to two years. Harry, I am thinking of moving back to Indiana. Do you think we could be friends there?" He made no reply. "Harry, please forgive me for running out on you in Florida after all you did for me," desperation in her voice.

Harry eyes were roving over her face. He was remembering the rebuff in her attitude after the children had been returned safely. Remembering the hurt. *Was she in earnest about returning to Indiana as a friend? Could he forget the length of time it took for him to recover, after coming home from Florida? Another rebuff would be more than he could stand.*

Indifference on her part was something he couldn't handle anymore.

"Harry, you haven't answered me? Can you forgive me leaving you in Florida so abruptly?"

"Laurie, I can't deny you hurt me and I went home in an unhappy frame of mind. I guess we could be friends if you came to Indiana." He had too generous a nature to deny her anything.

"How is Todd taking my memory loss?"

"Todd doesn't quite understand it so he is frightened by it." She wanted to put her hand in his. Would he be offended if she did?

"Todd stayed away yesterday because I thought it was for the best to distance ourselves from the hospital for awhile. They had the gala event in the community park, we went there instead. The children needed a break from having to sit still in a hospital and talk in whispers, which they had been doing for hours since Betty first arrived here."

Laurie reached over placing a hand lightly over his. Harry didn't remove his hand immediately so she left it there letting her fingers cling more tightly.

"The activities the town put on occupied them for most of the day. They supplied us with a wonderful BBQ picnic dinner. The gold key to Merritt, Todd accepted on your behalf, was quite an honour bestowed on you."

Harry grinned for the first time since she had arrived to visit. "How about that and I missed it?" *Was Laurie changed or would she revert to herself and her indifference when this was over?* He had thought there could be so much for them, after the closeness they had achieved in Florida, but she had walked away ignoring both Todd and his feelings. He was afraid to give her the opportunity to hurt Todd and him ever again. His heart couldn't take the wound. But the hand over mine did feel warm and caring. He wanted a connection with her. He would just have to buffer his heart till she faded away from their lives again. He knew Todd would feel the same, and he was too young to protect himself. *Get real Harry it is your heart that you want to protect not him!*

What do I say now? What is he thinking? Has he driven me from his heart forever? No, Jack said Harry had told him that he loved me. He intended to win me over when he got back from the fire. When they had arrived in Merritt, she and Harry had spent the afternoon together. He had been affectionate towards her. The showing of this was by fondly accepting the saloon couples assumption that we were married and neither of us correcting them. What could she possibly do to win him over now?

Dr. Connolly noted the couple were linked by hands, but he felt not linked in mind. There was a blanket of emptiness over the room. Harry added to the feeling when he quickly removed his hand from Laurie's touch upon seeing the doctor. The situation had not changed. He must not have recovered his memory yet, which the doctor had hoped for. He felt sad for them as he hid his disappointment. His patient wasn't improving in that sphere.

"Good Morning. How is my patient today?" The tension was thick the closer he came to the bed.

"Fine."

"How is the head? Have the headaches settled down yet?"

"The headaches are receding, accept when I try to make a constructive effort to remember, then the headaches flair up again hampering me."

"Give it time Harry, it will return. The body is a wonderful entity that way. How are the leg and the arm?"

"My leg doesn't bother me much but my arm is a different story. The discomfort can be mind boggling. Maybe I have a low tolerance for pain but I have never thought so?"

"I would let you up to help keep your muscles toned but I am afraid with your head injury of you blanking out and falling."

Dr. Connolly turned to Laurie. "How is Baby Anthony? I haven't had a chance to inquire this morning."

"He is doing well according to Betty. I haven't seen him this morning either. He gained a half a pound which is pleasing everyone."

"That is good news. I am glad to hear that. Harry, I am going to leave you now. My advice just be patient, the body will heal itself when it is ready."

"Take care, Laurie." He placed his hand on her arm and gave her a gentle squeeze of compassion. Even if Jack had not told him about this couple, he could read the pain in her eyes. Her goodbye was little more than a murmur with tears in her throat.

The silence after the doctor left was torturous, neither saying anything, her bubbly manner dissipated. Laurie didn't want to leave but Harry wasn't encouraging her to stay. She had to brave it out; she just couldn't walk away not now. If she did it might never be possible for her to enter that room again.

"Jason and Todd were excited about going to the forest fire area. It is hard to envision the devastation until you see it firsthand I suppose. Hearing is not enough, you have to see it to believe the extent of a destroyed forest I'm sure. Besides the boys have been at the hospital too much since this all started and they both needed a break. Todd will probably be in to see you when they get back, as Jack will want to see Betty and the baby." her voice petered out. He made no comment. His eyes were closed. *Was he hoping she would leave?*

Just when she was ready to give up he said. "Yes, I hoped Todd would come today. I missed him yesterday. Thanks for being there for him while I am laid up. I don't know what I would have done if anything happened to him. He is the only one in my life that matters." Harry paused as if to punctuate what he had just said. She felt the wrench all the way to her heart. Then he continued his eyes still closed. "You probably think the same about Jason and Bethany?"

"Yes Harry I do. They mean the world to me but I think I am ready for more." Laurie paused to let that sink in before she continued. "So that is why I am thinking of moving back to Indiana?" She ended making it into a question.

Dead silence. Harry opened his eyes then closed them again. There was glitter of warmth but only for a moment, then steel grey eyes.

"Harry, I had better go to see if Jack is back yet." She almost stumbled on her way to the door, after hearing no reply to her Indiana query.

"You do that and if Todd is here send him in. See you Laurie." His eyes were on her receding back.

Laurie wasn't about to let him see how much he was hurting her. She caught herself enough to walk proudly out the door. The tears fell instantly she cleared the door, the tears cascading down her cheeks in rivulets. She moved to the window at the end of the hall, so he wouldn't hear her and nobody would see her broken heart exposed for all to see. How could she bear the hurt? Was this the way he felt when she walked out on him in Florida? She was so sorry now. If only she could turn back time. To do what...? Go back and never have disappeared the way she had? Yes that is what she wished now. More important, would she be given another chance to show him? She headed back to Betty carrying an outer veneer of calm hiding the hurt.

Laurie continued down the corridor her steps becoming steadier as she built up her resolve. Jack and the boys were just entering the hospital. The boys rushed excitedly towards her. They were talking about the devastation of the fire. "Mom, the experience was really weird. All those miles of blackness and spurts of smoke and grey ashes, burnt-out trees standing like a sentential of death." "No foliage for wildlife if any survived." Todd spurted out.

"Uncle Jack took us to the house. It is okay. Only the houses before you reached town were burnt but the houses in town escaped." Jason chirped out. Laurie stood gazing at their vibrant faces, taking the message in.

"That is good news. Hi Jack. These two are certainly animated about the fire and all they viewed."

"Yes, they took quite a shock at first seeing all the damage. The scarred earth will take quite awhile to recover. Thankfully the house is fine. There is still a strong smell of smoke, but not much smoke clouds in evidence. Some of the neighbours have returned already and are cleaning up as best they can with the air not being pure yet. It is best that Betty stay here a few more days."

"Yes it is probably best, but Jack I think I will take the boys and Bethany back to the house. I have had enough of motel living. I could get the place ready for Betty's return." She looked at him imploringly. "Do you mind?"

Jack had been studying her face. obviously Harry had not recovered his memory. The signs were evident. "No, of course you can go home. Maybe I will move back too, even though Betty and Anthony are staying here." Jack was thinking Laurie shouldn't be off by herself, brooding.

"Yes that would be fine. Todd, your father wants to see you. Why don't you and Jason go in to see him?" The two boys took off quickly down the corridor towards the elevator.

CHAPTER TWENTY-FIVE

"So things didn't go well with your visit with Harry I presume." Jack's eyes were scanning her sad face. "I'm sorry Laurie. I had hoped he had recovered his memory by now. Maybe it would be for the best to distance yourself for awhile."

"Yes, when we go to your place, I'll be able to clean and air the rooms for Betty and the baby's homecoming. Is there much dust and ash in the house?"

"Actually it is better than I had visualized. We will have to take all the things from the motel plus get delivery of the gifts the townspeople gave to Anthony. Merritt's residents are such thoughtful people. It makes my heart burst with their kindness."

"Yes. It makes you have faith in people again, when something like this happens to you. I lost it quite a bit after Dennis and the abduction."

"That is understandable. I better go see Betty. Where is Bethany?"

"With Betty, so I will come too. Harry hasn't forgiven me for my mode of leaving him in Florida." She went on dejectedly as the elevator eased up to the third floor. "That is what is uppermost in his mind. I can feel the resentment burning under the surface of his manner. Now I know how he felt when I was so distant, after the children were returned. I did this to myself, and now I wish I could wipe out that memory. But the truth is that it is the memory he is stuck with, my fleeing out of his life." Laurie's expression was of distaste for herself. "I didn't even say goodbye. I just ran away back to you and Betty."

"Laurie quit beating yourself up. If Harry hadn't fallen, the story would be entirely different. He told me he was going to persuade you to enlarge on your relationship. He had no intentions of letting you get away this time. He said he loves you. Right now you will have to believe me. His mind will recover, then he will remember he forgave you. You will have to hold onto that thought and forget the rest." They had come to Betty's room. They could hear Bethany exclaiming over the baby. They smiled at each other realizing that they would have to put Harry behind them and just be glad to see Betty which they both were.

The smiles still spreading across their faces as they entered the room, Betty looked up with a special smile for her husband. Jack bent over to ease her out of the chair and into his arms for a loving kiss, his fervour encircling them both. When they finally broke apart Betty said. "I missed you too." With a little laugh and no embarrassment.

"How is our son?"

"Oh Jack, he is so wonderful. Anthony is doing so well he will soon be out of the incubator. All the wires have gone and they let me hold him longer today when I fed him. I let Bethany help me hold him for a few seconds."

"Yes Uncle Jack I had my arm around him." Bethany said excitedly, giving bouncing motions with her expressive body. Laurie smiled at her daughter's face of pure joy.

Laurie said. "Jack, let's go see that son of yours." She was ready for some happiness, to blot out the sadness she was carrying inside.

He grabbed her arm. "Be right back, my sis and I are going for a viewing of Anthony. My son awaits his Daddy." His jovial voice filled the room as he whizzed Laurie out into the hall, the nursery their destination.

Jack's heart melted when he saw his son. He was still so tiny to him. "Hi, Anthony Stewart Wilson that is a big name for such a little guy like you." The nurse lifted him out of the incubator. After wrapping him in a warm blanket, she placed the baby in Jack's arms with an encouraging smile. "Here daddy, your son wants to greet you." Jack was thankful for the oversized blanket so he wouldn't squeeze Anthony too tightly. "Well Sis, what do you think of my handsome son?"

Laurie laughed. She knew he was quaking inside with that precious bundle in his arms. "Brother, he is pretty wonderful, much handsomer than you were when you were born, as I remember." She teased.

"Do you want to hold him?" Passing the bundle over to Laurie trying not to show his haste; still hesitant in handling this tiny new life that was still too new to him.

"Hi sweet baby, your father is afraid of you. You keep getting bigger and then you will be more than he can handle." She continued billing and cooing to the baby in a soft voice, until the nurse came back to place him back into his warm incubator bed. Jack was bursting his buttons, he was so proud of his son. He could see the little bundle had captured his sister's heart.

"Doesn't he make you realize how amazing this world we live in is, to produce someone as special as Anthony?"

"I think you and Betty are the special ones to produce someone special as that. Wait till you get home with him. When he puts on a few more pounds you'll be wrestling with him. He is a fighter, as he has shown in defeating the odds that were against him, when he was born and since."

"I know he is special. I can't believe I'm a father yet. I am still trying to let it sink in. Just think Anthony is a celebrity too. You know I always envied you, Jason and Bethany. Now I have a son of my own." His face was wreathed in an expansive smile.

"Let's get back to Betty. I want to rave about my son." Jack hurried along the corridor on flying feet. Laurie sped up. She was laughing at his haste to get to his wife to praise her.

"My love you have given me the best gift ever in my life. That son of ours is beautiful. Thank you." Bending down he gave her a big kiss and a hug.

"Betty I add my praise as well. Anthony is an unbelievable miracle."

"Thank you, I had help." Smiling Betty looked up at her husband. Bethany came over to hug her mother.

"The boys aren't back yet?" Laurie asked looking down at her "No Mommy."

"I hope things are going okay in there?" with a concerned voice.

"Of course why wouldn't they be?' Betty inquired.

Jack interrupted. "First things first, Mrs. Wilson that son of ours is beyond words. I am so proud of him and you." Kissing her fervently, this wife that had created such a wonderful son.

"Thanks honey. We did produce a handsome son didn't we? So you really love him?" Breathlessly Betty said, recovering from the amorous kiss.

"I can't find the proper words to express all that is in my heart right now. When do you think you and the baby will be coming home? Has the doctor given you any indication?"

"Anthony has to be out of the incubator for at least three days before he leaves plus he wants him to gain more weight. So it will be a few days yet."

"That is good because there is still too much smoke in the air at home. Anthony Stewart Wilson. I think it has a ring to it for a celebrity. Oh by the way, the rest of us are moving back to the house, when we leave here. Laurie and the kids have had enough of motels. We want to get the house ready for you and the baby to come home. But I will be back to see you tonight."

Laurie thought it was time to give Betty and Jack some time together. She had recognized Betty's look of astonishment at being left behind. Jack would have to do some fast talking. Turning to her daughter, holding out her hand. "Come on Bethany, let's go find the boys."

Laurie hesitated, just a fraction of time before they entered Harry's room. The boys were perched on his bed, one each side of him, drawing designs and sayings on his casts. The boys were working with such concentration. His expression was that of a proud father of two. The boys were taking turns talking about the fire area, and the things they had seen that day. When Bethany saw what they were doing, she raced up to the bed. "Can I do some? Please Harry? Can I?" Hopping from foot to foot.

"Sure Todd isn't the leg cast big enough for two?"

Bethany ran around to the side of the bed opposite to Todd looking pleadingly at her mother, wanting help up onto the high bed.

"Laurie, do you have anything in your purse that Bethany can use? The nurse just brought two pens for the boys." Harry was being very accommodating. So different from when Laurie was visiting him alone. Rooting around in her purse she came up with a pen offering it to Bethany.

"Harry, won't it be too much having all the children on the bed?"

"No lift her up and I will hold her."

Bethany settled in to concentrate on her patch of leg cast that Todd indicated, and Harry put his good arm as best he could, around Bethany to anchor her on the bed. He didn't seem to be bothered by any pain at the moment. The children seemed to be good therapy for him.

"I wondered why the boys hadn't returned. I should have known that they would enjoy leaving their personal mark on your casts. By the way Harry, I am taking the children back to the house. The fire is officially out and we are allowed to return. I am getting tired of motel living, and I am sure the children are too. I will be cleaning the house in preparation for Betty and Anthony's home coming."

"Does that mean you won't be coming back to the hospital?" Harry's voice was resigned Laurie was walking away again.

"No Harry. I'll be bringing the children in to see you while I visit Betty and Anthony."

The kids started to giggle. Todd had drawn a heart with Laurie's initials over Harry's with love in between. Laurie hoped Harry didn't notice, as she was disturbed that Todd had recognized her changed feelings towards Harry.

"Are you about finished? Isn't that enough? We have to be going." She was trying to cover up her embarrassment. She was sure her face had gone to a mortified shade of red.

"Will Todd be able to come in with Jack when he comes in to see Betty?"

"Yes. I will also be coming on occasion too and I will bring him with me. Goodbye Harry." Her formal voice was noticeable. Harry's goodbye wasn't much better. The boys were looking back and forth between the adults. Both their voices were strange and reserved. A sound not usually associated with these two.

"Mommy, I haven't had enough time to finish. Please let me stay? Todd will bring me to Auntie Betty's room when I am finished." Bethany was busily working on the cast.

"Just a moment longer Bethany that's all." Laurie was heading for the door, escape near at hand.

Harry accepted a kiss willingly from each of the children when they were ready to leave. "I will be awaiting your return." His borrowed family and Todd, he missed them already and they had just disappeared out of the door. He wished he could alter his attitude to Laurie but she had walked out on him too often and he needed a buffer against it. A pain in his head had him closing his eyes for relief, as his hand reached for the painkiller.

. . .

Laurie, Jack and the children went back to the motel to pack. They had accumulated more things with the new clothes and some of the baby gifts.

Jack expressed the advantage of station wagons for their belongings. "Laurie, the townspeople offered to send the cradle, stroller and car seat directly to the house, when I phoned the mayor's office to let them know we were leaving. So will you stick around for their delivery tomorrow?"

"Yes Jack. I won't be coming back for awhile. I want to concentrate on cleaning the house." Realizing that meant she wouldn't be seeing Betty either she added. "Perhaps I will be in to see Betty now and then. Will you bring Todd with you? Harry will want to see him."

Jack gave her a meaningful look. "Of course, I understand Laurie." He hated to see her so broken up. She was finding it hard to believe his explanation, that Harry had said he really loved her.

The cars were finally packed, Todd and Jason rode with Jack. Laurie and Bethany rode in her car following a safe distance behind them. She waved to a few of the townspeople that she had met at the gala. She looked around with a warm heart, having felt the good heartedness of this town, while she tried to ignore the hidden pain, of leaving an uncaring Harry behind.

The trip to Melville went quickly because most of the firefighting equipment had been removed from the area. Jack noted that only a skeleton crew were left behind to watch for any flare-ups. Trees can burn under the ground for quite awhile then suddenly appear where the roots are exposed as a flare-up. He had learned this from the firefighters that had instructed him in the beginning.

Melville was busy. People were shopping, some just talking and others cleaning their homes and yards. Jack waved to a few of his friends about town but didn't stop. He was anxious to get home. He handed things to everyone as he unloaded the car. The kids were running as Jason was impatient to give Todd a proper viewing of the house, now that they were home. With all their possessions taken inside Jack released them.

Laurie was standing on the driveway looking down the street wistfully, remembering the amazement of seeing Harry walking towards her. Harry, her saviour who came to her rescue, when she needed him. He was such a caring and kind man. He had tried to show her his true feelings. Why didn't she recognize her feelings for Harry sooner? She knew she loved him now. Why had that fact eluded her until too late?

Her running away in Florida was not from Harry and Todd, but from Dennis and the horror that he had put her through. She just wanted to get away from Fort Lauderdale and the helpless feeling she had suffered during the days of the kidnapping. The relief that he had brought them back unhurt, did not outweigh the distress, that he could have planned something so horrendous.

Harry had deserved a proper goodbye. It was no wonder he was treating her this way. That is the last memory he has of me. Laurie turned and entered the house with heavily laden feet.

Jason was showing Todd the layout of the house and Bethany was tagging along. When they got to the patio and the pool they could see remnants of the fire, ashes floating on top and some particles on the bottom. The pool would need extra cleaning. Jason got the net that was on a long pole, and tried to catch the floating ashes.

Bethany was telling Todd about how much her swimming had improved since Florida. Uncle Jack had spent some time during their stay, helping them to develop their skills.

Laurie went into the kitchen to make some coffee, and put the groceries away. They had picked them up in Eugene on their way through, giving the children a break from being cramped in their seats with all the abundant possessions around them. She kept busy, so she wouldn't dwell on Harry, although he wasn't too far below the surface.

Laurie quickly made the dinner. The kids' chatter at the table with Jack's bantering made Laurie smile. The boys were extra boisterous, when Jack put them in the shower together, laughing light heartedly as only the young can do, their pent up energy no longer curtailed by hospital restrictions.

He supervised making sure that they were indeed washing themselves by peering into the bathroom at intervals. He told them how much he appreciated their help with their Aunt Betty, and the events leading up to the baby and since while he helped with the towelling of their hair.

The boys were sleeping in the same room and Jack saw them into bed and shut off the light. They would talk for awhile he was sure. He would soon be doing this for his son. His heart expanded at the thought.

Saying goodbye to Laurie, Jack anxiously headed for the door. It was time to see Betty and Anthony again at the hospital, even though it was only a short time he had been away from them.

Laurie had spent the evening sitting alone, her thoughts searching for a way to change Harry's opinion of her? Will he ever get his memory back? What if it never returned?

Laurie knew she couldn't keep stalling. It was time to go back to South Carolina if she wanted to keep her job. The loudness of the commercial called her attention back to the TV.

Jack eventually came back. Laurie turned off the television. They sat discussing Betty and Anthony. He omitted telling her that he had gone in to see Harry, but nothing had changed there.

He hadn't regained his memory, but he seemed to be in less pain. Jack had avoided anything that might disturb his head but Harry had wanted to know more about the fire and what had happened to him when he fell over the cliff. So Jack recounted the details of his fall and the rescue. While Harry was listening, no enlightenment appeared on his face. Jack excused himself to say he had better leave and give him some rest. Harry had asked about the children and Laurie too, but only as though it was an afterthought.

The next day, Laurie recruited the children to help with the clean up. Jack had to go back to work that day. Work had been put on hold, while he had permission to help fighting the fire. His staff had managed without him under the circumstances.

The children wanted to concentrate on Anthony's room first. The walls, floors and curtains had to be washed. The boys took care of the windows and made them shine. Bethany was dusting the furniture off consisting of a chest of drawers and a matching crib, that Betty had purchased from a neighbour.

The cleaning of the baby's room took them almost to noon. Laurie told them they could have a swim before lunch, for all their help during the morning. This comment had them slipping into their bathing suits immediately. Jack had been up real early to clean the pool, concerned that all the debris would hamper the filter system.

She watched the two boys swimming back and forth from deep to the shallow end, while Bethany was paddling about in her attempts to swim. She was more sure of herself now. Jason was perfecting a new dive under Todd's tutelage. Bethany was being more adventurous and Laurie was swimming beside her. Todd was surprised because he recalled that she seemed to be afraid of the water in Florida.

Jason wanting perfection, kept diving over and over until Todd laughed at his eagerness saying that he had perfect form after the second time. He was a natural at diving, like his speedy grasp of swimming. Laurie finally called a halt, and they went in to get ready for lunch.

The afternoon was spent with more cleaning after a promise of another swim before dinner. The arrival of Anthony's gifts from the wonderful people in Merritt, made the afternoon pass quicker assembling and placing them in the baby's room.

CHAPTER TWENTY-SIX

*L*aurie couldn't keep apart from Harry. That evening they all went to the hospital. She didn't have to go in to see him, she could just be there in the same place was her reasoning. Bethany kept asking first Jack then Laurie could she hold Anthony again. The boys were looking forward to more art work on Harry's casts, switching leg and arm casts this time.

Laurie was going to see the baby and Betty. Todd and Jason proceeded straight to Harry's room. In Betty's room Jack embraced her, the light kisses flowing with love.

Laurie and Bethany arrived at the window of the nursery to see the incubator was empty. The nurse signalled for them to come in. Bethany squealed with delight. He was on his own now. They went in and the nurse lifted Anthony and placed the bundle in Laurie's arms. Bethany put her arm under him too when Laurie bent over a bit, it was like they were both holding him.

Laurie wished for another baby, as she held this little bundle in her arms, but that would never happen again. The nurse smiled at them, watching for a short time, then putting out her arms for the baby. "It is time for this little guy's dinner." Anthony was still being fed every two hours. She wheeled the baby off in the bassinet, towards Betty's room.

Bethany wanted to see Harry next. Laurie stood at the window in the hall listening to the children and Harry talking happily together. She wanted to give Jack and Betty time to enjoy the baby without interrupting them. Avoiding Harry was childish, but she wanted to keep part of her resolve.

Harry was enjoying the talk with the children but he also had one eye on the door. Was Laurie pulling her remote act again?

She was wishing she had begged Harry to stay with them instead of departing for the fire camp to retrieve his car. She should have known he would feel it his duty to help. Gone was the closeness that had developed recently. Knowing that he was in so much pain was hurting her too. Was there any possibility of a future for them ever again?

· · ·

The next few days passed without incident. Laurie seldom went near the hospital and if she did it was only to visit Betty and the baby. The house was sparkling, awaiting the arrival of Betty and her precious bundle.

The special day arrived at last. Betty and Anthony were being released from the hospital; the children's excitement was running high, as well as Jack and Laurie's. Everyone wanted to go. Piling excitedly into the station wagon, they were on their way.

Laurie went to Betty's room to check that she was ready, and to see to anything that needed packing. Jack took the children to visit Harry for a few minutes. He was off the painkillers and the IV pole was gone. The artistry on his casts was impressive, placed there happily by the kids on their visits. He was up daily now using a wheelchair or a crutch to manoeuvre around.

Dr. Connolly considered releasing Harry but felt it was too soon. He wasn't ready for the trip to Indiana alone with Todd. Especially as his memory hadn't returned in the days that he had predicted. The doctor's belief still was when the time is right it will happen. Dr. Connolly wanted to speak with Jack and Laurie, as indicated by a nurse, but the doctor had been called into an emergency operation and had missed them.

As Laurie came out of Betty's room, she saw Todd wheeling Harry down the hall with Bethany and Jason holding on to the wheelchair like they were helping too. Jack smiled at Laurie giving her brotherly support. Harry had come to wave the family off, he had taken them into his heart once again. He greeted Betty shyly as he didn't really remember this woman although she had come to see him a few times. At that time, he had told Betty that he still got the odd headache and he apologized for his memory loss, in not remembering her and the baby's arrival.

Many staff members grouped around to say goodbye, Baby Anthony's supporters that could safely leave their duties. The ones that had watched his daily survival, his fight to embrace life. Baby Anthony woke up to give a gentle cry, as though this was his final tribute to the staff congregated there.

As they drove away Jack and Betty's hearts were filled to overflowing with the farewell. Harry was looking and waving to the children as the car eased away. Laurie waved sadly.

That night Jack showed up with Todd and Jason to see Harry, because their visit had been brief due to Betty going home earlier that day. He was out of the room practicing with his crutch when they walked towards him. It was difficult with a cast on each side of his body, it seemed to make his balance off. The nurse was beside him with the wheelchair ready to ease him into it, when he got tired. When he was safely in the wheelchair, he tried to move it himself but the fingers on his right hand with the cast made it difficult so Todd and Jason took over enthusiastically. The hospital had ordered a wheelchair, for use when he got back to Indiana.

Todd and Jason took him to the lounge area, Harry didn't want to spend any more time in his room than need be. The nurse arranged for drinks from the kitchen. When the nurse returned with the drinks she handed a message to Jack. Reading the message Jack excused himself. "The doctor wants to see me." He didn't elaborate which doctor, it was from Dr. Connolly and he didn't want to tell Harry, until he found out what the doctor had to say.

Laurie and Jack were down as Harry's next of kin as Todd wasn't old enough to assume responsibility for him. Dr. Connolly greeted Jack and asked him to have a seat. "You have probably figured out why I wanted to see you. Harry is ready to be released. There is no further treatment that can help him here. His memory will take time, that is all that I can say. I am sorry his memory didn't return as I hoped."

"My concern is that Harry is still having headaches, so he should not be left alone for at least a month. I am hoping during that time that his memory will return. We still don't know if he will have blackouts in his mobility. His right arm is going to make him incapacitated for a short time longer. He is doing fairly well with one crutch but his balance is not good because he should have two."

"What would you suggest?"

"I have spoken to Harry and he is insisting on going home to Indiana. He is indicating that Todd and he will manage. Granted Todd seems mature for his age. More so than normal but he is only thirteen. I think this is too much for him to cope with. Todd doesn't have the strength to help Harry should he fall."

"I couldn't find any record of family, as next of kin, other than Laurie and yourself. So that is why I am talking to you. I know you have responsibilities with your wife and baby, but I don't know who else to call upon?" Dr. Connolly looked questioningly.

"What you're saying is that Harry is determined to go back to Indiana even without help, except for Todd?"

"That's right."

"That is not feasible. I can see your point, it is not wise. I know in the past Harry has helped my sister and her children on a couple of occasions. Taking them into his home and nursing my sister when she was ill and hardly knew her and helping her in Florida. I know if I approached Laurie she will be only too happy to help him now. Besides she is talking about relocating to Indiana anyways. She could suggest if he let her stay with him until she found a place, she could help in his return home. To alleviate the cost for her she could help out with the housework in payment."

"That might work, why don't you suggest that to Harry tonight. Perhaps you can phone Laurie to get her input on the matter. I hesitated asking her due to their situation, that is quite evident between them." Dr. Connolly pushed the phone towards Jack.

Jack put the proposal to Laurie, when she answered the phone. She drew in a deep breath and held it. The hesitation was obvious, until Jack reminded her of how Harry came to her rescue a couple of times. Harry had been there for her when she needed him, and now he needed her. She agreed with some apprehension, but knew she had to assent gracefully. Laurie specified that she would call her boss about this latest development.

Jack put down the phone with a satisfied smile. He felt like he was playing cupid rather than organizing help for a disabled person. "It's all set with Laurie now I just have to convince Harry."

Dr. Connolly and Jack shook hands like fellow conspirators.

Harry and the boys were out in the corridor taking turns wheeling him around. When they saw Jack coming they zipped back into the lounge. He soon met them there.

"I think Todd and I are heading back to Indiana. I think we can manage don't you Todd?" This was news to Todd but he quickly responded. "Yes Dad, we always have in the past." Harry, anxious to leave the hospital, was obviously awaiting Jack's comments.

"You mean drive back to Indiana? How can you manage the drive?" Jack pointedly looked directly from one cast to the other, Jack's puzzlement very obvious.

"Of course, I'm more than ready to go home. Dr. Connolly and I have already discussed it. He is in agreement that I can be released." Harry was being blasé about it knowing the driving would be impossible.

"Well in that case I will miss you both, but I was hoping you would stay with us for awhile at least until you were more mobile."

"You have your hands full looking after your wife and new baby. No I prefer to go home to Indiana. I have already phoned Marvin to let him know I will be back soon and he will pop in to see if I need anything. He is good that way."

"I don't believe that drive is for someone with two casts. By the way your car is at my place. I meant to tell you that sooner."

"Thanks, I was wondering. I really haven't thought seriously about the driving. Perhaps you're right, it would be risky. I could call Marvin, my partner. He could fly here then drive the car or if someone here would be willing then I could arrange for them to fly back."

"Gee Harry, I was just thinking Laurie is seriously planning to move back to Indiana. Maybe she could drive you. She needs to find a place to live."

"Laurie? Well I don't know. She probably isn't ready to go yet, and she has her own car. Doesn't she have a job that she has to get back to?" Harry muttered.

Jack jumped up. "I'll phone Laurie right now, it will be no problem I am sure." He sped out of the room ignoring Harry's. 'Not right now.'

Harry was shaking his head. How did that happen? He couldn't have Laurie driving him. He would just have to put Jack straight when he got back, besides she would probably say no. Meanwhile Todd and Jason were trading high fives behind his back.

Jack had gone to the phone pretending to make the call in case Harry had the boys follow him. A voice kept repeating 'Insert a quarter then dial the number including area code.' After three repeats of the message Jack stopped the pretence and hung up the phone receiver, and returned to the lounge.

"Well that's all set Laurie is driving you." The boys were jumping up and down. Their close relationship was due to continue this time.

Harry looked thunderstruck. What could he do now but thank Jack and consent. He just wasn't up to arguing. The conversation moved to Betty and his son skilfully by Jack. Mention of the trip was avoided although it was still weighing on Harry's mind.

Jack tried to tell him that Laurie was trying to make up for the hurt she caused him in Florida rather than say Harry had already forgiven her. He didn't want to cause the usual headache, which he knew happened often, when he tried to remember past events.

Harry knew he had successfully worked Laurie out of his system before his memory loss. It was just the time since meeting her again that he didn't remember, how had they acted towards each other? She seemed to want more from him this time. Why couldn't he remember?

He wanted to believe that something good could happen between them, but it had taken him too long to get over her and get on with his life after that last time. Flashes of the wilderness trip were invading his mind. But they were brief and he didn't seem to be retaining them. A headache was zinging through his head. It was easier to accept those missing days than to try to find them.

Jack wound down quickly when he noticed the pain on Harry's face. "Is your head hurting? Can I ask the nurse for something to help you?"

"No. I'll be alright. Just trying to remember, it always ends with pain."

"That's it boys. Todd, wheel your father back to his room and I will speak to the nurse. Harry, you need something to help you rest. I'm sorry if I caused you pain, leave the missing memories lost. They aren't important right now. Just accept life day by day. When you get home it may all come back to you."

Harry wanted to believe him but his headache was draining his ability to think. Maybe a painkiller and oblivion was what he needed after all.

. . .

Todd, Laurie and the kids arrived at the hospital; it was Harry's release day. A wheelchair was part of his release. Todd and Jason were only too happy to help push him in a wheelchair. The hospital came up with one for him. Harry promptly donated money for the payment of a new one. He had every intention of returning the wheelchair when he no longer needed it, as he was very appreciative of the hospitals generosity towards them all.

The hospital staff gave him a hero's send-off with wishes for a good life which embarrassed him a little. Dr. Connolly included some instructions to Laurie for his injured limbs and head which he had already discussed with Harry.

Harry was giving everyone the full treatment of his normal self and his good humour. Laurie was even included in some of his smiles. They were to stop in at Jack and Betty's for a meal before hitting the road. Jack wanted to assess the way Harry was acting towards Laurie before sending them on their way.

Seeing the devastation of the forest fire with its sentinel of burnt trees and beds of ashes was difficult for Harry. Like all people, the destruction vetted there was incredible but for Harry it did not help him penetrate the fog in his mind as he hoped it would.

He wanted to go home now. They were on their way with a slight detour back to Melville to say goodbye to Jack and Betty. Todd and Jason were his guardians doing whatever they could to make things easier for him. He was gratified and proud of the boys in their nurturing. Bethany, not to be outdone by the boys, offered Harry a hand pulling his meal closer and filling his glass with iced tea. Everyone held their breath on that feat. The meal was very tasty and the conversation lively. Anthony in his cradle was waving his arms a bit to the children's delight. However, they didn't delay once the meal was ended. Hugs and kisses were exchanged freely, and they were finally on the road.

The first day was to be short, so Harry could adjust to the change of being cooped up in a car. He was in the back seat with his leg cast across the seat but angled out so Bethany could be squeezed into the corner. Betty had supplied a couple of pillows to elevate his head and right arm. It was not the most comfortable position but Bethany, the smallest, did need a place to sit.

The car was whizzing along. Laurie had the children singing. Harry was saying little. *Why had he insisted on going home? Now Laurie would be back in his life, in close proximity for a brief while. How often could he keep doing this?*

Laurie kept glancing over her shoulder at Harry, but he was avoiding any eye contact by concentrating on the scenery. Laurie's repertoire of songs was fast running out, but she kept on for the children's sake. They were enjoying themselves. Finally she asked. "Harry do you know any songs the kids might like to sing?"

Harry's head swivelled towards her voice. "Songs?" He asked as if it was a foreign language.

"Yes, do you know any songs?"

"No, I don't think so." Silence.

In desperation Laurie spotted a Dairy Queen up ahead. "Anyone want a milkshake?"

"Me! Me! Me too!" Were the chorus of children's voices with yells of preferences.

"Harry what kind do you want?"

He wanted out to stretch and change his position if only for a few minutes. Then considering the rigmarole of getting him in the car he forgot that idea quickly. "Vanilla will be fine." He felt so confined and uncomfortable. He was trying to master his feelings of dissension, or this trip he had insisted on would be never ending. "I would come with you but my body won't cooperate." He flashed her a grin. Laurie almost swerved the car in shock. Harry had been so glum and unresponsive so far. Her heart gave a leap at his sexy smile.

When they were parked Harry said to the boys. "Go and help Laurie and be my stand-in." The boys scurried out of the car chasing after Laurie. Bethany stayed and kept Harry company. He opened his door to get rid of the enclosed feeling and a rush of hot air filtered into the car making him aware of his enveloping casts. Ignoring these he asked Bethany about her life in South Carolina. He wanted to know if she would miss it if she came back to Indiana permanently.

Bethany wasn't the shy girl she used to be with Harry. "Since Uncle Jack and Aunt Betty moved, things didn't seem as much fun there anymore. I have a few friends and Jason has more but Mommy hasn't many since Uncle Dennis hurt her. We called him uncle but he really wasn't our uncle and he turned into a bad man."

"Do you want to be back in Indiana?"

"If you and Todd will be with us I will. Mommy said she would go back to Indiana if she could meet someone there to make her as happy as my Daddy did."

"How do you know that?"

"She told Uncle Jack last night. Mommy said she was hoping things would be different in Indiana. She said she hoped that her personal relationship would improve. So I guess she hopes to meet a new daddy for me."

Harry was flabbergasted, was she talking about him he wondered? Did she know someone else from her past? A friend of her husband's maybe? Or was she hoping to meet someone new?

CHAPTER TWENTY-SEVEN

The conversation ended when Laurie arrived with fries while the boys carried the milkshakes. After the fries and milkshakes had been distributed, Laurie said her fries were to be shared by her and Harry hoping he didn't mind. He wanted to say he didn't want any but before he could she sat on the floor beside him in the open car doorway with her legs stretched out.

Being one handed, Harry was holding his milkshake and Laurie was teasingly feeding him fries. It was most erotic the way she would devour him with her eyes as she held out her hand invitingly and he would have to lean over to take the fry. Then she would eat one herself licking the salt off her finger with the tip of her tongue.

Harry was melting inside. This was certainly a new Laurie. They had never had this kind of contact before and in such a suggestive way. Never in all the time he had known Laurie had she been the erotic female, that she was playing at the moment. She had been strictly a platonic friend.

They hardly noticed the chatter of the children's voices or the cars coming and going around them. Harry knew these were just fries, but they tasted better than ever before. *What had gotten into her? This was definitely not the Laurie he knew.* When the fries were finished, he sat there dumbly looking at her.

Laurie put an end to the scene by picking up a napkin and wiping her hands then offered one to Harry by drawing it over his lips and chin. He took a drink drawing strongly on the straw as if it was the most important thing in his life. He needed to recover from this unusual experience.

She gave him an endearing grin before she eased into a standing position. "Is everyone ready to continue the trip?" He gave her a sick grin.

"Why not," dumb answer, but Harry's mind was mush.

Laurie was enjoying a chuckle as she moved around the car. *Gotcha Harry! That put your austere manner out of kilter.* Laurie was wearing a expansive grin, when the car eased back into traffic.

The trip progressed without much communication between Laurie and Harry, but she knew that he was giving her appraising looks. Every once in awhile the children would ask about the scenery or how much further they had to go? Otherwise the children talked amongst themselves and Laurie and Harry could be in their own thoughts.

She was amazed at how very helpful the motel was when they stopped for the night. They showed their concern for Harry's comfort. The nearby restaurant had given them special service because of his incapacity. They came up with a special dinner for him where a knife was not required. He was getting more proficient with his left hand but Bethany made sure everything was within easy reach. Harry complied with this treatment not wanting to hurt the child's feelings, only too glad it wasn't Laurie.

He had manoeuvred the seating so that Laurie was seated first, opposite the two boys with Bethany beside her. The wheelchair was close to the table. After dinner Laurie and the kids all congregated in Todd and Harry's room to watch television.

When bedtime came Bethany and Jason gave Harry a hug and kiss on his cheek. Laurie gave Todd a hug and kiss. She raised a hand to Harry but didn't approach him, although she sent him a wistful look. He raised his hand casually in reply.

The next morning they were back on the road early. Harry had been pretty tired and uncomfortable after yesterday's ride but he felt he had hidden his discomfort well. Regardless, today he intended pushing Laurie to make the ride all the way home. The incident of the fries kept preying on his mind and he didn't know how much more of that he could take. He couldn't believe, that eating something as simple as fries could end up in an erotic experience.

Laurie was talking brightly as though she could read Harry's thoughts, and was enjoying herself. When they stopped for lunch he insisted they go inside this time.

"I need to get out of the car. I feel like I am glued to the seat." The boys helped Laurie get Harry into the wheelchair. No more intimate feedings for Harry, regardless of the problems negotiating getting in and out of the car was causing.

Bethany sat beside Harry, naturally to perform her duties. Laurie separated the boys so she could sit on the end near Harry's wheelchair. She kept accidentally brushing his hand reaching for her drink. *What game was she playing?* He wondered. This was not the platonic Laurie he knew.

Now more than ever he intended to push her to complete the trip home today. It was tiring and difficult but they made it. The boys got him into the house with only a bit of help from Laurie.

"The arrangements will be that Bethany will help me get settled in the living room while Laurie, you and the boys go out for takeout dinner, after picking up some groceries." She complied at his abrupt suggestion with a direct look of surprise, taking the boys with her as helpers.

Bethany followed him around as he tried to totter around on his crutch which was easier than the wheelchair in the confined space. This house was not designed with a wheelchair in mind. He needed to be more proficient at moving around, in order to gain his independence. He got the impression that Laurie intended sticking around for awhile. Jack had stressed her being there was to look for a place to live, and in the meantime help him till he conquered his handicap.

He had asked about her job. Jack had replied. "Laurie phoned and quit yesterday." At this news, he had wished it had only been his leg and not his arm too. He could have managed alone then.

It felt so good to be at home, in familiar surroundings seeming to give him more strength. He tried harder to move around with the crutch. One crutch wasn't enough. He tired so easily and then the pain crept up on him. Ignoring the pain would be difficult. He needed to be more mobile without a brain fogged by painkillers. His muscles needed toning but he realized at last that he was over doing it and asked Bethany to get his wheelchair which was fairly close at hand. She was game for anything to do with Harry, but it was difficult for her to move it without bumping into things.

The others arrived and the Chinese food and drinks served by the children appeared on the table. Laurie showed up with an open bottle of wine and two glasses. When the wine was poured in their glasses Laurie proposed a toast. "Let's drink to being back in Indiana and a great future together." The children joined in happily at that positive thought. Harry just stared at her. The children prodded him to join in the clinking of glasses before drinking the toast. Laurie stared deeply into his eyes while their crystal glasses sounded an angelic ring. Her face wreathed in a special smile that spoke volumes.

She kept trying to catch his eyes during dinner but he was deliberately avoiding hers. Evidently this was not going to be easy. She would just have to ease off and bide her time.

. . .

The days elapsed but not quickly enough for Harry. He was not making the progress in self-sufficiency that he had hoped for. His mind went back to the first night, when Laurie shooed the boys off to bed before Harry was ready for bed. He really hadn't thought about it until it came time for him to negotiate the stairs. Laurie eased under his good shoulder and helped him hobble upstairs. He also needed help preparing for bed. He told Laurie he would sleep in his clothes but she ignored that message and entered his room right behind him. Humiliation set in when she stuck around to help.

She worked his T-shirt over his cast after releasing his good arm. Her hands seemed to be touching him everywhere while easing the T-shirt over his head. Next item the removal of his pants. Even though they were loose fitting elasticized waist joggers, he couldn't manage their removal on his own. They kept clinging to his cast.

"Just leave them on I will be fine."

"Harry you can't sleep in your pants." She firmly put her hands to his waist pushing them down over his hips. Harry pushed her hands away. "I'll do it myself after you're gone."

"Harry why injure yourself unnecessarily? I'll do it." Laurie's hands were pushing once again against his hips. His efforts to pull them up again were causing her hands to rub up and down his sides.

"You are only making this undertaking even longer. I have seen men in under briefs before." He had to stop struggling just to get her hands off him. She was easing them down over his cast while admiring his leg as the pants slipped slowly downwards revealing his long limb. He was worried about her fingers making his blood boil, rather than the fact she was studying him so intently.

He was going to coordinate his bedtime with Todd's from now on until he could manage better with his left hand. It was just the inflexible cast on his leg that produced the difficulties.

"Excuse me I will have to go to the bathroom first then I will wash myself in private," he said tellingly. "I will call you if I need help."

Laurie said fine and stopped outside the bathroom taking his crutch. He eased inside holding on to the doorknob then the vanity and closed the door. She stood waiting until she heard the toilet flush then gave him a few minutes to straighten himself then she opened the door and popped in.

He was mortified. Laurie was very matter of fact grabbing a cloth and soap preparing to wash him. He made a sputtering sound which turned to a gentle purr almost as the cloth gently caressed his face. She rinsed the cloth and proceeded to push the cloth over his face again only this time at a normal pace.

"I hope I didn't get any soap in your eyes or mouth?" Breaking the spell, Harry tried to talk. Stopping to clear his throat and starting again. "I don't think so." He finally managed hardly breathing.

"You need a shave." Laurie said but the startled look on Harry's face made her say. "Perhaps we will leave that for tomorrow."

"Maybe I'll grow a beard." Harry grumbled quietly.

She rinsed the cloth then soaped it again. Reaching for his left arm she washed it vigorously until she reached his hand. When she washed his fingers the cloth slowed right down with a caressingly touch.

Laurie was staring at his hand. He was staring at her. Then the cloth was rinsed, she dragged it over his fingers on his right hand gently.

When she reached for the towel he whipped it out of her hand and dried himself as best he could knowing he was so inflamed he couldn't possibly be wet. She let him and acted busy cleaning the sink. She placed the crutch under his arm and walked away from him.

The covers turned back, she waited to tuck him in. She was reaching to lift his legs as though nothing untoward was happening. "See Harry, I didn't hurt you a bit and we did it together."

Right!!! Thought Harry.

"Well goodnight Harry." She leaned over and planted a feather kiss on his lips before he could object. She flipped out the light and exited the room before Harry could recover. He groaned. *Was this the same woman who did the disappearing act?*

She walked part way down the hall then leaned against the wall taking big gulps of air. Now why ever had she done something like that? She wasn't that type of woman. Finally she eased off the wall and headed to the other bathroom. The water she used was cold to ease the flame of embarrassment.

There had been no further repeats of the bedtime ritual with Laurie. Harry made sure of that. He sat around in the evenings in a housecoat thanks to Todd so that there would be no repeat of the first night.

Each day he worked hard at becoming skilled with his left hand. The boys were willing to be at his beck and call when they were around. Bethany was still his mealtime companion not that he really needed her but he had to admit he liked her attention as much as the boys administering. He was trying to be independent even of the boys so that he wouldn't have to get ready for bed quite so early. He was becoming quite ambidextrous with his left hand and with the help of the fingers on his right.

As a result the boys were finding more time to go exploring and hiking. Todd was teaching Jason survival techniques although they were only allowed to go to the nearby forest with a small imaginary cliff near the river. The cliff was really a pile of rocks but the way they traversed them up and down the rocks it could have been twenty feet high.

Laurie was giving Harry space now that he was more active on his own, taking Bethany with her looking for a place to live. Each day when she arrived home, she said she just couldn't find anything as nice as her old house.

Harry would hide his pleasure at this news, with a scowl and a comment such as. "Are you being too selective?" or "Are you looking in the right place?"

Laurie would watch him practicing with his crutch on the driveway. She could see the tension and the painful jolt in his shoulders, the unused muscles in his leg making it difficult. When his legs tired, he made it over to his wheelchair and sunk down gratefully.

Laurie realized that he was driving himself too hard. She had backed off since that first night, not pursuing him in any threatening way. She wasn't good in the role of the femme fatal anyway. It was a role she didn't feel comfortable with. She just wanted to be a part of his life.

He was treating their relationship like an armed truce. Consenting to her presence but not quite welcoming any overtures that weren't totally necessary.

How could she keep ignoring her feelings? In her heart she knew that she wanted to live permanently with Harry and Todd. Todd had accepted the situation readily, wanting Jason and Bethany around forever. Laurie squared her shoulders. She knew she had burned her bridges with her escape in Florida, along with Harry's memory loss of his forgiveness. Harry was spending so much time trying to be self-sufficient.

She had contacted a real estate friend Nancy Brewster in South Carolina. Laurie had met her socially on several occasions and felt she trusted her to sell the house and arrange to have her possessions shipped to Indiana. It had sold in two weeks and the house had been packed up. Nancy had informed her yesterday to expect the moving truck in four days. Laurie asked her to stall things for a month until the closure on the house. Because nothing had been settled here yet, she had arranged for them to go into storage in a month's time. Except for some of their clothing which Nancy had marked for special delivery directly to Laurie now. She had even opened a bank account in town and had all her funds transferred from South Carolina.

There was no turning back, and her stratagem to delay finding a place was not panning out. Time was running out. She was getting desperate. Harry why can't you remember that you asked me here to

Indiana? Would she really have to start looking in earnest? Bethany was getting bored with the charade. What could end this stalemate? Should she revert back to a femme fatal? No she couldn't do that even if she knew Harry seemed to respond to her that way.

Several of his buddies and his partner Marvin had come on a number of occasions. His partner especially was keeping him informed on the happenings of the business and encouraging him to get back even if he couldn't use his right hand. They had all seemed to accept Laurie as part of his life now.

Denise was another matter. She grabbed at Harry's accident as an excuse to be back in the picture. She seemed to accept Laurie as a caregiver and tried cuddling up to him as though there was a permanent relationship between them, but he seemed to be rebuffing her efforts. Laurie didn't understand if his behaviour was because she was present or Denise wasn't really what he wanted in his life. *Was she missing something here?*

Harry was out walking again with his crutch. Trying ever so hard to get a rhythm going in his gait. Resting for a moment, he remembered that he had almost fallen three times during the time he had been home and each time it had jolted his right arm.

He knew he was pushing himself too hard and perhaps preventing his body from healing as quickly as it should. Why was he torturing himself? Laurie was here to help. In fact, he was dreading her leaving. He liked to look across the table and watch her animated face listening to the boys and their adventures. She always laughed easily at their escapades. Jason was a real cutup in his story telling, his stories usually had them in stitches. His embellishments that were harmless, but funny.

What would he do when Laurie left? Would he get over her this time? Or could he try again with suggestions of a life together? They had lived in too close a proximity for much longer this time. Now that she was going to be in Indiana, they would be seeing each other on occasion he hoped. The bond between the children should not be broken this time.

While he had been standing there reminiscing, he had let the pain seep through him, so much that now he would need Laurie's help getting back into the house as the boys weren't around.

CHAPTER TWENTY-EIGHT

*L*aurie could see Harry was trying to swallow his pride and ask for her help. Her heart went out to him. She had to end it for him, by rescuing him with the wheelchair.

"Harry, isn't it time for a drink? You have been out here a long time." She lifted his leg to place it on the wheelchair extension after he plunked down. She put the crutch across his knee then pushed the chair knowing he didn't want to be left alone in his exhaustion. "You're doing fine."

She patted his shoulder. He braced himself as she propelled the wheelchair up the ramp and into the house.

She gave him the crutch that he used to steady himself as he mastered the way to the living room. She knew he would want the privacy to recover. It was slow but he made it. He relied heavily on the pain pills, though on fewer occasions now. He was trying harder each day not to give into the pain and its addictive pills. He knew Laurie would be arriving with a fruit drink and insisting he lie down.

* * *

In three weeks the cast would be removed from his leg. Then it would mean going for physiotherapy and more time spent toning the muscles of his left leg. The doctor wanted to wait another week after his leg before the right arm cast would be removed because it was still causing him pain. Meaning self-sufficiency would have to wait. Would his life ever get back to normal? Was he being pessimistic? He just knew he wanted it to be over and his life back to normal.

Harry was leaning on his crutch looking out the window. The sun was shining through the trees dancing on the flowers and shrubs. It was a beautiful day but she felt sure he wasn't seeing the sun or trees or even the blooms in their multitude of colours.

When he became aware that she had entered the room, he turned his body with a wince as he accepted the drink that Laurie had brought. She pretended to ignore the flinch, she stood beside him enjoying the view that took in the forest to one side and the creek beyond the shrubs on the other. She had to say something. "Harry don't you think you are trying too hard? Is it necessary for you to drive yourself this way?" She paused. "Perhaps if you waited a while then the pills would not be necessary."

Knowing from his intake of breath that he knew she had guessed he had taken more pain pills. "Yes perhaps you are right." She patted his arm and walked out of the room.

Harry's attempt at sleep was unsuccessful, so he decided to go search for Laurie. He discovered her doing mending in the family room while listening to classical music. Chopin seemed to be one of her favourites along with Beethoven and Strauss. She had brought her own CD's with her. When he crossed the threshold she rose to change the CD's to one of his but he stopped her.

"No. Leave it." Realizing why she had risen so quickly. "I like this type of music too. I just don't seem to buy them for some unknown reason. You are enjoying the music don't change it because of me." His voice trailed off. He closed his eyes and let the music flow over his senses.

Absorbed in the music, he felt the contentment of knowing that he had learned something new about Laurie and her preference of music. He glanced at her immersed in a serenity of the music pulsating throughout the room. He closed his eyes indulging his senses.

"Harry, will you tell me something?" He opened his eyes looking at her questioningly. "If I am able." he replied.

"If I can't find a suitable dwelling, when you are capable to be on your own, will you let me still stay here? I know you have worked hard to attain your self-sufficiency. You are more successful each day while I am not able to find what I need in a comfortable home."

Harry paused. *What could he say? No? Besides he never wanted her to leave the truth be told. Wasn't he secretly happy when she came home with failures in house hunting?*

"Of course you and the children can stay here. I would never make you leave after unselfishly helping me these past weeks."

Then why are you working so hard to be independent? "That is nice of you Harry. I will go out again tomorrow, but I am getting discouraged that there is nothing out there for us. The disappointments diminishes my strength to keep looking." *Laurie you are a terrible liar. You spend your time at the mall or the library rather than house hunting.* She hoped he would never find out.

She was enjoying this quiet time with him. No children to inhibit the music or make demands on her. She was in a quandary as to why she just couldn't seem to penetrate the shield he had put up around him since he lost his memory, which didn't seem to be returning anytime soon.

"Harry, do you ever regain any of the missing time in your memory? We haven't talked about this lately. Whenever we did the headaches came back. I haven't pressed it for that reason. You never share your thoughts with me, so I don't know if there are incidents that filter back to you."

How do I answer this? Do I lie and say I really tried when I haven't. Was he avoiding it because he secretly did not want her to leave? The flashes were there at odd times, mostly of the wilderness trip also his falling over the cliff and free falling in fear. Odd fragments of memory came to him which focused on flames of the fire leaping around the peripheral of his mind.

"There are flashes now and then but nothing of significance. The headaches that come with it, make me not try I guess." He decided to be evasive, but not lie. He didn't want that between them.

Laurie's heart fell. Jack said everything would be okay once Harry was back in his own natural surroundings. How could she help him if he wouldn't even try to remember their relationship had changed?

How long could she stall her leaving? Surely he would catch on soon the ruse of finding a house? Her frustrations were building so she closed her eyes and let soothing music flow over her.

My gosh he thought. Laurie is so beautiful sitting there. I want to reach out and touch her. Can I keep her here? Why don't I share my feelings? He knew because he didn't want her to walk away again. Maybe it was time to let her know his feelings? No, and yet, maybe it would be yes instead of no this time? Harry didn't ask instead just enjoyed looking at her in silence.

. . .

The weeks passed. The casts on his leg and arm were removed. He was able to negotiate the stairs with a cane. The therapy was success-fully working on the lax muscles, with constant work firming them.

Each day he improved Laurie went quieter and more withdrawn as though hoping not to be noticed, leaving the room at the first opportunity not wanting to face the reality of the situation. Instead of a closeness occurring, the distance between them was widening from a gully to a canyon. Her leaving the room, he knew meant it was inevitable she was leaving soon. *How could he stop her?* She wouldn't stick around with him long enough to broach the subject? The children were buffers when they were around.

"Harry, why do you not like my mom anymore?" Jason asked one day when they had a moment together with just them. Jason was one to speak his mind. Apparently even the children were noticing.

"I like your mom." Shock was evident in his voice.

"Well you hardly talk to her, so you make her feel uncomfortable and she stays away from you." Jason replied accusingly.

"I am aware of that, but what would you suggest I do to change it?" Curious to hear his answer before Todd or Bethany put in an appearance.

"Well I can't suggest dancing with your leg, so maybe a catered candlelight dinner like the ones you see on TV."

"Do you think it will work?" Harry was amazed at his ingenuity, and he was willing to try anything at this point.

"How about we, meaning Todd and I serve dinner for the two of you like we were waiters in a restaurant? Bethany can help us too. We will serve wine. It should be a late dinner after we have had ours, then we can disappear." Harry was warming up to the idea noting the silly grin on Jason's face. "It always works on TV."

"Will you let me think about it?"

"Okay." Satisfied Jason left the room to find Todd.

Well. Well. That boy is a smooth operator. I never thought of such an idea but it just might work. The silence between us seemed to be thicker and more uncomfortable.

Now a special meal, where can I get the food? Denise? No, Harry shook his head that definitely wasn't a wise decision. Marvin's wife? No, he knew that wouldn't be very romantic. He would phone the French cuisine restaurant on Kennedy to deliver. He knew that was where his friend Loren worked as a waiter. He would phone Loren to consult about the menu and wine.

Harry was getting into the spirit of the idea. Maybe just maybe this would succeed with Jason, Todd and Bethany's help. Friday night was far enough away to get things in place. The time to make the call, without Laurie finding out, shouldn't be too difficult the way she was avoiding him lately.

He would need linen, candles, dishes and music but Loren can arrange all that. Thank heavens they were good fishing buddies. Loren would do this for him.

While Bethany and Laurie were making dinner Harry, Todd and Jason were making plans. Todd was going to be in charge of the wine and the music. Jason was to be in charge of serving the meal with some help from Bethany. Harry had to get in touch with Loren tomorrow while Laurie was out house hunting. The boys were giving each other high fives.

Laurie entered the room to call them for dinner. "Hey what's going on here?"

"Just male stuff, Mom." Jason supplied sheepishly.

Harry made all the arrangements for the menu and wine with Loren the next day. Loren offered to deliver it personally on his supposed smoke break. Not being a smoker this would be no problem. He would get one of the others to cover his tables until he got back. Loren was thinking this was romantic of Harry, so he too was getting into the spirit of the romantic evening, knowing that Harry's mobility was still a hamper.

During one of the planning sessions Harry asked Jason for suggestions on how to get Laurie dressed fittingly. "What if you tell her that your partner and his wife want to take you both out to a late dinner? While she is dressing we will set the dining room table if Loren can bring the settings ahead of time. Mom won't go in the garage so we can get him to put them in there. The food should arrive then too if we time it right." Jason was excited that his idea was accepted so readily by Harry.

"You know Jason, you are to be commended for your cleverness in thinking up this brilliant idea, isn't that right Todd?"

"You bet." Todd was anxious to put forth his thoughts. "Dad, do you need any pointers on how to woo Laurie?"

Harry's mouth dropped open. "I'm almost afraid to ask." Harry said with a chuckle. "But I do think I can manage to handle the conversation with a woman."

"Don't blow it." Jason chimed in.

Looking from one boy to the other Harry noted that both were quite serious about this. "Maybe I do need instructions after all." He wanted to know the boy's thoughts on the subject. This project seemed so important to them. He knew it certainly was imperative to him.

"You reach for her hand across the table and caress the back of her hand gently with your thumb. Then you raise her hand to your lips and place a kiss tenderly on the back of her hand." Todd said in all seriousness.

"Which TV show are you getting this from?" Harry was having trouble keeping a straight face. He was afraid what would be coming next.

"Dad, don't you ever watch the movies on television? They do it all the time like that in the movies. You have to dress for the occasion too."

"I think you boys have handled enough of the planning. I will handle the personal actions myself, I promise. I won't blow it." The two boys sat thinking it over.

"If we hire a tux from that place in town that rents formal wear. Todd can be your valet while Bethany and I set the table." Jason said with a positive voice.

"You have the mindset of a true romantic." Harry said to Jason. "This dinner just might work with all your cooperation and planning."

Laurie knew they were all up to something but she couldn't find out what. They seemed to clam up when she entered the room. Bethany was given the task of alerting them when Laurie was approaching.

She gave up trying to find out, instead directed her concerns to a suitable dress for the dinner on Friday night, with Marvin and Louise at the new night club in town. She would have to go shopping. The prospect of dinner must be what had put Harry into a more jovial mood of late, although he still didn't say much to her directly. The thought of getting out with Marvin and Louise should be a good break in the routine for both of them. She knew there was dancing too, maybe they could get up and sway a bit. Laurie sighed.

She forgot the strange goings on and concentrated on finding the appropriate dinner dress for the occasion, which she found at the mall Thursday afternoon. It was a knockout type dress quite out of character for her but she felt so good in the dress. Hang the cost. Harry just had to notice her in this ensemble. She hoped that Louise wouldn't think it was inappropriate of her to be quite this risqué. She went to bed that night with a feeling of hope.

Harry was under a stressful condition unrelated to Laurie and the dinner party. That evening as he sat watching the television with the kids and Laurie he was getting more profuse flashes of the forest fire and the evacuation. Betty's fall and the trip to Merritt flashed in the mirror of his mind. He didn't say anything as he didn't want to get their hopes up only to be dashed if the images disappeared again. He kept waiting for the headache but his head stayed clear. He had hope at last. Maybe he should not expect too much too soon.

He went to bed with an odd feeling. This was the first time since he had arrived home that these flashes were so consistent, although he had a few in the hospital. Was this a good sign or was there to be more disappointment. He was just dosing off when he saw flashes of Laurie and he in a saloon drinking with two couples. He lay there awake waiting.

He didn't know what he expected next but then the flashes were of Jack and Harry in a truck on the way somewhere. His head felt like there was a pressure inside. What was transpiring here?

Then his head cleared and he remembered everything. The cloud over his brain had lifted. Should he wake Laurie and the kids and let them know? What if it didn't last?

He lay there remembering the time he had lost. Now he realized he had forgiven Laurie. He had been ready to tell her that he loved her. Then with horror he realized, he had been treating Laurie so badly since they came home, and before in the hospital to alleviate his fear that she would walk away again.

He viewed the remembrance of memory as positive, that things were going to be okay from now on. Now he was really pleased about the dinner as this would be something to celebrate. No he wouldn't say anything just yet. He would keep it as a surprise till after the dinner. If all went well he would reveal that his memory was back, but if it didn't stay he would pretend nothing had occurred. He felt he needed that buffer just in case things weren't as clear in the morning. He felt the underlying dread that this might not be permanent. Would sleep ever come? Turning over pushing the pillow under his cheek, the thought this might not be permanent still with him.

CHAPTER TWENTY NINE

*F*riday night the children gulped down their dinner and helped Laurie by cleaning the kitchen. Laurie thought it was so considerate of them, as they were suggesting that she needed more time to pamper herself with a shower, and manicure. She was thankful as it was something she had been neglecting lately. She was looking through a magazine for ideas in the latest hairstyles when the boys announced they were going to Todd's room which was of course Jason's room too.

Laurie just said 'humm' absently continuing to read the magazine. She had found a style that she thought she could manage without too much difficulty and only a bit of trimming. She was secretly excited at the opportunity of going out with other adults. They needed a diversion from each other. Who was she kidding? That dress isn't for Marvin and Louise, it was definitely to get Harry's attention.

Bethany was in the bathroom early getting dressed, before Laurie arrived to pamper herself. The two boys were getting dressed in black suits supplied by the formal wear rental. It had been Harry's responsibility to direct Laurie to get dressed as a signal to the children who were hiding their new attire that they would emerge in, when the coast was clear. The boys had to suppress the giggles that kept leaping into their mouths.

At last the all clear came with a knock on the door, their cue to emerge and start the evening. Their bedroom door had been shut in case Laurie looked that way on her trip into the bathroom. Trusting

Laurie would bypass the closed door and not see what was behind it. Jason and Bethany headed for the kitchen. Todd went to his father's room to supervise the dressing of his father, the right arm was still a bit of a hindrance. Harry had showered earlier.

Jason and Bethany were setting the table in the dining room with the place settings Loren had dropped off that afternoon. Everything was ready. The silverware was shining in the glow of the candles. The crystal wine goblets were twinkling with prisms of light. Jason switched off the light as they headed to the kitchen to await Loren and the food. He rapped twice at the kitchen door just in case they didn't hear him the first time.

Loren was admitted quickly. He had brought the food in special heated containers that he immediately set up with the lit sterno underneath to continue the heat. He told them that all the restaurant staff had been let in on the secret so he would be able to stay longer to help with dinner because his friends were going to cover for him. He wanted to put the food on the plates in a decorative fashion while the soup was being served.

Harry appeared in the kitchen doorway dressed in a tux, he looked handsome. His gait was laboured with a cane for balance.

"Everything all set here?" Harry asked with an anxious voice. It had been hard all day not to let anyone know he had recovered his memory. But he had kept it to himself so his anxiety for tonight was twofold.

Loren came over and hugged him, slapping him on the back. "Relax just do me proud when you get in there with your pretty lady." Harry gave him a sick nervous grin. Then he limped out of the kitchen as Laurie came down the hall. Harry looked surprised with awe.

She was gorgeous in a red dress with flecks of gold simmering through it, when she moved it clung to her body like a second skin showing her curves to their best advantage. Her blonde hair was pinned on top of her head with springy curls hanging down around her face. Her face was a picture of artistry highlighting her features. He realized that he had never seen Laurie in evening attire before. There had not been any special evening occasions during their short encounters.

"Laurie you look ravishing." Harry continued to stare. Todd was making a quiet exit behind Laurie through the living room to get to the kitchen.

"Why thank you Harry you look pretty ravishing yourself." Laurie replied with a giggle. Partly because of the spectacle of their clothing and partly because of her nervousness, thinking she may have over-done herself with the scarlet dress.

Harry held out his hand and Laurie put her hand in his. "Right this way mademoiselle." A wicked gleam entered his eye.

As they proceeded to the dining room Laurie could hear romantic music coming from the stereo. Instead of heading to the front door and their coats, he guided her into the dining room.

Laurie's eyes flew to the table as if the candlelight drew her like a magnet. The candle lit table was set for two. Then she spied the two boys attired in their black suits and Bethany in a pretty dress. The boys had napkins over their arms and Bethany was dipping a curtsy in their direction that she had been practicing for days. Laurie was looking at the children's smiles of glee wreathed on their faces.

"Bonsoir, mademoiselle and monsieur." Jason said in his best French accent that Loren had taught him. Todd was holding out her chair awaiting Laurie.

"How did you arrange this?" Laurie enquired as Harry led her gently to her chair, Todd gallantly seating Laurie with a wide grin.

"With a lot of help from my French staff." Waving his hand towards the children, as Harry chuckled.

Todd placed a napkin over her lap with a flourish.

Harry bent over Laurie's hand that he had retained and raised it to his lips, placing a caressing kiss on her hand. "Mademoiselle." Turning his head to wink at the children.

"Oh Harry." She looked up at him with laughter in her eyes.

"This is what you all have been planning." Looking around at them all with a glow Laurie smiled. "What a lovely surprise. No Marvin and Louise?"

Harry slid into his seat. "No Marvin or Louise just you and me . . . and our French staff of course."

Todd was back with the wine. "Monsieur le vin." Holding the bottle Pinot Noir wine out for Harry's inspection.

"Merci, trés bien." Harry was playing along.

Todd easily pulled the cork which Loren had removed to let it breathe then recapped so Todd could serve it in proper style of a famed sommelier, pouring a bit in Harry's wine glass. Harry tasted the wine. "Bon."

Laurie was having a hard time not to break out in laughter at the French accents and the performance as Todd poured the wine, placing the bottle on the table near at hand.

Jason appeared with a plate with an individual soup tureen on it followed by Bethany at a much slower pace so as not to spill any. Jason served Laurie then quickly retrieved the other soup tureen from Bethany for Harry.

Jason bowed formally. "Bon appétit." Then the three children left the room.

"Harry, this is wonderful. I don't know how to ever thank you."

"Then don't just enjoy." Harry raised his glass to her. "A toast to my lovely lady." He took a sip then he sat just drinking her in. The candlelight was dancing over her hair and into her eyes, the wine moist on her lips. The contours of her body gloved in the flaming red dress, Harry had to pull himself together if he was to continue without some embarrassment.

"Shall we start? There is more to come and the French staff will be anxious." A giggle came from outside the door.

Laurie and Harry started eating their French onion soup with a layer of bread topped with melted cheese. Laurie's eyes met his intently as they raised their spoons together. Their intense gaze of fascination preoccupied them, so only a part of the onion soup vanished before the French staff appeared.

Jason asked if they were finished.

Laurie and Harry said "Merci" in unison and laughed. Todd was pouring more wine and Bethany was helping Jason remove the soup bowls. When Harry lifted Laurie's hand to his lips to place a kiss ever so gently in her palm, Todd and Jason gave a 'yes' as they left the room.

"Harry, why do I get the feeling the boys helped choreographer this evening's event?"

"Well they thought I might be out of practice so they gave me a few tips on wooing a lady."

"Harry this is priceless."

He squeezed her hand. Jason and Todd appeared with dinner plates held by a napkin. After they placed the plates before them, Jason said. "Please be careful the plates are very hot. Would you like some pepper on your meal, mademoiselle?"

Bethany appeared magically carrying a peppermill and rolls.

Laurie chuckled. "Merci"

Jason worked the peppermill over her plate with a flourish then went around the table to repeat the performance for Harry. The staff disappeared after Jason said "Bon appétit."

"There has to be someone in the kitchen. Who is it?" Looking down at the skilful presentation on her plate.

"The French chef of course." Harry's tongue in cheek comment, he had trouble keeping a straight face.

"I can't wait to see who that is." They both started eating. The food was so tempting to their palate they ate with gusto in case the French staff arrived too soon to whisk it away. There was very little conversation except their eyes were devouring each other.

Right on cue as they finished their entrée, the French staff materialized. Todd topped up the wine while Jason and Bethany removed the plates.

Harry raised his wine glass and signalled to Laurie to do the same. Then Harry saluted "My compliments to the chef and the staff for this wonderful meal." Then he took a drink of the wine with zest. Laurie repeated "To the chef and staff." Raising her glass to her lips she sipped while her eyes danced with merriment.

Jason bowed. "My staff thanks you mademoiselle and monsieur." Turning they departed the room. They were back shortly with a dessert of peach torte bathed in a brandy sauce. Todd was pouring coffee and Loren emerged with the Cointreau.

"Laurie may I introduce the French chef Loren, and Loren, this is Laurie."

"Pleased to make your acquaintance at last, lovely lady, but I have to run as I must get back to the restaurant. I really am on duty tonight. Knowing Harry's surprise for you, the staff covered for me." He gave Laurie a sparkling grin.

"Merci Loren." Laurie smiled luxuriously for his help in presenting the meal.

"Thank you, Loren." Harry added with his heart brimming in gratitude. A chorus of thank you's came from the French staff to Loren.

"Don't botch it" Loren said winking at Harry, Loren departed laughing.

Jason said. "My staff and I will be leaving you to enjoy your dessert."

As he passed Harry's chair Jason shoved a box in his hand saying in a whisper. "Don't blow it." Then Jason shooed his staff out the door. Harry and Laurie's loud 'thank you' ringing in their ears. Laurie looked back at Harry.

"Blow what?"

Harry lifted his hand onto the table. Flicked the box open with his fingers and Laurie saw the ring displayed there, the diamond twinkling with rainbows of colour in the candlelight.

"Laurie, will you marry me?"

Laurie couldn't say anything she was too stunned her mouth open. The silence was broken when a voice prompted from the hall. "Answer him, Mom."

"Harry I would love to marry you." He got up and went around slipping the ring on her finger. Then he bent over and kissed her lovingly.

There were a chorus of loud cheers from the hallway. Harry went to the door to look out. "Did I get it right?" A hand appeared to give him a high five to Laurie's laughter. Harry whispered. "Where did you get the ring?"

Jason replied. "The jeweller gave it to us on loan." To Harry's look of amazement Jason continued. "Loren's uncle is a jeweller. Do you like it?"

"You made a good choice. Thanks." Gave them all a wink and returned into the room. Harry had a satisfied look on his face that was almost a leer. When he reached Laurie he pulled her into his arms, kissing her like he had always wanted to, passionately. He pulled back saying. "I do love that boy of yours, he has class."

Laurie had tears of joy in her eyes. She had her Harry and three children to love. She was here to stay with her Harry, to share an everlasting love. She settled more deeply in his embrace that had tightened around her locking her there forever.

The children entered the room with big grins on their faces. Harry and Laurie included them in their embrace with much laughter. Harry pulled back a bit. "I have an announcement which is the topping on the cake I am sure. I have my memory back and my dear lady, I want you to know that I intended on asking you to marry me ever since Florida."

"Oh Harry, that's wonderful." Laurie said as Harry hugged her close again and the children echoed her sentiment boisterously.